TIME OUT OF MIND

SHIRLEY WRIGHT

Published in 2012 by FeedARead.com Publishing –
Arts Council funded.

A CIP catalogue record for this title is available from
the British Library.

Acknowledgements

A big "thank you" to everyone who has ever supported my writing. But very special thanks are also due: to Bristol Women Writers, for unfailing encouragement, coffee and cakes; to Sarah Duncan, a born teacher; to Jim as my official "techie", for ensuring that all things IT keep functioning; to Sylvia Dyer, my editor, for believing in this book.

Disclaimer

Cover Design

The past is not another country;
it is a familiar that walks daily with us,
by our side.

Chapter One

I slide the desk drawer out for another quick fix. There it is – Penmaris, sitting four-square in the middle of fields, with nothing else in sight. Almost the air changes and I can breathe. I gulp down the whisper of a summer breeze, peer closer at the photo. You can tell the front door's open; I imagine that Paula has just walked through it with her camera to take this very shot from the end of the drive, framing the cottage in the landscape so it appears to rise naturally from rough grass and ancient stone.

Since acquiring the snap a few days ago – "Here, Rose, have this one, it's recent. Nice sunny day in July. Be a bit nippy this time of year, though" – I have become obsessed with a tiny holiday cottage in the middle of nowhere. A place I've never visited, never seen, yet it haunts me like a melody I can't quite catch. In the office I'm unable to focus on deadlines or art work and at home I cringe, suddenly overwhelmed by space. Our Clapham Common terrace has morphed into a cavernous sprawl I find intimidating. Instead, I pretend I'm living in this country cot, moving through its diminutive rooms, strolling the quiet garden to pick flowers, descending steep cliffs to the seashore to sketch the view: rock formations, a perfect seagull, waves breaking over shingle.

And always I am alone. Completely alone. Which is fine, because that's how it feels right now. After Peanut and the ghosts in his wake.

Dear God. Six months on, and I'm still assigning gender based on instinct. I bite my lip. Focus on breathing. The fact is, we'll never know.

Somewhere in the open-plan office a phone rings. I drink coffee and try to appear busy. One more peek at the photo and I promise myself I'll shut the drawer and get on with the Hansen contract. But this time when I glance at it, the picture seems different. A shadow lies over Penmaris and – how odd, I've not noticed that before – at the upstairs window, what looks like a face, someone's head and shoulders…

"Hi, Rose. What's up? Got your note."

My arm jerks, coffee spills. "Shit. You made me jump." I slam the mug down.

"Sorry. You okay?" Ellie drags a chair over to my desk and sits close. Her knees bump the drawer. "So, what can I do you for?"

The jokey manner disarms me, threatens my resolve. It's embarrassing to let her down. No, worse than that. I hate people who take advantage of friendship, and here I am about to exploit hers. Again.

"Well, actually, I'm thinking about… I know it's going to be a nuisance, but…"

Words skitter like autumn leaves. Ellie places a hand over the tangle of my fingers. "Stop picking, Rose.

6

You'll make them bleed." She rummages in the open drawer and throws me the tube of hand cream. Then she sees the photo. "Pretty house. Where's this?"

I grab the snap from her, dismayed to find it splashed with coffee. What I had seen as a face at the window is now a blob of disintegrating celluloid. But the small disaster restores my voice. "I'm toying with the idea of going away, Els. Just for a while. Down to Cornwall. Next week, maybe, or the week after? Paula's said I can…"

"Paul?"

"Paula. And Chris. Our next-door neighbours?" Ellie nods. "They've said I can stay at their cottage. They don't get many bookings in October, so they're happy for me to… I need to be on my own, you see. I… I need to pull myself together, else I'll fall apart again."

People have hammered me with that phrase: *pull yourself together* – as if a broken puppet can repair its own strings. And I have tried – I've gone through the motions, knotting frayed ends with numb fingertips. But I feel like Pinocchio and I suspect my nose is getting longer.

Ellie is already tapping on her BlackBerry. "How does Oliver feel about this?"

"He can't possibly take time off, he's up to his eyebrows in work." Someone else I'll be dumping on, which is another reason why I'm hesitant. But Oliver's a workaholic, so he'll get by. I should be grateful he has a place to bury grief.

After punching a few more keys Ellie says, "All sorted. Viv can finish the Trueform job. Ah, what about Hansen?" A pause. More key punching. "Okay. Also sorted. Just give me a bell when you've decided."

I want to thank her but she cuts me short. "What are friends for, Rose? It's all right. I understand. Send me a postcard."

* * *

Next morning I psych myself up for parental concern.

"Be back teatime," I yell from the bottom of the stairs and grab my coat. "Bye now."

As I slam the door I catch the end of Oliver's "…them my love." He's still in bed, having got home after midnight from a long Friday of meetings in Birmingham. Not that he needs an excuse; he tends to cry off lunch with the in-laws on the grounds that I'm the one they really want to see, he's just the other half. In truth, he hates Mum's fussing and the way Dad criticises everyone else for not having the good fortune to be him.

First stop petrol. While there, I buy a garish bunch of flowers and a bottle of plonk, which is stupid because they shriek bad taste, but perhaps we can argue about that instead. Diversion tactics. Then I join the Saturday morning crawl to Dulwich, during which I consider simply not telling my parents about Cornwall. Since I'm not sure whether I'm going to go, why rock the boat? And if I do, chances are I'll be back before they miss me. Oliver can field any flack. He does a good line in schmooze. Let's restrict conversation to the usual battle grounds, like who's doing what for Christmas.

Before I've even parked the car, Mum has the front door open. She must have been watching for me.

"Hallo, darling. I did phone, but Oliver said you'd…"

8

"Hi, Mum. These are for you." I thrust the outrageous bouquet at her, then notice her red, watery eyes. And that she is blocking my way.

"Daddy's got the flu, and I'm coming down with something." She sounds croaky. "I think you should go home, Rose. We don't want you ill too."

"Don't be silly. Let me in. You need a hot drink. Got any Lemsips?"

"No, Rose, you're not coming in. The last thing you want right now is to catch our germs. You're not well enough as it is, you're not…"

"Not what?"

Her voice drops to a whisper. "You still haven't recovered from losing…" Her last words fade into air. She thinks a quiet voice means a quiet life.

"Mum, will you stop trying to—"

"Don't argue with me, Rose. You need to look after yourself. Go home and I'll ring you in a few days."

"But by then I might be in—"

"Go on. Shoo." She flaps her hands at me. "Go home early. Give Oliver a nice surprise."

Which I do. He's making for the bathroom as Ellie strolls, naked and dishevelled, out of our bedroom.

* * *

I'm not remotely calm or contained, though I am trying to hold it all together. Catastrophes keep happening to me. Out of a clear blue sky, oh Lord. Anger fires adrenalin so that I blaze with a kind of mad energy as I throw things at the MG, not caring what goes in or what gets left behind. I make sure I have my painting stuff, though. That's important. The easel fits in last, somehow, through sheer brute force and swearing, and I am smug that my girlie sports car is really a Tardis. Oliver, in dressing gown and bare feet, keeps getting in the way, saying "Please, Rosie, please. Will you just stand still and listen to me? Rosie, please." As if repeated begging will make a difference. Ellie is hiding, I suspect in Oliver's study. A good idea. Otherwise I might have to kill her.

It would seem that I've made my decision. Or rather, it's been made for me; dithering has been superseded by events. With the coffee-stained photo of Penmaris Blu-Tacked to the dashboard, I settle myself behind the steering wheel and turn the ignition. This takes several attempts because my hands are shaking so much I can't get the key in the lock, but once the engine roars to life so does something else, a voice inside urging me to run, shouting at me loud and clear to get the hell out of this damned place and leave it all behind.

All of it. The whole bloody mess.

I head for the M4. Traffic is dire, and for hours we crawl through road-works and red-cone disease. Stop, go, stop, go. Stop mainly. But I don't care and it's probably safer if I'm forced to drive slowly. What matters is that every mile takes me further from London and closer to Cornwall. Unable to think about what has just happened, because it's a black hole, and unwilling to because I need to concentrate on the road, I enter the limbo world of motorway reality and let it bear me away.

* * *

It's nearly midnight when I pull into the drive. High hedges and a maze of winding lanes mean I almost miss my turn. I swing the car abruptly, wheels scattering

10

gravel. Killing the engine, I slump back in the seat. My hands are shaking again. In fact, everything is shaking and there's a buzz in my ears. Tiredness overwhelms me. I've been on the road for eight hours.

As I lie there, eyes closed, head back, the tremble of exhaustion leaks away and a new sensation takes over. At first I can't identify it, then I realise – I am sitting in the middle of silence. I drag myself out of the car. My legs wobble as if I've been on board ship, and I cling to the door for support, listening all the while for any sound. The silence and emptiness are astonishing, producing a sense of disorientation. The quiet is palpable – the tangible absence of the press of bodies. In London you're never alone; on seemingly empty streets people breathe their nearness through brick walls, in the pulse of all-night traffic, in the hum of humanity that never dies.

A large garden stretches behind Penmaris, partly visible in the moonlight and winding away into blackness. Once my legs feel more normal, I walk down the path, brushing my arms against damp leaves from overhanging trees and bushes. Every few steps, I stop to listen, I breathe deeply. The heavy, moisture-laden air carries salt and the bone-marrow essence of earth. At the end of the path is a wall that separates the garden from the field beyond. Leaning against the stones, I strain to hear what might lie on the other side; cows or horses, maybe, or the sea somewhere in the distance.

But the field is quiet. The more I strain to hear, the more the silence itself seems to open out and take weight. Stretching a hand in front of me, I stroke darkness.

Paula drew me a sketch-map, showing the cottage in relation to the landscape. From what I remember, the cliff top is straight ahead, presumably on the far side of this field. From the bedroom window I should be able to see the Atlantic. Something I'll check in the morning.

A sough of air brushes the open ground. I hold my breath, listening intently. And there it is in the silence, far away, the rolling rush of waves.

I let out a sigh of relief, like a thank you. I've made it, despite the odd little difficulty, to where I wanted to be. Penmaris: my crazy fixation. I turn to look back at the cottage, hunched at the other end of the path. With no points of reference, it seems distant and isolated, a dark smudge in the tangle of garden which appears to stretch in all directions. There are no other signs of life, just endless shadowy space and, up above, a million stars glittering in the night sky.

Brittle. Indifferent.

A shiver of doubt pricks my spine. *The odd little difficulty!* An earthquake in my marriage and the journey from hell; how on earth will I manage, on my own, here in this lonely place? What can I possibly do, stuck in the middle of nowhere, to mend the disaster that has become Rose Little?

I tell myself to calm down. Don't start freaking out already. Everything's going to be fine. Unpack the car and settle in. Do your Scarlett O'Hara. Tomorrow is another day.

I push off the wall, ready to head back, and catch a hint of perfume. Nose tilted to its note, I follow the scent until I bump into and graze my shin against a stone buried in the long grass. Its top is round and smooth to the touch. About the height of a small stool, it invites me to sit. When I do so, I find it surprisingly comfortable, as if carved to my shape.

The perfume floats all around. I sit, engulfed by bushes and overgrown shrubs, drowning in a delicate, elusive fragrance. The smell is heavenly and I feel so tired I could fall asleep right here. Except that, after a few minutes, damp from the grass starts to wick up my jeans. As I make to stand, a flicker of light snags my eyes. Grey-white wings flutter past, quivering round the bush in front of me. Insect wings. A moth, maybe. Leaves stir where the creature moves, alighting then darting off, flitting in and out of the branches in a halo of moonsilver.

Then, through the layers of darkness, comes the faintest sound of a woman's voice, singing. Someone out for a late-night stroll, I assume. The voice seems far away, as if carrying across huge distances, and although I can hear the lilt of melody, I can't make out the words. Not Lily Allen, though, that's for sure. There's nothing modern or estuary-English about it. An old folk song perhaps, in a sad, haunting, minor key.

Which reminds me – with the song fading into air, I go back to the car, dig out the key ring Paula gave me and let myself into the cottage.

Chapter Two

Next morning my mobile wakes me, wittering and juddering on the bedside table.

Bugger.

I fall out of bed, ready for action: who's sick, what catastrophe, which meeting, where? Then – strange shapes in the gloom, bare walls – and I remember. When I see it's Oliver on the phone, I switch the thing off before padding carefully down the unfamiliar wooden staircase. My mouth is a sand-pit. Despite a deep and dreamless sleep, I feel grotty and exhausted.

Filling the kettle with one hand, I dig through my box of supplies with the other, rooting around for teabags. The kitchen is *that* small. But I am not *that* co-ordinated and manage to knock over the cereal box which topples against the coffee jar and sends the whole lot crashing to the stone floor. I cornflake-crunch down to the cupboard under the sink for dustpan and brush.

Afterwards, dangling a teabag in hot water, I observe just how violently my hands are shaking, wonder if I ought to ring Oliver back (and give him a chance to – what? Explain?) and fight off the strong desire to go back to bed and sleep for a week. Give in to the latter.

Sipping as I go, I carry the mug carefully upstairs. The bedroom is still dark thanks to heavy curtains; the bed's crumpled duvet invites. Once again I am struck by the silence. Normally there would be noises everywhere: air brakes wheezing or car doors slamming, the clank and chink of London waking. Something always disturbs my sleep. Whereas today I'd still be dead to the world were it not for my bloody awful mobile. Its current ringtone, demented wasp on speed, was a birthday joke from an irritating colleague, and I'd wipe it off if only I knew how. Glaring down at the phone and sending hate messages, I remember Paula's map and the promise of a view. With a tingle of premonition I walk over to the window. Leaving the mug on a bookcase, I stretch out both arms, shoulder high, and grasp a curtain in each hand. I close my eyes and pull.

As if someone had thrown a pot of yellow paint, sunshine splashes my face and chest with such force that I instinctively step back. I am bathed in liquid light. Oddly, it feels both warm and cool at the same time. I pause, prolonging the moment until I can wait no longer, then open my eyes.

An arc of deepest blue sweeps the horizon, splitting earth and sky like a bow. I gasp. Pressing my hands against the windowpane, I gaze out; to my left, black rocks jut like saw-blades into blue air; to the right, away in the distance, a tip of coastline hugs sheltered

15

bays and soft sand. I could go swimming. If it stays warm enough. But ahead, straight ahead, is the sea, the endless blue blue sea, except... over there it's cerulean lapping turquoise then changing to purple, thick and foaming white where it pounds against the rocks and, well, that patch... why, it's more like aqua-glass shading to green then grey then inky blue again.

So much... blue.

My gut knifes. Why, I had almost forgotten.

Fancy nearly forgetting...

Forgetting Blue. *You think to paint that, little laydee?* comes the mocking whine. A taunt clawing at my skull, telling me I might as well throw my brushes away and give up before I start. The spark of an idea kindled a few weeks ago during rush hour on Chelsea Bridge is in danger of being eclipsed by Cornish light. What am I doing here? Faced with solitude and this prospect of the sublime, *what on earth do I think I'm doing here?*

Glancing to the right again, I notice boats on the water. The nearest big town lies in that direction; "frightful tourist trap", according to Paula, to be avoided "like the plague, darling, full of ghastly grockles." But a source of human contact, nonetheless. The cottage might feel isolated, but Porthallen village is down the hill less than a mile away and towns like Penzance are a short drive along the coast. I'm hardly marooned on a desert island. There's no need to panic. I should give myself time.

Blue is just another colour.

Opening the casement window, I lean out. The garden looks smaller and less interesting this morning. Last night it seemed endless and mysterious. A trick of the imagination presumably, caused by the distortion of evening shadows. And it's an absolute mess, overgrown and untended, something of a jungle really, though a few late blooms are poking through and autumn colours have started their burn.

A cottage facing the sea. I repeat the phrase several times, like a mantra. To be in sight of the ocean, to hear its music in the deep of night. I am fortunate. Yes, I am. I must keep reminding myself of that. I have *some* good friends, if not the ones I'd presumed, and I have Penmaris, a place of safety to lick my wounds and mend my heart. A place to think. I have both time and space. I can damned well survive this. Somehow.

I shiver in my flimsy T-shirt, throw on some clothes, finish my cuppa, and go outside to fetch the rest of my stuff from the car. Slinking round the side of house is a black cat which dashes off, startled, when I open the back door. Nearly tripping over him I manage a laugh, pleased to meet my first local resident.

* * *

Once unpacked, I decide to go for a walk and see if any shops are open on a Sunday. Beacon Road curves in a long, slow descent towards Porthallen, picking up for the last hundred yards or so and sending me tumbling headlong into the village. It feels like free-wheeling on a bike, all motion and no effort, just irresistible speed, heels barely touching the ground. I bowl past a couple of houses, then a chemist's next to a fishing-tackle shop, swing round a lamppost and abruptly I'm facing the crossroads where the village proper begins. On the opposite corner stands Coleforth's Minimart. A mother and son are coming out.

Shopping list in hand, I take a wire basket and determine to fill it. Having been a contentious issue in recent months, because everything I eat tastes like ashes, food is usually a no-go area. So today I choose fresh fruit, bread, eggs, cheese, thin rashers of smoky bacon, healthy staples of which even my doctors would approve. They're always telling me to eat properly, so I'll give it a go. Might even keep some of it down. Then, after a furtive glance behind me, I add a couple of ready meals and a box of white wine to sit in the fridge. Finally, my willpower crumbling entirely, I select a bottle of vodka. I was going to buy gin, *Mother's Ruin* as they used to call it, but I put that back on the shelf. Vodka, by comparison, tells no tales, and I want no reminders of ruined motherhood.

Oh, sod it, why fart about? I take two. At the till, I pick up a local newspaper.

"We'd best put this lot in a couple of carrier bags, my dear." A broad face, wearing a pitying smile. "One for each hand. Then you won't come over all lop-sided. That'll be thirty-eight pounds forty, please." Is this Mrs Coleforth, I wonder?

The plastic carriers sag as I heft them to the ground. Stuffing my purse into a back pocket, I brace myself.

"On your holidays, are you?" asks the till-lady. She wears the look of one who recognises a fool at twenty paces. No car has drawn up, no car keys are jangling. Besides, she probably watched me flying uncontrollably down the road.

"Not exactly," I snap, then regret my sharp tongue. "I'm staying at a friend's place," I explain, lifting the bags, "for a… for a while." The square lady, squat as her cash register, unzips a smile as if she's heard it all before. "My next-door neighbours in London, Chris and Paula Benning. They own Penmaris Cottage," I continue, "up the hill there." I point, having put the bags down again in case they break before I even leave the shop. "You know it?"

With exaggerated deliberation, the woman follows my finger, then looks down to the shopping on the floor. "You carrying that lot up there?" It's not so much a question as a punch line. To the private joke she's probably enjoying at my expense. Stupid. Stupid. Why do I never think first?

"I know. I'm silly." I shake my head to cover embarrassment. "I rushed out because the sun was shining and I didn't realise..." My appraiser looks unimpressed, so I add, thrusting out a hand, "I'm Rose, by the way. Rose Little."

There is a distinct pause, then, "Yes, I can see that." Po-faced, deadpan. I don't know whether to be offended or not. Any response is forestalled by the bell tinkling over the shop door. Greetings ring out.

"Morning, Mary!"

"Phil."

"Got my favourites?"

"Came in last week. Down by the cake shelf."

"Cheers, Mary." Phil disappears down an aisle.

I pick up my shopping again. Best to say nothing. "Bye then, er... Mary? I expect I'll be in again soon. Nice to meet you."

The woman nods. "You watch yourself, Rose Little. You take care, up by Penmaris."

The remark sounds odd. "Oh, I'll manage." I shrug. "I'm stronger than I look. Or at least I will be, after I've climbed that hill a few times."

Calling the parting sally over one shoulder, I set off at a brisk pace, determined to look, from the rear at least, like the capable person I wish I could be.

Roughly halfway back, however, I'm forced to stop. Both hands are red and swollen, with groves cutting my skin where the thin plastic has dug in. I spit on my fingers, then wave them in the air to cool them. Propping the carrier bags against stones on the verge, I sit on the grass and wait to get my breath back.

Tucked into the hollow behind me lies Porthallen, now visible only as a geometry of roofs pierced by the church spire and quartered by four intersecting roads. Three climb sharply into open countryside; the fourth meanders down probably to the beach. I'll use the car next time. There's no way I'm going to climb this hill again. I'm here for a rest, which doesn't include lugging shopping up a one-in-four. Look at my poor hands. I owe them better, a few words of explanation for such mistreatment.

Yesterday I'd been pushed for as many as a few words. God, was it only yesterday? Less than twenty-four hours, in fact, though a chasm separates then from now. I remember how inadequate words seemed. How I couldn't find them, how I couldn't actually get anything out of my mouth, as if my tongue had swollen and was blocking my throat. Just like I wanted to block Oliver's throat to shut him up – chop his balls off and stuff them down that great open, protesting, red gullet. I also remember the expressions on their faces, Oliver's and Ellie's, when I materialised on the upstairs landing. Ellie's reaction was immediate, one of total shock, her mouth a perfect O and her eyes stretched wide in horror. But for a split second Oliver had looked cross.

He'd not been able to prevent it, that flicker of annoyance with me for daring to arrive home early, that lip-curl which implied it was all my own fault – oh yes, among the many salacious images scrolling down my mind-screen, that's the killer. Oliver, pissed at being caught out.

I've made rather a mess of this nice patch of grass, tugging it up by the handful. A shower of green trickles through my fingers, feeling damp and soft. And gentle.

Thank goodness I'd already made some plans, squared things with Paula, been organised enough to tuck the keys into my bag along with her directions for getting to Penmaris.

No wonder arranging time off work had been so easy.

To think, Ellie and I have been friends since school. I've known her even longer than I've known…

Originally the idea was to spend a few weeks in Cornwall to get my head together. I'd hole-up in Penmaris and do some painting, start to feel grounded again, touch base with sanity. A bit of rural peace and quiet was all I needed to get over… Then, when I felt strong enough, I'd go back to London and carry on with my life.

I hadn't seen it as running away, though it may have looked like flight. But not flight from Oliver. Well, not then. Rather, flight from the pain in my head and hands and heart, from a pain so intense I thought my body would fly asunder and everything that had ever been Rose Little would break into a thousand pieces. I just needed some time.

But yesterday all that changed – the past got rewritten and now the future's a blank sheet of paper saying nothing much. Nothing much at all.

Seagulls are shrieking overhead. I pull my trainers and socks off, put the trainers back on my bare feet and wrap a sock round each palm. When I stand up, the gulls are wheeling, big and ugly, watching for easy pickings. "Go away," I shout at them, "go and catch fish, or whatever seagulls do."

In a fifteen-minute burst I cover the remaining ground, drop my bags as I fall through the cottage door and rush for the kitchen tap. I swallow thirstily, then prop my arms on the edge of the sink and dangle my hands under the water. Panting like a steam engine, I'm ashamed to realise how unfit I am. Slumped over like this, I catch a flicker of movement out of the corner of one eye. Then it happens again. And again a few moments later, this time followed by a thump. Curious now, I fling the window wide open and lean out as far as I can. There is a man in the garden, hacking into the bushes, tossing severed branches over one shoulder.

"Oi! What do you think you're doing?"

My voice fails to carry above the sound of his axe thudding into wood, and he's wearing a silly hat that covers his ears. Even when I stomp up the path, he doesn't notice me till I'm close enough to poke him. "Excuse me, but do you mind telling me what you're doing?"

The man spins round, his axe scything air. "Well now, I might ask the same question," comes the reply, his voice the long, slow drawl of fading summers. He stands his ground, waiting.

Thrown on the defensive, I start explaining *my* presence to *him*. Then I try again. "And you are?"

"I do the garden. For the Bennings. Needs a bit of pruning, this time of year, a garden does." Ignoring me, he scoops an armful of leaves and tosses them into a wheelbarrow.

Now I bother to look, I notice a shed tucked against the side fence, its door open to reveal an assortment of tools. Last night, in the dark, it had not been visible.

"Mr Benning. He sees me right. Every time they comes down, he pays me. Mr Benning and me, we've got an *understanding*." He stresses the word, as if to establish prior claim.

Paula said nothing about a gardener. He's a tall lean man of about sixty, with hair poking out from under his red woolly hat. He resembles one of the branches he's busy chopping; beneath a muddy green sweatshirt, muddy brown corduroys are tucked into Wellington boots – all the colours of the earth. Despite warm clothes, he manages to look cool and comfortable.

"Is this your day, then?" It would be helpful to know when he might suddenly materialise in the back garden.

"My day?" he repeats, as if he doesn't speak the language.

"Sunday. Do you usually come on a Sunday? Only then I'll know to expect you." It's like pulling teeth. And I haven't learned his name yet. "Would you like a cup of tea? I've just got back from the shops and I'm gasping." I think of butter and milk that need fridging and head for the back door, assuming he'll follow. "I'm Rose, by the way." I introduce myself, for the second time that morning, but at the door I realise he's walked in the opposite direction and is wheeling the cuttings down the path. At the bottom, he tips them over the wall into the field.

I'm filling the fridge when I next become aware of him. His presence seems to fill the doorframe, casting a shadow over the floor.

"I'll be off, then," he says. He has a way of not looking at you when he speaks, as though his eyes might wound.

"Oh. I've just put the kettle on." I try again to coax him. "Are you sure I can't persuade you to a cup of tea, Mr… er…?" I wait. "I'm Rose."

"You said."

"Yes, I did, didn't I? Sorry."

"I've locked the shed. You don't need to go bothering about that. Or the garden."

It sounds almost like a threat. Or a warning. I watch him as he stomps off, then I turn and finish emptying my shopping bags.

Chapter Three

"Rose darling, are you going to be all right?"

Out walking, I had picked wild flowers and was busy arranging them in a chipped, blue-and-white jug when the phone rang. "Of course I'm all—"

"Only it's such a long way away." My mother croaks pitifully down the line.

"It's Cornwall, Mum, not Corfu." Why does she act like I've gone to the ends of the earth? Though given the journey down on Saturday, Corfu might have been easier. She's miffed, I suppose, because she's only just found out. "Anyway, listen, I want to know how *you're* feeling. You still sound a bit rough."

She ignores me. "Whatever is this place like, Rose? Oliver gave me the number, said it's a *cottage*." Synonymous with *hovel* in my mother's mind, civilisation being bounded by the M25. Clearly Oliver has delivered the pre-Saturday-caught-*in-flagrante* spiel: poor Rose, convalescing, let's cut her some slack, leave her in peace, blah de blah. Bastard. But I decide to play the game, rather than add to my mother's worries. Her cold seems worse.

"It's tiny," I say, "like a box. And I love it."

Or like two boxes really, one on top of the other. I describe how the front door opens directly onto the sitting room, from which a small rectangle has been walled off for the kitchen. Upstairs is the same, one square bedroom minus a corner for the bathroom. Connecting the boxes, a wooden staircase climbs the right-hand wall, beginning by the front door and breaking through the ceiling to end at the rear of the cottage.

That's it. Two squares, two rooms: one for living, one for sleeping. And the ceilings are low, adding to the sense of the place wrapping itself around you. I love its neat, compact simplicity, the stone walls which seem to grow from the soil. That's why I'd slipped out to pick flowers, answering a need to bring the outside in, to complete the circle. It's only Tuesday, but already the cottage feels comfortable and I wonder why anyone should want more.

The voice on the other end of the phone sounds dubious. "Strikes me as a bit pokey."

Having raised two daughters in a gracious Edwardian residence, my mother has no understanding of a word like *compact*. I say, "It's fine, Mum, don't worry," and ignore the maternal sniff. "I don't take up much space." Sunlight through panes of glass falls onto orange petals. Colour spills across the white gloss paint of the windowsill.

Of course, with half a dozen unruly kids it would be impossible. I can see that. But many of my friends are like me, singletons or childless couples who live in what now seems, by comparison, a palatial splendour that is both unnecessary and vulgar. Why, the entire ground floor of Penmaris would fit into our Clapham kitchen.

"… *and* I managed to cook my supper last night."

I make it sound like a culinary triumph, though for *cook* read: *warmed a pizza*. Then I threw most of it away. But she'll hear what she wants to hear. This is a woman who swears by halogen hobs and who would have a fit if she saw the kitchen at Penmaris. It's minute. Not-enough-room-to-swing-a-cat minute. Two cupboards, a sink, a small fridge and an old-fashioned, solid-ring electric cooker. Instead of worktops, there are tops to work on: the top of the fridge, the top of the floor-standing cupboard, and a sheet of Formica to cover the draining board when not draining. Best not to tell her that.

Because the cottage lay empty for several years before Chris and Paula bought it, Chris insisted on certain basic repairs straight away. He didn't want the place crumbling to ruin, taking his investment with it. New roof tiles, the external rendering, a decent bathroom, modern plumbing, were all deemed priorities. While a local builder got busy with structural work, Paula splashed diamond-white paint round the living room and bedroom, leaving the cottage clean, bright in bright sunlight, but somehow startled, with the bemused air of having been woken abruptly.

In the first flush of enthusiasm for their new acquisition (which they promptly named their *bolthole*, though what they were bolting from was unclear, since nowadays they only use the place for a fortnight each summer), Chris and Paula used to set off once a month for the country, taking down odd pieces of furniture, rugs, curtains, bargains found in antique shops or picked up at junk sales. As a result, Penmaris is randomly furnished and lacks cohesion. To my mind, the bare walls scream for relief and the rooms feel cold and unloved. Central heating, once discussed, has never materialised, but there is a fireplace and, according to Paula, a portable heater somewhere, probably at the back of a cupboard. When I asked her about staying at the cottage, Paula was almost indecently keen.

"Oh yes, Rose, yes of course. Yes, of course you can." I couldn't help noticing the guilt in her voice, the quiver of regret for having abandoned the place. "We did get the chimney unblocked once, so I'm sure you'll be able to light a lovely fire. But we've not bothered. Not in July."

Rustic charm will never win Paula's heart. Penmaris has already lost out to the urban imperative and slipped in her affections from bolthole to millstone. Chris'll hang on to it for as long as the property market remains buoyant, but the future for Penmaris is friends or relations, colleagues after a cheap break, and the holiday-brochure market. When I glance around the room, I detect sadness in the air, a sense of neglect and betrayal. Knowing exactly what that feels like, I resolve to fill the place with flowers, to light a fire in the empty hearth. Already I'm being proprietorial.

My mother switches modes to *making the best of a bad job*. "I dare say you'll manage for a few days," she says, "and the fresh air will do you good." I let it go. I have no timeframe in mind. "But make sure you eat properly, darling. You will take care of yourself, won't you?" Anxiety squeaks down the line. Then a bout of

28

coughing. I watch a money spider spin thread among the orange petals.

"Daddy sends his love. He's feeling much better, by the way. In fact, he's doing battle with the decorators, or else he'd be on the other phone."

"Well, my love back, and tell him not to worry."

"We're having the dining room done, did I tell you? So exciting. Of course, Daddy's much too old to be up ladders, and Oliver recommended this firm in Battersea but... well, between you and me..."

Well, bully for Oliver. Not that I can recall a single instance of my father up a ladder. He's always been too busy, too important. Decorating is what you pay other people to do. There's always someone else to dig you out of a hole, repair your burst pipes, fix the central heating, mend your broken life. Practicalities. My parents are good at them.

Penmaris might not be practical, but to me it speaks enchantment. Having never lived anywhere before with low ceilings, I realise now why I've always found the big, airy rooms of my London existence vaguely intimidating. At five foot one (well, nearly), I've long been the butt of aphorism: "the best gifts come in small parcels" (mother); "perfectly petite" (dad); "titch-snitch" (Megan); "less is more" (Oliver, when feeling sexy); and a host of other jokes over the years. My hands and feet used to be called "monkey paws" and only my long pointed chin, which entered rooms before me, permitted any sense that I might be able to compete. Growing up in grand houses, I tried to ignore the cathedral spaces above my head; here in Penmaris I can stand tall, comfortable with the proportions of my environment, not diminished by them.

Saying goodbye with a "take care," and a promise of postcards, I put the phone down and go and get a glass of water. Mum's cough has made my throat dry. While at the sink I rinse my breakfast cup and spoon. I ought to put them in the cupboard; there isn't space to leave things lying about. I picture our kitchen at home: the gleaming wastes of stainless steel and contrasting crimson, fitted to within an inch of their lives with every culinary device known to man. Oliver had the work surfaces specially commissioned to harmonise with the hard-edged, two-toned theme: metallic grey flecked with scarlet. It makes me think of mediaeval knights doing battle, of rapiers and armour and weapons for cutting flesh and slicing muscle through to bone. The other day I was scrubbing for minutes to remove a stain after chopping meat, before I realised the surface was perfectly clean; what I had taken for blood was part of the design.

I lay a hand gently on one of the cottage walls and repeat its name, soothed by echoes of permanence and mystery. Penmaris. A warm resonance. A yearning. I draw it round my shoulders like a protective cloak.

* * *

Two days later, I hurl my sketchpad onto the couch in despair. An entire morning wasted drawing pathetic clichés: inky-black mussels commuter-packed on a rock; scraggy plants clinging to the cliff face; seaweed which I'd hurled only to watch it flop disconsolately; dead lumps of jellyfish. Despite my best intentions, I've produced tight, fussy drawings crowded with a degree of forensic detail more suited to the prosthetics' brochure I've been designing at work. Body parts.

Precision. Anal art. And I suspect we only got the Hansen contract because of Dad; I dread to think of all the palms he had to grease. Ellie always says she rates my skill as an artist, but she's just proven herself incapable of good judgement, so sod that.

I grab the book again, flip a couple of pages, chuck it back on the sofa in disgust. Out walking along the harbour I'd come across a rusty anchor, resonant of the high seas. It had shrieked adventure, its colours the corrosion of metal fatigue and the streaked sky at sunset. How had I so utterly failed to sing its song?

Perhaps on Sunday I was right – I no longer have any talent and I'm kidding myself. Having squandered the gift, it's gone. Perhaps I'm no more than an expensively trained fraud, with skills suited only to the commercial world of mass-produced junk. Any claim to artistic flair lies on the far side of Paris, ten years ago.

Perhaps I should just go home and confront Oliver.

Huh! Oliver.

And while we're on the subject, why am I not more bothered about Oliver? Who is a cold-hearted shit. Who is currently fucking my best friend. Who is undoubtedly an unfaithful, grade A, lying, cheating bastard. I should be screaming and weeping, tearing my hair out over Oliver, going potty, so why does it all seem rather distant and out of focus? Because it *does*. Because, actually, I can't be bothered with any of it. I can't be bothered to be bloody bothered, not about that or about *anything else, for goodness sake, enough is enough. I can't think about any of that shit right now.*

I march into the kitchen, slap bread and cheese together, pour a large glass of wine, grab the newspaper. So what, I hiss at the cooker, so you're not

Leonardo da bloody Vinci. Who was another *bloody man*. Stop stressing. Stop beating yourself up. You are going to go and eat lunch in the garden, you are going to relax and enjoy the view.

I storm through the back door.

Once outside, I notice the wind has a sharper edge. Just as well I took advantage of the early sunshine, then, wasn't it? Even though I have absolutely nothing to show for it. And as for all that blue...

Sheltered against the back of the cottage is an old wooden bench. Perched there, I spread the *Kernow Gazette* across my knees and bite into my sandwich. I munch with slow, deliberate jaw-circles, chewing one small piece of dry crust till it turns to pulp. Ruminants chew a lot, and seem pretty calm on it. While I'm reading about road-widening schemes and an increase in parking fees, the black cat I've spotted several times from the kitchen window appears suddenly by my feet, winding his tail round my legs. I pretend not to notice and chew on. I turn the pages, ignoring him, and continue to read; there's an advert for an art exhibition in St Ives on Saturday. Might be worth a visit. I breathe quietly, as if absorbed. The cat is a thin creature, a bag of bones, though he's obviously not feral. Perhaps he once belonged to someone in the village who's turfed him out to fend for himself. When I take another bite, the cat jumps up next to me, sniffing with interest.

"You'll have to earn it," I say softly, my hand poised. The cat approaches and allows himself to be stroked, rubbing against my fingers and indulging in that uninhibited, sensuous pleasure only cats understand. A deep purr rumbles from his belly. I break off a few pieces of bread and throw them onto the grass.

Sitting back to drink my wine, I watch the cat nibble each morsel with what looks, absurdly, like appreciation.

A sudden gust of wind lifts the *Gazette* off my lap and blows it across the grass. The cat, abandoning lunch, dives after it, ready for a game. Leaving my plate and glass on the bench, I run to collect the flying pages, one of which spins down the garden and hooks itself on a bramble. The cat gives chase, leaping and ripping the paper. He scurries around in excited circles, ears back, stopping every now and again as if to check I'm following. But once away from the house, the wind whips and no sooner have I bent to pick up one sheet than the next whirls away. The paper seems to come alive, flapping round my legs. There's no time to worry about getting it creased; I simply shove each sheet under one arm, freeing my hands to catch the next, heedless of the printer's ink rubbing off on my T-shirt and staining my fingers. Hair flies in my eyes as I bend down, twist round, turn, grab and turn again.

Lurching towards the last sheet, I feel dizzy and have to stop. Legs apart and with a hand on each knee, I hang my head as the garden dips and bucks around me. I fight to maintain my balance, waiting to get my breath back and for the world to stop spinning. Shapes flit past as I blink, as my eyeballs wobble, bright specks of light that prick and buzz and chirrup: *Now you see it, now you don't*, a high-pitched sound that rings deep into the shell of my ear. *If you will, or if you won't.* The cat, thrashing his tail, dives into the bushes and runs out again in a second, hissing with anger. He skitters crazily round my legs before leaping over the wall as if chased by demons. A cackle. I hear a voice cackle, followed by a softer sing-song: *Let the maiden join the dance.* Warm against the calf muscle of my left leg, I become aware of the rough mass of the round stone insisting and, almost without intention, I sit down.

I have ended up, by accident, at the same spot where I sat the first night, shortly after arriving at Penmaris. Since then, absurd as it may sound, I have failed to find the stone, hidden as it is in the long, wet grass. I've come out several times with the intention of looking for it, but each time I've been distracted, by flowers or birds, by my own lack of concentration, by the way the day seems to wander. But here it is. I try to fix its location but my head is spinning and when I move, the stone seems to rock, as if loose in the ground. I make an effort to keep still until the spinning sensation goes away. I sniff the air, but there's no whiff of the perfume I smelt before. Just a dank odour. I scrape my hair back and rub my eyes, then drop the tattered remnants of the *Kernow Gazette* onto the grass, anchoring its pages beneath one foot. My fingers are black as are, I guess, my face and hair and, well, probably, the rest of me. Why on earth, I mutter, in the technologically advanced twenty-first century, can no one manage to produce ink that stays on newspaper instead of…?

Mid-rant, I hear it again: *Let the maiden join the dance, join the…*

An explosion rips the air.

My outstretched hand flies to my chest to prevent it bursting open. Gasping and startled, I shriek as something lands on my head. And again. And then again and again. Pounding onto the top of my head.

Fat drops of rain the size of golf balls are coming down. They beat a cadence through the bushes, drumming on the dense foliage and pattering to the ground. They nail me to the spot. Thunder and lightning crack the sky above and the rain gets heavier.

Once over the initial shock, I calm down and actually start to enjoy the downpour. Sitting in the garden in a thunder storm is not something I normally do. The sounds are hypnotic, as though an orchestra is playing a watery tune specially for my benefit. And it's working; I am more relaxed, almost overcome by a sense of lethargy. Sitting amid the rhythms of dripping greenery, I wish to do nothing more than give myself up to the weather. This stone seat could have been placed here expressly, like a focus for the elements. I shuffle, make myself more comfortable. Then, leaning forwards, I hold my hands out, palms up, to be cleansed. Sooty runnels of dirt and sweat and printer's ink trickle to the ground. In the washed spaces between, where pale skin glistens, the veins on my wrists thread blue beneath the criss-crossing scars. I offer them up, travel down their blue waterways, drifting with the rhythm of the rain. My pulse slows, my eyes close. I let my mind float and idle, see shapes and colours in the hinterland, hear crying on the wind.

My head comes up with a jerk. Yes, I can hear crying. I can definitely hear a baby crying. Not a fanciful daydream but a real baby. And it sounds in distress. There are no houses close by, but there could be people out walking, caught in the sudden downpour, carrying a cold, damp, fractious infant who's getting wetter by the minute. Soaked through, drowning in water, drowning in a river of water.

Drowning, like…

Then all that matters is getting indoors again. Grabbing the soggy newspaper, I rush back to the cottage, collecting the waterlogged remains of lunch on the way. Dumping everything in the kitchen, I run upstairs, pull my wet clothes off and, without bothering to wash, throw a towel over my hair and slip my dressing gown on. Gathering what I need from a box in the corner, I clamber into bed and start to draw. There's no plan, but I decide to use charcoal which is smooth under my fingers and which, for the moment, feels right. Feels safe. Means I can avoid using colour. I sketch quickly, each sweep of my arm a long outrush of breath. My hands shake as my concentration deepens. Around me the cottage draws in its walls against the worsening weather.

* * *

I work fast, producing brisk lines which I smudge and blur, my fingers reacting to ideas as they come, in long arcs of thought and sudden frenzied application. This is what I wanted, what I've wanted for so long. To be able to draw again, and lose myself in the drawing. I see a face emerging. It seeps into my consciousness unannounced, revealing itself only after shapes have been offered to the page and I've rubbed away any firm suggestion of ridge or curve. It exists in the spaces between, where the creamy white of the paper remains. The face leaks through like a ghost unsure of its welcome.

I hold the sketchpad at arms' length and sip thoughtfully from the vodka bottle in the bedside cupboard. The light is fading fast and I'll have to stop soon, or continue in artificial light which will alter perspective.

Something nags at the back of my mind.

"Who are you, I wonder? Where have I seen you before?"

The pale face of a woman.

Chapter Four

The gallery is quiet for a Saturday afternoon. I accept a catalogue and glance round. Outside the tourist season, in early autumn, this is probably one of the last exhibitions of the year.

After an early lunch, shared once again with the cat, I'd set off for St Ives in optimistic mood, keen to see a small, seaside gallery and compare it with the sophisticated London collections I'm used to. I suppose I'm expecting to find raw talent on display, something unpretentious and direct. And I could do with an injection of creative energy right now. My charcoal sketch is progressing slowly, painfully even, following Thursday's initial burst. As yet it's all outline and shape; the distinctive features refuse to show themselves. I've slept badly for two nights and this has translated itself to the page. The woman remains elusive, evading me, though I can't help thinking I've seen her before.

I decide to start with a huge canvas that dominates the far end of the room, demanding attention. At first sight it seems to depict a typical holiday scene, hackneyed, unimaginative and depressingly predictable. I feel let down. Is the exhibition going to disappoint, after all? Prejudice, like the sea in the foreground, laps over me in waves. But to my surprise, as I walk towards the painting, I'm forced to reassess with every step. Suggesting a family playing beach games on the sand, the stereotypes resolve, or rather dissolve, upon closer inspection into confusing undulations. Leaning on one hip, I stand not too close and stare at the canvas, trying to absorb what's going on. The painting undermines sensory input. The longer I look, the more it disturbs me. After a few moments an elderly man, clutching a notebook and pen, ambles up and starts whistling under his breath. This is irritating and I wish he would stop. We stand side by side considering the picture.

"What do you think?" he asks at length, not looking at me.

"It's… unexpected," I say, sure this is not the right word.

"Why unexpected?" He scribbles a few rapid notes.

I shift to the other hip and sigh. "I suppose because from over there I'd assumed it was going to be—"

"Never assume," he says.

His tone makes me jump. "You're right," I concede. "I'm being crass."

"And patronising."

That's a bit strong. My annoyance returns. I wish he'd go away and leave me to look in peace. His thin whistle sets my teeth on edge.

"Well, come on. What does it say to you?"

Persistent, this man. But at least he's turned to face me. Grey hair and beard, narrow lips, filmy blue eyes. Then he shuffles off to one side.

"Well?" he demands on his return. His expression is earnest, as if he were truly interested in my answer.

"Well," I say after consideration, "it makes me think of Salvador Dali. His bendy clocks and sandscapes." There's one painting in particular, *The Persistence of Memory*, whose genesis is the stuff of anecdote. I smile as soon as I think of it. Apparently Dali had been eating a Camembert whose exceptionally creamy texture had provided both lunch and inspiration. I concentrate on the painting in front of me. "It's the dissolution of form, nothing coherent or lasting. But it's darker than Dali, there's no humour." I feel my mood change. "It's full of despair," I say. And suddenly the room is cold.

"You prefer the easy comforts of Monet or Constable, then? Pretty sentimentality?"

Now who's making assumptions? Who the hell is this guy? He starts writing again, resting the pad awkwardly on his thigh as the biro flies across the page. Some know-it-all art critic, no doubt, getting off on mocking the plebs. I move away to another picture, only to find him following, steering my course. We wash up in front of a bold modern design blasting geometric shapes. Okay, so contrast can be a useful tool, although I've always found abstracts more difficult to read. Too subjective. My insistent companion seems to be having the same problem; he paces backwards and forwards, viewing the painting from different angles.

"Does this one cheer you up?" he barks. "The lighting's all wrong, you know. They've got it all wrong." He tugs his beard in frustration. Then he gets down on one knee and squints up at the canvas, muttering.

Putting space between us, I go and sit on a bench to study the catalogue. To my surprise, it turns out that both paintings, although so very different, are by the same artist, a Cornishman by the name of Alec McConnell who signs himself Mac. He is exhibiting four other works here, all six being explorations on the theme of time. According to the biography, Alec McConnell is a former student and more recently Professor at the Royal College of Art, now back in his native Cornwall where he's researching a book, an illustrated exploration of Cornish mysteries. Accompanying the blurb is a small black and white photo. I lift my eyes to the vibrant canvas and to my putative "art critic", who is scribbling again. When he's finished, I watch him tuck the book into a back pocket then wander off. Ah well, *never assume*. Provided I can keep out of his way, I'll go and find his other four works to compare them.

It turns out his paintings are dispersed throughout the gallery, so tracking them down leads me past the entire exhibition. As an artist, Alec McConnell is an enigma. Each painting is bold and distinctive but completely unlike all the others; thematically linked, they could have been painted by six different people. This leaves me intrigued, wanting to know more. In the end I spend about three hours in the gallery. By four o'clock I'm footsore, thirsty and ready to go home.

Home. The word causes me to stumble. Last Saturday it meant a sprawling pile near Clapham Common. How can it simultaneously refer to a tiny cottage by the sea? Especially if home is where the heart is, as those embroidered Victorian samplers wanted us to believe. Pernickety art, tight-arsed. Hung on frowning walls and forgotten beneath a coating of dust. Home might be nothing more than the roof over your head, where you hang your hat, like in the song. I'll settle for that, for the time being.

I leave the exhibition, buy an ice cream and climb winding backstreets that seem to ache with sunlight. I emerge into the car park at the top of a hill overlooking the town. The sea glitters in the distance. People have told me about the light in this place, that it's a transforming light, that it goes a long way to explaining why St Ives became an unlikely Mecca for artists. Scientists have even taken measurements, apparently, in an attempt to find out if the effect is real or a trick of the imagination. Right now, reflected through the windscreen, the October sun seems to pierce my eyeballs as it slides towards the horizon. I'll have to drive back carefully.

Except I can't get the car started. Several turns of the key, but nothing. Probably I left the side-lights on the other day and drained the battery. Damn and blast it all. Why do these things keep happening? Why is technology out to get me? I reach automatically for my mobile, then drop it back in my bag when I remember. Its battery is dead, too. I forgot to charge it overnight. Bloody hell.

Locking the car, I head back towards the gallery. I might pass a garage on the way, and if not, surely one of the gallery bods will help. The lady on the door did smile at me.

No garage. No phone box. No lady on the door either – she's on a tea break. Instead, I find myself explaining to a man with a deaf aid, asking him if he knows where there's a... if he could point me towards the... if he can hear me properly... when Alec McConnell walks past.

"Problem?" he asks.

I have no desire to explain. "It's nothing," I say. But my deaf friend is already reaching across the counter for a street plan. He turns it round several times to get it the right way up.

"Long walk, I'm afraid," he says, indicating the other side of town.

"Can I help at all?"

"Lady's got a flat battery."

Gee thanks. Tell the whole world, why don't you. "Not a problem," I mutter. "I just need to find a garage."

"I've got jump leads in the back of the car," Alec McConnell says. "Follow me." And without waiting for my response, he marches off to a private car park tucked behind the gallery, leaving me no option but to tag along behind.

"Hop in," he says. "Name's Mac, by the way."

"Yes, I know." His eyebrows ask so I answer. "It's in the catalogue. At first I thought you were some pompous art hack, preparing scathing copy for the local rag. Oh, yes, go that way, follow the road up the hill." I nod as he eases into traffic. "Sorry," I add, "to have assumed." I give a small cough.

"You don't know much about local rags, do you?" He honks at a dithering cyclist. "They don't have art critics. They have spotty youths who also cover weddings, school sports and the WI. But you're right about the pompous."

I laugh.

"I'm as guilty as you." A screech of brakes and he swears at pedestrians for daring to cross the road. "I assumed you were a brain-dead tourist."

And now? I dare not ask. I cast around for something to say. "I suppose you must get sick of summer visitors invading this place." I realise I'm clinging to the seat as he swings the battered Ford through narrow streets. One by one, I uncoil my fingers.

"They schlep round the gallery in their flip-flops and sunglasses, chasing a nice little souvenir. They don't want art; they want wallpaper."

"You're rather cynical, Professor."

"Mac, for crissakes, and what's cynicism got to do with the price of fish, Miss er…?"

"Rose," I say.

"Want my advice, Rose? Always think the worst of people."

"Isn't that the ultimate assumption?"

"Touché," he says, loosing a grin. "But that way you might get the occasional nice surprise. Now, which of these is yours?" The smile transforms his face and twenty years fall away. The brisk walk to his car, the energy he radiates – is he fifty? Sixty? I have no idea.

We draw up next to the MG.

"Huh. Posh motor."

"Oh, no." I hate when people say that. "My… Oliver… we…" I dig the keys from my bag, wishing I didn't sound pathetic. While Mac rummages in his boot for jump leads, I slide behind the steering wheel, praying for the bonnet release to be where I think it is.

The engine catches quickly, suggesting the battery isn't completely dead. The job is done in minutes.

"You ought to get a mechanic to check it out, just to be sure."

"I can't thank you enough. You're very kind." I watch him stow the leads and slam his squeaky boot.

"That I am, dear Rose," he says. "Not the crabby old bugger you assumed, eh?"

Perhaps a bit of both, I think. I hold my hand out. "Thank you, Prof… Mac. Maybe I'll see you again." He has a firm handshake, which encourages me to add, "I do love Monet, by the way, sentimental or not. Sorry to disappoint you."

"Ever been to Giverney?" His face brightens.

"Yes. Yes, it's wonderful." I grin back. We seem to share the moment, the excitement. "I lived in Paris for a year, when I finished training at the Courtauld." In my mind's eye, a bridge floats over a lily pond. "It was my sort-of… gap year."

A gap which, every so often, opens up to swallow the world. A bloody great gap I still tumble into. A pit so deep it sucks you down.

"Good. Good," he says, getting into his car. Then through the half-open window, "I'm often here at the gallery. Next time we'll have coffee."

All the way back to Penmaris, I observe the Cornish countryside soften under an Impressionist's brush. I remember Monet's garden, blossom drifting on a spring breeze, the warmth of fingers interlaced, Jean-Yves bending to kiss me. When I swing into the drive and kill the engine, I am startled by a dark shape framed in the small, upstairs front window.

* * *

45

A flash of panic. That icing of cold steel through the gut. There's someone in the bedroom. Shit. Someone's broken into the house. Then I look again. What I had perceived as a shape is more like a gap in reality, a memory in outline. Perhaps my own confusion. I get out of the car and raise a hand to shield my eyes so I can see more clearly. There's nothing there. It must have been the sun setting through cloud, or reflections on the pane of glass. As I move and the angles change, the window alternates between black and dazzle.

Suddenly I remember Paula's photo of Penmaris. I haven't seen it recently. It must be in the car somewhere. That day at work I'd imagined I could see a face at the very same window, so there must be something opposite that's causing a weird reflection. While I'm hunting for the photo down the side of the passenger seat, on the floor, under the mats, the phone in the sitting room starts ringing. Its insistent trill drags my feet through the front door.

"Hallo?"

Oliver, breathless. "Rosie! Oh, thank God. Please, darling, don't hang up. I've been trying to get you on your mobile but—"

"Oh, the battery's de—"

"Rosie, please. We've got to talk."

We quickly establish that you can't actually mend a whole life over the phone. You can't talk about what matters. We stick strictly to business. Oliver's business, anyway. He's babbling about bloody mobiles.

"I'll make sure my mine's switched on next week," he's saying, "just in case. But I'm afraid I won't be much use to you."

Not much use to me – that's quite funny, till I remember his DNA lacks the gene for irony. I glance round the empty room, listen for noises upstairs. There's nothing. It must have been my imagination. There's no one here.

"Which is why I had to get hold of you today. To check you're all right before I leave. I've got a meeting in Paris on Monday, then I'm going to Germany. If things drag out, I might have to stay over with Klaus and come back—"

"Paris," I whisper. "I see."

Jean-Yves's face stares out through shadows under the Pont Neuf. Blue hovers behind him, always in the background. Those billiard-ball eyes, that rictus smile. So many faces staring through shadows.

Damn the exhibition. And damn Alec McConnell, for waking memories. Right now I'm remembering the way Jean-Yves used to quote poetry. Whenever things got tough, he would spout Baudelaire: *"Entends, ma chère, entends la douce nuit qui marche."* And make love to me as if that night signalled the end of time.

Oliver's off on one of his riffs about check-in times, body searches and dangerous liquids on airplanes. But he'll be fine on Monday morning. Oliver is always fine. Cocooned inside the techno-bubble of his existence, Oliver leads a charmed life. A successful businessman, the marketing arm of a thriving video games company, video dreams are his daily bread. He inhabits a very different world, a virtual universe of electronic connections that are permanently fizzing, uploading or downloading, inputting or outputting, charging, recharging, discharging. A place where reality is

47

silicon-thin. However did I come to be part of that pseudo-existence?

If you cared, I tell myself, you'd be down here now. Sod work, sod meetings and Klaus Bruhler and contracts and megabucks. You'd be here. Now. And nothing would stop you. Not if last Saturday was just a silly mistake. Not if you really loved me.

At some point I put the phone down and go back to ransacking the car to find my coffee-stained photo of Penmaris.

Chapter Five

The photo was on the floor, wedged into the mechanism for adjusting the seat. It must have got caught when I pushed the seat forward last weekend to unload the car.

I've ripped the corner, pulling it out. And it's got a bit creased. Heigh ho.

Studying it now, I wonder why I thought I'd seen a woman's face. All the front windows in Penmaris are small, probably original, and they look out onto the drive, the lane, the hedges and trees which are threaded by roads. In other words, onto nothing very interesting. Whereas at the back, replacement picture windows afford panoramic views of the garden, the cliff top, the sea. Instinctively one gazes out there, not at the front. Besides, if Paula took this photo then it would have been Chris standing at the tiny window, perhaps peering down to find out what his wife was doing.

And I had seen long hair; a bold, feminine silhouette.

Or a mark on the surface. A blur on the lens. A figment of my over-active imagination since erased by coffee stains.

Although, yesterday afternoon, arriving back from the gallery, the shape that caught my eye was quite…

Oh, for God's sake, Rose, stop going round in circles, you'll disappear up your own arse in a minute. Oliver-speak, after another bout of soul-searching. He says I obsess, that I expect rational explanations for everything. Whereas shit happens.

So, that was Peanut, was it? Just more shit happening?

Right. Oliver and Ellie. Shit happening.

* * *

It's nine o'clock, but dark as hell. I fancy an early night and a trashy novel because I've spent all day out walking, climbing the steep slopes between then and now, and I want an end to it. To the turmoil stirred by thoughts of Jean-Yves and Paris, to flashes of Oliver and Ellie, bodies entwined and writhing on our sheets. To memories of death. Tomorrow Oliver will be in Europe and I can start a new week free from shadows.

The paperback fails to intrigue. The devious machinations of a well-endowed air-head battling the might of corporate America make increasingly less sense the more I read. I'm actually quite shattered, and soon my eyelids are drooping over a fourth attempt at the same paragraph, so I give up, switch the light off and quickly plummet into sleep. But only a light sleep, because I wake at the slightest disturbance and fidget across the mattress before dozing briefly again.

Then I'm wide awake, roused by the sound of a bell ringing. It seems to come from far away, but it fills the room. I sit up and become aware of the house moaning and creaking around me, making noises that are strange, frightening even, though the explanation is obvious – wind in the rafters, the old building shifting and groaning under its own weight, reverberations you'd never notice in the bustle of day. To one whose unbroken lullaby for thirty years has been the background roar of London traffic, these disturbances are easily explained – I'm not yet accustomed to silence, or to the sounds of silence. But ignoring them is harder. Each time I'm on the verge of tumbling into sleep, a thin cry snags my attention. The more I listen, the less clear it becomes, a vague squeak that fades the moment I turn my head or try to identify it. Then another noise, like footsteps in the attic, and the scrape of something being dragged from one side to the other. The ceiling boards crack.

I get up and peer through the curtains to check whether the trees are swaying as violently as I imagine they must be, proving it really is a blustery night and what can you expect in the middle of nowhere but a sough of wind and weather? I open the window to admit the roll of the sea, hoping it will lull my anxiety. But sleep skitters away, slithering from my grasp.

At two in the morning, I give up. On the opposite side of the room, leaning against the dressing table, the wide white rectangle of my drawing pad beckons. I get up again, pull my dressing gown on and try once more to bring a feeling into existence.

Sitting cross-legged on the floor, I angle the sketchpad to catch moonlight leaking through the open window. The rough outlines of a head and face confront me; now I proceed to work on the eyes. My hand feels fluid, my drawing arm swings free. Whereas the paper is a slab of white that seems to glow, the rest of the room, the carpet, the box of charcoals by my feet, sink in contrastive gloom. Emerging piecemeal from nowhere, the drawing absorbs my attention, sucking me under its skin at all those places where my fingertips touch to blur the brow line, soften angles, graze the heavy-lidded, liquid eyes. While outside the wind howls, for a time during the long night I am lost to myself as another woman's face comes to life under my hands. The forehead emerges prominent and proud beneath heavy hair, thick and wavy, luxuriant, insistently there; it almost draws itself and curls around the face, obscuring the features. The right eye proves the most difficult, stubborn in fact, less willing to be drawn than the left; the lower lid droops in a persistent tangle of lashes, the eyeball looks rough and sore and weeps a permanent tear into the crevice of the cheek where a ragged scar snakes towards the top lip.

I glance up at the window as if someone might be watching. Then gently, with my index finger, I trace a line down my own cheek from eyebrow to chin, leaving behind a charcoal stain and an ache deep inside. The ache of loss, of a child crying.

But it's too much, way too much. Suddenly I want rid of this ugly drawing, this ugly woman, I want deep oblivion and for tomorrow to come. In the cupboard behind me sits a half-empty bottle of vodka. I know it's there because I can feel it taunting me, whispering promises. I swing round and grab the bottle, upending it down my throat. If that's what it takes, then so be it.

Enough booze to pass out, to forget Oliver, forget… What I need is sleep. Oh please, please let me… With each swallow, fire slides down my gullet like hot kisses, urging me to drink and drink.

As alcohol threads my veins, and despite its numbing effects, I grow pathetically more exhausted and dissatisfied, angry, frustrated, unable to contain myself. And sleep creeps further away. Now I want to tear the picture into a thousand pieces, resentful of its intrusion into my mind. I feel the face accusing me, feel its eyes upon me. The room has grown cold, the wind rattles the window pane and rages over the cliff top, the distant bell tolls once more, one last mournful ring, and I shudder. There is a presence here, an unwelcome ghost watching from between gusts of night air.

I jump up and throw the drawing pad onto the bed. Staggering, I almost tumble on top of it, grabbing the bedpost to steady myself. Then I remember the easel which I left in the car boot. Last Sunday I assumed I wouldn't need it straight away. I unpacked suitcases, walking boots, grocery box, coats, a couple of anoraks; I'll bring the easel in later, I told myself.

So at four in the morning one week later, that's exactly what I do. Sneaking downstairs (why am I sneaking? There's no one here), I tiptoe outside while it's still dark. (Why am I on tiptoes? I'm so drunk I'll fall over.) Keeping as quiet as possible (who am I going to disturb?), I drag the large, paint-spattered easel from the boot. The night air proves sobering, slicing through the cotton wool that packs my head. Despite the vodka and with surprising dexterity, I manhandle the easel from car to sitting room without dropping it and manage to erect it in the alcove by the fireplace. Then I go upstairs for my sketchpad which I carry down and prop on the pegs. And all because I've convinced myself I have to get the face out of the bedroom. Before I destroy it. Because I'll never sleep knowing the eyes are watching me.

When eventually I crawl back to bed, I pass out in seconds.

* * *

Next morning I wake up feeling surprisingly clear-headed. Over black coffee I decide to spend part of the morning locating the nearest garage. If my car battery really is on the blink, I need to get it sorted. I should stop procrastinating and get on with it. I resolve to be practical; I shall dress quickly and set about the day in a purposeful manner. Although I can't believe I slept, clearly I must have because I've no memory of dawn breaking, yet here is the sun, heralding a fine day. A bright Monday morning. A trip to the garage might be all I need to start the week on the right note.

Swallowing a yawn, I make sure I have my cheque book and keys, open the front door, then come to an abrupt halt. Even with my back turned, I can feel the eyes watching me. I spin round and grab the crocheted blanket from the back of the sofa and throw it over both sketchpad and easel, arranging it so that nothing can be seen. Or can see me. The blanket reaches the floor, falling in soft folds to the carpet. Immediately I feel better. With the face obscured I can forget it. Concentrate on practicalities. Get some jobs done. God, I sound like my mother. For good measure, I also slip Paula's photo into a drawer out of sight.

My second attempt at leaving is uninterrupted; the car starts without a hiccup and I ease smoothly onto the road for Porthallen. At ten in the morning the village is quiet. I decide to drive straight through the centre and out the other side, the route most likely to take me past a garage. The road winds past St Michael's Church on the village green, across a hump-backed bridge, then turns sharply left. There, hanging off a broken fence-post, is a rough, hand-painted sign indicating Brian Brothers Autos. I follow the pointing finger down a narrow lane by the side of the river. Fast-flowing and glinting in sunshine, the water tumbles in a rush of white dazzle. Where the lane ends I draw into the garage forecourt. Inside I explain my problem to the two friendly mechanics, nearly identical brothers who finish each other's sentences and laugh reassuringly as I stumble over mine. Is the battery actually dead? Did I leave my lights on and run the thing down? How would I know? The Brian Brothers must think I'm an idiot, a typical woman driver.

But they nod energetically. Shouldn't take too long, they promise, just, you know, driving in like that, without ringing first, I'll have to wait till they can fit me in, right?

So I walk to the sea to while the time away.

* * *

The tide has turned, uncovering firm, golden sand which shelves gently to the water's edge. Pristine and biscuity in colour, it crumbles around worm holes and blows in soft drifts from the tops of ridges formed by the retreating waves. A demarcation line of pebbles and seaweed splits high-water shingle from the growing expanse of beach.

The place is a tourist's dream. Empty on a Monday morning in October, Porthallen Sands must be a magnet for summer-holiday makers. I can almost hear the shrieks of excitement, see the sandcastles, the buckets and spades, smell the factor fifteen and the sweet stickiness of melting ice cream. I slip my shoes off and paddle over to sit on a rock exposed by the falling tide. Wedging them on a dry ledge, I lean back to watch the sea roll in from the horizon, its belly taut and smooth all the way to the shore where it breaks in a froth that pits the sand. The waves sound different from here, visceral, like blood in the veins or like wind blowing from the beginning of time. Last night, what I heard through the bedroom window was an altogether more alien music, thin strains that carried the chime of church bells – which is ludicrous at three in the morning.

Gradually my eyes close, lack of sleep catching up on me. The sun feels warm on my face and I begin to drift like flotsam, rocked by the water's rush and fall. Against my eyelids come strange shapes surging from the deep in colours that splatter and clash like sword blades and the gleam of glory. There is music, a woman singing, her long hair whipped by the wind, and I long to…

"Hallo, Rose. We meet again."

"Christ," I shriek, nearly falling off the rock.

"Sorry. Didn't mean to startle you." Alec McConnell is standing there, hands in pockets, looking out across the water. And he is wearing his shoes. The sea has disappeared.

Half a beach away now, the tide has continued its long retreat, leaving firm sand encircling my seat, with rock pools that glint in the dips and gullies by each outcrop. I check my watch; I must have dozed off. The world seems to spin.

"Professor McConnell. What are you doing here?" I jump down, rather unsteady, and grab my trainers, tying the laces together to sling them over my shoulder. "I must have fallen asleep in the sun. Isn't it a nice day?" My heart is racing, for no reason, because the air is balmy and the sand underfoot soft and inviting. Nothing strange. Nothing out of the ordinary. Everything's fine. "It's almost hot enough to swim, isn't it?"

"Global warming," he says. "Bloody water's probably like ice. And I might well ask you the same question."

"Sorry?"

"I *live* in Porthallen. What are you doing here?"

In unspoken agreement we start walking, side by side, across the beach towards the other end of the cove.

"So do I, sort of. For the time being. I'm staying at a friend's place, up there somewhere." I point towards the cliff. "You can't see it from here, but away in that direction." While I'm trying to locate Penmaris, I realise what he's just said. "You mean you actually live in the village?"

"I have to live somewhere, Rose."

"Yes, of course you do. Sorry. I'm just surprised by the coincidence. When I met you at the gallery I *assumed* you lived near St Ives." Then I look at him, at his raised eyebrows, and we both laugh. "Actually, you'll be glad to know I've just taken my car in. To Brian Brothers?" He nods. "Don't want to get caught out again." He grunts something unintelligible and resumes his off-key whistling. "So I'm idling the morning away. They warned me it could be later this afternoon."

Barefoot, I wander to the water's edge to paddle and, since Alec McConnell is pursuing his own path, I venture further in. He's right. The sea is cold at first, shockingly cold, but I persist and soon I'm splashing like a kid, and in over my knees. The hem of my skirt gets drenched and I hitch it up.

Then suddenly, "Tell me about Paris, Rose," and he's right there, standing in inch-deep ripples, getting his shoes wet, addressing me.

I wade back to the shallows. "Are you always so abrupt, Professor McConnell?" I ask. "You don't waste words, do you?"

"My mother's old adage: if you've nothing to say, say nothing. I try not to blather. Most people don't really talk. They create noise to avoid silence, because they can't stand the sound of their own soul."

I think of Oliver, plugged into his iPod or his computer, of pointless phone calls, of office babble, the electronic whirr of machines and the clack of tongues. Okay, I can go along with that.

I head up the beach towards drier ground. "Well, when I finished at the Courtauld, I didn't know what to do next, except I fancied leaving home." Mac nods at that one. "I've lived in London all my life, really, born and bred, you know? So I went and did the starving-artist-in-a-garret bit in some rat hole off Montmartre. It was great at first, though I discovered starving's not much fun. I managed to sell a few crappy paintings, tourist stuff, quite meaningless, but it helped keep me over there and I did all the galleries and museums and churches and… everything." My hand sweeps in a wide arc that rises on a tide of memory.

"And fell in love?" he asks.

Encroaching on the sun is a patch of dark cloud. Perhaps the weather won't last.

"Yes. Of course I fell in love. With Paris. It's the most beautiful city in the world." My feet kick sand in the air. "Subjectively speaking, of course. To be honest, I've not seen all that many." Jean-Yves showed me his city, unwrapping it like a gift for my delight: the monumental madness of Père Lachaise; tartes au citron, mouth-melting, in a hundred street-markets; gold-leafed wingtips over the Seine; the blues of the Sainte-Chapelle, the oldest stained-glass windows in Paris, drowning me in their deep glow, sea and sky, aqua and sapphire, azure and cerulean and blue on blue on blue, till the earth fell away and you were lifted to paradise. Some things endure. Some things speak in the silence.

"So why didn't you stay?" He's still firing questions at me.

I gaze out across the sea, to where there might be room enough to accommodate the past. Splendid in his Parisian arrogance, Jean-Yves flicked me from his life like the buzz of an annoying fly. Then landed up in jail. And Méline? She would have been a teenager by now. My heart breaks when I remember Méline.

"Well, eventually I had to come home, of course." An attempt at defiance in my voice. "Had to earn a proper living. Couldn't just play at it for ever, could I? Time to grow up and all that. So now I design corporate brochures and advertising material. Back in London." I spit the words out. They sound shameful, and I feel ashamed. "I earn pots of money. And I live in a big house in Clapham. And before you say it, yes, I sold out, I compromised my art." I glare at him.

Alec McConnell lifts both hands in protest. "One has to survive," he says.

"Yeah," I murmur, "but it's a question of how."

We walk on, side by side, the professor whistling tunelessly.

When it becomes clear he's not going to help me out, I mumble, "Oh, I don't know. My life's such a mess at the moment. I've had a… I'm staying down here for a while. I've run away, if you really want to know. To think, get a different perspective."

"To listen to the sound of your soul."

"Perhaps." It's an odd phrase, but that's the second time he's used it, and I get the impression it's anything but a throw-away line. I wonder what he's running away from.

Having reached the end of the cove, we wheel round to walk back. The tide is on the turn, waves rolling up the beach. Alec McConnell crosses the high-water mark to collect dried branches that have washed in and bleached under the cliff. Some pieces he tucks under one arm, the rest he throws back on the shingle.

"Firewood?" I ask.

"Mostly. Though I'll see if anything can be used first. Look at the grain in this piece." He hands me a thick, twisted limb. "Carve it, sand it, the right varnish, might be saleable."

I look at him in astonishment. "But you're a painter, an academic," I start to say.

"I'm Mac, all right? Forget the Professor crap. That was then, this is now. I do what I have to do."

We progress along the beach in silence, Mac darting off whenever he spots a likely chunk of wood. In no time there are splinters in his beard, twigs poking out of his shirt pocket, sand dripping from his hands and arms and drifts of detritus down the front of his trousers.

Where tarmac meets the entrance to the cove, I see his battered Ford parked in a lay-by. "Right. Well, I'd better go and find out if my car's ready," I say, glancing at my watch. "They've had an entire morning." What else should I add? I'm unsure how to close the encounter. Here is a complicated man, a man who's had art exhibitions, publications, a professorship, and who now varnishes driftwood to sell to tourists.

Mac drops his treasure trove, fishes for his keys and opens the boot. I bend to help him throw the wood in. Then I dust my hands, hesitate about whether to hold one out but change my mind and put my trainers on instead, making a big show of brushing sand off my feet and fiddling with my shoelaces.

"I'm off to the pub," Mac says, "if you fancy a pint." He, too, hesitates for a moment, then guns the car up the hill, leaving exhaust fumes behind.

Chapter Six

My car is sitting exactly where I left it, on the forecourt next to a Toyota with its side bashed in. I'm guessing they haven't even started on it yet. A metal grill covers the garage entrance and there's no one around to ask. The Brian brothers are probably enjoying a pie and a pint. Indeed, lunchtime seems to have swept the streets of Porthallen clean and all the shops are closed. That such an old-fashioned tradition should persist I find delightful. London never closes, and I'm so used to buying whatever, whenever, that I take twenty-four-seven for granted. If my local store dared to close for anything less than an Ebola outbreak, there'd be riots – with me among the first to slag off shopkeepers and rant about slack attitudes. But today, instead, I smile. For an entire village to observe a proper lunch hour strikes me as civilised and entirely to be desired. I shall do likewise.

Mac offered to buy me a drink, so I head for the Ship's Anchor. Several patrons look up when I walk in.

The Brians are there, as I'd guessed, playing cards in one corner. They acknowledge me with their beer glasses. An intense group of middle-aged guys in overalls are throwing darts as if the result matters and jostle my access to the bar. Some teenagers, who should be in the school canteen, are swapping headphones and crowding a table by the fire. Half the village seems to be present and most of the barstools are taken. The room is hot and bibulous and expansively comfortable with itself. Canned pop music whines in the background.

One of the Brians stands up to get refills. I want my car back in one piece, so I pursue him. "Hi there," I shout, elbowing my way to the bar. "How's my battery?" There might be a tinge of accusation in my voice – that he's not sober enough to remember me.

"First thing this afternoon," the Brian grins broadly. "Count on it." He leans across. "Same again, mate. What are you having?"

"Oh, no thanks. I'm looking for… a friend. Though I can't see him anywhere." I'm on tiptoes, but with no success.

"Try the snug," suggests the Brian. "Through that door." He points past the dartboard. "Yeh, I'm coming, keep your hair on." His brother is waving a pack of cards. "My deal," he says. "See you later."

He seems *compos mentis*. I'll just have to cross my fingers. I duck past flying darts and turn the brass doorknob.

The very idea of a snug is charming. Another anachronism, like shops closing for lunch. And true to its name it proves to be a small room, cosy and old-fashioned, which probably hasn't altered in fifty years.

No piped music, just a murmur of voices and an ancient patina of nicotine. Mac is there, deep in conversation, so I order myself a half – not that I like beer but because it seems the thing to do. When in Rome and all that. Gulping back a smooth mouthful I realise how thirsty I am. Two more gulps and it's nearly gone.

At this point Mac glances up and notices me. He waves me over. "Looks like more beers all round." He grabs the empty glasses. "Rose, meet Carne Tresawna, farms up back of me. Carne, this is Rose, a fellow artist."

I'm about to protest such a grand title, when I recognise the red woolly hat on the table and its owner who turns round. "Oh, hallo again. Nice to see you. Carne, did he say? What an interesting name. Is it Cornish?"

Carne Tresawna jumps up, grabs his hat and backs away. "No more for me." He shakes his head at Mac. "I best be off. Busy afternoon."

What did I do? Is the man allergic to me? More sharply than intended I ask, "Would one of those things include Penmaris? Because I was going to suggest, on your next visit, that you cut the grass. If it's not too much trouble." He hovers like a naughty schoolboy, shifting from one foot to the other. "It was Sunday, wasn't it?" I continue. "Your day for gardening? Only you didn't turn up yesterday." He's staring at the floor as if confused, and I wonder if he's all there.

"Right oh," he says after a lengthy pause. "I'm away then. 'Fore it starts raining."

"It's not going to rain." Now he's making silly excuses. "It's a lovely day."

He nods at me and stumbles out, pulling his hat down over his large ears.

Mac comes back with pints and pasties. I doubt I'll be able to manage much more liquid, but I take another long pull, eyeing my companion over the rim of my glass. He's eating with relish, steam rising round his face as he breaks the crust and munches hungrily on all the bits that don't flake off into his beard. For a brief moment I think he looks more like a vagrant than a distinguished painter, but I put the thought aside as unworthy. Oliver is the one obsessed with appearances, not me.

"Your friend seems a bit…" About to say "peculiar", I change it to "taciturn" and make a start on my pasty. "God, this is delicious." I'm mumbling, my mouth flooded with saliva. "Must be all this fresh air – I didn't realise I was so hungry." With the back of one hand I wipe crumbs off my chin. "Your friend, Carne Thingummy. He wouldn't tell me his name last week. I barely got two words out of him. Is he always so… quiet?"

Mac digs a paint-stained cloth from his trouser pocket to wipe his lips. "So you're staying at Penmaris," he comments, ignoring my questions.

"Yes, didn't I say? Up the hill, behind the cliffs where we walked this morning. It's a lovely cottage. Amazing views from upstairs. Belongs to friends of mine in London. They're letting me stay for… as long as I like, really." I attack the pasty again. "This is the best thing I've tasted in ages." After several minutes of munching and silence I venture, "Do you live in that direction?"

Mac shakes his head and continues with lunch. We finish eating and drinking without another word being spoken. I decline the offer of a third glass. "I'll explode." A few more moments of silence float past, then I try again with, "You know Penmaris Cottage?" My voice upbeat and engaging; it must be possible to hold a conversation with the Cornish. I'm used to Londoners being unfriendly; they have every reason – overcrowding, urban alienation. But this rural mutism is getting on my nerves. And it's such a cliché, that country folk shun outsiders. But Mary in the shop gave me an odd look, Carne does no more than grunt at me. Now Mac has started clamming up. Why won't they talk?

Then I realise. Of course. It's obvious. "It must be really galling for people round here," I say, "to see local houses being sold off to tourists as second homes, then left empty half the year."

"Penmaris was left empty long ago."

Do I imagine a change of tone? "Oh, really? In what way?"

I wait for a count of ten.

"You said, *long ago*?"

He glances at me, so I flash an encouraging smile. "Well," he drawls and then proceeds to drain his glass very slowly. After a further pause during which he appears to consider my eager face, he relents. "The previous family, they'd lived there for generations, you see. Like lots of people do in these parts. But, gradually, they died off or moved away, leaving just the one. Then she… disappeared."

"Disappeared? What do you mean, disappeared?"

Mac is concentrating on his paper napkin, folding it with care. "Carne used to be… very fond of her. Cut up, he was. Suppose you could say he never really got over it."

"Got over… what?"

"Her disappearing. That's why the place stood empty for so long. Like it was waiting for her. They found the skeleton eventually, up the coast, trapped under rocks. Police identified it from dental records. Couldn't tell if she'd drowned or if she'd hit her head, fell off the cliff. The body must have got buried in a landslide, after a storm maybe, and lain there undiscovered for years." From the folds of his red napkin Mac produces a flower, a huge tropical bloom. "A rose for Rose," he says, handing it over with a flourish. "Don't look so sad. It was a long time ago."

"But it's a sad story. I wonder what really happened to her. Do you think they'll ever find out?"

"Once the legal stuff was done, the cottage went on the market. Took ages to sell, by all accounts. I was teaching at the RCA in those days, so I'm going on what people told me, but the place must have been a ruin."

I remember Paula's delight at the amazing bargain they'd pulled off. "Talk about going for a song, darling. It's a real snip. Needs a bit of emergency work, you know, but then we'll have ourselves a proper little nest egg." Nest egg. Bolthole. Someone's home, waiting for her all those years. And now I'm living there, moving through the shadows of tragedy. On the table in front of me, the exotic red flower strikes a discord.

I glance at my watch. Fiddle with the strap. Hardly a sound can be heard from the main bar. The pub has emptied while we've been talking. Lunchtime is over and hopefully my car's receiving attention. To cheer myself up, I decide to look round the village for half an hour, explore the shops, before wandering back to the garage. I feel unexpectedly low.

"Well, I'd better be off. Thanks for lunch, Mac." I scrape my chair back and stand up. "It's been good to chat. Drop in some time if you're passing Penmaris. Please, do. Come and see what my London friends have done with the old place." He nods, head bowed over his empty glass. "And thank you for… this." I pick up the flower he's fashioned and twirl it round. "Bye, then."

* * *

With a new battery and two new tyres, my MG positively races up the hill from Porthallen. I hadn't realised there was anything wrong with the tyres but I paid the bill anyway, being in no position to dispute it and lacking the energy for a fight. Besides, a fight was exactly what I walked in on, some hulking great apparition in bikers' leathers revving his mean machine and bawling insults at the Brian brothers, calling them rip-off merchants. He'd screeched past me in a roar of exhaust fumes, giving two fingers to the world.

"The youth of today. You'd think you'd get a better class of yob in the provinces. Now, here's your key, milady. Car all done and dusted. Shouldn't have risked those bald tyres, you know, might've had a nasty accident."

Cute, the Brian brothers, in both senses of the word: redheads with freckles, sandy skin and bright blue eyes, though one is taller than the other and possesses the *savoir faire*. From the headed invoice I learn their

68

names are Derry and Colm, though which is which I have no idea. Derry and Colm. Unusual.

Come to think of it, many of the villagers have unusual names. I wonder about the previous owner of Penmaris, the woman who disappeared. What was she called? I can't get her story out of my mind, though I never got round to asking Mac her name. It had seemed inappropriate, too nosey. But driving around this part of Cornwall, I have noticed some interesting towns and villages. They sound enchanting. Lyrical and somehow all of a piece, with patterns of prefixes and suffixes that must have local meaning. Penzance, Penhale, Penhallow. And, of course, Penmaris itself.

In the hope of learning more I did try the village bookshop before collecting the MG, only to find they had nothing appropriate in stock. The bookseller directed me to the nearest library, but "since you're here, how about a paperback on Cornish myths and legends? Best I can do, I'm afraid." Well, why not? I'd recalled the exhibition catalogue saying Alec McConnell was working on a similar theme. If I saw him again, we'd have a ready-made topic of conversation. Antique lore might be an appropriate antidote to virtual reality.

Back at the cottage, I hope to find Carne at work. Now there's another interesting name. I wonder what it means. Can I use my new interest in etymology to coax him into conversation? There has to be a way to bypass the awkwardness, hostility almost, that he displays. Does he resent me for living in the home of the woman he once loved and lost? Not that Mac used the word "love", but I can read between the lines and I'm regretting my rudeness. I want to apologise to Carne, without making him feel even more awkward. Presumably his offer to tend the garden for Chris and Paula was a final act of devotion.

But there's no sign of him. Nor has he been here during the morning. The garden looks as messy as ever, the grass still long and uncut. For a devoted swain, he rather lacks commitment. Chris wouldn't be impressed if he knew his odd-job man was slacking on the job. As a hard-nosed businessman, he believes in value for money, in getting "plenty of bang for his buck". A gardener who doesn't garden would be a waste of space, simple as that. Chris would excise him with one snap of his mercenary secateurs. Commercial acumen doesn't accord with compassion.

I turn the key in the back door and ponder making coffee to counteract the effects of rather too much real ale. Good idea. Kettle on, I wander into the sitting room.

"What on…? Oh!"

It's like I've walked into a kaleidoscope. Catching sunlight from the window, the patchwork blanket which I'd draped over the easel is splashing colours round the room. Reds and greens and yellows flash onto the bare white walls as rays of sunlight catch each square of crocheted wool. I'd forgotten all about my drawing, and now that I'm feeling relaxed, the idea of covering up a sketch because it upset me seems ridiculous. How could I possibly be frightened by the product of my own imagination?

Lifting a corner of the blanket, I study the face once more, striving for objectivity and distance. The French have a phrase, I recall, for women like this: *jolies laides*, women whose ugliness is part of their beauty.

70

While their features verge upon the grotesque, it's the very excess of proportions that underlies their sexual appeal. This face, for example: broad, dominating brow, heavy bone structure, thick mane of hair, strong angular jaw-line. Not a woman to be messed with. I feel both fascinated and repelled. But it's the scar, carving the face in a line of pain, which demolishes any sense of power and introduces a tragic note. A hint of vulnerability. The damaged eye pulls me like a magnet. Attempting to assess planes and angles of forehead and cheekbones, I find myself compelled again and again by that dreadful wound weeping from eyeball to chin. And I hear Mac's voice, telling me about a woman who vanished twenty years ago.

I let the blanket drop, felled by a wave of exhaustion – lack of sleep, I suppose, sea air, too much beer at lunchtime. Thinking I might just lie down for a minute and flick through my new book, I go upstairs, kick my shoes off and flop on the bed. Within seconds, I'm fast asleep.

When I wake up, it's pitch black outside, so I must have slept for hours. And I had this weird dream. I was in a house with a never-ending central hallway that just meandered on and on without ever going anywhere. Rooms led off it, on either side, some completely empty, others devoid of people but furnished like stage sets waiting for the actors to appear, or perhaps recently abandoned by them. One turned out to be my old maths classroom. I recognised it straight away. A couple of times my form room and part of the maths suite, it had been the focus of my personal purgatory year upon year. There was my desk, with "Miss Lyons is a cow" etched into the fascia, and the rolling blackboard (dull green, in fact) covered in symbols and numbers that were meaningless, row upon descending row of them, down to the inevitable equals sign that screamed at me: "Come on, Rose! You must know the answer. What does it mean? Work it out, girl, don't just sit there." A code demands to be cracked, and I knew it was a message I had to decipher, but it made no sense.

On the verge of tears, I fled to another room which contained paintings except, when I looked carefully at them, the canvases were bare. Then I was in the corridor again, trying to reach the end. Corners and bends blocked my view, but slipping provocatively around each curve of the wall was the tail of a black cat. I ran after it, calling, but I couldn't catch it. The tail lingered just long enough to be seen, then slid away, always out of reach, always leading me on. At one point I heard the creature miaowing. Maybe he was hungry; but I had nothing for him. And the corridor wound ever on. I thought I recognised stretches I'd already passed, so was I going backwards?

Perhaps I should turn round. *I don't understand*, I whined. *How can 2a plus b equal 10 if x squared is greater than y?* The passage ahead seemed to be narrowing and squeezing me on either side. Soon I would be crushed. Just in time I slipped through another open door, certain that's where I'd seen the cat vanish, then I heard a loud thump above my head, like the closing of a heavy lid. The noise made me jump and that's what woke me up.

It's starting to get dark. That's odd. I roll off the bed, my head aching, and I open the window for a breath of air. Down in the garden, weaving through the long grass, I can just make out the shape of the cat, nearly invisible except for his tail swishing. He's still miaowing, and I consider going downstairs to put food out. Perhaps he isn't a family pet at all; perhaps he's a stray who depends on scraps to survive. Poor, starving thing. He certainly sounds hungry; he needs feeding. The longer I listen, the louder his cry becomes. In fact, it isn't outside at all; it's in the house. And it sounds more like a baby crying. I spin round, honing in on the sound. It is. It's a baby crying. Insistently, here in the room. It's *in this room*. I rush to the other side of the bed; carefully, so as not to alarm, I bend over the cot.

Oh my God! Oh my God!

I'm awake. And it's still broad daylight.

My elbows dig into the mattress, trying to push my body backwards, through the headboard, out though the wall, in a kind of reflex action to get away. Scrabbling against the bottom sheet, my heels slip and slither. The sound of my heart whomping fills my skull. I've been having one of those awful dreams where you keep waking up only to find you're still asleep, still dreaming. And each dream is scarier than the last. Only they're not dreams, they're nightmares. When my legs finally stop kicking, I pinch my arm. Then I pinch it again, much harder. Ow! That bloody hurts. I must be awake this time. And my mouth feels disgusting. Too much beer, that's why. I stagger off the bed to go and brush my teeth, then stop dead. Above the dressing table mirror, a thread of blood is trickling down the wall.

* * *

When I finally wake up, gasping and confused, I rush down the stairs, two at a time, out into the garden and

73

onto the wet grass. I take several long, shuddering breaths before I realise I'm getting soaked. To my surprise, the weather has changed. My watch says three fifty, which means I've been asleep for scarcely an hour, in which short time the blue sky has disappeared behind low cloud from which splatters a cold, hard rain. Carne was right, after all.

Back inside, and hot coffee fails to warm me. My teeth are chattering and I feel sick. Dampness seeps through the cottage walls and the old-fashioned, one-bar electric heater, which I eventually unearth behind the boiler, doesn't work. Its cable is frayed, with stretches of bare wire hanging loose. When I wiggle the plug in the socket, sparks flash ominously. Burning the place down, or even blowing a fuse seem like bad ideas. I look speculatively at the fireplace. There's a pile of dusty logs on the hearth, doubtless arranged years ago by Paula as a homely touch, and I've seen matches in the kitchen. I could risk lighting a fire. To my immense relief (for I fear the chimney might be blocked, even if Paula did once have it swept), the dry wood catches immediately and flames rush upwards, along with the smoke. In no time I'm sitting cross-legged on the mat, thawing out.

Waiting for the shakes to stop, I focus my thoughts on the present. On the here and now. The only way I know to beat nightmares. I try to imagine Alec McConnell relaxing in front of a fire like this one, somewhere near by, though I still don't know where he lives. Bet he has plenty of wood though, whereas mine will soon be gone; I'll have to restock tomorrow. Or buy bags of coal. You can usually pick them up at a service station, and I need petrol. After that, a trip to the corner shop and a trawl along the beach for driftwood. I'm being rational, thinking sensible thoughts, groping my way to solid ground. Everyday practicalities, something I can hold on to.

I lost a baby, not my entire life. Peanut. We loved that name; a tiny kernel of life inside me.

After the miscarriage, at fifteen weeks, it felt as if the universe had turned red. After the mess had finished oozing from between my legs, the thick, viscous, bloody baby mess (*no,* the *ex*-baby mess – foetal matter, one doctor had called it – matter? what's the matter? never mind, dear, doesn't matter), all the heavy, crimson-black death stuff that dragged and dragged and took my heart with it, after all that misery had finally evacuated my body, then I swear I cried red tears. The whites of my eyes turned red, I was weeping blood. Once the escape route of my vagina had dried up, the blood simply turned north and carried on leaking from eyes and ears and nose and every orifice of a body that could no longer contain hope.

So, for the second time in ten years, I am being required to *hold on*. First Paris, then London. Capital cities, capital punishment. If only I could escape the nightmares. Awake or asleep, I'm haunted by the sound of a child crying: the French child I was unable to hold on to, the English baby I failed to keep safe inside.

My parents took a robust attitude to Paris, Mum in the Gare du Nord supervising mountains of luggage while Dad bought tickets. Their brisk common sense organised my despair, breezing like an east wind through the rank confusion of my mind. And it was my mind that confounded thought; I could no longer be sure of what I'd seen or done. Did Blue have the knife

75

all along? Had I let the tiny hand go, fingers slipping unnoticed through my own? I'd glimpsed Méline's body when they pulled it from the river, limp and streaming. Then my sanity had crumbled. Other people, oh, they were caring and supportive at first, but they didn't understand. They kept telling me I must stop being hysterical, I must grow up, settle down, wise up, knuckle down, cheer up, calm down, up down up down up down up down like a sea-saw, guts churning, throw up, chuck up, give up. "*Calm down*, Rose, you'll be all right. Come home with us, darling, we'll look after you. Get yourself a proper job, forget all this nonsense, everything will be all right, you'll see. Just *calm down*." And the downs have it, down, down, down the slippery slope. "Rose! Great to see you. How was Paris? Looking a bit down, Rose, down in the mouth. Bit of a come down, chez ma and pa after gay Paree? See you down the pub. Come on down. What, you, settle down? Oliver? Job? Mortgage? It's all downhill from there on!"

And I had come down to earth, done as I was told. Played the game, followed the rules, too eagerly, some would say, going over the top again, till fate slapped me down a second time. "Just a miscarriage, Rose, happens to a lot of women. Try again. No reason you can't bring a baby to term, just one of those things." But I know it was my fault, working too hard, playing too long, burning the candle at both ends and thinking I could have it all. Not looking after myself, not paying attention to innocence. Forgetting Paris. And now it's time to pay. Crushed beneath the weight, squashed flat by the stone dumped on my head, will I be able to crawl out from under this time?

Outside the circle of firelight, the cottage lies in darkness. I draw the curtains against the early evening gloom, sealing inside the walls a cosy crackle of flames. The clocks go back soon, at the weekend, marking the death of summer and the long descent into winter. The bookseller reminded me this afternoon, as I was paying for *Old Kernow: Myths and Legends*, and we'd started chatting about the solstice and Halloween traditions. "Don't forget to put your clocks back on Sunday," she'd said.

Spring forwards, fall backwards.

The patter, learned as a child to remind me which way to move the hands on my watch, comes back to mock me.

Chapter Seven

Despite my good intentions, it's Wednesday morning before I'm able to make it as far as the shops. I have a hangover the size of Africa. When I turn the corner by the pub, I am confronted by a crocodile of children bobbing along the pavement in twos, bundled up in coats and scarves, holding hands and chattering. As the crocodile reaches the end of the street, a teacher steps into the middle of the road to stop traffic. Bringing up the rear is the lady who served me in the bookshop on Monday. She smiles as they pass.

"Off to church to practise," she says. I must look as blank as I feel. "For Halloween? The Year Six class has written *a play*." She sounds vicariously proud. "Stephen, don't pull Michael's arm like that. Hold his hand nicely, please." She winks at me. "Little sods. But I'm sure it's more fun than doing sums." Then with breathy excitement, "Wait till you see the costumes."

Confused, I nod and wave goodbye, then go into Coleforth's store. Halloween sounds rather pagan for the Church of England. And that extravagantly dressed woman, is she a bookseller or a teacher? Both, perhaps. My head, already swimming, is invaded by ghoulish figures.

At the end of the fruit and veg aisle I came across pumpkins, stacked in their matt-orange bulbous glory. On impulse I decide to buy one. Choosing the biggest, I carry it over to Mary Coleforth at the till. "Can I leave this with you while I finish my shopping? There won't be room for it in here." My wire basket is obviously inadequate.

"Going to bake a pie?" Mary asks.

"I'm not sure. Might just hollow it out and make a lantern. We used to do that at home, me and my sister. I just met one of your junior-school classes going to practice their Halloween play and it made me remember." I roll the pumpkin onto the counter. "By the way, who's the lady who works in the bookshop? She was with the kids crossing the road."

Mary wrinkles her nose. "Only I can give you a recipe. If you want."

"Sorry?"

"For pumpkin pie." She starts fiddling with the cash register.

"Er… no thanks." I'm being side-tracked again, but continue undeterred. "The lady from the bookshop?"

Mary considers the matter, then, "Dresses like a gypsy?" she asks, snapping a new till roll into place. A hint of reprobation edges her voice.

"Well, brightly dressed. Yes."

A long pause. "That'll be Jan."

"Oh, yes?" I wait.

"Jan Freeman. Well, Jancis, her name is. Her proper, given name… though some…"

"So is she a teacher or what?" Blood and stones come to mind.

Mary shrugs and rolls the pumpkin off the counter, stashing it somewhere below. "She helps out," she says, vaguely. "Very into *drama,* that kind of thing." There's a dubious stressing of the word, as if drama were faintly improper. "Does a bit of this, bit of that." I recall Jan Freeman's cheerfulness in the shop on Monday. She'd seemed friendly and approachable. And, compared with Mary here, positively loquacious.

After shopping, I had planned to drive to the beach for some fresh air and to hunt for firewood (there's none left in the cottage; I burned the lot) so I'd parked the car behind the store, down a cul-de-sac. When I come to drive out again my route is blocked by a mud-spattered Land Rover, open at the back to reveal mounds of produce and Carne Tresawna hefting boxes. He seems to be making a delivery to Coleforth's. Alec McConnell said he farmed locally. Maybe Carne grew the tomatoes in my bag, which is a nice thought, that local produce means exactly that. Manoeuvring round him, I wind the window down and wave hallo. "See you at Penmaris soon," I call out, then regret it. I don't want him to think I'm criticising. Carne mutters and disappears into the shop.

Much of the driftwood on the beach is wet, either from the tide or from yesterday's rain. But sheltered deep under the cliff I find a few twisted chunks, bone white, dry for months. Excellent for firewood, they'll catch easily and burn well. I consider them with the professor's eye, checking for shape and grain. I try to think like a sculptor seeing the statue in the stone, try to imagine what might be carved from this piece or whittled from that. Perhaps I should experiment with wood carving. It might be fun.

Choosing what I can feasibly carry, after only three trips I've filled the boot. When I stand back to admire the load, it occurs to me that most of what I've gathered is far too big to fit the fireplace. How to reduce branches and planks into useable logs is a problem I hadn't considered. Perhaps Carne might be willing to chop the wood for me, or at least lend me a saw or an axe. I hope he'll call round soon.

Instead of driving straight back to the cottage, I detour past the bookshop. A man behind the counter informs me that Jan Freeman does afternoons. She'll be opening up after lunch, two o'clock prompt. He does mornings.

So I return to Penmaris to put the shopping away, but leave the wood in the MG hoping Carne will show up later. The pumpkin I sit in an armchair where it looks comfortable and where I can contemplate it over copious mugs of black coffee. At two-thirty I set off once more for the village.

Jan Freeman glances up from the pile of paperbacks she's unwrapping. "Hallo again. It's Rose, isn't it?"

"How on earth do you…?"

"Village grapevine, my dear. Mary Coleforth's a dreadful old gossip." When Jan Freeman shakes her head, her long earrings tinkle. "So you're the one staying at Penmaris?" She holds out a packet of mints. "Extra strong. Cover a multitude of sins. Go on, have one. I'm Jan, by the way."

"I know. Same grapevine." I help myself to a mint. "Thanks. It's really nice to meet you." There must have been more feeling in my voice than I realised, for Jan bursts out laughing.

"Getting the silent treatment, are you?" she asks. "Carne and Mary can be devils that way. Tight-lipped sods." A half-laugh this time, devoid of humour. I sense mutual dislike.

The peppermint is volcanic and makes my eyes water. I squint through tears at Jan who is stacking paperbacks in height order. Like a gypsy, that had been Mary's description. I admire the shock of dark springy curls which a dozen silver hairclips are failing to control. How enviable to have a real head of hair, compared with my own wispy drizzle. The clips reflect the shine in Jan's eyes and complement the dangly earrings bouncing round her face. Hair glinting, jewellery sparkling, she seems alight. Bright red lipstick and very white teeth add to the brilliance. On Monday when I'd first seen her, she'd been dressed head to toe in black, something dramatic and velvety, I'd thought, that matched hair and eyes. Today, the word flamboyant comes to mind. She's wearing a silky top over a full, wide skirt, both items made from some exotic fabric that rustles, flouncy and blousy and coppery orangey red. She burns behind the book counter like a flame.

"Did the rehearsal go well?" I ask, picking up a large-scale map of south-west Cornwall. It might prove useful.

"Hilarious," says Jan. "Absolutely hysterical. They've all got about *one line each* to learn, and do you think they can remember their words? Not a chance.

But little Stevie's a darling as the naughty pisky. He was the one pulling his mate's arm off, did you notice, this morning? Little bugger really, but cute as they come."

I recall Jan yelling at someone in the crocodile while they waited to cross the road. "So the vicar lets you do a play about Halloween in the church?"

Jan opens her eyes wide. "Well, bless you, my dear. The vicar's one of us." Laughter ripples down her throat. Then, in confidential tone, she adds, "Besides, we're in the church *hall*," as if that makes all the difference. "Let me tell you, Rose. The old ways, they're part and parcel of everyday life round here. Slide down with mother's milk, they do. We don't go making distinctions. It's all one, when you think about it. Tell you what, if you're still here on the thirty-first, come and watch our play. You'll be very welcome. And you can join the fun on the Green afterwards." Her earrings tinkle softly.

"What's the play about?" I replace the map and pick up a street plan instead. "I thought Halloween was trick or treating, like they do in the States. An excuse for kids to throw eggs at people's windows and stuff themselves with sweets."

Jan fingers a crystal pendant nestling in the hollow of her throat. "Yanks! What do they know?" As she leans across the counter, I catch a spicy perfume in the air. "Folk round here call it by the old name, All Hallows' Eve. It's the night that marks the passage from autumn to winter, when the souls of the dead come back and warm themselves by the fire. We leave food and drink out for them, and the fairies dance a welcome. There's music in the air, Rose, fairy bells and elf horns. And sometimes, you know," her voice sinks lower, spinning fantasies, "the piskies get up to all kinds of mischief, like…" She gives a dramatic pause. "Like making off with a sleeping child and leaving a changeling in its place." A sharp wind rattles the shop door. Jan's eyes gleam. "That's Stevie's part, the naughty pisky, stealing the baby from its cot. Only during rehearsals this morning he yanked the doll's arm clean off in a fight. He's got a thing about arms…" She appears to consider this defect in his character. "We're going to need something a damned sight more robust for the performance." She winks again as the phone rings. "Porthallen Bookshop, can I help you?"

Dolls and babies and changeling children. Could I request the fairies to leave a special Halloween gift? In the ache of my mind, the persistent cry of a baby lost in dreamland.

While Jan is on the phone, I wander across to a rack of postcards by the window, noticing with surprise how few of them depict anything like the typical holiday scene. Mostly they're representations from myth or fantasy: on the one hand, mischievous elves in pointy red caps and green jackets alongside flower fairies with butterfly wings; on the other hand, dozens of old black-and-white photographs of standing stones. The overall effect is to confound, like the bending of time. From archaeological sites on the Scilly Isles to local pictures of menhirs, cromlechs and burial mounds, inexplicable megalithic structures rise majestic over the bleak Cornish landscape. Lanyon Quoit, Mên-an-Tol, strange-sounding names that pique the tongue. Strange names on a strange selection of postcards. Where, I wonder, are the beach scenes to send home and make the

84

neighbours jealous, the kiss-me-quicks, the usual views of sea and sand? The rack is full of images from another world, a world of fey creatures and monuments "raised" (so it states on the back of one) "by the hands of giants for the god-kings of old."

Eventually, tucked away at the back, I manage to find some ordinary cards – pictures of crumbling pasties, scones swathed in cream and jam, platters of seafood. I choose one for my parents to tell them how much I'm enjoying my little holiday and how much better I'm feeling from all the fresh air and exercise. For myself I opt for standing stones. *The old ways*, Jan had said. These photos will remind me that Cornwall is, after all, an ancient land. The phrase seems to speak itself inside my head and take up residence.

I carry the cards, along with the street map, over to the counter to pay. While I'm digging three pounds sixteen from my purse, Jan slips everything into a crisp paper bag decorated with bold, swirling symbols.

"Didn't I sell you a book the other day about Cornish legends? It's all in there. Everything you need to know."

I've barely opened it. "Yes! Yes, you did. And after what you've just been telling me, I must read some more." As I pay, I notice how violently my hands are shaking. I'm drinking far too much. Yesterday escaped me in a haze of vodka.

Jan presses the package warmly into my grasp, which has the unlikely effect of calming the tremor. "Take care," she says. "Enjoy your stay in Cornwall."

Enjoy. I feel confused and go for something bland: "It's so peaceful here. So quiet after London," and I'm surprised when Jan raises an eyebrow and gives me a long look. "Really," I insist, "compared with the endless din of London traffic, it's wonderful. If I leave my window open at night, I can hear the sea. It's amazing, the waves sound like cymbals crashing or like bells."

This time Jan nods, a slow smile parting her lips. "Call in again, Rose," she says. "And I hope Penmaris stays quiet for you."

Where our hands touched, I feel a lingering warmth.

* * *

Curled up on the sofa, I'm keen to make a start on my book, to escape into another world. I'd like to light the fire, but Carne hasn't appeared and I have no proper logs. I think of all the wood in my boot and decide that if it gets really cold this evening, I can always jump up and down on a few pieces. Cursing myself for forgetting buy coal, I turn my attention to Chapter One. Cornwall, I read, *is an ancient land where the past lives side by side with the present.*

An ancient land. The words I had used in the bookshop. My mouth drops open.

Fairies and other mythological beings inhabit the cliffs and moors so that the county lies beneath an enchanted spell. First Jan this afternoon, and now the author of this tome; does everyone believe in pixies? Or piskies, as Jan had called them. *Separated from the rest of England by no more than the width of the Tamar, this westernmost corner of Britain is so different that some call it "the land outside England". From this place come the Arthurian legends, stories of Celtic gods and goddesses, Druids and Ley lines, rumours of Plato's Atlantis and the lost land of Lyonesse.*

86

I can hear a funny noise outside. A sort of dragging, thumping noise. A thud, then footsteps creeping away. I move the curtain aside, but see nothing. When I open the back door and call out, the garden seems peaceful and still. Pouring a glass of wine, I grab a packet of crisps and return to the sofa and my book. I flick forward a few pages to the chapter entitled "Lyonesse."

Legend has it that the Isles of Scilly are all that remain today of the ancient kingdom of Lyonesse, the sunken land of romance where some say Arthur was born. According to the Saxon Chronicle, Lyonesse sank without trace in 1089 when the sea flooded the land, drowning towns, people and animals. One hundred and forty villages and churches disappeared, and local tradition has it that fishermen still bring ashore parts of old buildings caught in their trawling nets.

There it is again, more like scratching this time. Then a thud at the back. Quietly, I extract the torch from the kitchen drawer and turn the backdoor handle slowly. Immediately the little black cat dashes in, eyes blazing and tail like a Christmas tree. He's miaowing his head off. "Has something frightened you," I ask, "or are you just plain hungry?" The cat pads round the kitchen, back arched in display, before coming to rub against my legs. When I bend to stroke him, he doesn't feel especially thin. Perhaps he's found another source of titbits. Although I don't want to encourage him, I equally don't want him to go hungry. He looks up at me and mews pathetically. That decides it. From the fridge I take a few scraps of ham which I chop up and put on a plate on the floor, next to a saucer of milk. The cat, after perfunctory sniffing, falls upon the food. I return to my book.

Today about fifty islands make up the Isles of Scilly group, although only four are inhabited. Archaeological evidence suggests human habitation there since prehistoric times. It is believed by many that what we see as small, individual islands are but the hilltops of a sunken landmass known as Lyonesse. Sometimes, at very low tide, the remains of ancient stone buildings, including megalithic structures, can be seen.

While I'm reading, the cat, now with a fat belly, creeps into the sitting room and onto the sofa to curl up on the cushion next to me. I pretend to ignore him. I learn that in 1990, scientists investigated the area of sea just beyond the Isles of Scilly as part of a mapping project to find evidence for a much larger catastrophe that may have affected the coastal lands of the so-called Celtic Shelf of northwest Europe. The cat starts to purr, very quietly. I stroke his head, though I know I shouldn't. This might be someone's pet and I shouldn't encourage disloyalty. But his company is welcome and completes the room.

I turn a few pages and read about the Breton legend of Caer Ys, a settlement which disappeared beneath the Bay of Douarnenez in Brittany, and about the lost land of Cantref, drowned in Cardigan Bay, disasters all occurring in the same timeframe. *The persistence of the myth of a lost kingdom might well be a folk memory of dry land that did once exist linking the Celtic peoples of old. Even today, locals claim to hear sunken church bells ringing on stormy nights.*

The book falls to my lap; the hairs on my arms prickle. Is that what I heard? The bells of Lyonesse ringing in the night? Jan Freeman had reacted to my casual remark about bells, had given me a knowing smile. But surely I over-imagined the odd noise, attributing qualities and descriptions without thinking. I got myself spooked from too much booze, from feeling miserable, because of the wind in the trees. The whole idea was ridiculous. Even if there were sunken churches off the coast, surely the sheer weight of water above them would make it impossible for bells to swing and chime. That is, if they hadn't already rusted away in the intervening thousand years. One ought to apply a certain degree of logic.

I sit quietly, listening to the cat purr. Lyonesse, birthplace of Arthur, the once and future king, land of Tristan and Isolde, the doomed lovers. Myth and legend are so seductive, mystery easily eclipsing reason. Common sense, by comparison, seems counter-intuitive, a wet-blanket virtue that has to be learned and imposed upon our secret yearnings to believe. I've always wanted to believe, to be able to shrug off my natural scepticism and simply believe in Father Christmas, the tooth fairy, guardian angels, magicians, wizards and old wives' tales, the numen leaking into everyday life with small, telling portents.

Another crash outside. Something thuds against the cottage wall, right behind where I'm sitting. Shuffling footsteps again. My heart pounds. The cat springs off the sofa and up the stairs in a blur, abandoning me without a moment's hesitation.

Chapter Eight

There's a sharp rap at the front door, followed by a very human cough. No Celtic wraiths about to attack, then. Unaware I'd been holding my breath, I exhale a long rush of air, switch the lights on and open up.

A very unspectral Alec McConnell is standing there, arms filled with logs and a bottle of wine tucked deep into one armpit.

"I come bearing gifts," he says. "Quick. Take this before I drop it."

"What a surprise. Do come in, Professor." I sweep him a bow. "Are you here to solve my problems once again?" I extract the bottle and note its respectable provenance. No plonk for Alec McConnell.

"Cold as bloody charity in here," says Mac, filling the room in two strides. "You said you were jealous of my roaring fires, so I thought I'd share. That chimney'll burn well, you wait and see." Dropping the wood, he's instantly busy scrunching paper from his coat pockets and laying a criss-cross of sticks in the grate. "Oh..." He sounds disappointed. "You've already had a fire."

I'm fridging the wine and temporarily filling glasses with Coleforth's worst, which has the merit of not being armpit warm. I call out from the kitchen, "Paula, that friend I told you about? She left a few logs for decoration. I burnt the whole lot Monday night, then wished I hadn't – it was freezing yesterday." Tuesday, and I'd been shivering with cold but too drunk to do anything about it. In the end, I'd curled up in the duvet and got even more drunk. Eventually oblivion had negated weather.

Now I place our drinks on the side table, then stand to watch the expert at work.

"Right, Rose Little, are you ready for this?" With a flourish, he produces a pack of firelighters. Unwrapping one, he tucks it carefully under the pyramid of sticks.

"Oh, honestly! That's cheating," I say, laughing out loud. "Here." I hand him a box of matches.

"And... abracadabra!" A tiny spark, a fierce crackle, and soon flames are leaping. Mac squats on the rug, hugging his knees. "I've left you a pile of logs, by the way," he says, extracting splinters from his beard. "Enough to last a while. And don't worry, I've put a plastic sheet over to keep them dry. Scouted all round your bloody garden in the dark, looking for stones to hold it down. Hope I didn't disturb you." He glances at his shoes. "Sorry about the mud."

But he always looks like that; leaves in his hair, jeans streaked with dirt. "I did wonder what the noise was. I was about to creep out and hit you over the head with my torch. Here, drink up. It's cheapo rubbish, but it'll do till yours has chilled." We clink glasses. "Thank you, Mac. Really. Thank you. For the third time." His origami flower is sitting on the mantelpiece in full view. Mac fidgets and waves his hands, but I insist. "It was kind and thoughtful. And very welcome."

Mac scans the room. "There must be some kind of heating here, surely?"

"An old electric fire, but it's broken. I don't think Chris and Paula have given much consideration to winter. Penmaris is a fair-weather cottage, summer hols, that sort of thing."

"Fair-weather friends, then," says Mac, shuffling backwards from the blaze.

"No. No. They're good friends. I've known them for years and they're letting me stay here rent free, for as long as I like. All I have to do is keep myself." Mac cocks an eyebrow. "Okay. So I'm not doing a very good job of it at the moment. I did mean to go into town and buy a fan heater, but I got sort of side-tracked." Then I remember. "But I do have a boot full of driftwood. I went back to where you collected all this." I gesture to the logs he's stacked by the hearth. "Trouble is, it needs chopping." I shrug. "Never mind. Carne'll be round soon; I'll ask him to help."

"Well, if he doesn't turn up in the next few days, give us a ring. Meanwhile, I've left you plenty to be getting on with. Can't have you freezing to death now, can we? What a way to go!" He rubs his hands together with glee, then starts on one of his tuneless whistles as he gazes deep into the flames.

I slip out to the kitchen and make a grab for the edge of the sink. Méline's body had been freezing cold when they pulled her from the Seine. I remember touching her icy cheeks, the waxy feel of her skin.

Think of something else. Be hospitable.

I bang cupboard doors in a pretence of purpose, then pop my head into the sitting room. "Something to eat, Mac? There's soup and cheese. Salad. A *very* good bottle of wine someone's just given me. *Please* say 'yes'. I owe you supper at least."

"Yes," he says. "Supper would be nice."

* * *

We eat, me on the sofa and Mac in the fireside chair, from trays balanced on our knees. In front of us the fire roars and crackles. On the coffee table I've placed Camembert and Cheddar, a bowl of mixed lettuce leaves, the Pouilly Fuisé that Mac brought, condensation dripping down the bottle, and in the centre, on an old breadboard I found while hunting for oven gloves, broken chunks of warm, crusty baguette. Mac already has a drift of crumbs down the front of his shirt. In the pauses between eating, he glances round the room.

"Very white," he observes. "Give me the willies, this would."

I laugh. "It's Paula's idea of decorating."

"Then paint some pictures, woman. Cover the walls with paintings. Brighten the place up." He points his soupspoon at the outline of the easel occupying the corner alcove. "You've made a start, by the looks of it. What's hiding under there?"

"Oh, nothing. Really." I dart a look at the blanket, at its edges brushing the floor. As far as I can tell, he hasn't touched it. "Really, it's nothing." I could kick myself for leaving him alone in the room with my work. The easel was bound to provoke curiosity. I reach for the bottle. "More wine?"

He nods, dunking a crust in the remains of his soup. "Didn't take you for a coward, Rose." He licks his fingers. "I'm interested, that's all, not judgemental. Let's have a squiz." I shake my head. "What are you afraid of, woman? Instinct tells me you've been here long enough."

"Long enough for what?"

"Long enough to start the journey. Art's all about the journey." He cuts a slice of cheese and spears it with his knife, which he jabs in the direction of the easel. "Just thought you might appreciate a bit of company along the way."

He shrugs as if to imply indifference, an offer made, take it or leave it, but I suspect a feint. I'm beginning to doubt the grumpy-old-man act. Alec McConnell might just be the real deal. I take a long drink while I wrestle with the impulse to show him what I've drawn. The wine is fabulous, though nearly all gone, and having consumed too much I know we're broaching dangerous waters, where confidences swapped in alcoholic free fall are regretted next day.

After a prolonged pause, "Tell me more about the woman who used to live here," I ask. "The woman who disappeared. What was her name?"

Mac peels off a small bunch of grapes, then slumps back against cushions, popping individual fruits into his mouth. Shifting shadows from the firelight darken his face. Muscles, slack from alcohol, sag unattractively, adding years and temper. I still have no idea how old he might be, though I change my mind each time I see him. "Sally," he says at last. "She was called Sally Hendry."

"Doesn't sound like a local name," I say. "I was expecting something more Cornish than Sally."

"Think it depends on the spelling." He appears to be considering. "With or without an 'e'. And there might be Celtic roots. The surname's local, comes from 'hendre' meaning 'old farm'. Or something like that. So I'm told." His voice tails off.

"I should have come to you all along."

"About what?"

"These place names, like Polperro and Poldhu and Tre-something or other. They're so distinctive and different. And repetitive. They're everywhere. Penzance and Penryn, and now I live in Penmaris. They sound so beautiful and old, as if they belong to the land. As if they've grown from the earth itself. I wanted to get a book to find out more, but Jan Freeman's shop doesn't have anything and she could only recommend the nearest library. Whereas all I needed to do…" I raise my glass to salute him.

Mac is gazing at the ceiling as if trying to pluck a memory. "There's an old rhyme," he says, "goes something like: *By Tre-, and Pol-, and Pen-, Ye may know most Cornishmen.* Don't speak the lingo myself; it's called 'Kernowek'. There's a few people trying to keep it alive, translating Beatles hits and writing Cornish poems. Daft idea, if you ask me. But I do know some of the old prefixes. You mentioned *Pen* just now? Think it means the end of a stretch of land, like a headland. Take Penrose for example, common enough name, means the end of the moor."

"So Penmaris?"

He scratches his head. "This is not an exact science, you understand. And that fire needs stoking." Dragging himself from the chair, Mac seems unsteady on his legs. We've both had too much to drink. If Mac came by car, he certainly won't be fit to drive home again.

"You see to the fire," I say, standing up. "I'll go and make coffee." I wish I had more to offer than spoonfuls of instant.

"I think it's one of those mixed words, like 'television', half one language, half another." He's leaning against the kitchen door, dusting wood ash from his fingers. "Pen-, now we know that's headland or some such, and the maris bit sounds suspiciously like Latin. Of the sea. Put them together and you have the location of this cottage, pretty much. I'll have mine black, by the way."

"Your name's not Cornish though." I hand him a mug and we settle again by the fire. Mac produces a cigar from his shirt pocket.

"Take it you don't mind?"

To my surprise, I shake my head and throw him the matches. As he lights up, I feel the room drop its shoulders. Mellowed by odours of cigar and wood smoke, leftover food and wine, the cottage is sighing a welcome.

"I'm part Irish," Mac explains, "on my great-grandfather's side. He came over to work in the tin mines and married a local girl from Redruth. But Irish, Welsh, Cornish, what's the difference? All Celtic in origin, part of the same language group. There's lots of shared words."

He becomes positively chatty, explaining local derivations. He tells me that Carne's name means rock or stone, and that Tresawna breaks down into…

In a voice low and sonorous, hypnotic almost, Mac seems to be leading the conversation gently away from its starting point. The cigar, the heat of the fire, the sense of wellbeing, all are lulling me into inattention.

I interrupt him. "Did you know this Sally Hendry well?"

"Went to school with her." An unhesitating response. If his misdirection ruse has been sussed, he doesn't show it. "And her brother and sister. And with Carne. And his sister, Mary."

I'm startled. "What? Mary Coleforth, you mean? From the store? She's Carne's…?" and Mac nods. "Honestly! That's typical of this place! No one told me. I did wonder about—"

"Village kids," Mac is saying, "so we all went to the village school, though we were in different classes. I was a couple years ahead of Sal."

"I know where the school is. I saw a class coming out this morning."

"That building's years old, Victorian probably. Nowadays it's only for juniors. After the war they built a big new secondary school out on the main road, for all the nearby villages. Had great facilities. At least, so we thought, us yokels."

"Especially the art?"

"Yeh, too true. Kick-started my… career, I s'pose you'd call it."

"And Sally?"

"Oh, Sal…" He flicks ash in the direction of the hearth. "She was more into poetry." He pauses, frowning. "Poetry and breaking hearts." A hand passes over his face with a gesture I've noticed before in bearded men, that of stroking a dumb animal. Or pacifying the inner beast.

I wait, but he falls silent again. "So, tell me more. What did she look like?"

"Wild. Unruly. Bit of a tomboy when she was young. Then she grew these long legs and this mane of chestnut hair. Like a wild horse, she was, like some magnificent animal. Difficult to control." It's an artist's impression, lacking detail. I'm deciding whether to push for more when he adds, "I'm told she piled the pounds on in later life." A shrug of the shoulders, to imply distance, detachment.

I stare into the fire. Alec McConnell and Sally Hendry, two village kids growing up together. No wonder the cottage knows him. He's almost certainly played here as a boy, visited on and off for years, been cuffed round the ear by Sally's father, helped her mother light the fire, proved a godsend, a pain in the arse, he's laughed and fought and maybe… loved here. I see an embrace on the rug in the heat of the flames.

At that moment the phone rings, startling us both from our daydreams. We stare at one another, bewildered. I can't remember where I've put the phone. Then it comes to me. I stumble across to where I dumped it, on the floor by the easel so as to clear the coffee table for supper. But I'm drunk and in my confusion I trip over the curled edge of the hearth rug. Shooting out a hand to steady myself, I sweep the blanket clean off the sketchpad and can only watch in dismay as it tumbles to the floor, revealing what lies beneath. My hand, flying past the easel, collides with

98

the edge of the chimneybreast, which checks my fall. Mac is already half-out of his chair to help me when, behind my head, the exposed drawing catches his attention. Suddenly uncloaked, two huge sad eyes stare into the room. I think I see shock flash across the professor's face, before he drops back into the armchair. Demanding attention, the phone shrills on.

I panic, try throwing the blanket back over the easel, but the crocheted wool snags on my jewellery, entangling my fingers the more I fiddle. "Hallo," I bark, grabbing the receiver and tucking it under my chin. Loops of coloured yarn stretch as I pick at them. "Damn." I'm yanking at a skein caught in the claws of my ring, pulling hard enough to break the thread. Mac leans forwards to help; our fingers brush and bump.

"Rose, it's me," says Oliver. "Are you all right?"

"Just dropped something," I mutter. "The phone startled me."

"I tried ringing earlier," he sounds aggrieved, "but your mobile's switched off. Did you realise?"

Oh God, not again. I am not going to have this conversation again. He breaks my heart then obsesses about telephones. My left arm is dangling awkwardly as Mac unpicks the last strands of wool from my bracelet. Having freed the blanket, he folds it with exaggerated care and places it over the back of his chair.

Oliver's sigh, from across the Channel, could be in the same room.

Mac appears to be studying my drawing, though fingers steepled in front of his face obscure his expression. I need to get rid of Oliver quickly, so I can ask the obvious question, so I can raise the silly notion that's been obsessing me.

"Listen, Oliver. I can't talk now. There's, er, there's someone at the door. It might be the gardener bloke. I'll have to go."

"It's nearly eight o'clock, Rose. It must be pitch black outside. What's the gardener doing calling round at…?"

Oh, for goodness sake. I nearly slam the receiver down, but notice the expression on Mac's face. He's on his feet, semaphoring his intention to leave. He looks embarrassed, as if he wished to be elsewhere. I flap a hand at him to get him to sit down again.

"I'll call you tomorrow," I snap down the phone.

Having slipped his jacket on, Mac is digging round for his car keys, which he finds and waves at me. With exaggerated, tiptoeing steps towards the door, he makes it clear he has no intention of eavesdropping my conversation.

"Look, I must go, Oliver, I told you, there's someone at the… I have to go, Oliver. No, now. I'll call later, okay? Bye, then."

This time I do slam the receiver down and run to the door as Mac is opening it. He pantomimes looking right and left, then purses his lips. "Hmm. Don't *see* anyone out here."

"Oh, shut up." I tug on his arm and drag him back inside. "Please don't rush off." I turn and point to my sketchpad with the drawing of a woman's face. "You wanted to know what I've been working on. Well, there it is. Go on, tell me what you think."

Chapter Nine

Next morning when I open the curtains I can just make out the figure of Carne Tresawna at the bottom of the garden, barely visible inside a pall of smoke. He's lit a bonfire and is busy burning last week's cuttings. Good. At least he's here, getting on with the job.

I throw some clothes on, make breakfast, and take tea and cornflakes into the sitting room, feeling peckish and not in the least hung over. In fact, I feel… cheerful. Yes, that's the word, relieved and cheerful. Surprising, considering everything Mac said, that I should wake in a positive frame of mind.

The evening had threatened to end badly. After persuading Mac to stay and look at my work, I ended up showing him the lot. Why be coy, I argued with myself? Either I do this or I don't. And I got exactly what I asked for, a critique delivered in spades that morphed, under the influence of more booze, into bloody great shovels. Never one to mince his words, the professor was forthright, uncompromising, typical Mac, telling it like it was.

Admittedly, here and there he inserted the odd conciliatory phrase. He even reined back at one point, seeing my head bowed, conceding my work had… *something*. But basically he was brutal. He was hugely underwhelmed, that was the truth of it, and I was battered by a verbal blitzkrieg that ought to have destroyed my confidence. Yet, amazingly, this morning, it hasn't. Having spent so much time alone since arriving in Cornwall, I really enjoyed Mac's company and the opportunity for a few hours' provocative conversation. And now I feel optimistic and strangely energised.

The crocheted blanket is back on the sofa. On the easel, my sketchpad openly displays the half-finished charcoal drawing which I might or might not get round to completing one day. In the hearth are drifts of silver-grey ash waiting to be swept. As I swallow a mouthful of tea, I reflect on how some people possess the gift of feeding the spirit.

Last night, after I'd tripped and knocked the blanket off my drawing, I yielded to the inevitable. Either Mac recognised the woman's face or he didn't.

"Go on," I'd insisted. "Tell me what you think."

He'd pursed his lips, tilting his head from side to side, taking his time.

"Why charcoal, Rose? Life isn't lived in black and white."

Of all the things he might have said, that was the last thing I'd expected. I mumbled while scratching round for an answer. "Because it was there, I suppose. This strange face came into my head and I felt compelled, I had to start drawing. The box of charcoal just happened to be the first thing to hand. Besides," I remembered squatting on the bedroom floor in the middle of the night, "I was after a smudged effect." Watching Mac closely, I'd added, "I feel she's a ghostly figure."

"Ah," he'd said, tilting his head again. There was another long pause. Then he tapped me on the arm. "So, could it be a witch, perhaps? A wizened old crone?" I blinked at him. "Might be your subconscious, Rose, making links with Halloween, throwing up iconic images which you…" Was he making fun of me? Then in the same breath, he side-stepped into a rant about rip-offs. "Bloody shops these days, have you been in them recently? Stuffed with plastic tat that wouldn't frighten a frog. I ask you, ten quid for some grotty Halloween mask about as scary as my aunt Fanny." He kicked back a burning log that was threatening to fall from the grate. "Reckon your ghost here," he waved a hand, "knocks spots off any supermarket rubbish. But the old mind does pick up on vibes, doesn't it?" After a few considered tugs of his beard, he rounded on me. "Well, have you? Have you *seen* the crap they're selling this year?"

Upon which, he had lost interest and turned his attention to my book of outdoor sketches.

I'd had difficulty believing what had just happened. Or rather, not happened. No reaction, no sign of recognition. Either he was an extremely good actor, (but why should he need to dissemble?) or this was not the face of anyone Mac knew. And where I sensed relative youth, he had seen age. An old woman's face? Surely not. How could he possibly say that?

"She's a caricature, is that what you mean? Symbolic? Not a real person?"

He wasn't listening. He was leaning back in the armchair, flicking pages.

"But I've never done cartoons," I persisted, trying to regain his attention. "That's not my style at all. I don't understand what you mean. This face, well, it sort of…" *drew itself* sounded silly. Daft, he would say. I couldn't tell him how I felt haunted by it, how I'd been driven to put lines on paper to afford *her* passage. Whoever *she* might be. Evidently not someone Mac recognised, anyway.

He was flapping my book, making a fuss. "You're far too tentative, Rose," he was saying. "That's your problem. Look at this." He'd pointed to a drawing of a robin pulling up a worm. A delicate cameo of which I'd felt quite proud. "Nature red in tooth and whatnot, survival of the fittest, life-'n-death struggle – and what do you do? Something dainty in pastel." He had hurled the book to the floor. "It's all charcoal and pastels with you, isn't it? Namby-pamby pastels, Rose. Pallid and insipid. Where's the passion?" His arms circled wildly as his voice rose. "You're lacking nerve, woman. Try living in colour for once, that's my advice. Slap some paint down. You've got a right arm, haven't you? Well, use it. Start painting. What have you got to lose?"

He'd gone on to talk in earnest about tension and underlying constraint, about the discipline and freedom of working in oil; he'd urged me to open my shoulders to let the art escape; he'd thrown down a tacit challenge. Then he'd hovered awkwardly by the front door as we said goodnight, me reluctant to let the evening end and both of us self-conscious and suddenly unsure. Energy streamed from his body and I wanted to be part of that force, that electricity; wanted it to envelope me. Instead, I watched as his car slipped away and I waved into the darkness.

Now, next morning, here I am, digging through my box of brushes and thinking seriously about paint and colour. I lift the sketchpad from the easel and bury it, for the time being, behind the sofa. A final glimpse of two eyes which stare an accusation. In its place I stand my first blank canvas for years.

Empty space, possibility.

It's absurd, the extent to which I'd convinced myself I was drawing the face of a dead woman. A dead woman I now know was called Sally Hendry. I had come to believe Sally's spirit was controlling my hand, guiding the charcoal, dictating the weeping eye with its lower lid tangled in raw flesh, forcing the dreadful, ugly scar that crawled down one cheek. But Mac had called Sally beautiful, and my dread vanished. Penmaris was simply a cottage, not a haunted house, and I had spooked myself, hearing ghosts where there was nothing but the unfamiliar. Mac hadn't gasped on seeing the face, he hadn't reeled back in shock because he knew the sad woman in my picture. Furthermore, by voicing his opinions so freely last night, he had somehow set me free.

He has a gift, I murmur to the room, for all his grubby clothes and bad temper. The gift to inspire. And he's right, I must be bolder, I must reach beyond my comfort zone and start painting again. Forget about ghosts and dead people – get painting.

* * *

105

First I decide to go for a run. If I intend to concentrate I need to burn off nervous energy. Shuffling into trainers, I leave the cat a bowl of scraps outside the back door then jog down the garden path towards the smoke.

"Morning!" I stifle a cough. "Nice day." Carne grunts. "I'm going for a jog along the cliff." He nods, busy forking leaves onto the bonfire, leaves that are wet from recent rain. The pillar of smoke turns to a mushroom cloud that engulfs us. I flap a hand in front of my face. "Just thought I'd let you know."

"Thank you," says Carne, as if he has no idea what for. "Got yourself some logs, I see." He points to Mac's blue plastic sheet.

"Alec McConnell brought them round yesterday," I say, appreciating the care he'd taken to cover them. Did I remember to thank him properly? "Actually, that reminds me…"

Without a quibble, Carne agrees to tackle the driftwood in my car boot. In fact, he doesn't actually voice agreement; he slips quietly into the shed, and comes out with a murderous-looking chain-saw which he plugs into an extension cable that snakes from the kitchen across the grass. Then he lifts the saw and swings it high to check it's running free. The thing screeches, its blade spinning through air with teeth that could rip your head off. I'm taken aback; I had imagined Carne chopping the logs with an axe, like some fairy-tale woodsman, which for some reason seems less menacing.

He sets to with a will. Soon a hill of logs is forming and the green grass turns yellow with sawdust. Clearly there's nothing for me to do, so I yell, "I'll be off then," bellowing over the high-pitched scream. "Won't be long. I'll make us a pot of tea when I get back."

Maybe then Carne might be persuaded to chat. He intrigues me. He's an unlikely romantic hero, sporting a tatty woollen hat and wellies, standing knee-deep in muddy grass wielding a chain-saw. But according to Mac, he's been constant in love; here he is, still tending Sally's garden. Such devotion speaks of passions that run deep. If I can find a way through his silence and win him round, I might persuade him to talk to me about Sally Hendry.

* * *

The weather is glorious for late October. Sun sparkles off a blue ocean where scarcely a ripple disturbs the surface of the water. The cliff path is well trodden, narrow in places and stony. Stretches are overgrown with brambles and cascades of old man's beard, opening out to bare scrubland that affords panoramic views of the coast. I spot gannets dive-bombing the waves for fish and inland, sky high, kestrels hover, seeking mice and voles, their wings juddering on the breeze. In one spot, where the cliff edge has fallen away, the fencing and barbed wire has gone with it and a nightmare drop plunges to the beach below. It's nearly high tide; waves crash and boom in the undercut, broiling in the cauldron of unforgiving black rock. Terrified, I step back, away from the edge. This is ridiculously dangerous. Whoever's responsible should do some urgent repairs or at least put up warning notices. I mince carefully past, clinging to the landward side of the path. But for the most part, I'm able to jog along steadily, the wind in my hair and oxygen powering through my lungs.

When I grow tired of running I revert to scouts' pace, twenty jogging, twenty walking. In no time I'm standing high above Porthallen Sands. The bay stretches away to my left, half-covered by the tide. Panting, I turn to look back in the direction of the cottage. Rising into the air I can make out the plume of smoke from Carne's bonfire, a grey spiral in the sunlight. Then my gaze wheels round. All my previous visits to the beach have been via the road leading from the village; up here, by contrast, I can take in at a glance the full sweep of the bay and the final outpourings of the stream that winds innocently through Porthallen but which here seems to have broken through the cliff wall like a dam burst, only to seep and vanish into the sand. The cliff path I'm on dips sharply out of sight, then continues on the far side climbing up again, as I can see from this vantage point, in a series of steps cut into the rock.

Assuming there are steps this side as well, I decide to pay another visit to the beach. As usual it looks practically deserted, just one person down there walking along the tide line, hands deep in the pockets of a full-length winter coat. I hope this isn't a further instance of local intuition. I know Carne foresees rain when the skies are blue; is this another villager wrapped up warm against bad weather? And me sporting only a lightweight tracksuit.

The descent, when I find it, is steep and direct, carved into the cliff face. I'm down on the shingle in moments. I wonder why I didn't notice the steps before, because I'm standing near the spot where I collected the driftwood which Carne is, at this moment, reducing to logs. In front of me curves the crescent of Porthallen Sands.

I set off to resume my jog but, with the firm sand now completely covered, I find it hard running through soft powder. Abandoning the idea, I start to walk along the water's edge, tempted by the sun to take my trainers off and paddle. From the opposite direction, the lone figure moving slowly towards me reveals itself gradually to be a woman in a thick coat with the hood up. After a few minutes a hand comes out to clutch the hood tighter round her face. The strange angle of the woman's body, tilted as if she's leaning directly onto thin air, gives the impression that she's fighting her way through buffeting winds. On her feet, heavy boots like anchors weight her to the shore.

For a moment I wondered if the woman is drunk. She seems unsteady on her feet, staggering almost into the face of a non-existent gale. Or maybe she's unwell; huddled into the tight-fitting coat, she hugs it round her as if she's cold. Then the front panels of the coat fly open, flapping wildly, caught in a sudden gust. With her other hand she wrestles to hold them together. Occasionally she raises her head as if she hears a voice calling.

Nearer the woman and, to my surprise, I too can feel the wind. With each step I take it grows stronger, slamming into my back, driving me forwards. And I'm shivering. What a contrast with the warm sunshine twenty minutes earlier. As the gap between us closes, I notice clouds overhead and the air, which has turned so chill, now seems to find a bitter edge that stings my skin. A sudden blast from behind delivers a rabbit punch, sending me tumbling head-first into a squall of rain that lashes my cheeks. To my left, pounding into the bay, the sea boils in fury.

That such weather can materialise within minutes from a clear blue sky proves why tourists need coastguards. I'm astonished; the sun has simply disappeared. What had moments ago been calm blue sea is now a heaving monster swollen beneath a blanket of rain that wipes out the horizon and obscures the sharp outline of the rocks. Halfway along the bay, and I don't know whether to plough on or turn back. I leap sideways from waves that threaten to drench me and run, slipping on wet stones and trying not to twist my ankles, up the beach towards the cliffs and away from the water.

Clambering into the dunes, I glance back quickly to see how the other woman is faring. But in the cacophony of wind, rain and pounding tide, my senses fail me; it's disorientating, I can barely see or hear. The sky has turned black; day has become night. But there is… something. Through the wall of sound comes a high-pitched shout that rings across the beach like a war cry, a cry not of fear but of defiance. Coming from where, though? Where is the woman? Visibility is reduced to peering through a veil of swirling, eye-stinging sand. With one hand held up to shield my face, I stare hard until I can finally make out a shadowy form hunched low, moving towards the cliffs – it must be her, the woman, though she seems to be crawling on her knees. "Here, this way," I call, stretching out a hand. "That's it, keep moving towards my voice." I am bellowing above the rage of the storm. "Don't worry, we'll be all right. We're not far from the road."

I feel rather than see fingers grasp mine and immediately I start to drag the woman along behind me, heading always inland, away from the shore, scrambling up through soft, deep wet sand, two steps forwards one back, until I can feel firmer ground under foot. "Keep going," I shout. "We're almost there." Up and up till we've nearly reached the lay-by; soon it will be gravel then tarmac, solid and level. And there's some kind of old building, I seem to remember. I noticed it before, a wooden shack or a disused public loo, when I was helping Mac load his car. It'll provide shelter. We can wait out the worst of the weather.

With arms and legs aching, I make a final effort to haul myself over the top of the dunes, only to feel the woman's hand slip away. Everything is wet and sweaty and slippery. My eyes are practically closed to keep out the sand and I don't want to turn my face into the wind. I have to assume my companion, wearing those sensible boots, has also found purchase and is managing on her own. "We're nearly at the car park," I bellow over my shoulder.

And then I feel foolish. The weather's roar has died away and I am yelling into silence.

When I pull myself up straight and open my eyes, I am indeed standing on tarmac – warm, dry tarmac, next to a Vauxhall saloon in the front seats of which sit an elderly couple in sunglasses sipping tea from a thermos. Their car windows are open wide and the man greets me with a salute from his plastic mug.

"Morning! Lovely day for it."

I look down at my clothes. I am completely dry. Behind me the quiet beach glows in sunlight and the lazy, incoming waves leave a bubble of creamy foam where the water ripples gently from blue sea to shore. Of the woman there is no sign, just far off, a voice singing.

Chapter Ten

Carne has disappeared when I get back to the cottage. I seem to have been gone a long time, and in my absence he's doused the bonfire and locked up, but left a tumble of logs in the middle of the lawn. I've taken advantage of him and he's telling me I can finish the job by myself. So much for good intentions.

In the sitting room I kick my trainers off and slump on the couch. By the fireplace stands the easel, waiting. Fixing my gaze upon the huge square of blank canvas, I force my eyes open wide and unblinking until eventually a single tear pricks and slides down one cheek. This is an old trick I resort to when I have trouble shedding simple tears. Hysteria, verbal fugues, a whole panoply of alternative emotional outbursts come easily to me and have to be curbed. The spontaneous relief of crying is less accessible. But I am shaking and I feel utterly bewildered.

What on earth is going on? Am I losing my mind? I've been blown and sand-blasted and soaked to the skin, yet here I am dry and unmarked. I've helped a woman on the beach make her way through a blinding storm, I held the woman's hand and pulled her to safety. For God's sake, it felt real, it actually happened. Didn't it? I stare at my own two hands which are trembling. I can still feel the sensation of the woman's rough palm rubbing against mine, the grip of the woman's fingers as she struggled to hold on. How can I deny the evidence of my senses? Every aspect of the storm felt real, looked and sounded real. Passing my tongue over my lips, I taste salt.

The yawning, empty canvas seems to mock me. This morning I woke up feeling so positive and hopeful, yet here I am, a few hours later, a trembling wreck. Perhaps they're right, Oliver, my parents, my friends. Perhaps I should go back to London and make another appointment to see the shrink. Clearly I haven't recovered from the miscarriage and I need help. I can't do this on my own. Hearing noises in the night is one thing; full-scale hallucinations are quite another. I am going mad.

But it seemed so real. I can't get away from that. Damn it, it was real. How can I not believe what happened, why should I call it a hallucination? I don't even know what the word means. Am I saying my mind invented the storm and the rain, or did I perhaps experience… some sort of vision? Before I write myself off as a lunatic, I could consider the alternative. Where many would claim evidence of mental disintegration, others might argue for a psychic encounter. I can see the woman quite clearly, struggling across the beach with waves like mountains breaking behind her in that explosion of rage. And in my head I can hear the water

114

and the wind. So perhaps something did occur, but on a different level from everyday reality. What, after all, are the parameters of reality?

This is scary stuff. Loony logic. I clench my fists till I can feel my fingernails digging into my skin, then I press harder. The pain is reassuring – cause and effect; I'm still here, and everything works. I've got to battle the impulse to cut and run because that's what I always do, I run away, back to people who will hold my hand and make the monsters vanish. My parents, Oliver, friends like Ellie and Paula. The safety of other people. But this time it's different; Oliver and Ellie aren't my friends and there is no place to run. This time I have to go it alone.

Well, one thing's for sure: there's no point crying, so I might as well abandon my stupid tricks. I rub the tears away impatiently. I've got to pick myself up, dust myself off, blah, blah, blah. Silly song. There's no point staring at a blank canvas, either. Nothing comes of nothing. Except…

Except…

From the white rectangle of nothingness floats the slow germ of a thought, a suspicion maybe – that it's *Penmaris all along, Penmaris that triggers these strange events*. The cottage itself.

I keep my eyes fixed on the canvas while my head tries to grab hold of the idea. *Think about it, Rose! Think!* Strange noises. Things that go bump in the night. Dreams and nightmares. The persistent sound of crying. A woman's face. From the very first day I've sensed something about this place, but I've consistently refused to pay attention. I've dismissed what I've seen, played down what I felt, ignored signs, shoved weirdness under the carpet, pretended everything was normal. Because normal is what I crave. But Penmaris isn't normal. There *is* an atmosphere, a sort of presence. No, perhaps that's going too far. Though sometimes in bed at night, the cottage seems… alive. I can hear it breathing, as though it's trying to speak to me.

Cornwall is an ancient land where the past lives side by side with the present.

From the very first evening, strange things have occurred. Almost daily I've been subjected to events that make no sense but of whose reality my senses are convinced. Things that defy rational explanation: footsteps in the attic, a baby crying, a face that draws itself, rain that leaves me dry, bells ringing on the night wind, a voice singing at the bottom of the garden. And Penmaris lies at the epicentre of this turmoil. Penmaris, sending forth ripples of distorted reality that force me to question, beg me to understand.

But understand what?

What, for goodness sake?

I don't know, I whisper to the room. Then I shout it out loud, *"I don't know. I don't bloody know, do I?"*

And I'm on my feet, making a grab for my art box, which I yank towards me.

Because I do know what I'm going to do next.

I delve into the box, selecting and rejecting, scattering tubes of colour across the floor. I'll paint the storm, right here and now. I'll recreate what I've just undergone, with all the intensity of a lived experience: the beach, the sea and wind and roaring waves, the woman crawling to safety.

Normally a canvas should be prepared first, but today there simply isn't time. The important thing is to paint. I select a brush and begin.

* * *

Much later in the afternoon there's a sharp knock at the front door. I'm not expecting anyone and it makes me jump. Clicking the brush between my teeth and keeping my eyes firmly on the painting to watch perspective change with distance, I back across the room until I slam painfully into the door handle.

Chris Benning is outside, scrutinising his window frames. "Rose!" he exclaims. "Hi there. You're in, this time."

"Chris! What a surprise." I catch the brush as it falls from my astonished mouth. "What on earth are you doing here?"

"Had a meeting yesterday in Penzance, so I thought I'd call in today, see how you are, check the old place over." Flakes of paint come away on his finger as he rubs the windowsill. "Salt in the air," he says. "Needs touching up." Then he notices the brush in my hand. "Sorry. Am I interrupting? Looks like you're doing a bit of painting of your own." I shake my head, rub my back. "Mind if I come in then, just for half an hour, cadge a quick cuppa before I hit the road back to London?"

Whether I mind or not, he owns Penmaris and I'm staying here thanks to his generosity. "Sure. Come in. It's good to see you. How's Paula?"

While I make tea, Chris updates me on the comings and goings of our social circle, his latest squash match, the progress of Freddy's mega-bucks divorce, the de la Hayes's new car.

"Bloody great people-wagon, so if Boris puts up congestion charges, then wey-hey, look out Michael! Oh, and did Paula tell you, she's thinking Egypt for Christmas? Top up the old suntan down at Sharm el-Sheikh. Ollie emailed, by the way."

He slips the remark in casually. I wonder how much he knows. Or guesses. Has Oliver sent him to check up on me? A worm of anger twists in my gut.

"You weren't here when I called earlier, but I spotted Carne outside. Went and had a bit of a chat, sorted some stuff out. He's a good bloke, really. Can't help being thick." I gasp, but Chris doesn't seem to notice and rambles on. "Says he'll be doing quite a bit of tidying up next week, by the way. Weather permitting. Get the old garden sorted before winter. So don't be surprised if you see him around most days. I bunged him a few extra quid, made it worth his while…"

Everything is always about money, one-upmanship, control. Nudge nudge, wink wink. I want to scream. Chris, the lord of the manor, doing his *noblesse oblige*. And checking on the batty neighbour while he's at it. Doing a mate a favour. As if I can't be trusted to cope for five minutes. Not with the least little thing. Has Carne been recruited to spy on me now? Bloody Oliver, bloody Chris. Bloody men. I *really* want to scream. I think the top of my head might come off.

Instead, I take a deep breath. "He's not thick," I spit out.

"What?"

"You just said Carne's a bit thick. Well, you're wrong. He's a quiet man and very private. Just because he doesn't mouth off all the time doesn't mean he's stupid." Chris raises an eyebrow. "There's lots like him round here, people who don't speak unless they've got something worth saying." I hand him his tea. "Here. I don't have sugar."

In the sitting room, Chris is at pains to remark on the jug of flowers, on the homely touches I've brought to the place in only two weeks. This painting I'm doing is *amazing*, could be by a professional. Paula'll be pleased to hear I've settled in and made friends. Have I met Carne's sister yet, the woman who runs the village shop? I nod, seething but amused by his discomfort. He's trying very hard to placate me, because he witnessed first-hand one of my more hysterical outbursts a few months ago and was, according to Paula, "shocked shitless". Right now he's gauging my reactions, trying to work out if I'm about to lose it. Accustomed to being the ringmaster, he'd run a mile if the animals bit back.

Interrupting him, I say, "I didn't realise you had business contacts in this part of the world, Chris."

"Oh God yes, I started here in Cornwall, years ago. That's one of the reasons why we bought this cottage, so I'd have somewhere local to stay. Though what with email and video-conferencing, I don't bother to come down much any more. But at one time…" He's flipping through my sketch book on the coffee table. "You know what, you're wasted on company brochures, Rose. You really are. You've got talent."

"Does that mean you're Cornish, then? I had no idea."

"What me? No fear. It was 'cos Mum and Dad retired to Penzance. I was flat broke after uni, so I stayed with them for a while till I got myself off the ground. But pretty soon…" He swallows a mouthful of tea.

"The bright lights beckoned?"

"The ackers, you mean. Couldn't wait to escape Hicksville. Cornwall's fifty years behind the action, at least. Not exactly the business capital of the western world." His vowels take on a transatlantic twang.

"So you must have known the previous owners of Penmaris?"

He looks up, surprised, then seems to find something in the corner of his eye which he knuckles viciously. "Er, yeah, vaguely. Harry? Henry? Some such."

"Hendry. An old Cornish family, lived in this cottage for generations, so I've been told. I think Carne was pretty good friends with their daughter, Sally. She was the last one to live here."

Chris stands up and pats his jacket for car keys. "Frankly, Rose, I got my PA onto it. She trawled the web and gave us a shortlist of properties. It was Paula who fell for the place. To be honest, I'd have preferred something more central and less run-down." He's scrutinising again, checking his investment. I imagine pound signs popping on his eyeballs as he checks the window frames. He seems obsessed with the state of the windows. Then he walks over to the chimney. "Had a fire, I see. Any problems with it? We never bothered, far as I can remember. Glad the place didn't burn down round your ears, though."

Did Chris know Sally Hendry twenty years ago when he lived in Cornwall? He remembers the surname, even if he's pretending not to. And if so, who else might he have known? He's trying to avoid my questions. And why, I wonder, would someone as wealthy as Chris Benning buy this insignificant little ruin miles from anywhere when he has the money to buy exactly what he wants exactly where he wants it. To humour his wife? Pull the other one.

Chris is heading out the door. "I'll be off then, Rose, unless there's anything else I can do…? When's Ollie coming back, by the way? We've got a squash court booked end of next week."

"I'm not sure," I mumble. "At the weekend, maybe."

"And you?" I frown so he adds quickly, "No probs, Rose. No probs at all. Stay as long as you like. I'm not trying to hassle you. Stay as long as you need." We're standing by his car, facing the garden and the end wall. Seagulls squawk overhead, then fly lazily off towards the cliff. Chris gazes after them. "Nothing like the peace and quiet of this place, is there?"

I have no idea whether that's supposed to be funny or not. Besides, I have a painting to get back to. Other questions can wait.

Chapter Eleven

"Rose! This is a surprise. To what do I owe the honour?"

"Are you going to ask me in, Mac? Or do I stand here like a prat while you grin at me?"

Colours, I have used: for grass, the dunes, the cliff face, distant trees. No problem with colours. Until it comes to blue. Then I have to stop painting, so I walked round to Mac's house. It turns out he lives only a short distance away.

Like an Elizabethan courtier, he sweeps me an exaggerated bow, outdoing the obeisance I made yesterday. Why, I wonder, are we playing this silly game?

"Do come in, Rose. Come in, come in. And welcome to my humble abode. Try and avoid the barbed wire." He kicks several rolls aside to clear the passage. "Might turn this stuff into something deeply symbolic," he says, tugging at his beard, "or else it'll help keep the riff-raff off my back fence. Follow me. Follow me."

He sounds perky, his left arm waving like a flag. At the end of the hall he opens a side door onto the back courtyard revealing, opposite, the entrance to his workshop ablaze with lights. I walk into a lofty, rectangular space, both artist's atelier and busy office. A messy desk, overstuffed bookshelves, computer equipment and a couple of dead armchairs are squeezed into the clutter of a working studio. A mini-kitchen in one corner suggests that he lives here most of the day; already he's filling the kettle. A half-smoked cigar lies smouldering in an ashtray-cum-paperweight. Once the kettle is on, he resumes smoking, perched beside the printer, waiting.

Where to start? "I wanted to say thanks, for the logs," I begin. "I was so preoccupied last night with what you were going to… well, with your reaction to my drawings, that I forgot all about…"

Only after he'd gone did I realise I'd never properly expressed my gratitude for the wood, or the fire he'd lit, or the evening spent in his company.

He hands me a steaming mug. "You provided the grub. Fair exchange, I'd say." He picks flecks of tobacco off his tongue.

"Well, here I am with my thank-yous nonetheless." He accepts with a nod. "And I've been thinking," I continue, "a lot, about what you were saying last night, about letting go. About letting the picture paint through me. As a matter of fact, I've already started…" and then my voice fails. Drawn to a huge canvas Mac appears to be working on, I've wandered over to admire it but am instantly struck dumb. "Oh! A storm at sea," I eventually stammer. "That's... amazing," for want of something to say and sounding inane. What the hell is going on? How can we both be painting the same scene? I flounder for words. "Your brushwork on the waves here, the way you're building up layers of paint. They look so..." I move closer, unable to believe my eyes. Surely this cannot be a coincidence? I continue to babble. "I've always had a fear of paint, to be honest with you..." There, by the rocks, the smudged outline of a lone figure on the beach. "I find it so messy, so difficult to control. It sort of takes you over, doesn't it? The way you've done the waves here, it's like they've got a life of their own. I'm not sure whether I could ever manage to..." In my head, the ocean pounds the shore. A woman's voice is screaming.

"Gotta go with the flow, Rose. Isn't that the expression?" He's standing behind me, peering over my shoulder. "When the urge is strong and the picture insists, you go with the flow. And that's exactly what *you* need to do." He pauses, as if about to elaborate, then starts cleaning brushes, turning his back on the painting. "If you want my opinion, you should throw all your crayons away, and all your footling bits of paper. Commit yourself to paint on canvas. It's what I was saying last night. Come off the fence and commit. Trust yourself. That's why you're here, isn't it?"

Good question. Why am I here, in Cornwall, and here tonight in Mac's studio? Is it to sort my life out or to hide from it? Before discovering my husband in bed with my best friend, I'd wanted to... well, before *nearly* finding my... Ten minutes earlier and they would definitely have been... To think, Ellie must know his body as well as I do, the curve of his bum, those long

124

legs, surprisingly strong too despite his lazy lifestyle, the way his thigh muscles twitch beneath a caress. And there's that sprinkle of moles on his stomach and in the hairs curling round…

Well, before all *that*, before…

…I'd wanted to come here to find myself. I'd wanted to lay my demons to rest. To be grounded by a sense of place. In the chaos of London I had naively imagined that a simple Cornish cottage would help me feel calm and rooted after cyber-space and techno-crap and tragedy. But now that I'm here, I seem to spend half my time reading about stones of untold power, discussing the behaviour of pixies, battling imaginary storms and hearing voices. My afternoon self might have been prepared to jump on board that roller-coaster, but this evening I'm in need of a reality check.

Reality check? Perhaps not.

Nevertheless, it *is* the answer to Mac's question – I came here this evening for a dose of robust sanity.

But not straight away, not after coming face to face with his latest painting. I decide to postpone the moment and have a look round the studio. Mac seems happy to let me be, whistling to himself as he gets on with jobs.

What immediately strikes me is the startling and almost contradictory range of his art. Bizarre, life-size sculptures sit amidst banal watercolours any tourist might buy – *for wallpaper* (his words; I remember them well). For all his cynicism, Mac is prepared to supply what the market requires. In one corner of the room I come across his pottery wheel and kiln. He obviously made the mug I'm drinking from; similar stuff is displayed on the windowsill. Then something moves

125

overhead and I glance up. Suspended from high in the roof, fluttering against bare electric light bulbs, is a menagerie of strange flying creatures, dragons breathing fire, mythical winged beasts with bony skeletons part-fledged in metallic feathers that flicker rainbows through the harsh lighting. Breeze from an open window ruffles their wings, setting the sheets of metal chattering like birds. Other weird animals prowl the floor, constructed from the driftwood Mac collects. Some he's varnished to enhance the grain, but most are painted to suggest primitive art, in bold primary colours that are both childlike and menacing.

The surreal animals seem to be placed like pieces on a chess board; I have to navigate round them to get to the other side of the studio. Against the far-end wall, with their backs turned to conceal their subject matter, are stacked several massive canvases, similar in size to the seascape he's currently painting. That he's not afraid of the grand sweep I already know from his work on exhibition. He, at least, has no problem being bold and committing to paint.

Nor, it seems, is he averse to detail. A few more steps bring me to his desk, its surface covered in pencil sketches of ancient megaliths resembling those I saw the other day on postcards in the bookshop. Although he's drawn them from slightly different vantage points, they're instantly recognisable. There, for example, is Mên-an-Tol, the curious round stone with a hole in the middle, said to be associated with fertility rites. A photo of this very stone is on the card I'm using as a bookmark. Is this yet another coincidence? How many more lie in wait? The most interesting thing is the angle from which Mac has drawn the central stone. He must have been leaning against one of the two uprights so as to align the second dead-centre through the middle of the holed stone. He's deliberately chosen to emphasise the phallic symbolism. I pick the sketch up for a closer look and find a second sheet of paper stapled to it. Printed in stylish calligraphy is a poem, ostensibly about standing stones. But in fact it's a love poem. Reading it, I feel time spin.

These stones are old;
their cold, sad, siren songs
seep into the evening air,
echo through the inner ear,
and I could swear I hear
your voice.
We came here solstice-seeking,
speaking of love and mysteries,
eager for glimmerings just beyond reach
to teach us arcane…

"You've gone very quiet, Rose," Mac says. "What have you found?" He's walking towards me, drying his hands on a filthy towel. "Place is such a god-awful mess, I've no idea what's where."

I hold the drawing out for him to see. "Is this for your new book about Cornish mysteries?" I ask. "It's a very powerful image. I was wondering, are you planning any written material, notes or… or anything, to go with it?" As if I haven't spotted the poem on the back. As if I haven't already read it. "I think I recognise this place. I've seen photos of it."

Throwing his towel aside, Mac snatches the pages from me. He seems annoyed, almost angry, but at the same time embarrassed, as if caught out in a misdemeanour. A wave of expressions I haven't seen before break across his face. At once I start apologising. "I'm sorry. I didn't mean to pry. I didn't realise it was…"

All these coincidences; all these overlapping echoes.

"You'll get everything out of order," he snaps, slipping the drawing into a pile of A4 papers. I wonder whether the thick stash might constitute the manuscript of his book, but don't like to ask. He seems unusually sensitive about the matter. But his vulnerability gives me an edge, which I decide to exploit.

"I had a visitor earlier this afternoon," I state, rinsing my mug in the sink. "Chris Benning. My friend who bought Penmaris?" I watch Mac's face. "He was in Cornwall on business and dropped by to say hallo." A grunt, a clatter of tools, a loud curse. "Do you know him, Mac?"

He's hunkered down on the floor picking up a scattering of drawing pins. "Watch out. Don't tread on them." He grabs a dustpan and brush and starts sweeping. "Yeah, we've met," he says, breathing heavily. "There, think that's the lot. See any more of the buggers?" He straightens up, glances at me. "In the pub a few times. With his wife."

"Paula."

"Whatever. And with Carne. The constant gardener."

Ouch. That sounds harsh. And puzzling. "I thought you and Carne were friends?" When he doesn't answer, I plough on. "I found out this afternoon that Chris used to live down this way. Must have been about twenty years ago. P'raps that's how you know him. Do you remember him living round here? Was that when you first met?"

More grunts, followed by silence. The drawing pins safely back in their box, Mac turns to squeezing blobs of paint round the rim of an old plate, completely ignoring me as if I didn't exist. He carries the plate over to the canvas he's working on, selecting a couple of brushes on the way. Smearing thick daubs of blue onto the sea, working the paint hard into the surface and stabbing with the brush, he mutters under his breath: "It's too pale, I need a bit more… might just put a touch of…" Then sharply, "Is there something on your mind, Rose?" The question barked in my direction. I thought he'd forgotten me, but his right arm freezes in mid-air. "For goodness sake, stop hovering, woman. I can feel you hovering. Say what you've come to say and get it off your chest. You can start by telling me why you're really here right now being a pest and not at home painting." He spins round, his brush flicking ultramarine.

I gasp. From somewhere, a faint cry.

"Rose? What is it? For God's sake, Rose, whatever's the matter?"

"Paris," I say, and look down at the front of my cream fleece, splashed with blue.

* * *

Dirty water splashed our legs, the wake of a Bateau Mouche turning. I caught a trill of laughter, the strains of a love song; dinner on board a late-night river cruise. Méline squealed and I yanked her away from the edge. The evening's high was wearing off, leaving me feeling flat and hopeless. And cold. Jean-Yves, striding ahead, arguing in rapid French, gesticulating, refused to listen. The child fidgeted, but he would have no patience. It was up to me to keep her close. Nearly midnight; she ought to be in bed. "Tais-toi, p'tite. Faut te taire."

He called me his good-luck charm, wanted me along, and I wouldn't leave the kid behind so it was like happy families down among the dossers and the crack-heads. My head was splitting and I wondered if Claude had spiked my drink again. Not that I minded babysitting Mélie, except when I needed a smoke or when I was halfway down a bottle. Julie, not really into motherhood, was back on the game, turning tricks in the Bois, and there wasn't anyone else. But for a two-year-old she did whine so, her thin arm twisting to wriggle free. I whispered hard, *"Mélie, sois-sage!"*

Claude and Jean-Yves were ahead. They'd nearly reached the bridge. Claude marched on but Jean-Yves hung back and I could see his whole body twitching. He couldn't keep still. Impatient, nervous. He glanced round, checking shadows.

"Merde! Dépêche-toi, Rose! On attend."

"I'm coming!" I dragged Méline along, her small tired feet stumbling to keep up. I felt scared as well as cold. *Be on time*, Blue had said. *Or else.* Pont Neuf, midnight. He wasn't pissing about any longer, he wasn't some low-life messenger-boy. Get the money and be there.

It was Jean-Yves who nicknamed him Blue, from the blue-black sheen of his skin. It was an amusing conceit, he said, a peculiarly Parisian joke. Especially choosing the English word.

Blue. It was all Jean-Yves could talk about at one time. The colour blue. He was obsessed. According to him, it was the colour of artists and the colour of Paris. Ultramarine – his thesis and his passion. When we first met, he dragged me round the entire city one day on his favourite Blue Trail, tracing the chronology of lapis lazuli. "First mentioned in the Epic of Gilgamesh four thousand years ago. Imagine! But so expensive, Rose, a prince's ransom. A precious stone used in Egyptian statues, jewellery, burial masks, the blue of stained-glass windows. Mediaeval patrons instructed their protégés to use only the very finest blue paint, pulverised lapis lazuli, to create the most intense dark-blue pigment, a pure colour that never fades. Tempera or oil paint – it gives the purest, deepest, bluest blue. Look at it, Rose!"

In front of a Renaissance Madonna and Child, he would stand motionless, transfixed, his face white with passion. "Today they produce this cheap, synthetic stuff. Pah! The colour is less vivid, it is not as permanent. The real stuff has lasted for ever. That is why I have to make it, Rose. With my own two hands. To keep faith with the past, you understand? With great artists like Leonardo, with the patrons and the pharaohs, with the Roman emperors who ordered perfection and NOTHING LESS." His clenched fist jabbed the air. "Mined in Afghanistan for over six thousand years. Imagine it, Rose! Can you imagine it? A substance so perfect? Look at the colour. Have you ever seen a blue like that?" Tears spilled down his cheeks.

Blue's face was a burial mask, frozen in the rictus of his blue-black smile. Teeth like glaciers flashed when he spoke. *Be on time, or else.* Up ahead, Claude had disappeared under the wide arch of the Pont Neuf and Jean-Yves was stamping his feet. He was scared, like me. He was sweating fear when I caught up with him, and he snapped at Mélie who wouldn't stop grizzling.

She'd tripped on the stone embankment, and would have fallen if I hadn't been holding her tight. Jean-Yves grabbed me and kissed me roughly, fumbling my breasts. I could smell fear on his skin.

"Viens. Il est là."

As we headed into the dark cavern of the arch, I could hear Claude's high-pitched squeak contrasting with the thick, incomprehensible growl of Tunisian French. They were both talking fast. Like a counterpoint to their jagged words came the hypnotic slop and suck of the river. I breathed in the smells from deep under the bridge; the stench of unwashed bodies, river smells, mounds of detritus, life's putrefaction. I felt disgust.

Claude started to shout. He was such a cocky bastard. He thought he could bullshit anyone, but I knew he didn't have enough money and he'd coerced Jean-Yves along on the promise of keeping Julie's secrets from the family. It was blackmail, that's all it was. Jean-Yves would do anything to protect his sister, so Claude was using him as collateral – the old French name, connections, that hint of the *ancien régime*, enough to make up the difference and persuade Blue to deliver. Then they'd divvy up and sell the stuff on the streets: Claude to finance a feckless lifestyle; Jean-Yves to purchase more lapis lazuli, kilograms of the very highest-grade rock he could buy, so he could continue night after night perfecting the laborious extraction process that would yield one of the costliest and most precious of artists' raw materials – pure ultramarine.

"You're mad," I told him. "Why take such risks for paint? I don't trust Blue. He's dangerous. And if the *flics* catch you dealing, they'll lock you up." He'd laughed at my English timidity, the glint in his eyes born of wine and passion. But when he kissed me, I forgave him everything.

Deep beneath the arch of the Pont Neuf, shadows moved through the smells and the slime. They were all three gabbling now, too fast for me to understand, but I could hear anger, and Claude, wheedling. Then Méline started to cry.

There was a sharp intake of breath. I heard Jean-Yves swear in my direction.

Into one ear I hissed, *"Tais-toi, p'tite, tais-toi."* Shut *the fuck up*. I shook the tiny frame and dragged Méline away from where they were arguing, away towards the edge of the quay and into the miasma of the Seine. It was nervousness making me so rough with her. I'd never have done it otherwise. Like kicking a dog, isn't it? Lashing out at small things easily harmed, when really we'd like to hurt ourselves. Or those who hurt us. I felt so cold and so scared. I knew we shouldn't have been there, not in that place, at that time of night. Behind us, reminding us, the slosh and pluck of the river. "Shush, Mélie, we'll be going home soon." Méline grizzled, struggled to get free.

I moved to pick her up. Was it guilt for the rough-handling? Or my own need of comfort? I wanted to hug her shivering body and bury my face in her soft neck, to drown out the men shouting. Méline still had that baby smell in the creases of her skin – the perfume of innocence, like in paintings of angels and cherubs. I was bending over when a scuffle of bodies cannoned into us. Suddenly there were people everywhere. Feet slipped, arms and elbows barged, someone nearly knocked me over, and as I struggled to keep my balance

I saw the glint of a knife. I saw it quite clearly, despite the darkness, a silver blade in the night, like a thin sliver of the promise of death. And I saw Blue's face smiling.

Jean-Yves' hands were slick with blood when he grabbed me and slid with a groan onto the cold stone of the embankment. There was so much blood. And footsteps running. Then a voice. A cry. Was it her voice?

Someone said: "Where's Mélie?"

* * *

The workshop is quiet. My voice peters out, dried up like a parched water course; a final trickle, then nothing, though my mouth hangs open. The only sound is the soft sweep of brush on canvas. Mac has switched off the overhead lights and, when it grows almost too dark to paint, he lights candles. "Never have liked electricity," he says. The cavernous studio shrinks to a pool of yellow in which the storm canvas looms.

To my surprise and relief, I am able to broach the absurd. "Do you believe in ghosts, Mac?"

"Hah! You've been spooked by the Porthallen witches, Rose!" He turns to face me. "You don't want to take any notice of Mary Coleforth. Or Jan Freeman, for that matter. Crazy as coots, the pair of 'em." He snorts in derision. "Why, Rose? Why should Penmaris be haunted?"

I shrug. "An unresolved death. No one knows how Sally Hendry died. Perhaps something terrible happened to her and her ghost is trying to…" A sentence impossible to complete.

"You sound like the script of a B-movie," he says.

134

"But there are too many odd things going on. Like what happened to me this morning. I can't explain what occurred on that beach, it doesn't make any sense, but I'd swear it was real, it was as real to me as you are now. And the coincidences that keep piling up – like this storm you're painting." I lean forwards in my chair.

"It's quite innocent, Rose, it's part of a long-term project. Something I've been working on for months, actually. I'm trying to show the beach under different conditions. It's one of a series, not a sudden psychic impulse. And I bet it looks totally different from yours. You must try to remain objective." From the canvases stacked by the far wall, he pulls out two further examples, one depicting Porthallen Sands at sunset and the other on a bright summer's day. "There's half a dozen of them here, all from the same spot. Sort of time-lapse photography, only in paint. Remember Monet's series of Rouen Cathedral over twenty-four hours? Well, I'm trying to capture the changing seasons, a whole year not just a single day." He goes back to work, painting with strong, vigorous brush strokes. "Don't let the local coven scare you, Rose. Too much in-breeding. They're all batty."

"But the noises I hear? Outside at night, and above me, in the attic?"

"Well, go up and investigate," he suggests. "Probably mice or birds. Or that cat you've taken a shine to. I can't believe Sally Hendry's up there trying to communicate from beyond the veil." He puts his paint and brushes down and sinks into the other battered armchair. Lighting a cigarette, he holds it out to me but I shake my head. So he puts it between his own lips and draws deeply, considering his next words.

135

"In France you saw this little kid... Méline? You saw her disappear and drown? It's a terrible story, Rose. I can't imagine how anyone comes to terms with a tragedy like that. A little girl whose hand you'd been holding only a few seconds before." He blows a perfect smoke ring which expands till it dissolves in the shadows. "So. For years you've felt responsible and overwhelmed with guilt. Then earlier this year you lose a baby of your own." He pauses, as if waiting for me to do the maths, to join the dots. "Are you really surprised you have bad dreams and hear babies crying? Personally, I'd be surprised if you didn't. Doesn't have to mean the cottage is haunted, though, does it? And it doesn't mean you're going mad, either. If you ask me, it's grief, that's all it is, grief finally coming to the surface. Better out than in, I'd say."

I grimace at him, feeling the scars on my wrists throb. Extending both arms towards him, I turn my wrists out so he can see. "Look. Look what I did. Now tell me I'm not mad."

The first time I have ever willingly shown my shame.

His thumbs feel rough where he eases them across the scar tissue, but he's trying to be gentle. Cracked skin and dried paint bump over the ugly ridges. I sit there passively, my two hands in his huge open palms like two small craft lost in a sea of blue. "It's sad, Rose. It's very sad. And probably bad." Then, just as gently, he lets them go. "But not mad. And some time ago, I'd guess?" I nod. "Right. Well, that was then. You've moved on. You got yourself down here, for a start."

A rare smile lights his face, and I want lay my head on that grotty paint-stained shirt and be held by him. Be safe. He takes another long drag at his cigarette.

"You're beginning to heal, I'd say, even if it seems like a scary process. I'm sure there's no ghosts out there waiting to get you, nothing to be afraid of." Metal feathers flutter beyond the candlelight. "Sometimes I think we artists are too sensitive for our own good. We feel things, sense things, then we try and give those feelings expression in our work and, funnily enough, it upsets us. Cuts us to pieces sometimes. Who knows, perhaps grief will become the vehicle for your best work. You can use this, Rose, you can turn your pain into art. Use grief to cure grief." He reaches behind him, patting the table top in search of something. "Here!" He throws me a tube of paint. "Ultramarine. Synthetic, I'm afraid. Your Jean-Yves wouldn't approve. I want you to go and paint me something blue. Anything you like, the madder the better. Exploit your visions, you might be on to a winning formula. But don't give them credence. There's no such thing as ghosts, just bad memories." He holds my gaze for a long moment. "And on that note," he hauls himself out of the chair, "here endeth today's lesson." He stubs out his cigarette. "Fish-'n-chip supper? Or do you have a better offer?"

Chapter Twelve

There's a ladder in the shed. When I peer through a knothole, I can make out a couple of its aluminium rungs. I rattle the padlock on the door but it holds firm. Carne has the only key and I don't want to explain to him what I'm up to. Besides, he might not come for a few days and I feel too impatient to wait.

I try picking the lock, which always looks easy when they do it on TV, but I mangle a kitchen knife and nearly cut myself. Yanking on the door handle comes next, but I'm nowhere near strong enough to budge the door, despite the shed having seen better days. Many of the panels are flimsy and rotting, but kicking fails to loosen them and when I curl my fingers round a crumbling edge and pull for all I'm worth, one measly corner breaks away, leaving me with a handful of splinters.

After a final hefty kick, I give up. The black cat follows me into the kitchen, jumps into the sink and starts licking Marmite off my discarded breakfast plate.

He seems to be filling out now he's sneaking regular feeds. I lift him out, then rinse the dirt and mildew off my hands and apply first aid.

After coffee and a think, I go upstairs, followed again by my shadow. The weather outside is uninviting, just the sort of morning for curling up with a good book or, if you're a cat, snoozing the day away on someone's bed. Or, in my case, snooping. I settle the cat on the duvet, then stand back to reassess the problem.

Because the ceilings are low, I reckon I can reach the loft by standing on the dressing table, provided it will take my weight. A ladder isn't essential. Getting from the dressing table into the attic is another matter. But first I need to find out how the access door opens, then peer inside to see what I can see. The space might not be boarded and I can't risk clambering about up there only to put a foot through the ceiling and come tumbling out the quick way.

While I'm sweeping make-up and toiletries into a drawer, I notice my hands shaking. The effects of booze, the DTs? Or anticipation that Mac is about to be proved right; that I'm not going mad and there's nothing in the loft but dust and mice? Then I can forget ghosts and the supernatural and trust my mind to heal itself, however painful the process... Because I've only given Mac half the story – at the last moment I shied away from telling him about Oliver, as if present pain were too raw, too embarrassing to share, compared with past history.

Late last night Ellie phoned, just as I was getting undressed for bed. Filled with blue paint and abstract images, my mind took its time to register her voice. The silence, the audible pause, must have spooked her and she babbled something then hung up before I had a chance to speak. I wondered if she'd phoned earlier, while I was out, or whether she'd taken all evening to screw up her courage, only to lose it at the last minute. How did she get my number? So far I haven't rung back.

Dragging the rickety dressing table across the room, I position it directly beneath the loft entrance. Stepping from chair to table, I try to ignore the slight wobble and concentrate on what I'm doing. Be careful, I tell myself, the last thing you need now is a broken leg.

Slowly I uncoil until my head hits the ceiling, which is pretty much straight away. Fumbling awkwardly, my fingers locate the square of white-painted wood and I push. The cover, sitting in a frame recessed in the ceiling, lifts easily and I'm able to manoeuvre it to one side, exposing a well of darkness.

Beneath my feet the dressing table teeters alarmingly. I grab the edges of the frame and ease my head inside. Once I can stand up straight, I feel more secure. A mixture of smells hits me immediately, the abrasive smell of fibreglass insulation along with other, more musty odours redolent of damp and age. As my eyes grow accustomed to the gloom, I can make out old beams twisting upwards towards the apex and cobwebby recesses filled with debris. Pinpricks of light round the sides reveal gaps between roof and walls; access for tiny birds, no doubt. Score one for Mac.

I'm amazed to think how much I've told him, far more than I ever intended. Comfortable in his baggy armchair watching him paint, I'd talked on and on, the shadows of evening coaxing my voice into a river of words that flowed irresistibly. And my reasons for being there in the first place, to pump him for information about Chris Benning, and Sally Hendry and the cottage? They got lost somewhere in the strong current.

"Look," I'd said, and I'd held my wrists out. Never before had I done that; never would I have believed I could possibly do that.

He'd poured wine to accompany take-away cod and chips, smoked endless cigarettes, listened while I reminisced, lifted his head to blow perfect smoke rings, but offered neither comment nor judgement. Just told me to go away and paint. That was his answer to everything. Nothing I said seemed to surprise him. As if he'd heard it all before. One might even think he'd shown indifference. But when I walked back to Penmaris under the stars, my footsteps were lighter.

The good news is that the loft appears to be part-boarded. New floorboards have been laid across the joists, stretching out from the entrance for several feet in all directions. There's also evidence that someone started putting down loft insulation, then gave up and left the job half-finished. Tufts of wadding poke out from between the boards, which are unsecured but bare and clean, and from whose farthest ends I reckon I can to reach into the eaves where piles of junk lie shoved out of the way. All I have to do now is get inside. Backwards seems safest. I move my hands behind me and place them either side of the entrance cavity, then push down hard, heaving myself bottom-first into the roof. Easy! I whoop with success, sitting with my legs swinging in mid-air and looking down at the cat asleep on the bed.

Now to explore. The roof slopes at a sharp angle, so there's not much headroom. I'd better crawl and keep low. Setting off on hands and knees, I edge into the gloom and immediately curse myself for not bringing a torch. Some sleuth I am, forgetting the tools of the trade. Never mind, I'll make do rather than waste more time. There's enough light for my purposes.

The first pile of rubbish I examine proves to be leftovers from the renovation – builders' debris, lengths of piping and timber, a roll of unused insulation material which someone dumped and which is shredded along the exposed edges. Might birds have used this to line their nests? It's ragged enough and I can imagine sharp beaks pecking away at it. But nest building takes place in spring, not autumn, so that doesn't explain the noises I've heard at night. I search for signs of feathers or bird droppings, but find nothing. My fingers, touching here and there, encounter only thick dust.

I back up and start crawling in the opposite direction towards a stash of cardboard boxes. My movements set the joists creaking and I realise I'm trying to move quietly, so as not to disturb anyone. Creeping through this gloomy space is eerie. I feel like an intruder. The attic seems private, as though it has a secret life all its own which I'm invading.

It occurs to me that people spend a fortune on decorating their houses, but ignore the attic. Home is about creating an environment where every nook and cranny is familiar and loved; whether a source of delight or dismay, every spot becomes an extension of its owner. Years ago my father fought a running battle with a recurring patch of damp in our sunken dining-room. Megan and I used to draw round it with colouring crayons when we were kids. Then one day Dad simply abandoned the fight and joined in the game; he turned a messy patch of wall into the scariest monster ever. It was one of those great family moments.

Everyone must have memories like that, special memories of houses and rooms. But who has memories of their roof? It's simply there, and so long as it does its job, perhaps storing empty suitcases, no one gives it a second thought. Yet a house is nothing without a strong roof to keep the world out. Its span describes a huge space hanging literally over our heads but which is largely ignored and disregarded, integral to and yet a mystery within the heart of the home. I am struck by the truth of this idea, that homes are made by defining space and staking one's claim: living space, sleeping space, work space, play area, kitchen, bathroom… but the biggest space of all remains unknown, left to brood secretly over the transient lives of those camped out below.

A sound. The air moves and I jump as a dark shape glides past. Something brushes against my thigh and I scream. Then my hand registers warm fur. The bloody cat! How has he managed to get up here? My heart racing, I sit down abruptly as if winded. The cat, snaking round me, purrs loudly, pleased with his adventure. "What are you doing up here, you monkey?" The same as me, probably. Exploring. "You gave me a fright. I thought you were fast asleep." He miaows and shoves his head against my hand. "Well, you can stay, provided you don't scare me again. And don't get lost where I can't find you." Visions of having to leave the loft open for days till he condescends to reappear.

Unconcerned, he bounds off, leaving me to continue crawling to the end of the boarded section, which is still considerably more than an arm's stretch from the pile of cardboard boxes stacked against the chimney bricks. So near yet so far… I can't possibly give up. Testing the joists, I advance slowly on one knee and lean forwards till my fingers almost brush the biggest box. A bit further… I stretch, inching my right leg along the joist, extending my fingers until… Got it! Hooking fingertips over the lip, I haul the box towards me, accidentally nudging the others at the same time and sending them deeper into the recess. Never mind. Satisfied for the moment with one prize, I lift it next to me and sit back to examine the contents.

The top is packed with layers of cloth to keep everything secure. I lift out the first one, shaking it to one side and releasing a cloud of dust. From the feel of it, I'm holding a piece of seersucker cotton. Its faded blues and greens open into a square about the right size for a tablecloth. Along the folds the colours has almost disappeared. Next comes, probably, another tablecloth, once white and now a sickly yellow-grey with clusters of hand-embroidered flowers in each corner linked by chains of embroidery round the sides. Someone spent hours on this, the needlecraft is exquisite, but one corner is missing, the material roughly cut away. Trying to make out what happened, I angle it into a ray of light slicing between roof and wall; a brown stain is visible, creeping over the bottom half of the cloth.

A scrabble of claws makes me look up. The cat is poised on the edge of one of the other boxes. Before I can call out, he's inside. I can hear him moving around, his fur brushing the cardboard. Hoping he won't do too much damage, I ignore him and return to unpacking the layers of material, slowly, to limit the dust cloud.

Once the final layer of tatty net curtains has gone, I'm looking at an odd assortment of knick-knacks, inconsequential stuff I can only suppose had sentimental value. There's a few hand-painted stones, the broad, flat kind ideal for skimming the waves, and handfuls of shells from the seashore. I put the biggest one to my ear and hear the sea. Up against one side of the box is a thin exercise book which proves, upon opening, to contain an assortment of pressed flowers, fragments of which start to fall off the moment I open the first page. Bugger, I must be more careful.

Next I take out some cheap, roughly carved wooden animals and a telescopic tube that rattles when I shake it. I point it directly into a beam of light and peer through one end, realise I can twist the other, and then I'm rewarded with a dazzle of changing shapes and colours. A kaleidoscope, and it still works. Back to the box, and more toys emerge, all equally old-fashioned. Did they belong to Sally Hendry when she was a baby or are they even older than that? I have no idea what kids used to play with fifty or sixty years ago. And what's this, a stuffed sock? But no, upon examination it proves to be a simple home-made doll with woollen hair and a face sewn on. Everything seems crude and pathetic, the sad relics of an impoverished childhood. As toys, they don't seem like much fun.

Then, underneath a clutch of empty photo frames, I come across a beautifully carved, wooden casket. I place it carefully on my lap and run my fingers over the design, tracing the intricate floral shapes etched deep into the surface. There's nothing cheap or crude about this. The hinged lid opens easily and inside lie several white sheets of… is it card? Turning the top one over, I find I'm looking at an old black and white photograph of children playing on a beach.

My heart starts to race. Is this a photo of Sally Hendry as a little girl? Quickly I flick through the other pictures, some more recent and in colour. They must surely be family snaps, of the Hendry family, and Sally's face must be there. Once more, I regret not having a torch. I'll have to contain my excitement and wait until I can study them downstairs. They go into my trouser pocket for later and the wooden casket joins the toys on the floorboards, to which a skipping rope is added, then a colouring book, a moth-eaten teddy bear, a collection of feathers, a cap-gun and holster.

Thinking this must be the lot, I tip the box upside down and a single marble bounces out, a smooth round glass ball encasing a bright lick of yellow. I catch it before it rolls away and vanishes. In case there's any more trapped inside, I right the box and run my hands around. Yes, there is something, partly tucked under the flaps of cardboard at the bottom. With the utmost care, because my fingers recognise instantly the feel of sheets of paper, I extract another exercise book. Despite the bad light I can see this one contains, not pressed flowers but handwriting, page after page of writing. And on the front cover, faint but legible, a name: Sally Hendry.

Sally's handwriting, her diary or notebook. The first page shows a firm, round, almost school-girlish hand.

By now I'm too excited to explore further. I want to examine the book and the photos right away, in the sitting room where I can see properly. Putting the toys quickly back in the box, I press the tablecloths on top, just as I found them, though why I'm bothering with such niceties I have no idea. It can't possibly matter. Then, with a hefty kick, I boot the box out of the way with one foot as I turn round, eager to be downstairs. The cardboard makes a rough, scraping sound as it slithers across the floorboards, *the scrape of something being dragged from one side to the other.* Then it bumps, thud, thump, along the joists, a sound *like footsteps in the attic.* My leg freezes, half-extended in mid-air. I've heard that sound before, in bed at night, a sound like footsteps crossing the attic floor. My exact thoughts: *like footsteps in the attic*. It's exactly what I said to myself the night I couldn't sleep, the night I lay there listening to the house creaking overhead, the night the sad ugly face first crept onto my sketch pad. Slowly I lower my leg and crouch and listen. Goose bumps ripple my skin. I remember why I climbed up to the attic in the first place.

Is Penmaris speaking again? Alec McConnell might not believe in ghosts, but he did urge me to trust myself and be bold. Now the cottage seems to be saying the same thing: trust, be bold, ask questions. With any luck, there may even be answers waiting amid the items I've just found. I stuff the exercise book under my jumper, into my trouser waistband for safety. Then on hands and knees I shuffle back to the loft opening. Trailing something from his mouth, the cat bounds past me and leaps easily onto the dressing table below.

Chapter Thirteen

The first photo I look at is also the oldest, sepia tints depicting a family group in stiff Edwardian pose, ramrod straight and ready to explode from the effort. A moustachioed man is standing erect, cradling a hat in the crook of his left arm while his right hand lies in proprietorial fashion upon the shoulder of the lady seated beside him. She's a bosomy, middle-aged woman with frizzy hair scraped into a bun, and is wearing a high-necked blouse with mutton-chop sleeves above a long, plain skirt whose waistband struggles to define an hourglass curve. The couple, tight-lipped and stiff-backed, ignores the boy and girl sitting cross-legged on the floor in front of them, staring aggressively at the camera.

This man and woman could be Sally's grandparents, or even her great-grandparents. I gaze at the long-dead family. There's no date or reference of any kind on the back, forcing me to make my best guess. I've seen pictures like this in Mum's album, formal compositions from the turn of the twentieth century when visiting the photographer was still an event to be undertaken with due seriousness and a consideration for the concerns of posterity. "The past at a glance," Mum always maintains. "It's important that we remember." She religiously dates all her own snaps, and any that are passed on to her she'll painstakingly track down – people, places, events, times, relationships – so that she can write a simple legend under every single photo mounted in her collection. Will today's digital efforts, so easy-come easy-go, have such long and cherished lives, I wonder?

I put the photo to one side and pick up another. This is more familiar, more modern and in colour, and I recognise the Instamatic signature. My parents used to own a Polaroid camera till they went out of fashion. I remember when Dad went through the embarrassing phase of snapping his children's every move and showing their antics to his patients at evening surgery. He'd appear from nowhere, click a moment of silliness, then pull the picture out and wave it with a flourish, like a magician producing a rabbit.

The photo I'm holding is of a gang of beach bums: a dozen hippy-looking characters in their late teens, I guess, or early twenties, sporting shaggy hair, wide grins and bell-bottom trousers, lounging on the sand with arms linked as the sea rolls in behind them. It could even have been taken on Porthallen Sands; I think I recognise the rocks to one side. I peer intently at the faces, trying to identify someone, anyone. Sally Hendry could be there. I search for the long legs and wild mane of hair that Mac described. Trouble is, they all have wild hair; it was the fashion. And all the guys have beards. A very hirsute lot altogether. Then it occurs to me that Mac might be in the photo, though from a distance of forty-odd years it's difficult to be sure. I pocket the snap to take round to show him later. He's bound to be able to help. I pick up another at random.

At that moment, the cat decides it's time to be let out. Still trailing whatever it was he stole from the loft between clamped jaws, he appears from nowhere and skitters to the back door where he miaows loudly, demanding attention. I follow him to the kitchen, but he refuses to drop his find or have it taken. He scurries away when chased, hovering out of arms' reach and growling deeply until I give up and open the door. As he flashes past, I catch a glimpse of narrow, satin ribbons floating from a plug of white wool in his mouth.

Hoping he'll drop his mouse substitute, I dash out after him. Rounding the back of the cottage, I career into Carne, who's servicing the lawnmower. "Whoops! Sorry, Carne. Did you see where he went?" My words come in a rush.

"See who?"

"The cat."

He pulls his grubby hat off and scratches his head.

"He just ran past you. Look, there he…" and I shoot off towards the bushes, somehow managing not to trip over the stone seat, still invisible in the long, waving grass. From the wall I scan the field beyond but, as usual, the cat has disappeared.

Carne has the mower in pieces and is sandpapering the blades, which must have been extremely blunt and rusted because he's frowning to himself as he rubs, puffing with exertion. He seems indifferent to my presence, absorbed in his task. The mower will need to be sharp; there's an enormous amount of very long grass to be cut. *I had a bit of a chat*, that's what Chris said, *bunged him a few extra quid*. What for? Gardening or surveillance? This is the first time Carne has done any serious work since I arrived. Is he really here to tidy up or to keep an eye on me, report back to Chris, who'll report back to Oliver, who…? Or am I being paranoid? I march up ready with a sarcastic barb, but his easy concentration disarms me. I bite my tongue. "Big job you've got on today."

Carne laughs. "No problem. We only ever mows this top bit." He looks slyly at me and gives a conspiratorial wink. "Keeps his missus quiet."

"Paula, you mean?"

"Come spring I'll put out a few pots and tubs, make it colourful. So long as she's got somewhere pretty to sit in the sun, she don't notice the rest, down there." He nods to the other end of the garden. "We're letting that half grow natural, see. Don't want to scare off the wild flowers, or the insects an' critters that live there." He squirts oil round the guts of the machine, then wipes his hands on a rag. "There. Reckon that'll do."

It's such an unlikely scenario – Chris Benning and Carne Tresawna as eco-warriors scheming to preserve the wildlife on this handkerchief of land – that I nearly scoff. Instead I bite my tongue again. I have no reason to mistrust him, just a silly suspicion, and he has no reason to lie to me. "So Chris… Mr Benning… he's into that sort of thing, is he?" Knee-high grass stirs in the breeze and there's a hint of perfume in the air.

"Pretty much. I certainly hopes so. We chatted about it, back when he first bought Penmaris. Nowadays he leaves it up to me." There's something about the way he speaks the cottage's name. *We've got an understanding*, that's what he told me once before, implying that he and Chris are partners in care rather than gardener and boss. Carne stands up. "There's no beating nature, you see." He surveys the garden. "She always wins in the end. Best to let her be." He stuffs the oily rag in a pocket and starts pushing the mower, making trial strips, nodding with satisfaction. "I'll be getting on then."

This is the most he's ever said, all in one go, and I smile encouragingly at him, even though I find it hard to believe Chris Benning gives a damn about wild flowers. More likely he doesn't give a damn, full stop. Out of sight, out of mind. Still, one assumption I've got all wrong; Carne is no lackey. He acts more as though he owns the place. My hand goes to the photo in my pocket; I could ask him right now if he recognises anyone. Save waiting till I see Mac. But scarcely is the thought formed than Jan Freeman appears, marching briskly round the corner of the house, and the moment is lost. Carne tugs his woolly hat down over his ears.

"Heard the old mower clattering, so I knew someone was about." She beams at us. "Dropped by to give you this, Rose." From a voluminous shoulder bag she produces a poster advertising the Halloween play. "A reminder. You did say you'd come, didn't you? I was wondering, would you mind sticking this in your car? Slap it on the back window. Bit more advertising never goes amiss." The poster has creased slightly in her bag. Instinctively I smooth it flat, admiring the bright-orange pumpkin lanterns and Stevie's impish face grinning out from the reds and greens of his pixy costume.

Carne makes no concession to Jan's arrival and is struggling on with the business of cutting the grass. Putting his full weight behind the mower, he's leaning at forty-five degrees, grunting encouragement as the machine rackets and whines with the enormity of its task, sending showers of green spray to right and left.

Jan sniffs appreciatively. "Mmm, freshly cut grass. Nothing better. Though why he bothers with that old thing." She shakes her head. "Daft bugger." Then she adds, "Lovely garden, this," with a degree of feeling that surprises me, since I can't quite see it. "Always did like it out here. You get a sense of peace, don't you, away from the house?" She starts to stroll at ease, touching leaves, trailing her hands through the bushes. "Evergreens, Rose, they're the soul of a garden. The part that never dies." Abruptly she turns. "Can you smell that? Gorgeous, isn't it? Winter-flowering viburnum, I bet. One of the blessings of autumn." She suddenly veers off across the lawn, following her nose, heading directly into the stone's path. "Be covered in flowers soon, you wait and—"

"Jan! Watch out or you'll trip over the…"

But she's already leaning against the wall, coiling strands of foliage round her fingers, eyes closed in an expression of rapture. And she has missed the stone as if by magic. Coming to join her, I notice long, thick eyelashes which nestle against her cheekbones like dormice curled in sunshine.

I say, "Well, at least now I know what it's called." She's plucking leaves from the stalk and hands me one. "I've been wondering for days." I sniff the leaf. It smells of nothing much, but around us the air gusts perfume. Wind is flapping the Halloween poster I'm clutching in my left hand, revealing underneath the photo I'd taken out to show Carne. Jan, opening her eyes, sees the photo and reaches for it. "Anyone I know?" she asks.

"Quite possibly." I pass it to her. "I found it in… in the cottage." No need for details. "And I was wondering whether Sally Hendry might be one of the people…"

Jan hoots recognition. "Reckon that's our Carne there, just look at him!" Her vermillion-painted fingernail jabs. "Even long hair can't disguise those ears." I must look blank. "You never noticed? I think that's why he always wears a hat." I glance in Carne's direction; the trade-mark red bonnet is hunched between taut shoulder blades as he clatters and shoves, strip after strip. "And if I'm not mistaken," another stab of the finger, "that's Mary standing next to him. Well, well. Quite the young thing there, isn't she? Must have been taken some time before she married her William. How about that! Brother and sister playing happy families by the seaside."

I had failed entirely to recognise grumpy, grey-haired Mary Coleforth in the slender girl in the photo, a teenager with tumbling auburn curls and easy eyes. But Jan is right about the young man, there's definitely something of Carne about the…

Abruptly Jan passes the photo over. "Can't help you with the others, I'm afraid," she murmurs, appearing to lose interest. She fiddles with her necklace that's snagged on the lace trim on her blouse. Viburnum leaves, clutched in her left hand, drift to the ground.

I'm both surprised and disappointed. "So Sally's not there?"

"I was only a kid, Rose. It was years ago. I was too young to know that hippy crowd. You can't identify anyone in a grainy old photo like that." She starts back towards the cottage, stomping through the grass, muttering. "The Swinging Sixties, eh? Peace, love and LSD. Wonder if old Carne here ever got stoned out of his mind?"

Carne has stopped mowing and is sweeping up. He glares at Jan as she approaches and brushes deliberately across her path so she has to side-step the broom. Turning sharply, she announces in an unnecessarily loud voice, "She must have been pushing forty by the time she settled back here."

"Sorry? Who…?"

"Sally Hendry. Chased off like a giddy teenager after some man, so rumour has it, then came back to Cornwall with her tail between her legs. Her with her high-flying ideas, but it all came to nothing. She never managed to escape Penmaris."

Carne's broom falls silent, the handle thrusting from his fist like a jousting pole. His head rears up. They stare defiantly at one another till I grab Jan's elbow and steer her towards the house. The elastic space between them stretches, taut and fizzing.

"Cold drink, Jan, cup of tea? Do you have time? Come inside and have a look round the cottage." By the back door I whisper, "So you knew Sally quite well?"

Jan hesitates. "Sort of. Yes. I suppose you could say that. I felt sorry for her. I know she tried to run away from all this," her arm waves vaguely, "wanting some fanciful life as a poet. But she ended up back where she started. She used to come into the bookshop a lot, that's how we first met. Everything had gone wrong by then, or so she always said. It was always someone else's fault. But when Jack Hendry died of a heart attack, Sal was forced to come home to look after Peggy, and she never got away again. She was the only one of the kids still single, so it all fell to her. Poor old Peggy'd had a stroke and needed twenty-four hour care. After she died, Sal stayed on and—"

"So who was the mysterious guy she ran off with?"

"Oh, I've no idea. Could have been one of many, I suspect." Jan chuckles. "She was a bit of a goer, by all accounts. Bit too flighty for Porthallen. There's many said good riddance when she left and didn't exactly welcome her back. But like I said, I was only a kid when Sally was cutting a swathe through the local males. By the time I knew her, the fire had dimmed. Well, buried deeper, anyway."

We're standing by Jan's car. I try again with "Tea, coffee?" in an effort to detain her, discover more about Sally Hendry. "Oh, I've just remembered, I bought a huge pumpkin the other day, to make a lantern for Halloween. It's still sitting on the kitchen floor. Come and see."

Jan brightens immediately and claps her hands. "But that's perfect," she exclaims. "Bring it to the Hall tomorrow morning and join us. We're holding a competition. There'll be loads of kids there, all needing help to make anything more than *an absolute abortion*. I'd be really grateful for some extra support." I'm about to protest, but Jan seems excited. "I can promise you, every single lantern will be used on the thirty-first. And that's next Tuesday, don't forget. Only a few more days to go. I insist you come and help. It'll be such fun. And yours might end up the star of the show. Now, I must be

off. Thanks for the offer of tea, but I'm late already."
She opens the car door, calling over her shoulder, "Ten
thirty tomorrow morning and no excuses." Then she
pauses, turns round again, hesitates. "I've got a photo
somewhere, of me and Sally, taken in this garden not
long before she… I'll try and dig it out for you." I hold
my breath, certain Jan is on the verge of saying more,
but she slides behind the steering wheel and waves.
"Bye now."

Halfway down the drive, she screeches to a halt and
dangles something out of the window. "Forgot to give
you this, Rose." It's a baby's bootee, knitted in white
wool and threaded round the ankle with shiny satin
ribbon. "Found it in the mud by your shed when I
arrived. Bit grubby, I'm afraid." She raises her
eyebrows. "Are we expecting a happy event?"

* * *

Carne spoons sugar into his tea then crunches on a
ginger nut. "Proper job," he says, sounding content.
Stretching his legs out in front of him, he sighs and
munches noisily. We are sitting on the garden bench
surveying with satisfaction the chewed rectangle of
lawn he's mown. The remaining long grass dances in
the breeze, its seed heads like fringes on a skirt swirling
round the apple tree and brushing the end wall.

"I found some old photos," I say. "Have a look at
this one. Do you think that's Porthallen beach?" I show
him the snap.

Carne nods slowly, a wide smile splitting his face.
"That's her, all right. See that rock there?" He points
with his biscuit. "Best spot for fishing when the tide's
in."

He seems relaxed and comfortable. It feels as though an understanding has been reached, a bridge crossed while I've not been watching, and here we are on the other side. More confidently I go on. "Who's in the picture then, Carne? Could that possibly be you?"

With surprising delicacy, he brushes crumbs off his fingers before taking the photo, squinting close, holding it carefully as if it's precious. "That's me all right, and Robbie, and Daniel. And Mary too." He laughs out loud. "My sister, Mary, when she were a girl." Then he pauses before adding in a softer voice, "And there's Sal. There. That one. That's Sal. Sally Hendry. She used to live here, you know," as if proclaiming a miracle. Gazing at the cluster of old familiar faces, he seems momentarily lost to the past, absorbed in the wash of stirred memories. Then, "Where'd you get this photo?" he asks, a hint of wonder in his voice.

"I found it this morning. In the cottage. I guessed you might recognise people. Do you remember when it was taken?" From the tray between us I pick up the teapot and pour a second mug of tea, creating a small ritual, lulling time. The bright, wide eyes of Sally Hendry watch me.

"It were the last summer before she went away. Spent every day on the beach that summer, we did. Longest summer I've ever known. Like it wouldn't never end." He smirks. "Huh! Just look at those daft clothes we wore!"

"How old were you?"

"Twenty-one," he answers promptly. "And Sal were just eighteen. Never forget it. Crowd of us used to meet up every day, drinking and laughing. Dreaming of the future. Making daft plans."

It sounds familiar. "Yeah. Yeah, we all do that, don't we?"

"Oh, I weren't that fussed. Not me. Never wanted to be anywhere else 'cept right here." He waves his mug in an arc that encompasses a universe. "Stick-in-the-mud they used to call me. Mind you, most of 'em are still here round abouts, for all their big ideas."

"But Sally left?"

Carne's eyes focus on a point in the sky where yesterday hangs closer than today. "I proposed to her that summer," he says. "Now I bet that takes you by surprise." He glances at my dropped jaw, shoots me a grin. "But Sal, well, she were itching to leave. Couldn't wait to get away. Few weeks later she went chasing off after him." He points to the figure standing next to Sally in the photo, a tall man, big-built, hairy like the rest of them, pulling a silly face at the camera.

I think perhaps I recognise him. "Who's that, Carne?"

"That's Alec McConnell, that is."

* * *

In a bowl of soapy water, flecks of dirt, grass and gravel float loose from the white wool of the bootee. It looks hand-knitted. In places the ribbon is pitted with tooth marks; the cat has been fiercely possessive. My mind bubbles like the soapsuds, bursting with questions I'm not sure I can ask and leaping to wild conclusions that are unwarranted but irresistible. Sally Hendry and Alec McConnell. They'd been lovers. Carne had all but said so. Sally and Mac, in London, in the early Seventies. He'd been a struggling art student then lecturer, she an aspiring poet. How long had their

159

relationship lasted? Imagining a Bohemian affair, I picture them in a dingy flat in Bayswater, consumed by passion as they fought and laughed and loved, as they painted and wrote amid drifts of paper that littered every surface, oil paint and water colours seeping into the pores of their skin. Shunning electricity, they would light candles that flickered in the gloom.

I start to rinse the bootee under the tap then realise what it is that I'm holding. I grip it hard between my fingers. A baby's bootee. Good grief, did Sally Hendry have a *baby*? Mac's baby? The thought makes me gasp. And if she did, what became of it? The Sally remembered by people in the village had certainly not been a mother. Jan described her as single.

A child born of flight from sleepy Porthallen? Could Alec McConnell be the father?

But the delicate garment, now clean and damp, squeezed hand-dry in my palm, came from the attic here in Penmaris, where the cat found it just a few hours ago. Perhaps Sally returned to Cornwall to give birth or… Another line of thought occurs.

Jan said Sally was forced to come home and look after her sick mother. Perhaps, when her mother died, Sally stayed in Cornwall because by then she was having another affair, because she became pregnant in later life? Ideas jostle in my head. Not Mac's baby, then. He was well established in London by that time, a college lecturer. It would have to have been someone else's, someone who lived nearby in Porthallen. Carne? Of course! He'd once lost the love of his life to the lure of teenage dreams, but maybe he found her again in middle age. Carne, the patient lover. And that would explain why Sally decided to stay here.

160

But according to Jan, Sally was alone and unhappy, so why hadn't Carne married her? What had gone wrong? And if she'd been a single mum, just think of the scandal. An illegitimate child in this close community. I could almost hear the wagging tongues. Poor little baby, whatever happened to it? Was it adopted? Did it even survive? No wonder the locals are quiet on the subject of Sally's life. And death.

The tiny kitchen feels claustrophobic, as if the walls are closing in. Placing the bootee on the windowsill to dry, I open the window wide and stare out. Instantly and everywhere, the smell of newly cut grass. But the smell is overpowering, nauseating. Instead of oxygen, so that I can breathe, the air delivers the stench of rottenness: wet leaves, decomposing vegetation, things left to decay and stink.

There's too much going on here that I don't understand and the only person I dare ask is Jan Freeman, because she'd been Sally's friend – she'd admitted as much, outside earlier today, almost as a direct challenge to Carne who'd looked as if he'd like to murder her. Jan had befriended Sally when she started calling in at the bookshop to fill her empty days, after Peggy Hendry died. When Sally was a much older woman.

An older woman – that had, roughly speaking, been Mac's dismissive take on my drawing. Disingenuous, I must now assume. I could show Jan the same sketch and get her reaction. And I could show her some of the old photos I've found. Maybe then she would talk more freely to me about Sally Hendry. Equally I could confront Carne's rival directly, I could challenge Alec McConnell about his relationship with Sally back in the

Seventies because, for sure, he knows more than he's letting on.

I wipe my hands and turn the bootee over to dry the other side. The cat found it in a small cardboard box which I'd ignored. Time to revisit the attic and see what other secrets it holds.

Chapter Fourteen

Jan Freeman is wielding a knife.

"Now, we are going to use these *very* carefully, aren't we?"

Some of the parents twitch when Jan waves the blade in their direction, emphasising her words with sharp jabs at the front row. It's Saturday morning in St Michael's Church Hall, where Year Six are gathered with their anxious mums to make pumpkin lights for Halloween.

I'm sitting at the back waiting to give my short demonstration. Having decided I want Jan on my side, not to say in my debt, I spent yesterday evening preparing stencils and arrived at St Michael's early, volunteering to give the children a brief lesson… if that was okay with Jan, if Jan didn't mind… to be smothered in her patchouli-scented hug.

"And *no one* is to touch *anything* until Rose has shown us what to do," she insists.

The triumph of optimism over experience. Already the children, cross-legged on the floor, are wriggling with excitement. Soon they'll be uncontainable. On a long table in front of them stand the pumpkins in all their bulbous glory, and at one end there's an assortment of knives, spoons, felt-tips, paper and scissors, cloths and kitchen towels. I feel as though I'm back at school. I can remember the excitement of craft lessons and the thrill of taking one's masterpiece home at the end of the day to show the family. And I know the kids can't wait to get their hands dirty. I'm hoping the plentiful cloths and buckets are for washing sticky fingers, not mopping up blood.

Jan is in full flow. "Now, who can tell me another name for pumpkin lights? Billy?"

"Jack-o'-lanterns, Miss." He pokes his tongue out at the boy next to him.

"That's right. And what were they used for?"

"For light, Miss."

"Well, yes of course, for light. But what's special about Halloween?"

I think about the souls of the dead. Last night, before going to sleep, I studied the beach photograph in detail, learning to read those happy faces from the hippy generation, the age of peace and love. It isn't a grainy picture, as Jan tried to make out. It's perfectly clear, especially the face of Sally Hendry, now I know where to look. All that teenage intensity, transformed into a woman who vanished suddenly twenty years ago in strange circumstances, in a manner unexplained and uninvestigated, whose broken skeleton was found under rocks, but who in life led an apparently unremarkable, some might even say unsuccessful existence in a rural backwater, and whose passing caused scarcely a ripple.

Or did it? I'm convinced now that there's more to Sally's story than local people want known. Something terrible happened at Penmaris, a tragedy perhaps involving a child, because when I climbed back into the attic yesterday I found the box of baby clothes. The box the cat had jumped into. Pieces of the jigsaw are coming together. I might even be able to uncover the truth, if I keep looking. And for some reason that seems incredibly important.

I sense her presence every day. In the cottage, outside in the garden, when talking to Carne or Mac – everywhere and nowhere, a shadow of Sally lingers. Now, thanks to the photo, I can see her clearly: prominent nose, high cheekbones framed by that wild mane of hair, a square jaw that brooked no denial. Strong features suggesting a forceful personality, a combative, animal attraction. A face that catches the eye.

A face which, under a different guise, I've done battle with myself. Although my sketch pad remains behind the sofa, out of sight, I'm always aware of it. Sally is never far away. The eighteen-year-old snapped on Porthallen beach was strong and perfect, a striking creature with huge eyes that challenged the camera and who, even as the shutter clicked, was making plans to follow Alec McConnell to the bright lights of London. The Sally I have drawn is a damaged version, older and broken. But I'm sure it's her.

It's easy now to pick Sally out as a little girl in some of the other photos. There are family portraits where she's posed next to, presumably, her brother and sister (are they still alive?), mementoes of birthday parties and summer picnics, groups of kids playing indoors and out, and a formal school photo of "Class 6 Miss Jenner", with the class tiered on benches looking gawky and probably about the same age as the children here today. In each case, Sally eclipses the crowd – everything about her radiates energy. Except there's one much later snap, taken in a garden. Older and fatter, her thighs bulging in tight denim beneath the bulk of a shapeless jumper, her face obscured behind a tangle of hair falling forwards, this is a very different Sally Hendry, standing alone, tired and faded at the edges.

Jan is busy explaining the origins of the Jack-o'-lantern. "It dates all the way back to the ancient Celts, they were the original Cornish folk who lived here thousands of years ago." Her voice sinks to a whisper. "They used to stick the skulls of dead people onto poles, which they dug into the ground all round the edges of their camp to drive away the evil spirits." Rich in sibilants, her words slither and snake round the hall. She's good at whipping up an atmosphere; one little girl in the front row is transfixed, sucking the end of a pigtail, eyes like saucers. Then someone goes "whoooo" and all the children scream.

They'll be having nightmares tonight, I reckon. It's time to interrupt and get practical. I rise to my feet and grin at their eager faces. "Okay, who wants to make a lantern?" Every hand shoots up as I walk over to the demonstration table. "We don't want nasty old spirits round here, do we?" Blonde pigtails in the front row smiles with relief.

I grab my tools and get started. Slicing the top off my pumpkin, I carve an opening large enough to insert a hand, then scoop out the flesh and seeds with a spoon, reminding the mums present about the wisdom of making soup with the pulp and roasting the seeds to eat – neither of which I have ever done nor have the remotest intention of doing. But I'm getting into role. I hold out the empty shell for the children to inspect. "See, I've kept the walls quite thick, so the finished lantern will be good and solid and won't fall apart if you knock it or kick it or… anything." I cut a flat base to show how it will sit securely on a table and not topple over. "I'm going to scrape inside too, just here at the bottom, and make a tiny hollow to hold the night light." My forefinger points. "And now for the good bit. The face!"

"Miss!" A hand waves. "Miss, can I do a scary face with big teeth?"

"You can do whatever you like. For those of you who want help, I've made some templates for you." I select a stencil from the pile and place it over the pumpkin, showing how to prick holes along the design using a nail as a guide for cutting. "But if you're good at art, you can draw your own face free-hand with a felt-tip," which I wave at them, "then cut along the lines. But cut slowly and carefully; ask a grown-up if you're not sure, because once a piece is cut out, you can't stick it back again." Taking a knife, I create two diamond-shaped eyes and push the pieces through, discarding them in the bin. The buzz in the hall reaches explosion point. "There. See? Now it's your turn. Come and…" My words are lost in the rush to the table.

While Jan organises the children, I finish my pumpkin. I punch holes either side of the opening, thread string through to make a handle, set a match to the night light, then carry the completed masterpiece to the stage where the lantern gives out a satisfying glow. One or two children clap, which I find unexpectedly moving.

While I'm clearing up, a small form appears by my side and a hand creeps into mine. A voice whispers shyly, "It's magic, Miss." It's blonde pigtails, beaming at me.

I bend down. "What's your name?" The girl whispers something, and I feel time shiver as her hand slips away.

Méline, slipping from my grasp.

Jan strides across. "Come along, Melanie, stop bothering Rose. I bet you haven't finished your lantern yet, have you?" She speaks over the child's head. "She's a funny little thing, this one. Slippery as an eel. Never where she ought to be." She addresses the girl again. "Show me what you've done so far, Melanie, come on," and she takes her by the arm, about to bustle her away.

Melanie twists round to face me. "The lights are beautiful, Miss. I can't wait till Tuesday, can you?"

As they move off, I drop heavily onto a wooden chair, my legs trembling too much to stand. I close my eyes, taking deep, measured breaths. I misheard the name, that was all. It was a silly coincidence. It means nothing. Around me the noise level is rising, but through the excited chatter I pick out Jan's voice relating a few more Halloween traditions.

"October the thirty-first marks the passing of the old year and the arrival of the new. On this night, so some people believe, the veil that divides our world from the next is at its thinnest, allowing the dead to pass through.

168

Those skulls on pikes I was telling you about soon gave way to gourds, turnips, pumpkins, all of them hollowed out to hold a candle to light the way home for lost souls wandering in the void."

Does Méline's spirit wander lost? Ten years ago, yet still she haunts me with the flutter of passing fingertips. *Tu veux jouer avec moi, Rose? Jouons au cache-cache. Cherche-moi, Rose! Trouve-moi!* Slip-sliding away in an everlasting game of hide-and-seek, a memory in peripheral vision. I would give much to feel Méline's fingers gripping my own. Like Melanie's just did.

I can hear Jan telling another anecdote about mischievous spirits said to roam the countryside at Halloween, causing havoc and mayhem. Parents are laughing at the absurdity. I wonder if I'm falling prey to malign devilment. Are ghosts of the dead messing with my mind? Or do I simply, as Mac would maintain, have an over-active imagination, a gullible psyche? Méline's death was not my fault; Sally's story, however intriguing, is not actually anything to do with me. Having set out this morning with the intention of questioning Jan, I sense my determination wavering. Perhaps I should let the dead lie and get on with the business of living. I open my eyes to see Stevie, naughty pixy *par excellence*, shoving lumps of wet pumpkin down the neck of someone's T-shirt. Perhaps he has the right attitude.

Forty minutes later, Jan is doling out coffee. With a sigh, she collapses onto the chair next to me and sticks her feet out. "Phew! Time to pick a winner, Rose. What do you think?" The front of the stage glows with flickering lanterns. "Bit of a mixed bunch, I'm afraid, but apart from the *totally hideous,* there's... maybe... a few possibles?" She sounds doubtful.

"Hideous is good," I say. "They're meant to be scary. I think they've done really well."

"Oh! Before I forget." She rummages in a pocket. "That photo I mentioned. Here. Me and Sal looking frumpy in your back garden."

The same tight jeans and grey, baggy jumper. Like the photo I found. I'm intrigued. And Jan looks as drab as her friend, the pair of them dumpy and glum, whereas today Jan dazzles in silver jewellery and electric blue. She seems to have reinvented herself in the intervening years.

"Thanks," I say, hesitating. "I was wondering..." So many questions I want to ask; where to begin? "I'd love to know more about Sally."

"Like what?" Jan's thoughts are elsewhere, preoccupied with pumpkins and the imminent arrival of the caretaker. She waggles a finger at two boys doing a kamikaze jump off the stage.

"Well, for a start, who took this photo?"

"Tell you the truth, I can't remember. Probably no one. Expect I stuck the camera on a tripod, then dashed into shot. I used to take a lot of pics at one time."

"You look—"

"Don't!" she protests, wincing in horror. "I'm living backwards, like Merlin. Getting younger every day. Old Celtic tradition." She winks. "Keep it, if you like. I've got plenty more. Think it must be one of the last pictures of Sal before..." She hauls herself upright. "So, are you fit? Time to do battle again. Yes, hang on, Billy, we're coming right now and no, you haven't won."

170

* * *

Returning to the cottage, I flop on the sofa and stretch my legs out, propping my feet on the edge of the coffee table. Next to an unwashed breakfast mug I place my Jack-o'-lantern which leers a zigzag grin. Dropping keys into my bag, I notice the photo Jan gave me: Sally Hendry, best guess, late thirties or early forties, leaning shoulder to shoulder with a younger Jan Freeman, their heads almost touching. Sally, home to care for a sick mother and stuck in Cornwall, disappointed and middle-aged.

I jump up to fetch the companion picture I found in the attic. I prop them side by side against the pumpkin, knowing now that Jan took them both, here in the garden at Penmaris in the mid-Eighties. Neither woman expected to be photographed. The whole thing looks spontaneous, a spur of the moment idea, no tidy hair or smart clothes. Yet the absence of glamour lends an intimacy to the awkward poses, a stripping away of pretence, the suggestion of a friendship much deeper than the casual acquaintance Jan implied.

What did Sally Hendry, wayward rebel and aspiring poet, do with the remaining years of her life? How did she spend the time, once her mother had died and she was left alone? Perhaps from a shared love of books and ideas, she and Jan became very close, the younger woman reminding the older of her passion for words.

I jump up again, this time for the exercise book I unearthed yesterday and to which, excited by the box of photos, I've given only a cursory glance, sufficient to see it contains poetry. Here, I hope, is the key to understanding Sally Hendry. I open the book at random. Words tumble in a waterfall down the page in front of me as if trying to capture a feeling, a sound, an image. I read them out loud, savouring them on my tongue, imagining Sally doing the same. On the next page are short verses, many seemingly incomplete, consisting of no more than four or five lines; elsewhere longer poems, which begin confidently only to peter out, perhaps because inspiration faded. Several pages are blank, others are crammed full.

One thing strikes me immediately: assuming Sally wrote all these poems herself, then she had been a woman obsessed with Cornwall's mythic past. The theme occurs again and again, the notion of a mysterious land set apart yet ever-present. Sally sings its song as if time were one and ancient Lyonesse no more distant than last week. Tristan rides his steed through forests deep beneath Mount's Bay; he dines with Arthur at Lanyon Quoit, the table where Merlin prophesied a gathering of kings before the end of the world. She describes local characters and customs as if time has buckled and then is now: a race of ugly spriggans are guarding treasure in moorland cairns; neighbours are baking a Groaning Cake for easy childbirth or a *cheeld's fuggan* for the christening to protect the baby from witches; an anxious mum pins her baby's nightgown to its cot to prevent pixies stealing the child and substituting one of their own.

Here I pause. The poem is entitled "Fairy Child", and its theme is the theme of Jan's play, the story of a changeling. I read it again. Coincidence? Possibly. Jan is equally hot on folklore. Though if she and Sally had been close friends, they might well have collaborated on a piece for Halloween. Now there's an interesting thought. How much of Jan's play is her own?

The poem is long compared with many in the collection, and full of specific detail, the writing factual and spare, devoid of sentimentality. All the more surprising, therefore, that the description of the baby asleep in its cot should be so touching. I read it for a third time and it makes my heart ache. Yesterday in the drive, after Jan handed over the muddy bootee, I'd been too stunned to come up with a riposte to her crack about a "happy event". But once she and Carne had gone home, I'd gone back to the loft and sorted through the box of unused baby clothes. The other bootee was there, as well as a matching knitted jacket, various bonnets and leggings, a delicately crocheted shawl, each item pristine and folded carefully between tissue paper now pinpricked with cat claws. And I'd felt unbearably sad. Here was evidence apparently confirming my suspicions, that Sally had expected and lost a baby. How terrible to face such a tragedy alone. I decided to leave everything where I found it, safe in the cardboard box – though I brought the bootee down to join its twin, now clean and lying on the coffee table alongside the photos and the Halloween light.

I glance up. In my head from somewhere far away comes the high, thin wail of a baby crying. Or a cat miaowing. At times it seems as though the cottage weeps for attention.

Sally wrote about cats. I flick to a page I spotted earlier full of rhyming couplets which link cats with the weather. Then I remember having seen cats and dogs in some of the family photos; Sally had grown up with pets in the house. I read eagerly. "Washing its face over-ear, tomorrow skies will be fair and clear." Well, that's wrong for a start. In my experience cats don't wait for good weather before having a wash. They're fastidious creatures, come rain or shine. On the other hand, "Running wild, a storm in its tail, tomorrow's sure to be wind and hail" has the ring of truth. My parents used to laugh at their "scat cat", as they called him, windmilling through the house on blustery days. I read on, sometimes agreeing, sometimes not. As a form of primitive weather-forecasting, the couplets make me smile; they seem no more and no less accurate than modern meteorology.

At the bottom of the page I come upon a delicate ode to feline beauty, a poem of great gentleness and charm, the work of someone who loved animals. Here then is another connection between Sally Hendry and old Cornwall; she borrowed its sayings, its nature beliefs, and turned them into the vernacular of her poetry. "So curves her neck in grace by firelight, back firmly turned on biting frosts that grip this night." Standing stones, animal magic, Celtic mythology; Sally's words have a way of diving beneath the surface of things into a deep sea of knowing.

Reading the poems fills me with nostalgia, and I experience a sense of kinship with Sally Hendry born of shared pleasures and pains. Two histories, different in detail but alike in experience: disastrous loves, dead babies, cherished pets. No wonder then, no wonder Sally's cottage speaks to me, no wonder its ghosts cry out. I lean back against the cushions, my head full of memories. Whenever I move, the sketchpad, which is tucked behind the sofa, shifts and clatters about on the floor. Sally, reminding me she's there. On impulse, I decide to phone Mum for a chat.

"I'm fine, Mum. Really I am. Did you get my postcard?" Silly question, I only posted it two days ago. "Guess what? I've adopted a cat! He's a stray, I think, but he finds me a soft touch so he's taken to hanging around. No, of course I haven't given him a name!" Why not, though? It's a good idea. "He reminds me a bit of Whiskey, do you remember, our black and white tom? Kept bringing home dead mice and birds? Whatever happened to him?"

"He disappeared, Rose, like all the others. Went under a bus, I expect. Now tell me, dear, are you eating properly?"

Afterwards I ring Oliver. Well, not so much Oliver as my home number, so I can hear the familiar message on the answerphone. Listening to it prompts a fierce pang of longing and guilt; I miss my life and it hurts. But as expected, no one picks up and I decide against leaving a message. Oliver won't be back from his trip abroad yet. I might ring later in the week. Or he'll ring me first. One of us has to make a move.

The room is cold. I light a fire, pleased with my newly acquired skill, then work for hours on a small abstract I'm painting. Having taken Mac's advice, I'm constructing a complex geometry in varying shades of blue. Scary at first, the colour is definitely becoming less charged, more neutral. The regular shapes seem to confine thought and prevent my mind from wandering; soon I'm absorbed in creating planes and angles. The ultramarine Mac gave me I use sparingly, aware of its bite and resonance, but overall I'm enjoying this latest project. It feels liberating; it builds my confidence.

Eventually, when the fire dies down, I clean my brushes and shower the day away. Then I fall into bed and sleep without dreaming.

Chapter Fifteen

It's late when I surface next morning and I feel good; a booze-free Saturday, and my head is clear. Halfway through boiling the kettle I even remember the date. Spring forwards, fall backwards.

The Speaking Clock announces nine, thirty-eight and fifty seconds. I reset my watch, pleased to have gained an hour which for some reason seems like much more, as if I've reclaimed the day. Instead of being nearly lunchtime, Sunday morning stretches before me.

I decide to make good use of the time. First I feed the cat who, having no watch to adjust, is pacing outside the back door growing impatient. He certainly has things to do, so will I get a move on? Watching him eat, I come up with *HeCat*; it's virtually what I'm already calling him and it neatly proclaims his being: "He, cat." Mum was right; he deserves a name. "All done, HeCat?" I ask, experimenting with it as I remove his plate. "That's enough breakfast. You're getting way too fat. Go on, shoo." Which makes me think of

FatCat. I try that one on him. As if in appreciation, he rubs against my legs before trotting into the garden. Whatever.

My car in the drive gives me an idea. After adjusting the dashboard clock, I fish out my super-scale, easy-to-use, brand new road atlas from behind the passenger seat. Oliver once suggested satnav as a birthday present, but settled on an atlas and a new pair of shoes after I'd fallen about laughing. Me and technology – you must be joking.

Back on the sofa with a coffee, I open the atlas where a fluorescent Post-it note sticks out from the side. On the Lands End page I search for the megalithic sites whose names I know from Jan's postcards. A surprising number are clustered in the extreme south-west, not far from Porthallen. Right then. That's what I'll do today. I'll go and visit them, experience first-hand the kind of stone monuments Sally described in her poetry. After that, back to Penmaris for more painting. Satisfied with my progress on the abstract, I also worked on the storm scene last night and it too is nearing completion. I'm looking forward to hanging them on the walls to cover up the endless white. I feel torn between the urge to stay indoors and carry on, and my spur-of-the-moment idea of a trip to see the stones.

In the end, the decision is made for me. I leave straight after breakfast because a weak sun has started to shine. Experience of how fast the weather changes in these parts tells me to seize the moment. Painting can wait till afternoon.

* * *

First stop is the Merry Maidens stone circle, described in *Old Kernow: Myths and Legends* as one of the few "true" circles left in England, being complete and perfectly round. From the map it looked easier to find than Mên-an-Tol, which involves wiggling down narrow lanes and getting lost.

The site is fairly busy when I draw up. Easy access from the road suggests it's a popular spot with Sunday walkers. Families stroll the field or march noisily down the path through the centre of the circle towards trees in the distance, shouting at dogs that ignore them. It's more like a local amusement park. Kids are playing leap-frog over the stones, and this in particular strikes a discordant note, like chalk on a blackboard. I feel uncomfortable, disorientated. In fact, I'm about to change my mind and go home when I notice a man sitting on the perimeter wall apparently drawing. Artistic curiosity prevails and I amble across to sneak a look.

"Ley lines," he says.

I had intended to wander past nonchalantly, but I can't resist peeking over his shoulder at the strange, vaguely geometrical chart propped on his knees.

"Sorry, I didn't mean to be nosey, I just thought you might be drawing…"

The man is elderly, his face a crease of wrinkles. From deep inside the greying folds I catch a glint from two specks of icy blue. "I'm plotting stone circles to see if they align," comes his scratchy reply.

"Align? With what?"

"With ley lines."

I haven't a clue what he's talking about. Then the blue eyes find mine.

"Ever heard of the Nazca Lines in South America?"

I shake my head. "No. I don't think so." Perhaps I should have gone home after all.

"What's the shortest distance between two points?"

It's like being back at school. "Erm… a straight line?"

"Right," he says, wrinkles splitting into a grin. "Now, there's a belief that ancient societies made use of these straight lines when travelling. They're often linked to the course of underground streams and magnetic currents, the Earth's geo-magnetic forces that criss-cross the planet. Neolithic man built monuments on them. Where lines intersect there's a strong psychic resonance, an energy. Dowsers can pick it up, so can people who are sensitive, in fact sometimes almost anyone can feel a certain… something." He grunts at my expression. "Come on, you must have been in a church or an old building and got a sudden shiver down your spine?"

"Well, yes. But that's because I was cold."

He laughs. "Many religious sites are located along these straight-line networks. Some stretch for hundreds of miles. Round here, we're right on top of the St Michael's ley line, probably the most famous one in the world. Look." A knobbly finger points to a line on the chart running from the east coast of England to the tip of Cornwall and across to the continent. "Passes through megalithic sites like Glastonbury Tor and Silbury Hill, as well as countless places named after St Michael himself." I can see St Michael's Mount highlighted in red, then Mont St Michel off the Normandy coast. "Stone is thought to amplify the

180

power. That's why people say you can touch the stones and feel them resonating, as if they're alive."

I start to edge away, without being too obvious. The man laughs again. "Don't worry, you're perfectly safe. There's no need to run. I'm quite harmless really. It's just a hobby." He flips to the back of his file and becomes once more absorbed.

I've touched the stones and felt nothing, only their cold, hard resistance. But then… there is the Penmaris stone, my favourite seat; it pulls me like a magnet. And sometimes I think I hear voices singing… Instead of walking off, I sit down next to the old guy and ask hesitantly, "So, these circles…"

His name is Diggory Welland (is anyone actually called Diggory, I wonder, or is he having me on?) and he lives near Bodmin. Since retiring he has indulged his passion for what he calls "alternative archaeology", travelling Britain and the continent to chart the topography of megalithic sites in an effort to link them all into some kind of pan-European system of ancient power. Quietly spoken and intense, he comes across as something of an ageing anorak, a well-intentioned nutcase with an impressive if unlikely wealth of evidence to support his off-beat theories. Though I can't follow much of what he's saying, I am drawn by his slow, hypnotic delivery, by his cracked voice filling my ears as I gaze at the stones in front of me. Nineteen in all, he explains, evenly spaced to form a near-perfect circle with a diameter of seventy-five feet; one of the best preserved circles in all England; dating from the Bronze Age, over four thousand years ago; *Dans Maen*, in Cornish. It means the dancing stones.

"Why?" I ask.

"For the nineteen maidens who were turned to stone for daring to dance on the Sabbath. Well, that's one of the local legends. Some people think it's the stones that dance." Then, to my surprise, Diggory coughs to clear his throat and, in a scratchy voice, starts singing. "*Dance, dance, wherever you may be, I am the lord of the dance, said he…* You'll have heard that one, I imagine?" He coughs again hard, then again, caught in a choking fit. "Very pagan, that is… oh, oh dear," and the next cough doubles him up. He fumbles for the handkerchief in his pocket. "Sorry, lass. But I've talked more this afternoon than I usually do in a month." He wipes his mouth and I notice his hand trembling. I feel slightly guilty for tiring him.

"I ought to be going," I say. "I've got a couple of other sites to visit before…"

"Not from round here, then?"

"No. Well, yes, sort of. I'm staying at a friend's place in Porthallen for a while."

Diggory riffles through the pages in his file. "Thought so." He jabs his finger. "Name rang a bell, soon as you said it. There's part of an old dance near there." He holds another chart up. "Not many stones left now, though. It's in a field on the outskirts of the village, if I remember rightly." A road runs close to where he's put a series of small dots; it's the road that leads past Penmaris, and the dots lie in the field at the bottom of the garden.

* * *

I drive next in the direction of Penzance, then turn left and climb steeply away from the coast. Quickly the houses thin and, apart from occasional farms, the area

182

seems quiet and unoccupied. Frustrated by my visit to Dans Maen because nothing happened, because the monument seemed overwhelmed by the present, by children and yapping dogs and I felt no reaction at all, I hope my next destination will have a bit more atmosphere.

If I can find it. The road meanders on, past more barking dogs, this time working animals patrolling farm gates. Is it to be a day of dogs? As far as I can make out, I'm on the right road. Hang on in there, I mutter, you can't possibly get lost.

Then Lanyon Quoit. A slow left-hand bend and I wonder if I've driven into Lilliput. The structure heaves into view like a gigantic dining table waiting for guests to arrive, a couple of gnarled Celtic giants, perhaps. Visible from the car, it dominates the entire landscape, only a few yards from the road.

I park in a lay-by and climb into the field where a well-worn track leads to the grassy mound where the stones stand. A tripod of pillars supports the massive, flat top-stone at a height sufficient to walk underneath. Half-buried in the grass all around are the remains of other stone slabs, possibly further uprights once part of the original group but now collapsed and broken into the earth. Flickering on and off through cloud, the sun catches specks in the granite and sets them on fire.

Despite the isolated situation, I'm not the only visitor. A middle-aged man is taking athletic photographs, leaping from one tuft of grass to another, twiddling the camera focus, crouching, changing from landscape to portrait, clicking away whilst an elderly lady, his companion, laments the poor quality of hotel service. "I did *ask* specially for *softly* boiled…" I walk slowly round the perimeter to avoid them both, until skirting a boggy patch of scrub leads me directly into the photographer's orbit.

"Still impresses, doesn't it?" he remarks, pausing to consider his next shot. "Last time I was here I actually climbed on top. Can't imagine how I did it now, but I've a photo of me and my boy standing right up there, on top." He smirks with naughty pleasure at the memory. Then he pats the overhang of his gut. "Bit fitter in those days, I suppose."

I smile and move on. "Makes you wonder what it's here for, doesn't it?" says the photographer to no one in particular. He scratches his bald patch, then kneels with his camera pointing up at the pillars, at an angle that will exaggerate their immensity. I lean against one of the three "table legs", my left hand pressed flat to the stone. If David Bailey here wants me out of the way, he'll have to ask. The stone feels like stone, cold, rough, unyielding.

Soon the couple wander off, so I leave too; the quoit is intimidating when the sun goes in. I want to find the third site on my list.

Only two miles further up the same road I notice a defaced signpost, but am half a mile past it before the first letter clicks in my head. A capital M. I turn round and drive back for a second look. I can only just decipher the name; many of the letters have been deliberately scratched out. But there's no doubt, the fingerpost points to Mên-an-Tol somewhere along a rough track that disappears over the hill.

I park and put my coat on. The path is muddy underfoot, with deep puddles and tractor ruts either side, evidence of local farmers delivering fodder to the herds that dot the fields. I climb steadily. In fact, I've been climbing ever since leaving Penzance; once my route departed suburbia, it rose dramatically into an altogether different country. Megalithic Cornwall.

Beyond the hilltop I emerge onto sparse, wild moorland. There's no sign of the stones and the path continues endlessly. Lost behind persistent cloud, the sun has abandoned the moor to grim pre-winter harshness. Despite watching where I'm going, my shoes and feet are already wet. Each time I jump to avoid puddles, I land in thick ooze which splatters my jeans. At the back of my mind a thread of worry begins to tug; what if I fall, what if I get lost or caught in bad weather? There's no one around. Not even cows, up here. Out loud I tell myself to stop being such a wuss.

After about another mile I come to a wooden notice which directs me off to the right, though there's still nothing to be seen apart from brackish grass and wilderness. I spin round, searching the horizon, expecting any minute that the tip of one of the two upright pillars will break the skyline. Nothing has prepared me for such a remote location. Finding only cloud, I zip my jacket up to the chin and turn my footsteps to the path, plodding determinedly on. The new track seems barely used, hardly there at all; it narrows quickly and falls away in a sudden descent into thick bracken, after which it rises again steeply and then, before I have time to panic, opens out onto an unexpected sward of green in the middle of which sit the three ancient stones of Mên-an-Tol: two upright pillars either side of a central holed-stone. As I approach them, there's a sudden wink of sunlight; the stones sparkle like jewels in a crown.

Surrounded by soft grass, the stones sit neatly and purposefully in the ground. That their placing on this very spot was a deliberate act is obvious, bizarre in one sense, quite artificial, but at the same time they seem to announce an ancient belonging. As if they own the land. Yet they're surprisingly small. In fact, the closer I get, the smaller I realise they are, all three somehow compact and tidy and no more than a metre high. For some reason I'd assumed they would be enormous. I experience an Alice-in-Wonderland moment – the magic and delight of small things.

It looks like a doughnut, comes the irreverent thought as I run up to the holed stone. The central aperture forms a perfect circle, perfectly smooth and perfectly welcoming to the touch, as if inviting entry. A child or slim adult could easily pass through. I am tempted. I glance round, but I'm quite alone. There's no one to see. Others have clearly tackled the challenge because the grass around the base is scuffed away, leaving two mud-and-rainwater hollows either side. Entering the stone is probably meant to be a summer rite, when the ground is dry and the air warm and irresistible, the passage easy. On the other hand, the ritual is said to confer not just fertility but general good health and spiritual wellbeing. It holds the promise of wholeness. I'm up for that. And my jeans are already covered in mud.

In seconds I've removed my jacket and dumped it, along with my bag, against one of the uprights. I find a spot off to the right from which I can step over the worst of the sludge and crawl through the holed stone. I'll emerge on the other side on a slight rise where tufts of grass remain. I crouch low. It'll mean a lot of wriggling to get through at such an angle and I can just imagine how ridiculous I'll look. But, if I shove really hard and keep my head up…

Stepping forward, I twist into the hole, curl in on myself, roll round then thrust my arms out the far side. I push and pull on anything to hand, kick with my feet and wiggle like mad till I managed to slither my top half right through to emerge, mostly, on dry land. My legs follow, flopping like dead weights into a puddle. I've done it; I'm out the other side. I let loose a shriek of triumph.

Propped on my elbows to recover, I stare back through the hole at the vertical pillar in the distance. It takes a few seconds to dawn on me that I've seen this view before. I can hardly believe it – the upright stone is bisecting the gap with the same erotic suggestiveness I noted in Mac's sketch, the one I found in his studio. This, I realise, is the very same angle from which Mac had chosen to draw the scene. Well, well. Now isn't that interesting!

I shriek again, roll over and scramble to my feet. More jigsaw pieces are falling into place.

After collecting my things together, I find myself hanging around simply to watch the stones. It's impossible not to. They hold the eye in this landscape a million miles from nowhere, and time slips away. My heart rate slows, the dizzy excitement cools. I succumb to the magic of the place. Can one actually fall under a spell? Do such things happen outside fairy stories? The music of earth and sky play in the wind that shakes the grasses.

Then I shiver. The sun has disappeared and the moor feels old, full of shadows.

I should go home.

* * *

By the time I get back to Penmaris, the car heater has dried my jeans. Although it's barely three o'clock, the afternoon is dull and grey, and mist is threatening to close in. If I'm to satisfy my curiosity, I'll have to do so straight away or wait till morning. Swallowing a quick glass of water, I grab a biscuit and the torch from the kitchen drawer and set off down the garden path.

I scramble over the wall and jump into the field. If I can trust to his accuracy, Diggory Welland had marked the circle in the right-hand corner, so I walk in that direction, peering down at my feet for anything big enough to qualify as a small standing stone. Hopefully I'm not trespassing or tramping down next year's crop; in the weeks I've been at Penmaris I've seen no sign of a farmer working this piece of land. Carne has no qualms about dumping rubbish on it, and there are never any animals grazing. The ground is uneven and seems to have been abandoned to rough grass and a vicious brand of thistle capable of penetrating denim.

The first stone I encounter by blundering into it; bent double, I'm shuffling along rubbing my ankle where a thistle has scratched red weals that sting like crazy. Using handfuls of wet grass I'm trying to cool my skin. When I yank up one particularly stubborn fistful, my knuckles scrape against roughness.

Like the stone in the garden at Penmaris, this one is also largely hidden because the field is so overgrown. I kneel down and push all the weeds aside so I can have a good look. Then I switch my torch on and shine it in an arc that might pick out other stones near by. The moment I spot one, I forget about thistles and run across. And then there's another. And another, teased into view by torchlight. In rapid succession I discover five more stones, and begin to imagine the size of the structure they might once have formed. A tentative circle starts to take shape; it's so obvious, once points on the circumference are clear. To think the remains of a Neolithic stone circle have been here all this time only a few yards from the bottom of the garden where I live, from the wall where I'd sat chatting to Carne and to Jan. I'm exhilarated, ridiculously excited.

I glance behind me to see how far I am from the wall, but it's almost disappeared in swirls of mist. I hadn't realised how much the weather had deteriorated in the last hour. Reluctant to stop exploring, I worry that if I don't head home soon I'll have trouble finding my way. Then a loud protest from my stomach decides the matter. One chocolate digestive since breakfast. No wonder I feel light-headed.

Clambering back over the wall at its lowest point, I walk straight ahead in the direction of the cottage. I'm walking across Carne's wild lawn; the path lies off to my right. It feels as though I'm passing through cloud, a shimmer of silver-grey that billows like lace curtains in the wind, blowing clear one moment, opaque the next. Add to this the fading daylight and the narrow torch beam I'm waving from side to side, and the sense of dislocation grows. Under such conditions, at times like these, I can believe that Cornwall is a land apart, a fairy place.

Kicking my feet out in front of me so I won't stumble, I soon kick against the stone seat. Here I am again; here it is again. Crouching down, I shine the torch onto it, brushing leaves off the top and pulling grass away from the sides to expose the entire thing. As best I can tell, there are no markings anywhere, though it does seem exactly like the stones I've just been looking at; similar size and shape, the same sort of rock, definitely the same colour. I run a hand over the surface and it even feels the same. The temptation to identify it is irresistible. It's possibly a bit smaller than the others and its top is rounder, smoother. But otherwise it seems on a par with the few remaining stones of the circle, situated not a hundred yards away.

So why was it removed and brought to Penmaris? And how? It might be small, compared to the massive blocks of Lanyon Quoit or even the neatly compact Merry Maidens, but it's basically the same, a lump of solid granite. Not something you pick up and put in your pocket. Perhaps somehow it was rolled into the garden, at a time before the wall was built. Is the wall contemporary with the cottage, or more recent?

I sit down. As a seat the stone is always comfortable, if currently damp. Water droplets in the torch beam glitter like diamonds. The world is hushed beneath the blanket of mist, the only sounds the drip, drip of leaves, and my heart thumping.

According to my ley-lines friend, you can find the remains of small circles in fields all over Cornwall. *The remains of*, because in recent times they've been plundered and the stones taken by farmers and local people for building purposes, or for use as way-markers, for aggrandising property, even for gravestones.

For gravestones. I can hear Diggory's patient explanations as if he were here, sitting next to me. And right now, in the thickening mist, the garden feels holy; might this small stone mark a small grave? A child's grave?

Am I sitting over the spot where Sally Hendry buried her baby? It seems macabre, in the latter half of the twentieth century, an act of such secrecy and desperation. But perhaps for Sally it was the natural thing to do, according to some ancient Celtic rite. For that's the impression I've gained from her poetry: a woman rooted in the old ways, for whom modern conventions mattered little.

In one of my coat pockets nestles Sally's book. I slipped it in this morning alongside gloves and an apple, thinking I might read the poems *in situ*, as it were. But of course, I forgot. I take it out now and turn to the last page. I'll start with an unread poem and work backwards. In the torch light, the paper gleams a startling white.

There's a rustle in the leaves behind me, a breath, a whisper.

Let the maiden join the dance…

I twist round in the direction of the sound, a high voice issuing from nowhere, from clouds of mist and nothingness, nothing visible, nothing happening. As always, the sound stops the moment I move.

The final poem in Sally's book is called "Storm off the Cornish coast". The narrator, down on the beach at night to watch a tempest out at sea, experiences not wind and rain and crashing waves, but a mighty fanfare:

see how the holy tide
rolls from the dungeons of Lyonesse,
smashing music from rock spume
tasting of ferocity and pride.

The holy tide. That word, holy, for the second time in as many minutes. Not a word that belongs in my personal lexicon, it came unbidden to describe the garden and is here again in Sally's poem. Stone sites, or so I've read, were considered by many to be sacred. Is this in some way a sacred place?

Join the dance, join the dance…

There it is again, that persistent, high-pitched, plaintive voice. Where does it come from? Then the words change; a soaring melody filters through the air, lingering on a final note surprisingly clear but incomprehensible, stretching out until it becomes the mist itself, a white wailing sadness, and the mist too thick to make out any signs of life or movement. Nearly every time I sit on this stone I hear a woman singing. Or at least I think I do. Is it just a tune going round in my head, a silly jingle I've picked up from somewhere and can't get rid of? Of course, that must be it. This afternoon Diggory Welland sung to me. He described the song as pagan, said it was called "The Lord of the Dance". But when I was at school we used to sing that one and I can't imagine our headmistress allowing anything pagan in her morning assembly. I shake myself, trying to concentrate. I turn a page to read Sally's next poem and the book falls from my hands.

These stones are old;
their cold, sad siren songs
seep into the evening air,
echo through…

It's the poem I read in Mac's studio! There's no doubt about it; I remember the lines perfectly. Lines I

192

first read a few days ago, when they were clipped to Mac's erotic drawing of Mên-an-Tol, alongside the papers I assumed to comprise his nearly completed manuscript.

Sally's poem all along! Composed in this old exercise book in her loopy handwriting, complete with crossings-out and alterations. I picture Sally hunched over the page, changing her mind, preferring one word to another, scrawling out "mystic" in favour of "siren". No wonder Mac looked embarrassed when I asked about the existence of text to accompany his drawings, no wonder he snatched the page back and buried it under others. Sally wrote of "fond imaginings, the lingerings, the long gone rememberings," about a love imprinted on stone that would outlast time:

> once you and I were here
> and thus will always be
> you and me,
> somewhere.

They had been lovers. Mac and Sally. Of course they had. It was obvious now.

I jump up. I want to go round to Mac's house and show him Sally's book. There's nothing to stop me going round this very minute. No way can he pretend any more, claiming to have no idea what became of Sally once he left Cornwall for university. Here is proof of their continuing relationship. Mac was involved with Sally Hendry the woman, not just the schoolgirl, involved at the very least to the point of stealing her poem and passing it off as his own. I feel the weight of Sally's words through my bones. And I feel something like outrage.

Then I remember the holed stone and the sensation of my body passing through it. The fierce, electric thrill when I emerged on the other side. Only hours ago and I had been there, at Mên-an-Tol.

Like Mac and Sally, once?

Let the maiden join the…

A stone circle used to be called a dance.

Chapter Sixteen

I knock again, but Mac definitely isn't in. I'm wasting my time. The house squats in gloom and there are no lights on; out back his studio hangs like a shadow. The mist has turned to thick fog and darkness is falling. I should return to Penmaris while I can still find my way. My torch battery seems to be fading by the minute. Another dead one, I assume. Why does everything work off batteries that never work? I shake the torch, which perks up briefly, enough to light most of the road home.

Before doing anything else, I strip and chuck all my muddy clothes in the washing machine, then take a long, hot bath perfumed with lavender oil. In its scented cloud, my sore legs ease and my mood mellows; perhaps I've been too ready to jump to conclusions. Mac provided jump leads to start my car, encouraged my painting, listened while I unburdened my soul. Why, he even brought the logs I burn. After the bath, I pad downstairs and light a roaring fire, then spend the rest of the afternoon and evening painting in front of it, finishing the blue abstract Mac set me as a challenge. And he's right; blue, it seems, is just another colour. How could I have been afraid of a colour, for all these years? I have plenty of reasons to be grateful to the professor, and no excuse for making wild assumptions about him. Except for curiosity, of course, and the nagging feeling that I'm being led down a path I have no option but to follow.

It seems certain now that Alec McConnell and Sally Hendry *had* been lovers back in the Seventies in London, thus confirming what Carne said. The affair eventually came to an end, but Sally's feelings for Mac lived on in her poetry. At some point there was a baby (whose?) which didn't survive. The body is likely buried in the garden, its grave marked with a stone taken from the circle in the field beyond. By the Eighties, Sally was back in Cornwall for good, disillusioned and living alone in the family cottage from which she suddenly disappeared and died in unexplained circumstances. Although the timeframe was vague, the downhill slide of Sally's life seemed inescapable. I wonder, for the first time, if she committed suicide. Surely Mac must be able to help piece some of this together? After all, he appears to have access to Sally's writing and is planning to include one of her poems in his book. I shall try again tomorrow.

* * *

Which dawns with low cloud that hangs about all morning, lifting only at lunchtime. The afternoon is dry, if dull. Rather than make another abortive visit, I decide to ring first. Amazingly, I realise I don't have Mac's

196

number and will have to call Directory Enquiries. Lifting the receiver I'm surprised by beeps announcing a recorded message: Oliver phoned yesterday while I was out. "Hi there, just to let you know I'm back." He sounded tired and preoccupied, his thoughts still in the skies somewhere over Europe. He rattled off a potted account of the week. "Well, anyway, sorry to have missed you." Then, as an afterthought, "Hope everything's okay? Right, well, ring me? Please."

For several minutes I hesitate, felled by his nearness, however far away. Then I bite the bullet. But there's no reply, of course, since this is Monday and Oliver will be at work. When I ring his office number, Tricky Dicky answers.

"'E's in a meeting, Rosie. T'rific news about Brussels, *nessee pas?*" He likes to impress me with what he thinks is French. Office noises clatter in the background. There comes a sound like a dog in pain. "Tell you what, Rosie, things are really buzzing round 'ere. We're going global now. Totally awesome. Trust Ollie to bring home the bacon, the old *lardon*, if you get my meaning. Eh? What? Oh, yeah. 'Course I will."

"Thanks, Rick, only I—"

"No probs, babe. Gotta dash, though."

"Right. Bye, Ri—"

But the line is dead.

I blink. It's like communicating with Mars.

Perhaps tonight Oliver and I will manage to talk, like grown-ups. Imagined conversations have been playing through my mind in recent days: I suggest he drives down to Cornwall; we meet on my terms, on my turf; Penmaris works its magic and we…

My eyes fall on the pumpkin lantern waiting patiently on the windowsill next to an arrangement of autumn leaves. Tomorrow is Halloween, I'd almost forgotten. Then the whole world will be given over to magic. The spirits of the dead will walk again. Right now I feel trapped in limbo somewhere between the living and the dead: the shadows of Sally Hendry and Méline crying through my mind; Oliver and my broken life dragging at my heart. I feel cornered, as if a weight is pressing down on me, making it hard to breathe. I need to do something. I need to get out, quickly. I grab my paint-stained fleece and walk round to Mac's house.

"Ah, Rose," he says, filling the doorway. I've just caught him; bundled in a thick coat, he's on the point of going out. "Is this a social call? Only… Come in, come in. Have to be quick, though. I'm due at the gallery in…" He rummages under layers of sleeve for the time. "Tea?"

On the way over, I've rehearsed what I'm going to say. We'll be in Mac's workshop near the desk where I previously saw the drawings for his book. Gradually I'll steer the conversation round to Sally's poem. I'll mention his drawing of Mên-an-Tol, make it seem natural, unforced, avoid any sense of accusation. Only now this isn't going to happen, because Mac is in a hurry. I shake my head. "No thanks. I don't want to make you late. Sorry, Mac, I'm…"

"Told you before, Rose. Stop apologising for existing. Here." A mug of something lukewarm appears. "Left over from lunch."

I've not been in his kitchen before, not his real kitchen. It's a dingy pre-war disaster. Like his studio galley, it's a clutter of artefacts from floor to ceiling, raising doubts about hygiene. A small, unwashed window favours cobwebs over daylight and the glass is cracked. Side-stepping a bag of cement, I try stuffing my gloves one in each pocket so I can take the tea, but the right-hand pocket contains Sally's book and there isn't room for a glove as well. Instead I shove it in my mouth and grab the mug.

Mac is leaning against the cooker, upon which sits a large black pot streaked with lumpy stains; leftover stew or clay mix? He's watching me, a wry smile creeping across his lips. "So, Rose, what progress with ultramarine?" His eyes flick to the shadow on my fleece. Despite two visits to the washing machine, an echo of blue remains.

I spit the glove out. "Fine. Actually. Yeah, I'm really surprised. Exorcising my demons, and all that. Once I got started, it was easier than I expected. Blue turns out to be... just another colour." The tea is foul. I put it on the counter, next to my glove, and continue to describe the abstract in detail. "Actually, I think it'll look quite good on the wall by the door." I realise that I'm rambling. "Or over the fireplace, maybe. You said I should hang some pictures, to cover the white."

I pick my glove up then put it down again. Mac nods, a shrug inside his coat.

"I finished it last night, actually. Come round sometime and tell me what you think." I must stop saying *actually*.

Mac is tossing keys from one hand to the other.

"Sorry, Mac. I'm keeping you."

"Don't worry about it, you could be doing me a favour. I foresee a tedious argy-bargy about next year's exhibitions, fund raising, stuff like that. I'm on some sort of committee, for my sins. Wind-bags united." He pulls a long face.

I laugh, aware that I'm dithering. Fiddle with my glove again.

Mac cocks his head to one side. "Come on, Rose, spit it out. You know you'll feel better with it off your chest."

Right, well then, I will. So much for sidling up gradually. "I found this," I say, "in the attic." I give him Sally's book. "I nosed around up there, like you suggested, and I found a couple of boxes shoved under the eaves, full of… Look, the name's on the front, can you see?"

For once, I've taken him by surprise. He flicks backwards and forwards through the pages, trying to disguise his shock.

"Told you Sal was into poetry," he mutters. "Juvenilia would be my guess. Typical schoolgirl's handwriting, that is. See, those loops." He points. "Fancy an old schoolbook surviving all these years."

Are his hands shaking?

"I'm not so sure it is from her school days." I lean across him and turn to the penultimate page. "This poem. I've read this one before. Don't you recognise it?" When he fails to answer, I add, "You should do. It was clipped to the back of one of the drawings I saw last week, on your desk." I wait for his reaction.

Mac closes the book abruptly and returns it, while his other hand ushers me from the kitchen. "So what's your point?" he asks, inching us towards the front door.

"My point is, this doesn't read to me like the work of a child. It's as much about love and loss as about standing stones. I felt that strongly when I read it last time. Remember? You caught me examining pages of your manuscript before you snatched them away?" Mac grunts something incomprehensible and switches the lights off, but I carry on, undeterred. "Right here, look." I open the book again. "Sally says *their love* will last for ever, she says she can still hear *his* voice when she touches the stones." I'm trying to hold the page up for Mac to read over my shoulder as we shuffle along the dark passage. "She's recalling a special time and place, isn't she? Mên-an-Tol. Special to her, in later life, because once it was special to both of them. Who do you think she's talking about, Mac?"

Our thick winter coats jostle as we squeeze our way past rolls of barbed wire on the floor. I let out a screech. "Ow! This stuff's scratching me." Right on top of yesterday's scratches too, which have barely started to heal. "Ouch! Ow! Oh God, now I'm caught." Wriggling to get free, I snag my trousers comprehensively on the sharp barbs and come to an abrupt halt.

Mac cannons into the back of me. He sighs loudly, a sound full of exasperation as he bends down to help. "Hold still a minute, will you? Stop kicking."

"My ankles hurt."

It's too dark to see much at floor level. While Mac tugs at my clothes, I fume silently; yet again Mac is digging me out of trouble. How does this keep happening? He isn't wearing gloves, so his hands must be getting ripped. Every few seconds he curses and swears, a string of oaths that explode when he stumbles backwards, banging his head against the wall. "Sodding bloody…" I try hard not to move, wishing I were a hundred miles away. When the last barb comes loose, Mac opens the front door and shoves me through.

201

"Gotta get rid of this whole fucking lot," he mumbles. Drops of blood well up through nicks on his fingers. "Whole fucking lot first thing tomorrow."

My calves and ankles sting as if bitten by a swarm of mosquitoes. I rub them hard, which only increases the pain. "Why on earth do you keep barbed wire in your hall?" I snap. "Of all the stupid places…" then I notice his hands. "You should go and run those under…" But Mac shakes his head. He's sucking the cuts, licking the blood away and avoiding eye contact.

During the kerfuffle I tucked Sally's book down the front of my fleece, out of harm's way. I become aware of the cover digging into my chest, like a prompt urging me on. *Don't forget me, don't forget why we're here.* Within minutes Mac will be off to St Ives. Because of this stupid incident, next time we meet I'll be too embarrassed to say anything and the opportunity will be lost. I might never get round to asking him about Sally. What to do? Mac is fishing in his pockets. I watch him, aware I'm dithering again and aghast by my lack of sensitivity; now is entirely the wrong moment, I should leave well alone, not push my luck. But my legs hurt, my trousers are torn.

In for a penny, I think. Why quit when you're losing?

And I know that I'm making a mistake.

"That evening you came round, last Wednesday, you told me you had no idea what happened to Sally after you left Cornwall." Mac has produced a grubby hankie and is wiping blood off his hands. "Yet here you are, about to include her poems in your new book." An intake of breath as the hankie catches a deep cut. "You seemed almost indifferent when you talked about her, you sort of shrugged her off as if she'd been nothing to you. But that's not true, is it?"

Damn. I didn't mean to call him a liar.

Mac's head jerks up, and he seems to swell with anger. "Listen here, Rose." His voice bites. "I'm not sure what you're accusing me of, but I'm bloody sure it's none of your business." He slams the front door shut and in two fierce strides is jabbing a key into his battered Ford. "You're like every other bloody woman I've ever met. Can't resist poking their noses in where they're not wanted." He wrenches the car door open. "What is it with you women? You take everything personally. What makes you the centre of the bloody universe?"

"I'm not…"

"You scuttle down here to escape your own problems, and you think inner angst gives you the right to play god and interfere in everyone else's life. Well, I don't remember inviting you into mine." He slides behind the steering wheel and jams the key in the ignition.

"Carne told me about you and Sally. And I found a photo, I found some bab—"

"Oh! The constant gardener!" He thumps the steering wheel then winces. "Aargh, bugger." Flicks his hand. Then, "Hmph! I might have bloody guessed."

"Why do call him that? I thought you two were friends." I'm holding on to the car door to stop Mac driving away.

"Want some advice, Rose? Don't believe everything Carne Tresawna tells you. Now, if you don't mind…"

I cling to the door as he tries to close it. "He was just reminiscing, that's all, because I showed him an old photo. He wasn't trying to…" Foot on the accelerator, Mac guns the engine. I yell above its blast, "Sally haunts me, Mac, she haunts Penmaris. If we work together, perhaps we can find out what happened to her, how she died. I just want the cottage to be quiet again. I want the ghosts to…" I'm nearly crying. The door swings from my grasp.

Mac lowers the window a fraction. "You've done the broken-doll bit, Rose. And the wounded innocent. Oh, I admit, you had me fascinated there for a while, even thought I could help." He sniffs. "Got that wrong. But please, not the psychic detective now. I'm all out of Oscars. If you'll excuse me, I have things to do. I suggest you bugger off."

Chapter Seventeen

The Green by St Michael's Church is ablaze with Jack-o'-lanterns flickering in the early dusk. Days are suddenly short and nights long and depressing, as the dark month looms. The pumpkins' orange glow spreads cheer, their colour strong enough, Jan had assured the audience applauding her Halloween production, to ward off any evil spirits.

Colm Brian is making his way towards me from the church hall. I know it's Colm from his red checked shirt, having been seated next to him during the play. His brother is still wearing work overalls, whereas Colm flames in pillar-box red.

"Is this as terrible as I think it is?" he'd whispered during a brief lull in the performance.

"Absolutely. Excruciating, but kind of cute."

"Fancy a beer after?"

"Shush!"

Now the play is over and the Halloween Fair beginning. Thus far, I've seen no sign of Mac. I doubt he'd have much interest in this sort of village gathering, so I'm not expecting him to turn up, but I keep glancing round all the same. I can't take back what I said and I'm dreading our next encounter. Serves me right if he never speaks to me again.

I wander over to a table where Mary Coleforth is supervising apple bobbing. Colm meets me there.

"Go on," I challenge him. "Bet you can't grab one." We join the queue of people waiting to get soaked catching apples with their teeth.

In between stalls set around the village green, fairy faces peek out, the cast of the play still in costume. Jan demanded they change first, but most of the pixies seem to have escaped her and are lurking in the shadows, eager to cause mischief.

Awaiting our turn, Colm and I are accosted by a trio of witches. Each wears a pointed hat decorated with stars and moons, a grey frizzy wig, and a plastic mask complete with long, wizened, wen-tipped nose.

"Trick or treat?" one of them hisses.

"Trick," says Colm.

"Treat," I shout over the top. From my coat pockets I bring out fistfuls of sweets. "Pick-n-mix from The Chocolate Shop," I whisper to Colm. "Never fails."

The wrinkled crone shoots out a tiny, smooth hand. She scoops the sweets into a supermarket bag which magically appears from beneath her cloak and which is already bulging.

"That'll rot your teeth," says Colm, scornfully. "I hope you're going to share everything fairly between the three of... Hey!"

He yells and leaps in the air, swinging an arm to catch the trickster, but the witches run off cackling into the crowd.

"Right down the back of my neck!" He wipes a hand between his shoulder blades, where the tallest witch upended an entire bottle of cold water. "There's no need to laugh. I'm bloody soaked."

"You did ask for it," I point out. "You should think yourself lucky. That's nothing to what they'd do to you in London."

"Go on, scare me." Head down, flicking rat-tails of hair from side to side, he reminds me of a dog with wet fur.

I laugh. "No, really, you don't want to know. How about fireworks through the letterbox? I seem to remember that was one of last year's favourites round our way."

"Charming. Remind me not to go there, then." He shakes his entire frame, from head to tail.

"Stop wriggling about. You're not making any difference. Here." I pull off my scarf. "Use this."

It's a long, hand-knitted scarf that goes round my neck several times. I jam one end down the back of his shirt. "It'll act like blotting paper and—"

A sharp voice interrupts. "Are you gonna be abobbing or not, Colm Brian?" Hands on hips, Mary Coleforth is glaring impatiently at us from behind an old tin bath filled with green apples sloshing about in murky water. "I'm not waiting here all day, young Colm. There's others in this queue, you know."

"Well, since I can't get much wetter."

"That'll be one pound fifty, if you don't mind."

207

"Mary Coleforth, you're a mercenary old witch."
Colm winks and fishes loose change from his jeans'
pocket. "Come on then. How hard can it be?"

"Hands!"

"I wasn't—"

"No cheating, Colm Brian. I saw you. Hands behind
your back."

"If I catch an apple," Colm mutters, his face
hovering above the surface of the water, "what do I
win?"

Mary snorts. "The apple, o'course."

While he bobs and splutters, I wave to Derry Brian
who has set up shop near the bridge, roasting chestnuts
in an empty oil drum from the brothers' garage. Lured
by the promise of hot nibbles, I leave Colm to splash
for fruit and stroll over to the brazier. Approaching
from the opposite direction, Jan reaches the bridge at
the same moment.

"The play was brilliant," I say, tempted to give Jan a
hug because she looks quite frazzled.

To Derry Jan asks, "Have you seen Stevie? His
mum's waiting to take him home, but she can't find
him anywhere. Little bugger's gone and run off. And
why are you still in costume?" Her right hand shoots
out to grab a hobgoblin by the scruff of the neck as he
and his mates dash past.

"Can I help?" I ask.

"Catch as many of these as you can," she shakes the
little goblin by his collar, "and drag them back to the
hall. Force them to get changed, beat them up, if you
have to. Thanks, Rose." Her smile, like her earrings,
flashes brightly; today she is all silver, like frost in mist.
"I've only got one pair of hands and I could do with a

dozen. Come on, you." She lifts the boy and marches him, feet dangling, towards the church. "Stevie, remember," she shouts over one shoulder, "keep an eye out?"

"Will do."

Derry shakes his head. "That woman don't stand a chance, not on Halloween she don't. He'll be off and away. There's ill abroad tonight. Can you sense it?" He stirs the hot coals from which sparks crackle and fly.

"Right, well, I'd better go and look for…"

"They say you can read the future in the way the chestnuts jump." Onto the roasting tray he tosses a handful of nuts which hiss and spit and skitter, leaping and crackling as if all the devils in hell are on their tail. "See what I mean?" he intones. "The spirits are restless. It'll come to no good, you mark my words." A gust of wind, which thus far has proved only a mild distraction, blows sheets of flame from the side of the brazier. Pumpkin candles in the wind's path gutter and go out. From trees by the river bank a final shower of leaves rattles to the ground, leaving black branches stretching bare into the sky. Derry shakes his head again, more doleful than before. "When the veil grows thin, they do say—"

"All manner of crap, if you ask my opinion." Colm Brian strides into the blaze of light, peeling an apple with a greasy penknife. "Are you trying to frighten the lady?" He slices off a chunk and offers it to me. "Your share of my success. Cox's Orange Pippin. Here, you might as well have your scarf back too." He drapes the scarf, damp and heavy, around my neck. "Thanks for the thought, but it's not quite up to the job any more. I'm soaked back and front now. Drowned, I am."

209

The word makes me shudder. A splinter of fear nicks my spine. From the shadows, eyes seem to blink then vanish. The sound of scurrying feet. Or is it the wind? "I must go and help Jan," I murmur. "Save me some chestnuts for later." I move off quickly towards a group of children who are spinning in circles, tugging on a length of rag. Closer I see it's a doll, which they're holding at all four corners, pulling its arms and legs as they dance round and round, the toy forming the hub of their spinning wheel. I recognise the doll from the Halloween play; it was the baby stolen from its cot by Stevie in his role as naughty pixy. Of Stevie himself there's no sign. I do, however, know one of the girls dancing in the fairy ring.

"Melanie! Have you seen Stevie? Miss Freeman's looking for him."

The circle spins, faster and faster, in a blur of squealing children.

"Melanie! Did you hear me? Can you stop, please. Where's Stevie?"

Faster and faster spins the wheel, round and round until feet scarcely touch the ground. The girls are flying on wings of streaming hair, shrieking at the top of their voices as they whirl in a vortex of energy strong enough to launch them to the sky.

Then someone trips, and the vortex dies. Bodies tumble onto the grass. On her back, legs in the air, Melanie clutches the doll.

I dash over. "Are you all right? Silly girl, you could have hurt yourself." I pick Melanie up, check she's unharmed. "What about the rest of you? Are you all okay?" The girls are staggering to their feet, rubbing elbows, panting for breath.

"That was cool!" Melanie beams at me. "Did you see how fast we was going?"

One of the doll's arms is dangling loose inside its old-fashioned, lace nightgown. I take it from Melanie to inspect the damage.

"I'm hungry," Melanie says.

"Where's your mum?"

She points to a brightly decorated tent, streamers flapping in the wind and "Madame Fortuna tells your future, one pound a go" on a hand-painted sign tacked to the canvas.

"She told me to play out here till she's finished."

"And I'm playing with her." A bedraggled pixy inserts herself between us. "I'm her friend." She's also one of Jan's missing cast, the remains of orange panstick now smeared over her clothes. The other children have wandered off.

"Tell you what," I put an arm around the pixy, "let's get *you* back to the church hall and out of that costume. And while you're changing, Melanie can give this back to Miss Freeman," I wave the doll, "then we'll all go and get something to eat. Who fancies roast chestnuts?"

"Can I have a Fizzy Fanta? I'm thirsty."

"Me too! Can I have a…?"

"Costume, drinks, food. In that order." I propel them towards St Michael's. In the short time since the play finished, it has grown dark and cold, a wintry chill replacing the balm of autumn. Beyond the lights of the village green lies blackness. Colours from the church's stained glass windows leach into the gloom, faint specks of warmth and welcome.

A few willing fathers are stacking chairs in the hall when we walk in. From on stage, where she's tidying

211

props, Jan cheers to see another costume returned. She jumps down to take charge, bustling us into the back room where leftover plates of biscuits and jugs of squash sit amid fairy wings.

The girls set about helping themselves, as if they haven't eaten for a week.

"What are these?" I ask as Jan offers me a biscuit. "They're very yellow."

"Soul cakes," says Jan. "Halloween tradition. Baked them myself for the kids as a treat after the play. It's the saffron gives them that colour. Alice, you are a naughty girl. I told you to get changed before rushing off with Melanie. Hold still while I clean this muck off your face."

"Why yellow?"

"For the dying sun. Or some say to symbolise autumn bonfires, or flame to rekindle the family hearth, warmth and light to guide the souls of the dead. Take your pick. But now that you've eaten one, you're safe from harm." Such a matter-of-fact statement, it floats over the space between us and I swallow the remaining piece of biscuit, not wanting to waste a single crumb.

"Here, Alice. I think these are your jeans."

"Any sign of Stevie?" I ask.

"Nope. His mum's going frantic. Either of you two seen Stephen Parker?"

The girls shake their heads.

"Ah, well. I expect he'll turn up. They generally do."

"We're off to try the Brian Brothers' roast chestnuts," I announce. "Care to join us?"

Jan pulls a face. "Rather have a gin and tonic in the Anchor."

"You're on. Meet you there in an hour."

212

"Great. That'll give me time to finish up here and have a last scout round for Stevie."

Jan is clearly worried, despite her smiles. My stomach knots. Another child who… No. No, I won't go there. Halloween is about having fun, its ghosts and evil spirits just an excuse for dressing up. Stevie probably pigged a dozen soul cakes and is already safe at home, watching telly.

The girls persuade me to buy them fizzy drinks from the van parked near the church, Jan's lukewarm squash evoking their scorn. We amble along a grassy track towards the river, the girls sucking pop through curly straws. About halfway there, a blast from over-revved engines startles us, disrupting the peace of evening. A blaze of light sweeps the sky and, from nowhere, a dozen motorbikes roar up in a whitewash of main beam so powerful it's blinding. Within seconds the fairground is surrounded. The bikers drive round and around the Green, the drone of their machines throbbing menace into the air. Leather-clad and anonymous behind bulbous crash helmets, they seem more like robots than men, their presence an alien, inexplicable threat. Over by the bridge, I spot Derry and Colm glance at one another. Colm fishes in his pockets then punches numbers into his mobile. I put an arm around Melanie and Alice to draw them close, and press on.

Suddenly three of the bikes break away and drive into the crowd. Visitors to the fair are starting to disperse to avoid trouble; the bikers intend to stop them. Skidding through gaps between the stalls, their wheels churning clods of grass and mud, they aim directly at the bodies of anyone attempting to leave, veering off at the last moment and hauling their machines round in a cloud of exhaust fumes. People scream and huddle together in confusion. Meanwhile the outer ring of bikes continues to circle the Green, their headlights a revolving barricade behind which they corral the villagers like animals.

"Quickly," I urge. "Derry and Colm will be waiting with our chestnuts."

"I don't like chestnuts." Melanie's face adopts its wide-eyed look. "What are those men doing?"

"Making a lot of noise. Now come along, stop dawdling." If we can reach the bridge, we can cross to the other side and put the river between us and danger. We'll be safer. The police will arrive in no time; the Brians aren't the only ones with a mobile phone.

When we left the church hall, I was going to lead the girls onto a narrow path that skirts the cemetery, intending to rejoin the Green near the river, close to where the Brians have their stall. But the chestnut stand is this side of the water and reaching it will at some point involve crossing the road being patrolled by the bikers. Instead, I decide to hug the cemetery wall, follow it as far as the field, then possibly scramble over the fence and sneak round behind some old farm buildings. Even if I can't get to the bridge, we ought to be out of sight most of the time.

"No, Melanie. Come this way."

"I want to go and find Mummy." She wriggles from my arm, intent on running across the road.

I grab her hand. "Your mum's fine," I insist. "She told you not to interrupt her, didn't she?" I adopt my most cajoling voice. "This route's much more fun. We've got to climb over that fence," I point up ahead, "and crawl through the long grass. Like playing cowboys and Indians." Melanie gives me a blank stare. "You know, like… oh, never mind, come on."

With Alice in the lead, we speed along the grassy track towards the field. The night is overcast, eerily dark, and the path unlit apart from watery illumination given off by a few stars between the clouds. Behind us, the growl of engines and high-pitched, hysterical voices.

"This is *scareeeeey*," Alice whispers. She starts giggling then hops up and down trying to see over the wall. "All those *dead* people." Scrambling up, she peers over the top at rows of tombstones cloaked in velvet shadow. "I can't see any though."

"Alice, get down. Stay on the path." I feel Melanie's fingers tighten round mine.

"My mummy says that dead people get up on Halloween night and *walk among us*."

Great, Alice, thanks for that. Frighten the life out of us, why don't you?

"She says they're ghosts and they come back and they're witches and they turn little children into mice and toads and things, and then we all…"

Oh, for pity's sake. "It's just a story, Alice. Like a fairy story. You're not supposed to believe every—"

"Scary fairy," says Alice. "*Whoooo*. Oh! I know, I know, I've got a really scary ghost story all about—"

"No." Melanie's voice is small. She squeezes my hand for support. "I don't want to hear. I don't like scary stories."

"No silly nonsense," I declare. "We haven't got time."

As I speak, the motorbike drone fractures with explosive blasts. I recognise the sound of engines backfiring, though knowing the cause doesn't help; it still makes me think of shots from a gun. Each blast makes me jump. I hurry the children to the fence, help them climb over and then we're on the perimeter of a recently ploughed field, its soil rutted and bumpy with thick clumps of grass just right for tripping over and pits of mud for stepping into.

"Oooh! Help!"

I haul Alice out. "Keep close to me," I order. "Walk where I walk, nowhere else. We'll stick to the edge."

"My feet are wet."

"Don't fuss, Alice. This way."

We progress towards the outline of a barn, slip round behind it, then stumble on towards a stile that marks the far corner of the field and offers an easy exit to a further track that winds, according to my calculations, along the river bank towards the bridge.

"Listen," says Melanie. The whine of police sirens, faint at first then insistent.

I hesitate. If the police are nearly here, is there any need to avoid the Green? Should I go back, or press on? The path underfoot seems firm and well used. "Nearly there," I say, gripping each child firmly by the hand. "What shall we sing?"

We swing arms as we march along. "… and if eight green bottles should accidentally fall, there'll be…"

"I don't know this song."

"Hush. It's easy. Just keep counting backwards."

Finally, up ahead, a suggestion of light, colour, movement. I point. "Look! I bet that's Derry and Colm wondering where we've got to." But instead of racing forward, we have to pick our way awkwardly through tangled undergrowth. The path narrows, forcing us into single file, then dips sharply, the ground crumbling away to our right. Trees and rocks lay dislodged in a scatter of debris that litters the bank down to the water's edge.

A loose stone spins into darkness. I am petrified. "Hang on to each other," I shout. "Grab clothes, anything." The ground dips again, slick with mud and studded with exposed roots. The track is descending steadily into the gorge carved by the river. Police sirens wail in our ears and now the area to our left, where the village green must lie, seems high as a mountain and shot with flashing lights. Telling myself I should have turned back, I feel I have no option but to carry on. We must be only yards from the bridge. Yes, there. I can make out its shape, arcing into air, specks in the stone glittering. Distracted by the sight, I trip and, arms flailing, grab a branch to save myself. The children scream.

"It's all right. I'm all right."

A few more steps and I spot the bulk of one of the Brians, outlined against the night sky, coppery hair picked out in a sudden flash of light. "Colm," I yell. "Down here. Colm!"

My voice is lost in the racket coming from the Green. We need to regain height. Pausing to get my breath, I gather Alice and Melanie closer as I peer through brambles and dead ferns for the easiest route. It isn't far, not really, a quick scramble. By my side, Melanie has fallen silent. Alice finishes singing, "… and if one green bottle…" then she's off, climbing like a monkey, undeterred by thorns snagging her clothes. "Colm 'n Derry!" she calls out, bounding from one tree trunk to another. "Colm 'n Derry!"

217

"Alice! Wait!" Pushing Melanie in front, I start the ascent. Using tufts of grass and low branches as handholds, I pull myself slowly upwards, though my shoes lack grip and slide on the wet ground. Lighter and more agile, the two girls quickly reach the top and run, shrieking, towards Colm Brian who turns at the sound of his name. A few gabbled words, small arms pointing, and both the brothers are there waiting to haul me up the last few, slippery feet.

I gulp as relief surges; I've done it, we're safe.

Even Melanie comes back to help. Her pigtails bob as she chatters excitedly, confident now that she's surrounded by grown-ups. She stretches her hands out, determined to do her bit. She's copying the Brians, shouting instructions, "Come on, nearly there. No, grab this branch, here, this one, no, *this* one."

Which is how relief turns to disaster. Inching forward, Melanie loses her footing and whooshes past me, slithering on a scree of mud and leaves that shoot down the bank and into the darkness of the water below.

Chapter Eighteen

There's no time for thought. I drop Colm's hand, spin round and scoot down the slope on my backside straight into the river. It's too dark to see and my eyes fill with water. All I can do is follow the screams, the plumes of spray churned up by Melanie splashing and floundering. Seconds pass. Or is it hours? Time out of mind.

The cold penetrates clothes, then bone. I gasp, spitting out strands of weed as I thrash and stumble, my water-logged coat slowing movement. Then an arm smashes against my side. I make a wild grab, catch hold.

"I've got you," I yell, flinging myself around Melanie's body, cradling it. "I've got you, I've got you." Hugging, dripping, shivering, sobbing, we cling to one another as if welded together, waist-deep in the icy flow. Melanie starts to howl. "Shush. It's all right, I've got you."

Then Derry Brian is there, guiding us to the edge and Colm is draping a coat over us. And somehow we're back at the bridge, where Mac appears with hot tea, and a St John's Ambulance lady administers first aid and thermal blankets, and a young PC bustles past muttering "Thank shit for that," as he clamps handcuffs on one of the bikers.

After a thorough check-up, we are both pronounced unhurt apart from cuts and abrasions. The bruises will take time to appear.

"A miracle," declares Mary Coleforth.

"My poor baby," croons Mrs Richards, the fortune teller, rocking Melanie against her ample breasts.

"Fucking brilliant," says Derry Brian. "Reckon you ought to—"

"Get a medal." Colm plonks a kiss on the top of my head, on my wet, tangled hair. "When you're ready, I'll give you a lift home."

"But my car… I was supposed to meet Jan for a drink." I peer at him, dazed with shock and blinded by police lights flooding the Green.

"Little brother here will see to all that." He nods to Derry. "You can stop off at—"

"The Anchor on the way back, let Jan know, then I'll meet you—"

"At Rose's cottage. Sorted. Keys?" Colm gestures to my bag, still slung over one shoulder and across my body, safe but sodden.

At Penmaris, I resist offers of help, food or comfort, and then somehow I'm in bed. I must have fallen asleep instantly because I wake, what seems like seconds after closing my eyes, to find the sun shining on a new day and a new month.

Everything hurts. With a groan I drag myself from the comfy mattress and hobble downstairs. My wet clothes, now drying, are hanging over the backs of chairs, my keys are on the coffee table amongst the contents of my handbag, which soggy item someone has turned inside out and hooked over one of the easel pegs, and a note is propped on the mantelpiece: "Car outside, sleep well! C & D." It's nearly eleven o'clock.

Too thirsty to wait for the kettle, I gulp from the tap then polish off a carton of orange in the fridge. The juice skewers my stomach like an ice pick and I shudder, barefoot on the kitchen tiles. Glancing down, I note bare legs, knickers, a baggy T-shirt. Someone has undressed me and put these on; I wonder briefly who, then decide I don't care and drag myself back upstairs for a very long, very hot bath.

In the steaming water, to which I add a gallon of smellies, I examine my battered body. Because I'd been wearing jeans and a jacket, my clothes have taken the brunt. Even so, skin has rubbed from my arms and legs, leaving angry red marks, though none seem deep or infected. My hands are scratched, with several broken finger nails and splinters that will need attention. Twisting round in the tub, I try to inspect my backside and spot a few angry scrapes, though it's impossible to see splinters. I'll just have to hope there are none – after all, who am I going to ask to dig them out? I roll over. Basically, the injuries are trivial; I appear to be in tact. Breathing deeply, I stretch out full-length, luxuriating in perfume: lavender and chamomile, jasmine, rose. Heaven. The tiny bathroom disappears in a white, scented cloud. Even my joints start to ease in the hot

221

water, though this is temporary. The next few days will be painful, as bruises and stiffness set in.

Ah well, it could have been worse.

Much worse.

I jolt upright, sloshing suds over the side. Melanie! *Oh, Melanie*. I whimper the name. How is *she* feeling this morning? She could have drowned. Dear God, she could have drowned.

From hot, I go cold. I should never have led the children to the river, in the dark, along a path I didn't know. Stupid. Stupid. Forget the hooligan bikers, forget the trouble on the Green, I should never have wandered off with Melanie and Alice. Most certainly I should never have allowed them to climb that steep bank, with nothing to prevent them tumbling backwards, nothing to stop them falling into… Oh God, oh God. Oh, God…

Gulping air, I duck underwater and lie flat on the bottom of the bath. Eyes tight shut, I try to recall the sequence of events that led to Melanie's fall. I see her safe and smiling, grinning with excitement, reaching out and calling my name, a bundle of wriggling fingers and blonde pigtails bouncing round that apple face. Then bang… her foot slipped. It just went. As if she'd been on ice.

Against the backdrop of my eyelids I watch again as Melanie slithers past me, straight down into the river.

I splutter to the surface, gasping.

I think my chest will explode. Hanging onto the side of the bath, I wait for the pounding to ease, track each slowing pulse, each fading thud against my ribcage, loosen my clenched fists, inhale deeply.

I got those children back safely. I did. I know I did. They were safe. They were absolutely fine. What happened, happened afterwards. I got them back safe.

It feels as though a space is opening inside my skull, like a clearing in the darkest wood.

Alice and Melanie both reached the Green, safe and sound.

The accident was not my fault.

Three words ringing in my head: *not my fault, not my fault.*

* * *

It's the front doorbell ringing, over and over. Someone who refuses to give up. Grabbing a fluffy bath towel, I hobble downstairs just in time to catch the Interflora man. In his arms, the most extravagant, preposterous bouquet I have ever seen.

How can we ever thank you? Love, Angel and Melanie Richards.

Angel, the fortune-teller. What a perfect name! I pop the note on the mantelpiece next to the Brian brothers' missive and Mac's paper rose. Who wouldn't want their fortune told by an angel? The bouquet rests in my arms. Where on earth am I going to put so many flowers? I glance round the room for inspiration. As far as I know, there isn't even a vase in Penmaris; I've been using jugs and empty jam jars.

While I'm pondering the problem, there's a knock at the door. Mac, with a bottle in one hand and a box in the other.

"To keep you warm, Rose, inside and out." He strides into the sitting room. "Though some clothes might help."

223

I'd forgotten I was half naked and tuck the edge of the bath towel even tighter. Mac starts ripping cardboard to reveal a brand new portable fan heater which he plugs in. Warm air wafts over my feet.

"Where on earth…?"

"From a shop," says Mac. "Coffee or tea?" He moves to the kitchen.

"Tea, please. And there's cake somewhere. I'll just go and get…" but I linger in the billowing warmth, enjoying its caress on the backs of my legs, feeling relief as the heat moves up through each aching bone. "What I meant was why have you brought a—?"

"It's a present, Rose. From me. Don't you think you deserve it?"

On the coffee table stands a bottle of expensive cognac; the label speaks class. I drop into an armchair, overcome.

"Found some biscuits too." Clearing a space, Mac puts the tray down, transfers the flowers to the couch and settles himself opposite. "Looks like I'm not your first caller." He stirs the tea pot.

"They're from Melanie's mum."

"Hmm. Very colourful. Oh, before I forget..." He pours two mugs of strong brew. "Colm Brian said he'll drop by later to check you're okay." He gestures at my bag and its contents, now shoved to one end of the table. "Bit of an admirer there, if you ask me."

"Don't be ridiculous," I bristle.

Had Colm been responsible for emptying the bag and hanging it on the easel? Did he lay my wet clothes out to dry? And if so, did he peel them off me? Embarrassed, I pluck my torn jeans from the back of the chair and pull a face. "Think these have had it," I

224

say. They're the same pair I wore on Monday and bear clear signs, among all the others – ripped seams, holes in the seat – of where I snagged them on Mac's barbed wire.

"Eat," Mac says.

We munch digestives and sip tea until his voice breaks the silence. "Look, Rose, about the other day, I'm—"

I jump. "No, no, don't—"

"Bloody rude of me. Shouldn't have shouted at you like that."

"Mac, it's okay. I'm the one who should… You and Sally, it's none of my business. Whatever you were to each other… or weren't," I add, seeing him frown again, "it's nothing to do with me. I didn't mean to barge in like that making accusations. I can't believe I said what I said. I'm the one who should be apologising." I gesture at the room. "Something about this place, this cottage. That face I drew, the photos I found, the poems… I've been a bit… obsessed recently." Mac harrumphs. "I know, I know. More than a bit obsessed. And for all the wrong reasons. I've been, sort of… taking my personal problems out on you."

The phone is ringing. Getting up to answer it, I try to finish my apology. "I'm hoping last night's going to change a few things for me. Things inside my head. You were right all along." I lift the receiver. "Hallo?"

It's Jan Freeman, calling to update me on the Halloween saga and to invite me over for tea. While I reassure her about my bumps and bruises, Mac studies the blue abstract which, completed, now hangs over the fireplace. Then I hear myself put Jan off with a silly excuse. "I'd love to come round, but not tomorrow. I don't think I'll be here. In a few days, maybe? When I get back." Mac snorts, then starts whistling to pretend he's not ear-wigging the conversation, though Jan's voice must be audible from the garden.

"So long as you don't forget, Rose. I'll hold you to it. Any excuse to do some more baking."

"I will ring you. I promise."

"Bye bye, my dear. Good to know my soul cakes kept you safe."

I hang up. Eyebrows raised, Mac turns to face me.

"They found Stevie," I say. "He'd gone off with a friend and not told anyone."

"That was coven chief, I presume?"

"Oh, shush." I flap a hand at him. "I like Jan Freeman. She's one of the few people round here who's not treated me like an outsider." Mac's eyebrows lift. "Amongst which number I include yourself, of course."

"Well, Rose, I reckon that's all about to change." He points to the bouquet. "Hero of the hour, local..." I shake my head, so he corrects himself. "Sorry, *heroine,* if you're going to be pedantic, resident saint, saviour of young children—"

"No, no, it's not the word, Mac, it's the *fact...* the fact that Melanie's alive." An uncontrollable grin is almost splitting my face in two. "She's *alive.* Isn't it wonderful? You have no idea what that means to me."

He steps towards me and takes hold of my wrists, rubbing his thumbs across the web of old scars. With great deliberation, he places a kiss on each, gently, precisely on the knot of skin and vein. "Oh, I think I do, Rose. I think I do." His leg, brushing my knees, catches the edge of the bath towel which lifts then drops back into place.

Something bursts inside me. "Atonement, Mac. A life for a death. I feel… free at last." Transfixed, I stand there, my upturned palms like a supplication.

"Whoa! Don't go all religious on me, woman." He drops my hands as if he's been burnt. "Some you win, some you lose. Accidents happen, they work out, they don't. It's not divine bloody intervention." He makes a grab for the brandy bottle, gives the lid a savage twist. "Drink this," he orders, sloshing brandy into our tea. "Sit down and drink this."

"How can you be so matter-of-fact?" I ask. A slug of booze hits me between the eyes.

"Because that's what it is, a simple matter of plain fact."

"You sound like my father; he reckons I ought to shake things off, because I'm a doctor's daughter. Life, death, pain, suffering – shit happens. Says I should take it all in my stride. After Méline's death, then the miscarriage, he pretty much gave up on me. Claims I'm 'negatively self-indulgent', whatever that—"

"Bloody jargon."

"Well, I think it means… Oh, who cares!" Sixty percent proof on an empty stomach is making my head spin. "Right this minute, I feel free, for the first time in years. It's a miracle." I tug the towel over my knees, then ignore it, letting it fall away.

Free.

"So what now, Rose? What happens next?"

The question, dropped into rushing air, causes a small click of silence. Like a gun being cocked. The room is stifling, claustrophobic, the new fan heater having already paid for itself by turning Penmaris cottage into a Turkish bath. Beads of sweat are running between my breasts. We stare at one another, waiting to see who will blink first, until I realise I'm holding my breath and have to gasp. The fireplace seems to tilt. Mac's eyes flick away towards the storm canvas which, like the blue abstract, is also finished and is propped against the wall by the door, waiting to be hung.

"That's good, Rose. Really good." His voice sounds thick. He coughs, clears his throat. "You must do more. I can help you get exhibited."

"Actually, I was thinking of going home." Where did that come from? The announcement surprises me as much as Mac, whose face registers shock. When I gulp more tea and brandy, I feel the top of my skull explode. "Might catch a train tomorrow morning." He looks appalled. "Spur-of-the-moment decision, but I need to go and see Oliver. We've got things we really ought to… to sort out." Speaking to Jan on the phone was when the idea first entered my head and already it seems fully formed. "We need to get stuff out in the open, me and Oliver. We've had… Well, I won't bore you with the details, but I can't… hide down here any longer. I've got to go back and face…"

Is that true? Am I ready now to confront the mess I left behind?

Mac stands up. He looks distraught and sways slightly, off balance. For some reason this pleases me. I want to goad him. "I think it's time for me to go and talk to Oliver. Really talk. Which is another kind of miracle."

Mac stumbles towards me. "But what about all this, your painting?"

I shrug. "Let's see how things go, eh? Maybe I'll bring Oliver back with me and he can help me pack."

Mac opens his mouth to protest again, but I interrupt. "Oh Mac, come on, get real. I can't stay down here for ever, can I? I've a life in London. I always knew I'd have to go home at some point and pick up the bits and pieces."

Lifting the heavy storm canvas above his head, Mac swings it towards me. His voice roars. "This is you, Rose. Look at it, woman. Bloody look at it. This is what you can do. You've just started to find yourself. Don't run away from *this*." He shakes the painting in my face. "Sod all the bits and pieces."

As quickly as it flamed, his rage dies. He puts the canvas down, carefully, respectfully, then staggers across the room and folds me in his arms. A hand slides under my bath towel, loosening it. His lips find mine.

Chapter Nineteen

The hairs of his beard, sweeping backwards and forwards across my breasts, make my toes curl and I try hard not to giggle. I've never been to bed with a beard before.

"Mac, stop! It tickles."

"Go on, laugh all you like. My manhood will not be offended. As a matter of fact, my manhood…" He rubs against my thigh.

"Again? Already?"

"Ah. There, see, now you *have* offended me. Might just shrivel up, crawl away and…"

A huge yawn escapes me. I clamp a hand over my mouth in horror. "Sorry! It's just that I'm so…"

"Now I'm *seriously* offended. You mean the earth didn't move for you?"

"Oh shut up and come here."

Languorous, satisfied, floaty, deliciously relaxed, still rather drunk, and so exhausted I could sleep for a week, I melt beneath his weight. Expert hands move slowly across my wrung-out body, stir fresh waves of excitement. I bury my face in Mac's heaving chest and pull him tighter, tighter, burrowing into his bulk like a wounded animal seeking refuge. And like a wounded animal, I emit small feral noises, squeaks and groans of pleasure and pain as we roll across the bed in a tangle of limbs.

Downstairs, the phone starts ringing again.

"'Nore it," one of us mumbles.

But it rings on and on.

"Might be Colm Brian," I mutter. "Checking I'm all right."

"Yep. You're all right."

Our lips reconnect. The phone rings on.

And on.

"Don't you dare…"

And on.

Until ignoring it is not an option. "Sorry, but I'll have to…"

"Bloody hell." Mac collapses against the pillows, then grabs his shirt from the floor and rummages for a cigarette.

"Such a cliché," I quip, and catch the shirt as he flings it at me. "Thanks. This'll do nicely." It fits me like a tent and I trot down the stairs wrapping it around me, glad of its warmth. The fan heater's been off for some time.

Tucking hair behind my ears, I lift the receiver. "Hallo?"

"Rose, sweetie. How are you? It's been ages."

"Paula!" The last person I expected to hear from.

"Hi there, darling. Spur of the moment thing. Simply had to call and check you're okay. Hope I'm not interrupting anything *important*…"

Nah, just fucking the local professor.

"… but I suddenly thought, I know what I'll do, I'll ring…"

My brain struggles to deal with Paula's unique brand of conversation.

"… only you left so suddenly I didn't have time to say goodbye and I'd got all these bits and pieces ready to bring round so you'd be comfy cosy in the cottage – it must be a bitch this time of year. Are you absolutely *freezing* to death, Rose? I was going to give you this super little heater Chris bought, totally portable so you could take it…"

Words descend like a snow-storm, closing me in, cutting me off. Far away the bathroom door slams, the shower rattles.

"…never seen Oliver so angry, what *is* his problem? Anyway, darling, I did try a couple of times to ring you, then I forgot, you know how absent-minded I am, till the other night when I saw a light on so I guessed he was back from… erm… was it Italy? Chris did tell me. And Ellie was there too, you know, your Ellie? Ellie… oh, God, what *is* her other name? Anyway, she said she'd dropped by because she's been worried about you, like I have of course. Because apparently *she's* not heard from you *either*…"

Her words are settling around me in drifts, isolating me. Before there's a complete whiteout, I make a grab for landmarks, signs of the way things are. "So when was that, Paula? When you went round. What time was it?"

"Time? Oh, I've no idea, darling. Late. Well, latish. I think. I was waiting for Chris to get back from squash and I went out to check our porch light was working 'cos we've got this dicky bulb and of course that's when I saw your lights were on so I thought I'd just pop in and say hallo. Anyway, they both looked sort of... funny. Worried about you, I suppose, and that got me *really* worried so I said to Oliver..."

Ellie wasted no time, then. Straight round the minute Oliver got back from France, never mind it was late at night. When the cat's away...

Felled by a sudden thought, I drop into the armchair. *Away.* Did Ellie go *away too?* Did she go to Europe with Oliver and turn up at our house, not after him, but with him? For that matter, did he even go abroad in the first place, or did the pair of them skip off for a week of sex by the sea? Not business deals in Paris and Berlin, but... Bournemouth, Bognor. Bonking in Bognor, which has a certain ring to it. Bonking in bloody Bognor. No, no, that's wrong, that wasn't what the king said. It wasn't bloody Bognor, it was something else, it was...

I think I must have made a weird noise, because suddenly Paula is shouting at me, very loudly, which triggers an avalanche. I duck as the weight of all that snow comes crashing down upon my head.

* * *

Mac has gone home. He left after taking one look at me and ordering me back to bed with a hot-water bottle.

"Christ, woman, look at the state you're in. You've had enough excitement in twenty-four hours to last the average person a year. No wonder you're bushed. I

233

should never have… Go on, upstairs and have a rest. I'll spread the word you're okay but you need some peace and quiet. No more visitors for a while. And no more extra-curricular activities!" The order accompanied by a sexy wink. "Get some sleep." Then he tucked me in as if I were about five years old, plonked a kiss on top of my head and departed.

I did sleep, too. For a couple of hours. Deep and dreamless, and I do feel better for it.

Well, no, that's not strictly true. Everything aches. Like that joke – I ache in places I didn't know I had places, and there's a stupendous bruise come up on my right arm where I tried to break my fall into the river. Plus I have to face the fact that I've slept with Alec McConnell, which makes me no better than Oliver or Ellie. Different, I'll concede, but I've lost the moral high ground. Whatever was I thinking? Why did I let myself…?

Speaking to Paula hasn't helped, either. Speaking to her twice, in fact. First time round I was too pissed to see through veiled remarks like "always the last to know…" and "no better than she ought to be…" and I let them pass. Only later did they seem freighted with significance. Paula knows about Oliver's affair. Does everyone know? Have they all known for ages, long before I did, and do they whisper about me?

So I rang Paula back ten minutes ago for round two.

Apparently it was Chris who first suspected Oliver might be playing away, though Paula refused to believe him. "Oh darling, I just assumed Chris was being blokey, seeing sex round every corner. Aren't they supposed to think about it every twenty seconds? How the country ever functions is a mystery to me. But yesterday I was in the garden, right down the end and I turned round thinking about our conservatory roof. It's been leaking, did I tell you? Anyway, I was worried that leaves might be blocking the gutter, so I was staring at it and wondering if I should call someone to come and clear them out and do the drains too, you know, have everything sorted before winter? And I caught a glimpse of movement behind your bedroom window. Just, like, out of the corner of one eye."

"Go on."

"It was about midday, lunch hour, I suppose, so I assumed Oliver had popped home and I nearly waved. Can you imagine? I nearly waved!" The image came of Paula's mouth wide open in astonishment. "Then when I looked again, well… I could see it wasn't Oliver." Paula was gabbling. "I'm sure it's nothing, Rosie. A stupid fling. It doesn't mean a thing. You've been ill and Oliver's felt alone and, well… you know what men are like."

Do I? Naively believing that Oliver and I jointly lost the baby, I've been under the impression we were both grieving and just needed time to get over the tragedy. In our own separate ways, of course. Now it seems, in our own separate ways, we both went careering off the rails in spectacular fashion, me deep into despair, Oliver deep into Ellie Carter. Apparently Chris had his suspicions back in the summer. He came across Oliver and Ellie in a pub one night. Cosy little *tête-à-tête* was how he described it to Paula who, loyal and trusting, had immediately pooh-poohed his doubts.

"I was absolutely sure Chris had got the wrong end of the stick," Paula said. "He usually does. But after what I saw yesterday, from the garden, well… *that* was why you left so suddenly for Cornwall, wasn't it? Without saying goodbye? You found out and you had a terrible row and, well, as soon as I realised, I got really worried about you… I'm so sorry, Rose. I'm so upset for you. What a bastard, I can't believe Oliver would… But thanks, Rosie."

"*Thanks*? For what?"

"For ringing me back. I was scared you wouldn't want to talk to—"

"No. Thank you," I said, "for being on my side."

"Oh, darling, we wronged women must stick together."

There was a moment of complete silence, a hiatus that trembled with the threat of something quite unpleasant waiting to make an entrance. Then Paula began her tale. Mac said I'd had enough excitement in twenty-four hours to last a year, yet bombshells were still falling, because Paula was telling me about the time Chris cheated on her shortly before they were married, about twenty years ago. She nearly called the wedding off when she found out.

"Long-distance relationships, Rose, that was our problem. They're never a good idea. Chris'd been sowing a lot of wild oats down in Penzance, 'cos he was stuck living with his parents and there was nothing else to do in winter. But once we met, he started making plans to move to London and everything seemed fine. Till I found out he was having an affair with an older woman. A much older woman. Some Cornish bitch he couldn't keep his hands off." Paula's snarl was almost visible. "A *siren*, that's what he called her, so he could pretend it was all her fault. He was just the coy youth helpless to resist; she seduced him with her wicked ways. Lying sod! I reckon he had a number of other women on the go, too, but I've never been able to confirm that one. Anyway, I went ballistic, Chris begged and crawled and swore undying love, moved up here pdq and that was that."

"*That was that*? You mean it was *easy*?"

"Course not. Learning to trust him again wasn't easy. The point is, no one's perfect, Rose. People make mistakes, but they can learn from them and grow up. Settle down. That's what I mean about Oliver. I'm sure this is just a silly… mistake, because he's missing you."

"Do you know who she was, this older woman? Did you ever meet her?"

"God, no. I'd have clawed her eyes out. I was a possessive little cat back then. Chris made sure our paths never crossed or I might have killed her. I nearly did kill him. Besides, I was based here in London so I insisted he join me *toot sweet*, as they say. Or else!"

But Chris still made business trips to Cornwall. He'd never completely severed the tie. Wasn't Paula bothered? He'd been in Porthallen only the other week, dropping in to see me, checking up on Carne. "Don't you worry about them bumping into each other, when he's down this way?"

"Hardly, darling. I'm pretty sure she's been dead for years. It's all water under the bridge, sweetie. You'll see. One does get over these things."

A worm of suspicion was creeping under my skin. Unable to stop myself putting two and two together, I made some rash assumptions, assigned identities, experienced a rush of excitement so strong that, for the moment, I forgot about Oliver. "So why, Paula, given that messy history, would you go and buy a holiday cottage in Cornwall? If it was me, I'd've picked almost anywhere else on the planet."

Paula laughed. "God, no, Rose, the cottage wasn't my idea. Too far from civilisation for my liking. It was Chris who wanted to buy it."

The worm crawled deeper. I distinctly remembered Chris telling me the exact opposite – that it was all Paula; that *she* had persuaded *him* to buy Penmaris, against his better judgement.

Paula was explaining: "He'd spotted this old ruin and reckoned it would make a good investment. I thought he'd gone mad when he first showed me. What a state! But it's worth a packet now. Nice little nest egg. And I've grown quite fond of the place. As for his naughty fling... well, the woman's dead, Rose. It's all in the past. Why should I care?"

* * *

Mac has left the bottle open on the coffee table. I've always hated brandy. It messes with your head. As well as other parts. Experimentally, I run the furred monstrosity of my tongue round the sewer enclosing it. Huffing into the palm of one hand, I sniff cautiously and instantly regret it, whipping my head back from olfactory contact. I seriously need to stop drinking.

Well, perhaps I will. It's time for a change. After Melanie, Oliver, Ellie, Paula, Chris, Mac, Sally. Jeez! It's definitely time for a change.

Everyone lies – that's what they say, don't they? And to think it's called cynicism! Being realistic, more like. Escaping one mess in London, I've landed myself in another a few hundred miles away, and now it seems likely the two are linked by a web of lies. In the middle of which here am I, hooked by sticky threads, and the question is, am I the spider or the fly? One thing's for sure. I won't be rushing to catch any trains for Paddington tomorrow morning. I can't face Ellie's toothbrush in my bathroom, Ellie's moisturiser on my dressing table. It was probably a silly idea in the first place, to try and run before I can walk. Sufficient unto the day… For the moment, there's a mystery down here that I can't seem to leave alone, and Chris Benning's involved. The timeframe is right. I know it. For no good reason, I just know it.

From behind the sofa I take my sketch pad and, for the first time in days, I look the woman in the eye. Really look at her. Really focus on Sally Hendry.

Chapter Twenty

Because it is the face of Sally Hendry. That's another thing I just know. But I don't know how I know.

Like I know that twenty years ago Sally and Chris Benning were an item. Their liaison explains why Sally stayed in Cornwall after her mother's death – to be near her lover. Then Chris ended the affair and high-tailed it to London to marry Paula, and Sally died. Though not necessarily in that order.

Chris. Sally. Oliver. Ellie. Oliver. Chris…

What was it Mac said the other day? *Instinct tells me you've been here long enough to start the journey.* He was actually discussing art but, as with so many things, he was spot on. The shadow of Sally Hendry beckons and on the way to finding her, perhaps I can bury my own messes under any convenient stone.

Instead of hiding the sketch once more behind the sofa, I carry the woman with the scarred face upstairs with me and prop her on the dressing table, from where I can see her when I'm in bed. Her face turned to one side, she appears to be half-staring out of the small front window as though she's keeping guard. Looking out for me, here inside with her. But she's not gazing out of the window at all, she's… The woman with sad eyes… Nothing to be scared of anymore… Our relationship has changed and…

* * *

Through the thin slit of my caked eyelids I can tell it's morning. I've slept for about a thousand hours. Perhaps there's only so much a body can take before it shuts down. I rub my face and crank my eyes wider. From across the room, Sally's face, bold and clear. She seems to be asking me what I'm going to do now. Shower, teeth, get dressed. That's what.

Once I feel nearly human again, I start sorting dirty clothes into "wash" or "make do" while ignoring my stomach telling me I've barely eaten in the last thirty-six hours. Three aspirin swallowed twenty minutes ago will sort the hangover.

November. New month, new life, new resolution: I hurl knickers into the washing machine and vow to give up booze for ever. One thing I've come to realise in recent days is the value of a clear head. If only I'd been more aware of what was going on around me, I might have noticed that Oliver was…

At least I can try cutting back.

There's a knock at the kitchen door. Alec McConnell? Come to resume where we left off yesterday? Or more likely find out if I really am going to London. My hand hesitates on the door knob; this may be a complication too far. Except… I conjure a wry smile and open the door.

"Here to inspect the tank," announces a middle-aged man in overalls. "Routine visit. Only I noticed the car." A nod to my MG, next to which a white van is parked.

I expect I look stupid. "Tank?"

"The septic tank, down there." He points down the garden. "Sewage disposal, waste water?"

"Oh!" I follow his finger. "I didn't even know there was one."

"Gets checked every autumn," he explains. "Saves bothering people in the summer. Place is usually empty by now, but when I saw the old…" Another nod towards my car. "Thought I'd better let you know. Don't want you thinking there's strangers prowling around, eh?"

"Right. Thanks."

"Shouldn't be long. Okay then?"

I shrug and shut the door. In the kitchen, making tea and toast, I watch him. The tank appears to be in the extreme right-hand corner near the wall, under bushes which the man is pushing aside. It's the neglected end of the garden, dank and overhung by trees, part of Carne's eco-plot left to grow wild. Buried somewhere beneath the rotting leaf-mould must be the control centre of operations I don't care to contemplate in too much detail. My stomach moves in protest. I turn the tap off, eying water that slithers down the plughole.

He noticed my car. He had the consideration to knock. People do notice things, I realise, especially when they're sober.

I carry breakfast into the sitting room. Slices of buttered toast smell of warmth and comfort. Heaping marmalade on top, I bite into tangy sharpness. I shall eat a proper meal, look after myself, get off the booze.

Waiting for my tea to cool, I fetch pen and paper and, balancing the pad on the arm of the chair, I draw up two columns. Lists, I have decided, are the way forward; I shall be systematic and marshal my thoughts. One column I head *facts*, the other *suspicions*. Under the former I write: C's affair 20yrs ago; SH disappeared 20yrs ago; teenage SH in love with AM; SH and AM in London together (late 60s/early 70s); SH back in Porthallen by 80s (sick parent); CT loved SH; SH's friendship with JF.

Footsteps outside break my concentration – a crunch of gravel, van doors slamming, more crunching. The guy must be collecting tools. I can't imagine what servicing a septic tank might involve, but it's not a job I'd fancy.

I flick my biro aimlessly, chew another mouthful of toast, stare at the phone. I know what – I'll check the cable's properly connected, and I'll go and charge my stupid mobile, just in case. If drawing up lists is supposed to banish pictures of Oliver and Ellie in bed, then it's not working.

In *my* bed, at that. In *my bloody bed*.

No. Our bed. Mine and Oliver's. I remember the day we bought it, along with the duvet and matching bedding, the way we bounced around on the display beds in Harrods while the sales lady smiled instead of getting cross with us. I remember... Mac's naked bulk, his grey beard and the thick grey hairs on his chest, the way his toenails scratched the sheets.

I need Oliver to ring me, damn it! Though if he does, I'll probably slam the phone down. It's going to take more than a few days and three hundred miles.

Still...

I continue to stare. Sip tea.

Back to the lists. Into the *suspicions* column I put: JF's play/SH's poem; AM's drawing/another SH poem; AM & SH baby; SH & CB affair/baby; JF knows about SH&CB; how much does CT know? Were CT & SH ever lovers????

Sex, love and jealousy, the eternal triangle everywhere you look. Including my own back yard. After yesterday's revelations, I must concede the ubiquity of passion. It strikes me there's a deep intimacy implicit in what both Jan and Mac have done, using Sally's poetry for their own purposes. Therefore, if I suspect a sexual relationship between Mac and Sally, what about between Jan and Sally? Word is that in her youth Sally had been promiscuous; Jan called her "a bit of a goer". Was Jan speaking from personal experience? I glance at my collection of photos on the windowsill, at the one of Jan and Sally side by side in the garden at Penmaris, looking very ordinary, like a couple. And as far as I know, Jan, who must by now be in her late forties, has never married, which might mean…

Then there's what Paula told me on the phone yesterday. To the first column I add a new fact: CB lied re purchase of Penmaris.

Another knock at the back door. Tank-man is wearing a frown.

"Finished already?" I ask.

"Might have a bit of a problem," he says. "Have you noticed any funny smells?" He steps past me and leans over the kitchen sink, sniffing. "Tell you what, would you mind popping upstairs and flushing the loo? And turn the bath taps on, while you're at it." He opens both

244

kitchen taps then marches off, reappearing five minutes later.

Apparently waste water isn't coming through at a decent enough speed and probing with drain rods has failed to clear the flow. He suspects a partial blockage.

"Could be tree roots, a cracked pipe, vermin. That's a very old tank, that is." He shakes his head in disapproval. "God knows what idiot sited it down there in the first place, near trees. Asking for trouble. Still, don't you worry. I'll get some big equipment round first thing Monday morning, and she'll be right."

"Monday?"

"Fully booked till then, I'm afraid. It's not an emergency."

"No, of course not." Will Chris have to be notified? I start to explain. "I'm not actually the owner."

He waves a clipboard. "Got Mr Benning's details here. I'll ring him later, let him know what's going on. He's sure to want a ball-park figure." He gives a canny laugh.

"Fine. Well, I'll see you on Monday."

"Oh, there's no need for you to hang around," he assures me. "Don't spoil your holiday on my account. I can get access from the key holder if I need to." When I look surprised he adds, "A Mr Tresawna? Got his details here too."

Which piece of information goes straight into the first column – my interesting list of facts. There's plenty of facts piling up. I scribble furiously. How odd no one thought to mention to me the fact that "CT holds spare key to P". On consideration, it's perfectly logical he should, along with the key to the garden shed. But it might have been useful if Chris or Paula had told me, or

Carne himself for that matter. Just in case I lock myself out one day, by accident.

I finish breakfast, put more washing on, make a desultory attempt to tidy up whilst staying close to both phones, and at odd moments I add to my lists. Then I devise a complicated system of arrows and asterisks to help clarify my thoughts.

Neither phone rings. In the afternoon, frustrated by electronic silence, I call the bookshop. Time to start asking questions.

"Hi Jan. It's Rose."

"Hallo, Rose. I wasn't expecting to hear from you till next week. Weren't you going away?"

"Change of plans. Are you free this weekend?"

"Could be. What do you have in mind?"

"How about tea, Sunday afternoon? I know *you* invited *me*, but I'd love you to come over to Penmaris. If the weather's nice, we could go for a stroll first, and if not, well, I'm sure we can find—"

"Sunday? Oh. That's firework night, Rose. Fifth of November."

"Strewth! Already? I hadn't realised."

"There'll be a huge display on the Green, great big bonfire, the works. I was watching Colm Brian chucking wood on the pile yesterday morning. It's already over his head. They started preparations straight after Halloween, so by Sunday night the fire…" She must have heard me gasp. "Ah, sorry, I can see how you might not fancy…"

"No, not much. I think I'll give the village green a miss this time."

"Wise woman! Listen, the party won't really get started till sixish, so there's nothing to stop me popping round for a cuppa."

"So you'll come?"

Jan doesn't hesitate. "We can have a good long chat. About time we got to know one another better. Smashing idea, Rose. I'm delighted to accept."

We agree on three o'clock, and already I have visions of a traditional tea party and wonder if the oven can be relied on for baking. But what if Oliver phones? Supposing he suggests coming down at the weekend? Well, too bad. I've made other plans. He'll have to fit into my schedule for once.

* * *

"Rosie! Don't hang up!"

Eventually. I knew he'd ring sometime today.

I say nothing, though my knuckles are white.

"Rose? Are you there? Listen, I can explain…"

He can't, of course. How could he possibly?

"Can we talk about it? Please? I never intended things to go this far… saw Paula and I knew that she'd… all been a terrible mistake. Why did you rush off to Cornwall like that, why couldn't you…?

I stare at the window and watch raindrops chasing each other down the glass.

Eye and ear; different messages from different worlds.

When I persist in silence, Oliver starts to back down. "Look, I know it's my fault, Rose, this whole bloody mess… if I'd made time to help you, to listen to you… Ellie was just sort of there. She doesn't mean a thing. It's you and me, Rosie, all the way. It's always been you and me, but, well, we were so wretched, and I never stopped to think what…"

And then, in mid-sentence, he bursts into tears. I nearly drop the phone.

"I'm sorry, Rose… Please, darling, please, talk to me. Rosie… Please…"

Not once since I've known him has Oliver ever cried about anything. His stony, dried-eyed self-control when we lost the baby made it seem like my loss alone, my baby, my miscarriage, my pesky tribulations adding yet another problem to his busy schedule. While others praised his stiff upper lip, I longed for him to show one tenth the pain I felt, to weep with me, just once. "He's so strong," Mum said, admiration for Oliver's fortitude barely disguising her implied criticism of my weakness. "A man to lean on, someone you can depend on."

My voice is a whisper. "We can't talk over the phone, it's too—"

"I'll come down."

"We can't—"

"How about the weekend? I'll come down this weekend. Or tomorrow. Damn it, no, I can't. *Damn it.* It'll have to be after… but tomorrow night. Yes, that's it. I'll leave tomorrow night and I'll be there first thing Saturday morning."

"No," I say. "No." After a pause I add, "I'm busy this weekend. Besides, if it really mattered, you'd be here *now*."

I hear the sigh, see him raking back his hair. "I've just explained about today, Rose." Has he? Exasperation loads his every syllable. "I can't just drop everything, not after all the work we've put in to secure these contacts. There's other people involved, Rose. It's not just me. I'm sorry, okay? I'm really sorry…"

"Fine. Well, you sort out when you can fit me in and let me know."

I put the phone down, carefully, so as not to smash the receiver to pieces.

Chapter Twenty-One

In the end I buy crumpets, for toasting over an open flame.

Jan arrives early with a bag full of goodies, just as I'm putting a match to the fire.

"Here you are, Rose. A traditional Cornish heavy cake, to celebrate you rescuing Melanie." As she hands the bag over, she studies the dark circles under my eyes and frowns. "How are you, my dear? Are you fully recovered?"

"Few bruises," I say, peering at what she's brought. "Really, you shouldn't have. I invited *you* to tea."

"To think I missed all the excitement Tuesday night! Too busy swigging gin in the Anchor." Jan tosses her purple cloak over the banisters. "Derry Brian was *agog*, bless the boy! The way he fell into the snug you'd have thought his tail was on fire. Couldn't get the news out fast enough. I did offer to come round and help, but Derry thought you'd had enough of people fussing." While she talks her gaze is moving slowly over the room, as if to feed. Angel Richard's flowers draw her to the windowsill. "These are canna lilies, Rose." Her fingers caress the petals. "What gorgeous colours."

"They're from Melanie's mum."

The huge display is bursting from a bucket of water just big enough to contain the long stems. I've wrapped coloured paper round the grey plastic and placed it on the windowsill, next to my Halloween lamp. The photos I decided to put away for the time being, in the kitchen drawer.

"Let's light the pumpkin candle," Jan suggests, "to complete the effect."

She does so, and the solitary flame dances with those flickering in the fireplace on the other side of the room. The cottage begins to glow. Satisfied with the result, Jan wanders around exploring, touching things, stroking surfaces. The air seems to tingle where her hand brushes the walls. I retreat to the kitchen, leaving my visitor to become reacquainted with Penmaris.

"I hardly recognise the place," Jan calls softly. "It's so clean and bright. It seems bigger somehow." Then in a louder voice, "Wow, Rose, this painting… Who…?"

The finished storm canvas is mounted on the wall near the front door. Jan must have turned round and suddenly caught sight of it. I chose the spot deliberately, so that visitors arriving by what I think of as the formal entrance will have their backs to the picture and not see it straight away. Whereas each time I walk down the stairs or from the kitchen into the sitting room, a blue-green crash of wind and waves greets me.

Carrying the loaded tea-tray, I return to the sitting room with a grin I can't disguise.

Jan realises straight away. "You mean *you* painted this, Rose? Really?" She rushes over, relieves me of the tray and sweeps me into a tight hug. "It's incredible, it's absolutely…"

She smells of flowers and sweet cake, and is wearing tendrils of something white threaded through her black hair. Pressed up against her, I experience a sensation of falling. When released, I am held at arms length while Jan once more studies my face.

"You are a woman of many parts, Rose Little. A constant source of surprise."

Embarrassed, I side-step towards the coffee table. "Come on, sit down. Cut your cake, I'm dying to try a piece." I start pouring tea. "It's not heavy at all."

"No, *hevva*, old Cornish. The *huer* were women who acted as lookouts, standing on the cliffs spotting pilchard shoals. They'd bake these cakes for when the crew came home with their catch." She hands me a generous helping. "The criss-cross pattern on top represents the fishermen's nets." Onto her own slice she heaps cream and jam. "Go on," she urges. "It's the way we serve it. Forget your tourist scones, this is the real McCoy." She beams through red lips coated in clotted cream. "Whoever he was."

For the next half hour we drink and eat and chat. Jan demands a potted account of diving into the river after Melanie.

"Nothing so dramatic, I'm afraid. I slithered in on my bum."

A miracle, apparently that's how the village is referring to it, that's what everyone is saying. "You saved a life, Rose. You've become our resident saint."

Not another one. Mac had used that very phrase.

252

"Hardly resident," I point out. "I'm just a visitor and," unable to resist the barb, "not always a very welcome one at that."

"We'll see," says Jan. "Who knows how long you'll end up staying now? Perhaps we won't ever let you go."

"Are you putting a spell on me? What's in this cake?"

She lifts a hand in mock protest. "Nothing, Rose, I promise you! Nothing but flour and currants, peel, butter... It's not like the soul cakes; there are no magical properties I'm aware of. Just currants, my dear. With perhaps a pinch of fairy dust." She winks.

I laugh and stand up, wiping my fingers. The moment seems right. "Actually, I'm the one with the ulterior motive today. Stay where you are. I won't be a minute." I run upstairs and return with the sketchbook clutched to my chest. For a few seconds I stand in front of Jan with the drawing hidden, then I take a deep breath. It seems as good a moment as any to broach the topic of Sally Hendry. "I wanted to show you this." Slowly I turn the pad around so Jan can see the face. "It may seem like a silly question, but does she remind you anyone?"

I've decided not to worry if the answer's no. Photographic likeness is only one version of the truth; there is also symbol and metaphor. Mac always stresses the importance of the abstract. In this drawing I've captured grief and torment, ugly emotions that can rip people apart. Sally's unhappiness may well have been invisible to those around her; I believe the face I've drawn is more a symbolic representation of suffering. I'm not expecting instant recognition. In fact, I don't

253

quite know what I am expecting, apart from the opportunity to persuade my guest to reminisce about an old friend.

What I get is the unexpected.

Jan's right hand flies to her mouth, followed by a low moan.

I'm babbling excuses: "It's not finished yet, I don't know how to finish it. I just wondered if you…" but my voice peters out.

Clenched so hard they shine white, Jan's knuckles are crushing her cherry-red lips into a bloody gash. There's a glimpse of bared teeth, the sound of a snarl. She starts panting in her struggle to breathe, she flings her head from side to side like a dog in pain. When her gasps eventually slow to a tremor, she ventures an arm, slowly, hesitantly, as if afraid of breaking something, and she touches the drawing. A small cry escapes her throat. With tender care she traces the shape of each eyebrow and eyelid, runs her hand through the mane of hair as though to loosen the tangles, slides a finger down the scarred cheek.

"Sal," she murmurs. When she lifts her fingers away, the tips are coated in charcoal. She stares at them, then runs them deliberately across her own face. She is transferring the drawing to her skin, rubbing the image bone-deep, smudging her makeup, leaving black streaks that turn to runnels.

For long moments I look on, horrified, frozen by the sight of such strange, visceral passion. Then I jump out of my chair, needing to do something. "God, Jan, I'm so sorry, I'm so sorry, I didn't mean to upset you. Let me get you a glass of water." Even in the kitchen, with the tap full on, I can hear the shocking mix of gasping and sobbing. "Here. Drink this." I wrap her fingers round the glass. "It'll help calm you. I'm so, so sorry, please don't… I had no idea that…" I hover, relieved when she finally manages a few gulps before offering a bleak smile.

Oh God, what have I done? A week ago Mac had seemed so genuinely unimpressed by my drawing, dismissing it an ugly old crone, that I'd believed him. I'd allowed myself to be persuaded it bore no resemblance to an actual person. It was a surrealist concept, not a portrait. I'd accepted his comments and re-evaluated the sketch on the strength of them. Whereas now…?

Jan is blowing her nose. The crisis seems to be over. "Sorry about this, Rose. How embarrassing. Oh help! I need a wash, by the looks of it." The tissue is black with mascara and charcoal dust, and Jan is out of her chair, desperate to escape.

"It's upstairs. The bathroom's… you can't miss it."

She clatters up the staircase, and in her wake a quiet falls. In the spaces between, I hear the room shift and settle back into a different place. The faintest of quivers, like a sigh. Flames in the hearth blaze.

I feel it too, and nod my head. Despite Jan's distress, I can't deny the surge of satisfaction. Vindication. I've known all along, in my heart and gut, that I've been drawing the face of Sally Hendry, the woman to whom something so terrible happened that her only voice is Penmaris, a cottage that whispers to shadows.

Mac, damn him, he fooled me last week, tricked me with his cool indifference, pretending he didn't recognise her. Not that I wasn't partly to blame. I could kick myself for adopting such a servile role in our pupil-master relationship. My pathetic need for artistic praise made it easy for Professor McConnell to dupe me, to play me like a violin and dictate the tunes.

Mac lied. Over that and what else, I wonder?

Everyone lies.

When Jan comes back, she looks brighter. "Damage repaired," she announces, tossing her bag to the floor. She steps briskly over to where I'm attempting to slide the sketchpad out of sight behind the sofa and she puts a hand out to stop me. "It's okay, Rose. Leave it. You don't have to hide it away. I'm… I'm better now. Here, let me." Propping the pad firmly against cushions, Jan sits down opposite. "Any tea left? Could do with another cuppa."

As I pour I try to explain. "When I showed that to… well, I didn't deliberately *show* it to anyone, but Alec McConnell was here one day last week, only because he'd brought me some logs for the fire, and I certainly didn't intend to show…" I can't possibly go into the whole being drunk, tripping over, crocheted blanket, sketchpad-and-easel thing right now. "Anyway, he didn't see any resemblance. Really. To anyone. In fact, he said it looked like a Halloween mask. He was quite rude, to be honest. So it never occurred to me you would actually…"

Who am I kidding? I showed Jan the drawing precisely because it occurred to me that if anyone, then maybe the reputed "Porthallen witch", one of Sally's last friends, might be the very person to see what I have always seen: the face of Sally Hendry. I wanted proof that I'm not going mad, and now I have it.

Sharing one mystery ought make it easier to share others. So I tell Jan about the nightmares I've been having, about the odd sights and sounds in the cottage, the history behind the sketch itself. After her emotional outburst, it feels right to reciprocate in some way, to lay myself bare. Besides, openness on my part might encourage further confidences. So what, if Jan thinks I'm odd?

"It's funny, really, but on my very first evening here I thought I heard... something, in the garden. A woman's voice, singing. And I've often sensed a presence in the house... not... not ghosts or anything like that." I laugh at the absurdity. "I don't believe in ghosts, it's just..."

"You do realise you're psychic, don't you, Rose?"

"What! No, that's ridiculous. I've never..."

"Then how did you know about the accident? You can't tell from that photo I gave you. We made sure. Sal arranged her hair to hang loose at the front and cover the scar. She never liked people asking awkward questions."

An accident, to her face. Oh, good God...

"So her face *was* damaged." Jan nods, and the truth comes as both revelation and confirmation. I reconsider my drawing, able to hold its gaze now without flinching. "I suppose I felt it. My hand somehow... knew to draw it." Out loud, the remark sounds ridiculous, fey even. The very idea of possessing occult powers smacks of junk American TV. I shrug, anxious to direct the conversation away from myself. "Would you tell me what happened?"

"She fell, out walking on the cliffs. She managed to save herself from going right over the edge, clung onto rocks or whatever she could grab hold of, but she couldn't save her face. Nearly lost the eye." Jan looks

257

up, with a nod to the painting hanging by the front door. "It was on a day like that," she says. "Sally loved being outside in stormy weather. Didn't give a damn about danger or getting blown to bits or soaked through. Wouldn't be told. She used to walk the beach in the thick of waves like mountains, or she'd scramble on the rocks so she could be part of the storm, standing right there in the middle of it, bellowing at the sea. Then one day she came a cropper. You might say it was an accident waiting to happen. Lucky she wasn't killed, to be honest. It happened a few months before she… well, you know, before she disappeared. For ever." Tears brim again. "That damned scar just wouldn't heal." Together we stare at the ugly gash carving a track through Sally's right cheek. "It wept and festered, got worse rather than better, despite the doctor's efforts. It was a terrible, terrible thing." Jan's voice breaks. "Sal called it her punishment. Not that it put a stop to her, she'd still wander off at all hours, day or night."

For a while neither of us speaks. Jan seems transfixed by the image in charcoal and, looking at my painting by the door, I am blinded by the memory of a woman on Porthallen Sands, wrapped in a long winter coat, buffeted by wind and rain, calling to the storm and listening for its reply.

Then I ask, "So you think she had a second accident, like the first?"

"That's what the police said, when she went missing. And years later, when they found her. A fall from the cliff top, they said. She must have *slipped*."

"You didn't agree?"

"Well, I don't actually know, do I? Don't suppose anyone does. But as far as I remember the weather was fine for once. We'd had a warm, dry summer. There was no reason for her to have a silly fall. The paths weren't muddy. I walked miles in the weeks after, looking for her." A long pause. "She'd been… very uptight for some time. I got the feeling something was wrong, something really bad, more than just her poor face, but…" Jan shakes her head.

Cradling my teacup in both hands, with the fire burning fiercely, I realise how hot I am, that I'm sweating. I put the cup down abruptly in the saucer, where it jitters into place, and I scrape my chair back from the hearth to be nearer Jan's. "You two were very close," I say softly.

Another pause. Jan's smile is bleak, hopeless.

"I loved her," she says. "I… loved her."

Ah. There it is.

The air in the centre of the room seems to shimmer. Almost to myself I say, "You and Sally Hendry, you were lovers."

Jan stiffens. "No need to sound surprised, Rose. Isn't it all the rage in London? Porthallen may seem like a rural backwater, but real people live here, you know, real people with real feelings."

I hadn't meant to put her on the defensive. "No, no, that's not what I—"

"Anyway, it was more a case of me loving her and her putting up with it." She is addressing the face on the sketch pad. "Always had to share you, didn't I? That was part of the deal." Then to me, "You know what they say about the grass on the other side. Well, Sal wasn't one for monogamy."

259

A bit of a goer… difficult to control… How many people had been in thrall to this woman? "That must have been hard for you."

"Took its toll, yeah. You saw what I used to look like in that photo. A real mess. In some ways I'm better off with her dead. She's all mine now."

In the hot room I shiver. Sally Hendry inspires passions beyond the grave. Carne still tends her garden. Mac denies her picture to avoid talking about her, and I've a pretty good idea now why he tries to…

"Oh, he wouldn't recognise her from *this*," Jan says.

How did she know what I was thinking? I could swear I hadn't spoken a word.

"Sally'd changed from the pretty schoolgirl he grew up with. Don't forget, Rose, Alec McConnell didn't move back here till a couple of years ago. He didn't know anything about Sal's life in the Eighties, about the woman she'd become. Professor High-and-Mighty McConnell!" There is deep scorn in her voice. "People got so excited, local boy made good, choosing to retire to the village where he'd grown up. Famous artist!" She spits the accolade from her cherry-red lips. "As if he was honouring Porthallen with his presence! He'd not been near the place for forty years."

If that's true, then maybe Mac didn't lie to me. Have I jumped to the wrong conclusions yet again? That Jan's intense dislike of the man springs from something more than parochial testiness, is clear.

"Carne told me Sally followed Mac to London, that she ran off to be with him because they were…"

Jan shrugs. "Perhaps she did. Childhood romance, schoolgirl crush. Who knows? It was a long time ago, Rose. More likely she was chasing dreams. She had

260

visions of sitting in a street café, scribbling poems on the back of a fag packet, arguing iambic pentameters with the literati. As an up-coming art student, Alec McConnell must have looked like her ticket to Paradise. But one thing I do know, whatever there was between them didn't last. Sal ended up as a trainee reporter on the Bristol *Evening Post*. She worked for a number of regional papers, and each move took further from London and closer to the South West."

"A journalist! So she did make a living as a writer?"

"Oh yes. And it was jolly handy when Peggy fell ill. She turned freelance, combined work with nursing her mum. Plus it left room for the poetry."

"She kept on writing poems, then?"

"You could say poetry was her life. Her one true love. Not Alec McConnell, that's for sure." Abruptly Jan stands up. "I need some air, Rose. Mind if we…?" and she rushes to the back door.

It's dark outside. Cold wind assaults my lungs and sends goose bumps racing over my bare skin. Pulling my cardigan tight across my chest, I bury my hands in its long, dangling sleeves. Lights from the cottage windows splash gold across the garden. Where the grass moves, quartz crystals in the stone wink on and off like a beacon.

Jan leads the way down the path until we're leaning against the wall, peering into the emptiness that is the field beyond. She cranes her head back to stare at the sky. "Perfect weather for fireworks," she says. "What a relief! The kids are so excited. Look, Rose! The Plough and, look, over there, oh, what's that one called?"

Tonight will be clear and sharp with, probably, a heavy frost, a night intensely black and pierced by a million stars. But I'm not here for astronomy.

"So, Sally… she never married, she never had any children?" Unsubtle, but I need to focus the conversation again.

"Just as bloody well, if you ask me." An unguarded response, barked into the air.

I must look surprised, because Jan graces me with an explanation.

"Far too wrapped up in herself, she was. She'd never have been able to cope with a family." The bark turns to a roar of laughter. "I can just imagine Sal with a parcel of kids. She'd have taken them to the supermarket then forgotten they were there and gone home without them."

"Your typical airy-fairy, absent-minded—"

"No, no, not really. Just, different priorities. As if there wasn't space inside her head for other people. Though she wasn't egotistical or anything like that, she wasn't 'up herself', isn't that today's ghastly expression? Well, she wasn't. She could be shy, uncertain sometimes. She was a complicated person, Rose, very intense, but often generous and warm and loving." Jan's voice softens. "Sometimes she was more like a child herself. Full of doubts and fears, always searching for something…"

"… she couldn't find?"

"No. Something she didn't believe existed. Not in this lifetime, anyway. Like Lancelot or Galahad. The perfect knight on a white charger who'd slay dragons to win her hand. The romantic ideal. She used to quote great chunks of the *Morte d'Arthur*. God, how desperately she wanted all that to exist. But instead she had to make do with imperfect mortals, like me. So she was constantly disappointed."

I notice Jan wipe her cheeks. Then she slaps them sharply, as if whipping them into line. "This is all getting too deep, Rose, and I'm turning into a block of ice. Let's get back to your nice warm fire. I'll have to be going soon."

There's a rustle of leaves, the atmosphere humming, singing. Jan turns in the direction of the sound. "Did you hear that? What was...? I think it came from over..." and she marches off, straight across the grass, heading directly into the path of the stone.

I shout a warning. "Careful. Watch out, there's a big—"

"It's all right, Rose. I know it's there. Quick, come and look at this. Here, can you see, it's a tiny... Oh, it's flown away." Across her palm lies a branch, thick with dark green leaves that sparkle with the first dusting of frost. "Do you think it was her, Rose? Do you think she was here, listening to us?"

"You know about this stone?" I hover beside it protectively.

"Of course I do. It's been here for years. That idiot Carne swears it's a grave, so he won't go anywhere near it. Ever wondered why he doesn't cut the grass down here?"

So Carne believes there's a grave. How interesting. So much for his story about leaving part of the garden to seed wild flowers. Already calculating how I can persuade him to tell me about it, I ask Jan, "Well, how else do you explain a lump of granite in the middle of the lawn?"

"Not you too, Rose. Has that silly old fool been bending your ear?" She blows into her cupped hands to warm them. "I expect it was moved from the field. Deliberately, I would imagine, to destroy the circle over there and break its power." Jan glances at her watch. "So many questions, Rose. Bit like the Spanish Inquisition this afternoon. And I've got to go. There's a firework party needs me." She strides towards Penmaris and I feel dismissed.

The old guy I met last week, Diggory Something, he'd talked about fear of the unknown causing people to desecrate what they don't understand.

And all along, Jan has known about the stone circle.

Chapter Twenty-Two

My alarm buzzes early. I scramble for the light switch, throw on jeans and jumper and stumble heavily down the stairs. I set the clock last night so I could be dressed and ready for when the septic-tank guy arrives, preferring not to be bleary-eyed in pyjamas when discussing drains. On reflection, perhaps it was not such a good idea. I function less and less well at break of day. I am becoming an owl.

Once tank-man has arrived, I think I'll drive into the village and do some shopping. Meanwhile, I rake the hearth, lay paper and sticks for a new fire, tidy round, return my sketchpad to the dressing table near my bed so Sally Hendry can watch out for me, go down and make tea, eat a wodge of leftover cake, which makes me feel like throwing up, swallow two aspirin, fidget about, pace the cottage, then suddenly remember HeCat. And yesterday's fireworks. Oh, crikey! He'd better be waiting outside the back door. I sweep him into my arms with relief. Bangs and whizzes had racketed all night, but he seems absolutely fine. I put down a bowl of Whiskas which he demolishes while I finish the washing-up from yesterday's tea-party.

Today marks the start of my fourth week at Penmaris. I feel as though I've lived here a long time. The cottage has become home. I speak the word out loud, tasting it on the air. Home. A mysterious, magical word. Four letters, one short syllable, the heart's ease. A word that has confused me for years yet now, to my astonishment, a word I understand. Here in Penmaris is where I want to be. My other existence in Clapham, with walks on the Common, endless bus queues, Starbucks coffee and West End theatres, seems disjointed and out of focus. Still there, of course, but like a once-familiar business suit that doesn't quite fit any more because it belongs to someone else. Though I realise I'll have to give serious thought soon to the hideous question of employment. To the business of earning my living. And to working alongside Ellie? No, not that. No way.

How can the daily grind possibly chime with life in Penmaris?

By mid-morning tank-man still hasn't come. Nor has he phoned to say he'll be late. With no way of contacting him, I don't know what to do. Wait or give up? He did tell me not to stay in specially, so maybe I should just get on with things. I must go the chemist's. I've been putting it off for days. Perhaps I'll avoid Porthallen altogether and drive to Helston, where I'm less likely to run into Mac. Our next encounter is bound to be embarrassing.

While I dither, HeCat ambles in, more of a swagger really, and sits hopefully in front of the cold grate.

266

"Not till this evening, HeCat."

But I switch the heater on for him. He settles down to wash, one careful paw flicking an ear, circling an eye, over and round in slow, hypnotic waves of pleasure. With his face turned away from me, the back of his head and neck curve to one side in a graceful arc exposing the soft vulnerability of his throat. Watching him, I have an idea. I grab pencil and paper and start to sketch the contours of his body, trying to capture before he moves away that exact pose, that particular quality of self-absorption in a task of pure physical delight.

Satisfied with the outline, I get up to fetch Sally's notebook. One of her poems describes a cat washing itself by the fire. I flick through the book till I find it. Yes, as I thought, an ode to feline beauty. With HeCat's help, I could illustrate this very poem and at the same time acknowledge Sally Hendry as my inspiration. I could bring Sally's cat to life as a portrait in oils. Now that *is* a good idea. Mac and Jan have used Sally's work for their own ends. Why shouldn't I combine my art with Sally's, and pay credit where credit is due? Just the other day Mac floated the suggestion of getting my work exhibited locally.

Ideas on the wind. Turning the page over, I jot down some crazy thoughts that gust around demanding to be taken seriously. Surely I can't really be considering…? But it would be a solution to a lot of problems.

As there's still no sign of tank-man, I grab my coat and car keys and set off. Lunch can wait because I feel impelled, as usual, by the need to *do* something, to expend the nervous energy fizzing inside before I can possibly settle to serious painting. First stop, Brian Bros

Autos. I haven't seen either of the guys since Halloween, last Tuesday. And I owe them.

Colm's greeting is warm. "Come on through, Rose. Mind that pool of grease." Grinning like a schoolboy he leads the way to the back office, past hoists and bits of engine and cables snaking the floor. "Derry's out chasing door panels at the breaker's yard. He'll be sorry to have missed you. Have a seat." Brushing his forearm over the top of a rickety stool, he motions for me to sit down.

I accept a mug of something hot and suspect. "I wanted to thank you for…"

"You. Are. A. Star. Fancy diving in like that and…"

"… all my wet things, my handbag…"

"Least I could do for the person who…"

"Can you believe it was nearly a week ago? I should have called round sooner."

He waves my apology aside. "Have you been to see Melanie?"

"Oh no. No." The idea hadn't occurred, and something makes me shy away from it.

"Derry'll be mad when he finds out…"

"Well, tell him…"

Colm mimes inspiration. "Got it! Drinks tonight at the Anchor. The three of us." I open my mouth to protest. "I won't take no for an answer. *We* won't take no for an answer. You absolutely have to come. Derry's paying!" Comfortable in his role, he looks smug.

"Okay. Thanks. That'll be nice."

We fix on eight o'clock, the phone rings, a customer arrives about an MOT, and I slip out. As I drive slowly down the lane, the church spire beckons above bare tree tops on the far side of the village green. When I wind the window down, I can hear the stream gurgling.

Only a week ago, feeling like yesterday, yet already long gone: the paradoxes of time, here in Porthallen. Far from linear – past, present, future – time feels ever-present, a cradle of possibility that rocks me to the rhythms of its unique beat.

Next stop, the bookshop to say "hi" to Jan. Nagged by feelings of guilt, I'd like to make amends for having exploited her yesterday. Then into Helston where I can stroll the High Street and still get home for some painting before meeting the Brians at the pub. At the back of my mind a plan is hatching, a possible long-term project that half-thrills, half-terrifies me in its daring.

The shop is empty of customers. How do places like this survive the long winter? What with summer-season trading and ebooks, it's a wonder there's any booksellers left in seaside towns. Jan is hunkered down in the children's section, clearing shelves. We exchange platitudes while I browse and Jan dusts, neither of us comfortable with the situation. After five minutes, I find my courage.

"I saw her," I say, replacing a paperback of crosswords and kneeling beside Jan, "on the beach one day during a storm at sea. I saw... something, someone... what I now believe was Sally Hendry. But... I don't know why... I left her out of my painting, because... well... because none of it was real. It never happened. There was no storm. It was more a sort of..." Jan stares at me. "I'm sorry, I'm not explaining this very well. I should have told you yesterday, but there's been a lot of... weird things going on."

Jan's usually wide, high forehead crumples. "It's not fair." She chokes back a sob. "I've tried so hard, Rose, everything I know, but I can't reach her. I can't get through to her. A whisper, a glimpse, that would be enough. I could live off that." More angrily she goes on, "Then out of the blue you arrive and straight away she…"

"I'm not trying to take her over, Jan. I didn't ask for any of this. It just sort of happened. It is happening, to *me,* and I'm desperately trying to make sense of it. Actually, I'm desperately trying to prove I'm not going mad." I lay a hand on Jan's arm. "Sorry about the interrogation tactics yesterday but, well, that's all I have, a load of questions. Questions I couldn't even *ask* most people, they'd think I was round the bend."

"Oh, you're not the first to see her. There's been others, other guests at the cottage, not many. The odd visitor complaining about a 'strange atmosphere' or 'funny noises at night'. So now rumour has it the place is haunted and certain members of our community are having a high old time whipping up ghost stories and having a good laugh."

I recall Mary Coleforth's veiled remarks the first time we met, and the odd looks she'd given me. But Jan had made comments too, equally prophetic. An outsider couldn't distinguish between motives.

Jan is hauling herself upright, pulling on the shelves as if her legs aren't strong enough. "I know all the theory," she says, sounding immensely tired, "I've got bags of interest, a lifetime's service to the cause, you might say, but… no gift, Rose, no natural gift." Her voice falters. "I can't actually *see*. Whereas you…"

"But everything you do seems intuitive, and… well, what about the soul cakes?"

"Coincidence. Stroke of luck." She sees my eyebrows shoot up. "Okay, maybe not, but… anyway…" A grin appears. "Enough! Enough of feeling sorry for myself." She brushes dust off her hands, sweeps tendrils of hair from her face. "Tell me about that storm, Rose. Please. Tell me anything and everything."

* * *

What the hell is going on? The drive is choked with cars. It's worse than Helston High Street where, in the end, I had to park illegally on double yellow lines and dash round the shops trying to outwit traffic wardens. Getting round Boots was like navigating Marble Arch at rush hour, with baby buggies the size of SUVs jamming the aisles and young mums crushed beneath industrial-sized packs of nappies.

Ratty, Rose. You're being ratty. Breathe.

So I take a very deep breath and nudge in behind Carne's Land Rover. The moment I open the car door I hear his voice raised in argument with another, which I assume to be that of septic-tank-man. His van heads the log-jam.

"Afternoon, Mr… erm?" I march forwards, expecting a reply. Rounding the side of the house, primed with a sarcastic *what time do you call this?* I'm silenced by the scene which greets me. The grass is littered with tools I can't identify, apart from a spade that Carne is in the process of wrestling from tank-man's grasp, the two men hanging on to their particular end and refusing to let go. As I approach, they turn towards me as if for mediation.

"Got a cracked pipe, lady. I need to take a proper look at the damage. Tree roots, I reckon."

"He can't go digging round here," Carne croaks. "Tell him." Wild-eyed, he swings on the spade handle.

"Get off, yer silly bugger."

"Carne, please. Mr… er… are you sure? Have you checked with Chris Benning?"

"You're not digging up my garden, you're not disturbing this ground."

"Phoned him twice, lady. He's given me the go-ahead, only…" Another tug on the spade.

"Well, that sounds… fine." I walk up to Carne and put a hand on his arm. "Let's go and have a cup of tea, shall we? Leave Mr… to get on with his job." Under my hand, Carne's forearm is a knot of muscles tensed with anger. The spade, finally wrenched loose, spins through the air and lands against the stone where it pings and bounces off into the bushes.

"He can't dig there." Carne's voice splinters, hoarse from shouting. "He can't dig there."

"I've brought some pipe with me, case I need to put a new section in. Been into the cottage, of course, checked all the…" The poor man seems at a loss to know what to say next. "So I'll just…" He eyes his antagonist warily in case Carne decides to pounce. "Don't worry about the lawn, I'll take the grass up real careful-like, lift it in turfs. You won't be able to see where I've been when I puts it back." He nods at Carne as if trying to placate a rabid dog.

Gripping him firmly by the elbow, I lead Carne away. He submits with surprising meekness, though I can feel him shaking. "I think we could both do with a cup of tea, and there's some leftover cake, you'll enjoy a piece."

Because he seems cowed and defeated I treat him like a child: park him on the kitchen stool while I put the kettle on, busy myself at the sink, maintain a steady stream of pointless chatter. From the window I have a clear view of the spade as it glints, sinks into the earth, turns, re-emerges.

Although I know exactly what Carne is afraid of, I can't rationally bring myself to act upon supposition. What possible reason could I offer tank-man to stop work? Besides, he's working for Chris Benning, not for me; I have no rights in the matter. Each time I glance out, I hope to see the spade veer off in a different direction. I trust the digging will end short of the stone, I hope the ground will yield nothing more sinister than a tangle of roots and rubble. A blocked pipe. For goodness sake, what else is he likely to find?

Turning my back on the garden, I start pouring tea.

"Sugar, Carne? Shall we go next door where it's more comfortable?" I'm feeling squeezed in this tiny space, the air thick with the sickly sweet smell of cake.

Carne accepts a mug in one hand and a plate in the other, resolutely remaining where he is.

"That stone's very old," he says, enunciating with care, reining in his emotions.

"Well, I guessed as much. It certainly looks as if… Fancy a slice of this? Jan Freeman made it." I slide a few thousand calories onto chipped china.

"Shouldn't be disturbed, that's the thing. Asking for trouble, what he's doing, you mark my words."

"Why's that, Carne?" I make a grab for his plate. The piece of cake is threatening to slip off. "Anyway, what does it matter? It's only a stone, a… a lump of rock." Playing devil's advocate, I'm goading Carne into spitting out what he's barely holding in. Either that, or I'm trying to convince myself I'm worrying about nothing.

Carne points to the keyhole and the back-door key, from which dangles a length of green garden twine. "That's my spare. I keeps it for Mr Benning, so I had to let 'im in."

"Of course you did. It's quite all right."

"Though if I'd known what 'e were planning."

"He'll put everything back when he's finished. He said so. Don't worry. And you can double-check tomorrow, make sure…"

"Be too late by then," he intones.

"Too late for what?" I try to catch his eye. "I wish you'd trust me, Carne. Can't you tell me what it is you're upset about?"

With his left hand, now free of crockery, he yanks his hat off and scratches his scalp. "That stone's there for a purpose." He crumples the hat between his fingers. "It's a marker, see. It marks… what's beneath. Under the ground."

"Okay. And what might that…?"

But before I can finish, Carne has jumped off the stool and brushed past me to the window. "Where's he gone now? I can't see what he's…"

There's a perfunctory knock and the back door swings wide.

"Think you better come and have a look at this, lady."

Chapter Twenty-Three

About a foot from the base of the stone is a shallow grave. The sewer pipe runs close by, as I can see from the trench already dug to uncover the drainage system.

A bundle lies partially wrapped in what must once have been thick cloth, now rotted, disintegrating and the colour of mud. The spade has scythed through the edge of the cloth, ripping it apart and exposing the contents, also wrapped in something finer, now just a tracery of fabric around bones.

I become aware of Carne behind me. His breath, in bursts, pumps over my neck as he cranes forwards to see.

"Now what am I s'posed to do about this, then?" A perplexed tank-man is rubbing his face over and over. "Not the usual sort of—"

A thin, high-pitched keening breaks from Carne, a sound not quite human. I turn to stare at him. He's rocking backwards and forwards on the spot, and his mouth hangs slack. A line of drool dangling from his bottom lip sways in time to his movements. The cry, so unexpected, draws attention away from the grave site which, momentarily, seems of lesser importance. I panic, not feeling up to the task of dealing, two days in a row, with extreme displays of emotion. My shoes seem to be gluing me to the ground while inside my head I am scrambling frantically to decide what to say or do. Behind me, Carne wails and groans. Then, as if to save me the bother of delicacy, tank-man bends down and grabs one of the bones, which he holds aloft. He opens his mouth to speak, when a commotion near the house causes us all to spin round.

"Rose? What on earth's going on out here?"

Clipped feet stride around the corner of the cottage and march towards our huddle on the lawn: Oliver – startling us all into looking guilty.

As one accustomed to dealing with such bizarre situations on a regular basis, Oliver extends his right arm towards tank-man.

"Oliver Marshall. Pleased to meet you. And you are?"

"Bill Fitzgerald, Mr Marshall. I'm here to…"

Goddammit. How does he do that? I watch the two men shaking hands like old friends, but not before Bill, as I must now learn to call him, has emptied his of the piece of skeleton it was holding. The bone drops quietly to the grass. Seething, I'm forced to acknowledge Oliver's superior skills. Ten seconds, and he already has the guy's full name.

"Well, well, well, what have we here?" Oliver elbows his way to the edge of the grave and hunkers down to get a good look.

276

"I was repairing that pipe down there," Bill begins, "and I—"

"You came across this interesting little find." Oliver peers into the earth, then stands up and walks around the perimeter, kicking at the grass and occasionally stamping the ground with his expensively shod foot.

"Oliver!" I hiss. "What are you doing here?"

He ignores me. "Makes me wonder if there's any more." He starts scraping away at a patch of bare earth.

"How can you possibly say such a dreadful thing? Isn't one enough?" I can't believe he just said what he said. I can't believe he's actually here.

Carne's wail has diminished to a whimper. Oliver seems content to ignore him too, and is preoccupied pacing the ground. "Pet cemetery is what I'm thinking," he says. "If there's one, then why not more?"

"Pet cemetery?"

"Yeah. Family cats and dogs. What else would you want to bury? Rabbits, I s'pose. Hamsters? Tommy the tortoise? That looks like cat to me."

"We thought it was a…" My voice fades to a whisper.

"Oh, Rose, honestly! Get real!"

These are the first words he's actually addressed to me. And they're full of that familiar tone of exasperation. I want to kick him.

"For goodness sake, Rose, when are you ever going to…?" And then he stops in mid-sentence, perhaps because this is too much, perhaps because three pairs of eyes, heavy with their private emotions, swivel in his direction and glare at him. I hope it's also because he's suddenly remembered why he drove all the way down

277

to Cornwall at the start of the working week and exactly how I'm currently feeling about him.

"Reckon you could be right," Bill offers, breaking the awkward moment. "A cat or a dog." He picks up the skull which he tosses from one hand to the other, weighing possibilities.

"Well, if you like, I could go and… I've got my laptop in the car." Is this his version of pouring oil?

A murmur drones from close to my feet. "All these years, Sal, all these years…" Oliver shoots me a confused look, but I shake my head and bend down beside Carne, who is kneeling, fingering tiny fragments, the fragile remains of a rib cage, leg bones, what upon calm reflection could be nothing other than a tail. His lament shivers the air.

I try to be gentle. "Come on, let's go. Let's leave Bill to finish up here. It'll be dark soon."

"And don't you worry, lady. If I find any more, I'll collect them all together, in this box, see? And I'll put them all back when I'm done." Poor Bill, he wasn't expecting any of this. "I'd better get a wriggle on, though. I'll have to come back tomorrow if I lose the light."

I nod in assent.

"She laughed at me." Carne is leaning on me for support as he hauls himself upright. "When I told her I'd stand by her, see her right, she just laughed, said I were old-fashioned." Abandoning the grave and its contents for Bill to deal with, he shuffles towards the far end of the garden as though wading through a dream. I flap a hand to dismiss Oliver and turn to follow Carne.

Spade in hand once more, Bill calls out, "Mind you, I would be quite interested to know whether…"

"I'll get on the Internet, straight away," Oliver says. "Shouldn't take a minute. Anyone fancy a drink?" His words are swallowed up in the light mist gathering, and he walks off to his car.

* * *

"You thought same as me, didn't you, Rose? That it were a baby?"

We're leaning on the wall, staring into space. Behind us, the sound of digging. Every few seconds, Carne rubs his eyes as if to wipe away painful images from the past. I decide to confess.

"Remember I found those photos? That one of you and… everyone on the beach? Well, I found some unused baby clothes too. In a box in the attic. And at night I keep hearing these strange…" No point in going there. "Anyway, I started jumping to conclusions and, well, looks like I got it wrong."

"Makes two of us."

"Why did you…?"

"We'd been sleeping together, that last summer, till she upped and went off with 'im." The degree of loathing invested in that one small word makes me wonder how Carne has tolerated Mac's recent return to the village. "I wasn't messing with her, mind you. I was serious. I wanted to marry 'er, proper like, have a proper family. I loved her, not like… I weren't gonna get her into trouble. Promised 'er I'd stand by 'er if she… you know..." I nod. "But she went off anyway."

"And you were worried all the time that she might be… pregnant?"

"She came home for Christmas. Round as a turnip, she were. So naturally I assumed… But she just laughed and said I didn't know what I was talking about, that I hadn't got a clue."

"And then what?"

"She came back again, in spring. I knew she were there," Carne glances behind him at Penmaris, as if seeking confirmation, "but Jack and Peggy wouldn't let me in. Said she didn't want to see nobody. Said she were ill, she'd come home for a rest, and we was all to leave her be."

Carne's devotion became obsession. Denied access to the woman he adored, he virtually camped out in the field at the bottom of the garden, peering over the wall for glimpses of Sally. He hoped to catch her outdoors one day so he could talk to her, plead with her, offer to help if she would let him. But that was the trouble. Sally refused to have anything to do with him. And the idea that she might be seriously unwell had been terrifying.

"One night Jack comes out and starts digging. Few minutes later Peggy comes out with an arm round Sal, real tight, sort of holding her together, like she'd crumble otherwise." I hold my breath, hardly daring to believe Carne is finally confiding in me. "Sal had this bundle she were carrying in her arms. Cradling it, you know, like you'd cuddle a new-born baby? And it were wrapped in something white that trailed on the ground. Matter of fact, she tripped over it once." Nearly a laugh at the memory. Carne wipes his eyes, but he can't erase the details.

"You had a clear view, then?"

"Clear enough. From behind that tree over there." He points. "Your eyes adjust, you'd be surprised how much you can see at night, if you try." Carne falls silent, lost to memory. Then he says, "She were crying, real hard. She were so upset she could barely walk. And she hugged that lifeless bundle to her breast, tight, but gentle and loving. She hugged it like it... I was so sure it were a..." He chokes on the words. "Silly sod. I really thought she were carrying our dead baby." A hand dashes the tears away. "What a bloody fool. They're right, the lot of 'em, I'm just a bloody old fool."

A rectangle of bright light startles the gloom. Oliver emerges from the side of house carrying his open laptop, its screen pouring forth dazzle. "Here you go, Bill." He marches across the lawn sounding pleased with himself. "Let's have another butchers at that skull. There, see that, see what I mean?"

Bill looks from skull to diagram and back again, nodding vigorously. "Exact match," he proclaims, sounding like an excited schoolboy. "You were right. It's definitely a cat. It's a cat," he calls out to Carne, waving the skull triumphantly. "Nothing to worry about, just a cat."

"And I'm just an idiot," Carne mumbles.

Oliver is patting the side of his computer like a proud owner rewarding his dog for performing tricks. "Never takes long to get answers nowadays. Don't know how we managed before Google."

"That's a fancy bit of equipment you've got there," Bill says. Admiration for electronics has trumped mere bones. From my vantage point by the wall, I can almost see him salivating. "I have enough trouble getting a signal on my mobile round here."

"Ever heard of Wi-Fi?" Oliver warms to his theme. "Signals are in the gigahertz range. The aerial in this thing runs right round the screen, so it picks up far more effectively than those tiny pencil-aerials they use on phones."

"Pricey though, I bet."

"Well, depends on your needs. Horses for courses in this business." Oliver is pressing keys and putting the laptop through its paces. I might not exist.

Rage makes me quiver as I stride over.

Bill is shaking his head from side to side. "That's amazing, that is. Look at the quality of them graphics. See that, lady? Cor, just look at that!"

"Be amazed, Mr Fitzgerald. Be truly amazed. This is a top-of-the-range, up-to-the-minute multi-squiggabyte market leader. This machine can communicate with the outer spiral arm of the galaxy. Forget your signal problems in remotest Cornwall; Oliver gets emails from Alpha Centauri, don't you, dear?"

Oliver and I glare at one another. In the vacuum of silence which descends, Bill Fitzgerald scuttles back to his broken pipe.

After what seems like a long time I spit out, "Why don't you go and put the kettle on? I'll be in in a minute."

"What have I done wrong now?"

"Just bugger off, Oliver. Go inside, will you?"

Without waiting for an answer, I turn on my heels and walk back to Carne.

"Sorry about that. Listen, Carne, there's nothing you can do here. Why don't you go home? You'll be more comfortable in your own front room. It's getting cold and dark. I reckon Bill'll still be at it tomorrow morning." I encourage him towards the house. "Come round after lunch and you can check the garden's back the way it should be. I bet there'll be some tidying up to do. You can check everything's... the way you want it."

Carne is tugging his red hat over his ears. "It don't change nothing, mind. He's still... *violated* my garden." A loud and deliberate choice of word that conjures images of abuse, defilement, pain. "My Sal's special place."

"I'm really sorry, Carne, I'm really sorry you've been so upset. What a god-awful day this has turned out to be. But now at least... well, perhaps that particular sorrow can heal." I pat his arm. "You might feel differently about things in a few days." Platitudes, that's all I have to offer. Useless platitudes.

"Huh!"

"Anyway, I'd better go and chat to Oliver. He's driven all the way down from London to see me, so I ought to..." What? Wring his neck? Engage in more pointless words? "See you tomorrow, Carne. Take care."

Chapter Twenty-Four

Slumped in an armchair, Oliver looks grim. We've just been playing musical motors to let Carne's Land Rover escape from the drive. "You're very thick with the natives," he grunts.

To which I retort: "Hallo, Rose. Hallo, Oliver. How are you, Rose? Actually, I'm feeling bloody awful, since you ask." I collapse into the chair opposite. The coffee table, occupying neutral territory, referees the space between us. "God, Oliver, I really am. I'm knackered. What an afternoon! I could do with a large gin."

"Sure." He's up and scanning the room. "Where do you keep…?"

My laugh startles him.

"What's so funny?"

"I don't actually have any booze in the house." Except the Courvoisier Mac brought but, hey, that's different.

"Oh, come on, Rosie! You must have the odd bottle stashed away."

That does it. Something about his tone, that expectation of normal service being resumed. Cold fury rises, alongside a tide of hysteria. I want to smack him in the face. "I doubt you're going to believe this, but I actually poured all the bloody boo…" anger makes me stumble, "I poured all the booze down the sink the other morning. After I heard *from Paula*."

Oliver shifts his gaze.

"Yeah, that's right. Paula. She saw Ellie at our bedroom window. I bet you didn't know that, did you? From her garden, she saw you. You and *her*, my dear friend Ellie Carter. Paula knows, Oliver. *She knows*. Does *everyone know*?" The question squeezed from between my lips, I sink back in the chair as Oliver sits down again.

"I could drive to the pub? A drink might help—"

"No, no, no! You don't get it." I'm shouting and Oliver throws his hands in the air. "I've given up, Oliver. No more drink." I take a number of measured breaths, fighting the impulse to explode. "New Year's Resolution. I came to the conclusion it was about bloody time."

Oliver frowns. "But it's November."

I gawp at him, then clap a hand over my mouth. I have to hold it back, the hysteria that wells up and bubbles through my veins like the champagne I can't risk drinking. I'm shaking with laughter. As I gawp and choke and splutter and stare, it's as though I'm seeing Oliver for the first time. I hadn't imagined this. Not a month ago in London, stunned outside our bedroom door, nor the other day waiting in this very chair for the phone that never rang, not even this morning waking from another wretched night of missing him and hating myself, not one single minute since catching him with Ellie had I anticipated this: that I would be laughing. Belting him about the head with *Old Kernow: Myths and Legends*, maybe. Scratching his face and clawing his eyes out. Screaming and yelling.

But not laughing. Laughing because somehow it didn't seem to matter any more.

My hands fall quietly to my lap. "You are a prat, Oliver. An utter prat. What I'm trying to say is, I need to sober up. I need to start seeing things as they really are. Not through a haze of gin. Booze has been one of my problems, or at least the cause of—"

"I'm sorry, Rose." His words blurt out as if they can't wait any longer. "I'm truly, truly sorry." He stretches across the table, making a lunge for me. "No pathetic excuses. No crap. I got lonely and I let myself be tempted. I'm so sorry, my darling. It's not Ellie's fault, it's all my—"

I scrape hair from my eyes. Shake my head. "I don't care about—"

"It's all down to me, I know it is. And I know I've hurt you and I'm so, so sorry. Oh Rosie, Rosie, I've been desperate, wanting to talk to you. You just drove away and I spent all night wondering where you were. I was out of my mind, Rose. I didn't know where you'd gone at first, if you were all right. You know how you sometimes…? I was so scared, Rose, I forgot all about this damned place, I couldn't figure out where you'd gone, I just panicked. I thought you might do something… silly."

286

"Oh, so it's my fault, is it? How unreasonable of me, causing you so much trouble." Angry now, I grab the book off the coffee table, its reassuring weight a ballast in my fingers.

"You know that's not what... Rosie! Look at me, will you? Put that book down!" He tries to take my hands, finds one of them. "I love you," he says. "Rosie, please. Please forgive me. I was a bloody fool. It won't happen again. I swear it. You know I love you." When I fail to respond, he begs. "Come home with me, Rose, where you belong. I've missed you so much. Everyone's missed you. Let's go home. Let's get back to our life together."

"You think I can just pick up again where I left off? Working all day with Ellie and living with you? The two people who betrayed me?"

"Well, we could go away for a while, how about that?" He's improvising. "Grab some time together, just you and me. A holiday. Chance to talk. Anywhere you like so long as it's warm and sunny. Get you away from this dismal place." He glances round the room which, in semi-darkness and sub-zero temperatures, scowls back with icy contempt. "I work too hard, I know I do. That's been one of the reasons why... I know I need to set more time aside for us. For you. And I will. Please, Rosie. Please give me another chance."

I'm not used to hearing him plead. I never expected to. I get up and switch the fan heater on, creating a pause in which to compose my thoughts. "How can I go back, Oliver? For a start, I've no job to go back to." He protests that at once. "No, no, it's too late. I've made my mind up. I'm resigning. I'll write to Ellie next

287

week. Sod two months' notice and severance pay. She'll be lucky if I don't use poisoned ink."

"Okay, well, that shouldn't be a problem," he stammers. "You can easily find another—"

"She was my *best friend*."

"Oh, sweetheart…"

"And us. You talk about *us*. What *us*?"

"How can you even ask me that?" Oliver seems to pale visibly, and I am struck by how thin and drawn his face looks, shadowed with dark smudges that stand out like bruises against his waxy skin.

I draw the heater up to his chair, then retreat to my own.

"Oliver, I can't make plans yet. I'm not ready. I'm not really sure what I'm going to do. There's a lot of… unknowns."

He frowns again. "I don't get it. All the way down here, I thought you'd bombard me with questions, put me through the wringer demanding to know every single gory detail. But you're so distant, you don't seem… very interested." Oliver is struggling with the concept of doubt. "You do still love me, Rosie, don't you?"

"Oh, Oliver!"

"What? It's not so hard. Yes or no."

"There's a saying, isn't there? About having to love yourself before you can love anyone else."

"That's a cop-out."

"No, it's not, it's not. I'm trying to explain, if you'll just listen. I want to explain. I didn't even know I was thinking any of this till…"

288

What a strange afternoon. I'm no longer sure what's real and what isn't. Words speak themselves; I grant them space.

"I've spent most of my life doing what other people expected of me, because I had no idea who I was or what I wanted. Parents, teachers, everyone else's plans for my life. And the one time I tried to be independent I got it spectacularly wrong."

"Christ, Rose. You're not still hung up on that French creep, are you?"

"I'm not talking about Jean-Yves. I'm talking about me."

"Bloody bohemian, drug-crazed nutter. It was years ago, for God's sake. You got in with the wrong crowd. It happens. Get over it! When are you ever going to stop fixating on that one stupid incident?" His voice rises. Unable to sit still, he leaps from his chair and storms to the other end of the room where he comes face to face with my painting. The surprise, or perhaps the art, has a salutary effect and he calms down. "Blimey, Rose. This is good. I didn't realise you were… " He sounds almost contrite. "Sorry. Carry on."

"Because I couldn't handle what happened in Paris, I scuttled back to Mum and Dad and sort of buried my head. Like a kid hiding under the blankets, afraid of the big bad wolf." When I realise what I'm going to say next, I almost falter. "That was you, Oliver. One of the blankets."

"Christ, Rose."

"Settling in London, getting my first job, meeting you, the posh house, the lifestyle, all those things… I was acting a part someone else had written for me. And feeling just that little bit safer each time I got my lines

289

right. But I'd caved in, hadn't I? I'd caved in under the pressure of expectations – what *you* wanted, the life Mum and Dad envisaged for me – playing safe, heaping more and more blankets over my head to keep the wolf at bay."

"We all make compromises. It's part of growing up."

"Don't lecture me on grown-up behaviour."

He has the grace to look abashed. "What I mean is, we're always playing different roles, aren't we? Fitting in, trying to find our place."

"But it wasn't me. *Isn't* me. Down here, in Cornwall, I've started to find out who I am – it's only taken thirty-two years – who I am and what sort of life I actually want to lead, what makes me happy. I'm even learning to forgive myself. I can't go back to hiding under those blankets. You must see that."

"So you don't love me. You never did. Is that what you're saying? That I was just… convenient?"

We look at one another, horrified.

I stumble on. "I wanted to talk to you last week. I nearly caught a train home. I'd rehearsed this little speech, I had it all prepared. Then Paula phoned and…" I discover that I'm on my feet, standing near the kitchen. We're about as far apart as it's possible to be within the confines of Penmaris. "You're right, about putting the whole France mess behind me, and I think I can now. There's this little girl in the village, she's called Melanie and she… well, I was going to tell you about Melanie when I got home, about what happened to her."

"And were you going to stay?"

A beat. "Oh, I don't know. Yes, at first I was. I think I was. I honestly believed we could sort everything out and start again, but then Paula…" I lean against the wall for support. "I don't know. Hell, I don't know. I'm so sorry, Oliver. I'm sorry I used you, because I lacked courage. I suppose that's what it comes down to. You and my crappy job and our great mansion of a house – it's crazy, Oliver, that place is crazy. All those rooms, for two people! Like props in the pantomime that was supposed to be my life."

"That mansion you're pouring scorn on was intended to be our family home, for us and our children. I lost a baby too, Rose, or had you forgotten?"

I bite back the retort – you don't understand, you're not listening…

"So you'd rather be down here," he sneers, "with village idiots, dodgy drains, no heating and not enough room to swing a cat? This," his arm sweeps the cottage in mockery, "makes you happy, does it?"

I wish I knew. I think so. It may not be the answer, but it feels like a step on the way.

"You don't mean that," I protest. "They're not village idiots. You're hurting right now, and I'm sorry, I'm *sorry, all right?* I'm sorry."

* * *

Steep hills, winding lanes, potholes. I'll twist an ankle if I'm not careful, and my second bid for independence will end before it's started. I force myself to take care as I pound the streets of Porthallen in the dark.

Told you before, Rose. Stop apologising for existing.

It feels as though I've done little else recently: *I'm sorry* – my personal mantra. Well, let today be an end

291

to it. Mac's right, I've done nothing for which to feel guilty.

A left turn at the end of this track, then I'll be on the home straight. The path takes me past the rear of Carne's smallholding, alongside a copse of trees beyond which hangs the outline of Mac's studio. The lights are on.

For several hours I sat through Oliver venting months of pent-up anger. It's true, I have been a poor companion, an unloving lover this last year. He's quite right; he has plenty to complain about. Locked inside my own misery, there was no space for anyone else. But now I've cracked the door open, and to my surprise a different landscape beckons, borne upon a salty wind. SW4 and red buses and urban angst lie far away. Against all reason, right here is where I want to be.

I didn't exactly say I was leaving him, but I implied it. Perhaps I also offered the consolation of hope: it's too soon to decide… I need more time… let's wait and see… I'll phone you…

In my stomach, a queasiness; I think I might throw up. But in my head a cold wind blows. I knock on the door.

"Ah, Rose! The lovely Rose. A Rose by any other name."

Mac is pissed. When he lurches towards me, I instinctively recoil. Second-hand alcohol rolls over me in waves. Beneath the studio lights, daggers flash in his eyes. Then some sixth sense kicks in because he changes in a flash and ushers me to one of the battered armchairs as though he's shepherding an invalid. "You all right, Rose? Coffee? Beer? Something stronger?"

"Nothing, really."

"You sure you're…? Only you look…"

"Really. I'm fine. I wanted to ask you…"

He plonks down opposite, all concern. "Ask away, ask away."

"Last week you said something about helping me get my work exhibited, here in Cornwall. Did you mean it? Is there a chance I could…?"

His eyes gleam. "*Yes*! Yes, of course I meant it." Then, "No guarantees, though. The general public's bloody fickle. I can't turn you into an overnight success. You never know with the great unwashed. Loads of blood, sweat 'n tears."

Is he backtracking already? "So you don't think I…?"

"It's not up to me, Rose, 'sall about what *you* think, what you want. And if you want it enough, if you're prepared to take risks." He lights a cigarette. "Sure I can't get you anything?" He stands up, pulls the cork from a half-empty bottle of red on his desk and takes a long swig before carrying bottle plus dirty glass back to his chair. "But I'll do everything I can to help, swear to God." He sloshes wine into the glass and over the floor.

"Good," I say, "that's good."

"Do I take it from your question there's been a change of plans?"

I shake my head. Sit quietly. Then, after a long pause, "Tell me about Sally Hendry."

* * *

At last Mac relents. "Yeah, okay, so we had a fling. I was home for the long summer vac and she was… around." He laughs. Wine has loosened his tongue. "All over me, in fact, gagging for it. Wasn't me, though, so

293

much as my coat tails. Sal was a hanger-on, a… whadder-they-call-'em? A groupie? Chasing the art scene, the bright lights. She thought I was her ticket to freedom. When I went back in the autumn, she followed me. Wasn't my idea, I can assure you. I had a life to get on with, university, girl friends, stuff. Last thing I wanted was Sal butting her nose in. But she had this fantasy about living in London, doing the whole Sixties thing down the King's Road, being hippy and arty and cool." Mac empties the supermarket plonk, then squints down the neck of the bottle to check. "Had a thing about my beard, too. She liked hairy men." Stroking his grizzled barb, he grins suggestively at me.

So, Sally had been sleeping with both of them. Porthallen's two likely lads. "Carne was heartbroken," I say. "Did you know he'd asked Sally to marry him that summer? He'd even convinced himself she was pregnant."

I tell Mac about the grave we found in the back garden, about the state Carne is in, the fears he's been carrying around half a lifetime. "Why did Sally come home so soon, why wouldn't she see him, what was the matter with her?"

"Sulking, I expect," Mac says. "Jealous. Disappointed. Pissed off."

"Jealous?"

"She was too wild for me, I tell you, I didn't want to get involved. Not long term. She was always gonna cause trouble and fuck my life up."

"But you said *jealous*. Of who?"

Mac heaves a sigh. "You are tena… tena… You don't give up, do you, Rose? Give you that one. Like a

294

little terrier. You even have the nose for it." He tries tapping the end of his, misses mostly.

"Well?"

"Well… she found out I was having an affair with Grace." I look blank and Mac cackles. "Ah. Now there's something you've not managed to winkle out, Miss Marple."

I grant him a moment's triumph. "Go on then, spill. Who the hell was Grace?"

A ghost of sadness slips by. "Grace Hendry. Sally's sister." He attempts to light another cigarette, fumbles with the lighter. "No love lost between 'em, I can tell you. Grace hated Sal for being the much-adored baby of the family, Sal hated Grace even more for being her bossy big sister." Flicking the cheap Zippo impatiently, he finally catches a flame, touches it to the tip of his cigarette and inhales deeply. "Though not enough to avoid rocking up on Grace's doorstep demanding a place to stay."

"In London, you mean?"

He nods. "Grace had a flat in the East End. She was working for Save the Children, or Save the World. I dunno. Some such. Anyway, Sal assumed she could crash there for a few months, till she got on her feet. What she didn't realise, of course, was that she'd crashed straight into the middle of our little… of us, me and Grace."

"What, she had no idea? Her own sister?"

"Nope. Not at first. We'd kept it all very hugger-mugger. I'd bumped into Grace earlier that year, some exhibition in the V&A, it was. Just one of those chance encounters – I'd completely forgotten she was living in London. Things got pretty intense pretty quick. Like they do when you're a student. Grace was adamant we tell no one, especially not the folks back in Cornwall. She wanted the two halves of her life as separate as possible."

"Then Sally arrived and found out?"

"Bloody ridiculous it was, us trying to keep it under wraps, what with Sal camped out in the middle. We were skulking round like naughty school kids, it was never gonna work. I dunno exactly when Sal twigged, but at some point we knew we'd been rumbled. Then piece by piece, we started uncovering all the nasty little goings-on, all the mind games she was playing with us, trying to break us up. Scheming, manipulative bitch." He spits tobacco off his tongue. "Like I said, Sally Hendry was trouble. Reckon Carne had a lucky escape. Though he'll never see it that way."

"So you're sure there was no baby, no—"

"Enough with the babies, Rose! Jesus Christ! I thought you said you'd unearthed a cat's skeleton? Sally Hendry was a bitch, not a baby killer."

But it's hard to stop the pictures coming: a box lovingly packed with tissue paper, shiny ribbons threaded through white bootees, a knitted shawl.

"Read my lips, okay? No baby. Well, not as far as I know. Not by me or by Carne or by any of the other countless men she screwed. In all senses of the word. She fucked with people's lives, Rose. And now she's fucking with your head."

I need to move. I stand up, start to drift round the studio. "So what happened to Grace?"

Mac slumps in his chair. "No idea. And that's the truth. After Sal did her worst, there was no way Grace and I could patch things up. It all fell apart, like a house of cards. Within a few months Grace found another job and moved away. Then Sal buggered off and I shut the door once and for all on Porth-sodding-allen."

Now that isn't exactly true. The itch of curiosity prickles again. "Yet here you are, in your retirement, settled back in the village. And despite what you've said, despite how much Sally hurt you, you're planning to include one of her poems in your new book." Last time I raised this topic, Mac had gone ballistic. But I'm not doing apologies any more, and our relationship has changed. "It is her poem, isn't it? Because, remember, I found the original, in her handwriting? That book I found in the attic at Penmaris."

Walking over to Mac's desk, I remove the paperweight anchoring his manuscript and flick through the top few sheets. It must be here somewhere; he jammed it in between these pages: Mac's drawing, with Sally's poem on the back.

Mac throws his hands in the air. "She sent me the bloody poem, if you must know. After she'd ripped through my life like a fucking tornado then moved on. It might have been her idea of a joke, I s'pose, or else she was rubbing my nose in it. We'd been there, that's the point, we'd been to Mên-an-Tol one night during that mad summer, high as kites on LSD. Or p'raps it was…? Oh, I dunno. Something that blows your brains out, I don't remember any more." He pauses. "That was where we first…" He pushes me to one side, opens the desk drawer and pulls out the two sheets of paper clipped together. "Like she was staking a claim on me, like she bloody owned me and I'd never be free of her." He thrusts the pages at me.

My eyes fall on the last verse, which I read out loud.

297

Let the granite slabs berate me,
intimidate me and my fond imaginings,
the lingerings, the long gone rememberings;
once you and I were there
and thus will always be
you and me, somewhere.

Mac snorts. "Bloody mumbo jumbo. She used to say things like 'the imprint of desire on stone'. Oh, and the classic 'can you feel the vibrations?' She was into all that daft occult stuff." Mac is busy opening another bottle of wine. Cheap, with a screw cap, hinting desperation. "I came across the poem last year when I was unpacking boxes after the move. It's as simple as that. I thought I could use it in the book, exorcise a few ghosts."

"What, forty years on?" I find his *simple as that* explanation rather hard to swallow. "And you're the one who scoffs at Carne for carrying a torch!" I put the poem down and go over to the sink. "I'm making a coffee. Fancy a cup?" He looks wrecked and suddenly older. "You really don't need any more booze, Mac. Have a hot drink." Advice that sounds sanctimonious, so I add, "Trust me, I'm an expert." I turn the tap on hard to block out the glug-glug of wine he's pouring, its swirl into the glass, its promise of oblivion. How confidently I announced to Oliver my good intentions.

Mac is saying, "… see how you can possibly compare me with that silly old fart. He acts like Sally Hendry belongs to him. Like he owns the damned cottage, turning the garden into a bloody shrine. He spends more time at Penmaris than he does working his

298

farm which, let me tell you, is going to hell in a handcart. You should hear Mary give him an earful…"

I place a large mug of coffee in front of him, which he ignores and tops up the plonk. Bleary-eyed, stumbling, a shock of hair over his face, he seems to fill the studio with anger. Time is supposed to heal. That's what they say. But neither Carne, nor Mac, nor even Jan have found much peace from the passage of years.

Collecting my things together, I prepare to leave. A discreet withdrawal seems appropriate. If Mac is going to get maudlin and drink the night away, he'll be better left to himself. As for me – oh, bugger! I was due at the Anchor twenty minutes ago. With a swift "good bye" I open the door with one hand and pull my coat on with the other. Mac doesn't seem to notice. The sudden gust of wind sets flights of metal birds chattering in the air above his head.

* * *

Forced to park at the wrong end of the street, I leap from the MG and start walking quickly towards the pub, faking energy I don't have. I feel exhausted after running from Mac's back to Penmaris for the car, then driving too fast round dark country lanes. I'd like nothing better than to crawl under a duvet and go to sleep. A pulse is thumping in my head like drumsticks pounding a message which I'm too shattered to understand. I must be at least an hour late by now. Leaning against the wall outside the Anchor is the distant figure of a man, slouched in an attitude of extreme boredom, waiting. Colm Brian, perhaps.

But instead of hurrying faster, I notice my feet are slowing to a stop. Then they refuse to budge at all. Inside my head, a drum still beating.

Like he owns the damned cottage. The phrase tom-toms on my skull.

In my bag I locate my mobile, which works. I punch numbers.

You're not digging up my garden. I hear his voice clearly. He actually said *my garden.*

"Hi, Paula, it's me."

"Rose! Are you all right?" Paula sounds anxious. "Have you seen Oliver yet? What's happening?"

Get access from the key holder if I need to.

"I'm fine. Really, I'm fine. Listen, Paula, this might seem like an odd question, but—"

"What? What's wrong?"

"Nothing. Well… I… Listen, have you got the deeds to Penmaris?"

"What?"

"You know, the deeds to the cottage. Have you got them at home somewhere, in the safe, or in a desk, I don't know, somewhere…?"

There's a confused silence. "Er, no, I don't think so. I imagine they're lodged with our solicitor, along with all the other—"

"Have you ever actually seen them?"

"What on earth are you on about, Rose? I'm not with you."

"Well, like, did you have to sign official papers when you bought Penmaris?" I'm starting to sweat.

"No, Chris did all that. Officially it's his house. He bought the place. Siphoned off a bit of business money, between you and me, you know how these things work, darling, one doesn't ask too many questions. I always leave the boring legal stuff to Chris. Why?"

Mr Benning and me, we've got an understanding.

The figure outside the pub waves. I semaphore talking-on-my-mobile.

"Paula, do you think you could get hold of the deeds? Ask to have a look at them? You could go and see your solicitor and make up some reason why you needed to check… like, erm, some detail about… about property boundaries, or… something." I recall Mum and Dad once doing battle about the precise extent of their back garden and a neighbour's fence.

"But why?"

"I'm probably being daft, but…" My confidence is ebbing away. "On the other hand, it might just be important. And you must go on your own, you mustn't say anything to Chris."

"Rose. Are you sure you're all right?"

"Please, Paula, bear with me. Go and check the deeds, will you? Will you do that, for me?"

"Bit cloak and dagger, darling."

"I know. But will you? Please? Then get back to me?"

From the other end of the phone come strange noises; the line crackles. Outside the pub, the lounging figure peels itself off the pebbledash and starts to saunter my way.

"Trust me, Paula, and thanks." I'm shouting above the crackle and hoping Paula can still hear. "Got to go now. Bye." Stuffing the mobile in my pocket, I run up the road. "Sorry, Colm. I know I'm late."

He's tapping his watch. "We started without you. Reckon it must be your round by now. Mine's a pint of best."

Chapter Twenty-Five

Halfway along the cliff path between Penmaris and Porthallen Bay is a large boulder roughly shaped like an armchair. Affording wide unbroken views of sea and sky, this is a favourite spot when I go walking on the cliffs. In summer it must be a sun trap, a place to doze and get a suntan at the same time. Even on cold days, tucked snugly into the rock face, it offers shelter from which to daydream.

I'm sitting here sketching. Well, that's the theory. In fact, the A4 pad is gaping open on my knees while I gaze idly into the distance. *Sometimes I sits and thinks, and sometimes I just sits* – Dad's joke, told in his all-purpose country-bumpkin accent, usually followed by that quote about having no time to stand and stare. Well, today all I can manage is to sit and stare.

Tank-man arrived sharp at nine o'clock as promised, declaring he'd have to work *like billyoh* to get the job done; apparently it's going to rain later. After an hour or so of peering through the kitchen window at him, I'd had enough. The grass looked like the Somme, and I dread to think what will happen if the heavens do open. Rather than stay and watch, I grabbed a few things and set off trusting, though not entirely convinced, that on my return the garden will be back to normal. Something about Bill Fitzgerald fails to inspire, but I'm probably misjudging the poor man.

Overhead, flights of seagulls scoop the sky. I wonder what Paula is doing at this precise moment. Did she dismiss last night's call as madness? Or is she even now sitting in her solicitor's office in earnest conversation. Or flirting with him, which is more likely. He's doubtless an old friend and they'll be on first-name terms and Paula will gush and twitter and bamboozle, at least until she gets her hands on the deeds. Or doesn't, if Chris has lodged them elsewhere. Or if Chris never bought Penmaris in the first place. I have only suspicions and Jan telling me I'm psychic – which is just a word. It doesn't explain anything.

Bloody mumbo jumbo.

The flock of gulls dwindles to the horizon, leaving a trail on the inner eye – like the logic of what Mac said yesterday. At least his story now seems to tally with Jan's; he really did avoid Cornwall for most of his adult life and never saw Sally again once she left London for provincial journalism. Chances are, therefore, that he's been telling the truth all along. The Sally he knew was a beautiful young girl; it's no surprise he failed to recognise the face I'd drawn.

But Sally Hendry in her mid-thirties ended up back at Penmaris, from where she conducted, according to Jan, a variety of sexual liaisons. With whom, that's the next question? I'd bet money on Chris Benning being one of them. He lived near Penzance in the Eighties and had an affair with an older woman, he lied about his interest in buying Penmaris, and now it seems he's involved in a complicated relationship with Carne Tresawna. What exactly is the deal between these two? That Carne holds the answers to many questions, I feel increasingly certain. He'll be round later to check the garden, so I can try again, at the risk upsetting him further. The sight of Carne wielding an axe comes to mind.

Blinking the image away, I see instead Alec McConnell slamming his car door in fury. He cursed me for being a *typical bloody woman*, poking my nose into other people's business. Was that fair? Am I just idly interfering where I have no right? Even if I give the impression, it doesn't feel like that to me. I've never considered myself to be nosey, I'm not one for office gossip or neighbourhood tittle-tattle. Paula, on the other hand, now she *is* the guru of the grapevine. Paula makes insider-trading seem uninformed. Whereas me, withdrawn and under-confident, I've always felt like the one left out of the loop, the person who hasn't been told the latest scandal, the last to hear all the goss.

Across the sky bundles of cloud are rolling in, bearing the promised rain. It's turned dark all of a sudden, and windy. The weather has changed, the way I've come to understand it does in this part of the world. Having drawn not a single line on my clean, white pad, I throw it into my shoulder bag and gather my belongings. No point getting soaked. I might as well head back. As I'm about to leave, an unexpected blaze of sun bursts from between two roiling cumuli and descends in a vertical shaft of light that plunges into the waters beneath. Through the gap in the clouds the sky has turned gold, an unearthly greenish-yellow tinged with deep amber that pours like molten metal down the rays of sunlight all the way into the sea. Day becomes night, save for that golden blade which glitters and blinds. Carried on fierce winds, the waves begin to pound against the rocks, smashing themselves into white oblivion. Stacked behind them another cavalry charge rolls in, and then another and another, relentless, driven. I imagine I hear shouts of triumph, the clash of armour, the canter of horses' hooves. I see…

I blink and have to look away, so bright is the blade of light.

And then the clouds knit together and the moment is gone. The sky is uniform pewter on a dull November morning. But the sea continues to heave like liquid muscle and hurl itself to the land like some mighty being. I whisper lines from one of Sally's poems.

> See how the holy tide
> rolls from the dungeons of Lyonesse,
> smashing music from rock spume,
> tasting of ferocity and pride.

The awesome power of the sea. My blood tingles. I feel lifted out of myself.

No, I decide, I'm not being nosey. I'm not out to make idle mischief or cause trouble, nor am I a typical sticky-beak, whatever Mac might say. I'm not a typical anything. And Sally Hendry, the woman who wrote those words, died here twenty years ago, for no apparent reason. Everyone else seems content to ignore what happened whereas I, Rose Little, shall continue to find out. Sally believed the past endured, that it could speak to the present. I shall do my damnedest to listen.

* * *

On the way back my mobile rings. Paula. Wasting no time on niceties.

"It's me. How *the hell* did you know?"

I groan quietly. "Okay, tell me exactly what you've discovered."

"What do you think I've bloody discovered? You must have—"

"I don't *know* anything, Paula. Not for sure. It was a shot in the dark." There's a clacking sound; Paula's long fingernails drumming the table. Drumming hard. She'll break one in a minute.

"There's two names on the deeds—"

"You mean you've actually *seen* the papers?" Bugger. I've got this all wrong. Evidently Chris *is* the legal owner. He did purchase Penmaris and lodge the deeds in London.

"Of course I've seen them. How else could I have read the *two signatories*?" Her voice is high-pitched and getting higher. "It's Carne, for God's sake. The other one. It's Carne Tresawna. That dozy gardener. He's got joint ownership of *my cottage*. What on earth was Chris thinking? Why should Worzel Gummidge own half of Penmaris? Rose? Rose, are you listening?"

Bribery, blackmail, hush money. Words whose meaning I barely understand. Carne Tresawna and Chris Benning.

"I can't tell you yet, Paula. I think it might have something to do with—"

307

"And I can't get hold of Chris anywhere. He won't answer my calls. I must have left a million text messages. What the hell's going on, Rose?"

* * *

Tank-man is stowing his gear in the van. He waves at me as I dash up the path. The damaged pipe is repaired and the garden looks back to normal.

"All done just in time, as promised." He gestures at fat raindrops bouncing off the bonnet.

I'm panting, having run most of the way from a sense of urgency, though the nature of the urgency is confused. "Right. Well, that's great." It seems like a thing to say. "And thank you, for all your hard work. Do I need to… do anything? Sign any…?" I open the back door and edge into the warmth of the kitchen.

He waves his famous clipboard. "I'll be posting my invoice this afternoon, straight to Mr Benning. Nothing for you to worry about. Shouldn't think you'll have any more drainage problems." He looks pleased with himself, and I nod.

"Good. That's good. Well, if that's all, Mr… erm… Fitzgerald?" We've become formal again.

I put the kettle on and Bill Fitzgerald's van drives off.

Five minutes later, there's the sound of a car drawing up. I wonder if tank-man has left something behind, but it's Carne's old Land Rover. Carne jumps out, slams the door and, despite pelting rain, strides directly into the garden where he peers at the replaced turfs, bending over every few seconds to remove clods of earth which he hurls into the bushes. His bushes. His garden. Couldn't he have waited till the rain eased? I upend a few of his favourite ginger biscuits onto a plate and reach for another mug. "Tea?" I yell, cracking the window open.

He makes a big palaver of removing his wet coat and soggy hat and muddy shoes, though a trail of drips follows him into the sitting room. Accepting the tea, he perches awkwardly on an arm of the sofa, then thinks better of it and slides onto the seat. He avoids looking at me.

"Biscuit, Carne?"

We munch and sip.

"Job done, then." I nod in the direction of the garden. "Everything back as it should be?" Carne seems bemused, as though I'm speaking Martian. "The grass, I mean. Come spring, well, summer, I imagine you won't be able to tell…"

How to convey that I don't think any the less of him for crying, for having given way to strong emotion? Frayed shirt cuffs poke out from the sleeves of his jumper, itself grubby and holed at the elbows. Both sets of sleeves are far too short, exposing bony wrists scarcely strong enough to support his huge hands, like spades. His work clothes make him look thin and cold. I switch the heater on, offer more biscuits.

"I know how proud you are of… of *your* garden." A slight emphasis on the possessive. "Go on, have another ginger nut." Carne takes one, but otherwise exhibits no reaction. Sipping continues into a silence that grows heavier by the minute. I decide I lack investigative talent; I have no gift for subtle probing, for covert interrogation. I decide to be direct. "Funny thing this morning, I had a phone call from Paula. You know? Paula Benning?"

We stare at one another, then jump as a knock at the front door startles us. No one ever uses the front door, except…

Chris is standing there, warm and dry beneath a golf-sized umbrella. He's wearing a camel coat that reeks expense.

"Sorry to bother you, Rose. Just wanted to check on this drains business." He sweeps past me into the cottage, flapping raindrops off his brolly which he props against the wall. "Ah. Carne." Sliding out of his coat, he drapes it over the banisters.

"You've just missed Bill Fitzgerald." My voice sounds odd and squeaky. "He left ten minutes ago. It's all sorted."

"Oh, good. Only I got this crazy phone call last night saying work had been held up by… a *skeleton*? Can that be right?"

The two men glare at each other. "We're having a cup of tea," I say.

"Good idea. Don't mind if I do."

In the privacy of the kitchen I give way to panic. Is this a coincidence, Chris turning up today of all days? Has Paula spoken to him yet? She left umpteen texts, so chances are he's got back to her by now. Which means Chris knows that I know that Paula knows that… Oh, shit. Shit, shit, shit.

On the other hand, his phone might still be switched off.

From behind the closed door, I can make out their voices lowered in conversation. Talking quickly, urgently, snapping and impatient, the sort of conversation that's really a whispered argument. I pour a mug of tea for Chris, then realise I'm running out of milk. While I'm watering down what's left, the door opens.

"Hold that tea, Rose. Need to inspect the damage." Carrying his enormous umbrella, Chris blasts through the kitchen into the garden, followed by Carne who struggles into his shoes and grabs his coat on the way. I watch them head straight for the stone.

* * *

Damage. What a terrible word. So much in life can damage and so easily, especially people. In ways that leave no visible trace. Which makes the damage harder to repair.

There's an expression, isn't there, *the walking wounded*, used by the media in the aftermath of train crashes or motorway pile-ups? To my mind it chimes too closely with "the walking dead" and conjures unfortunate images of B-movie zombies swathed in bandages and moaning ineptly. Early Hollywood horror, before special FX.

But in our different ways we're all walking wounded. The phrase defines the human condition. At best we totter on, we try to walk tall.

But not Carne. Not today. He stands there by the cat's grave, arms dangling, head bowed (or is it cowed?), and his pain cannot be disguised. Chris, on the other hand, is gesticulating, his body language that of the playground bully, though my view is partly obscured by raindrops on the window and the swing of his absurd umbrella. I wish I'd marched out in their company, to turn two into a crowd. Or, more accurately, I wish I could overhear their private conversation, from the safety of the kitchen.

311

As I'm resolving to join them and interrupt their little *tête-à-tête*, the two men start walking back to the house. Chris actually waves to me as I stand, hovering ineffectually, at the kitchen window. I retreat to the sitting room.

"Well, that was a lot of fuss about nothing," he announces, striding ahead of his trail of muddy footprints. Carne, who at least has the courtesy to remove his wet things again, follows like a dog. His grey, woolly socks pad in the wake of Chris's tracks. "Gather Ollie was here too. Quite a little get-together. Down for a quick conjugal, eh, Rose?" Before I can answer, he goes on, "Never mind. I'll catch up with him in the next few days. Send him your love, shall I?"

The air crackles with suppressed tension. I can see muscles twitch in Chris's forehead, and Carne is slumped in silence.

Chris reminds me of a wilful child, picking at scabs till they bleed. "Right old gathering of the clans yesterday, and all for a pointless hole in the ground. High drama, according to Bill Fitzgerald. Poor sod had the fright of his life. Thought he'd dug up someone's grandma, all that weeping and wailing." He glares at Carne, whose eyes are fixed to the floor. "Goes to show what happens when you jump to the wrong conclusions."

Unable to remain quiet a moment longer, I interrupt. "How can you be so insensitive, Chris? Carne's been upset enough in the last twenty-four hours. He made a mistake, that was all."

Chris raises his eyebrows. "And there speaks an expert in wrong conclusions." A sneer twists his lips.

"Don't you think *you've* upset enough people for one day?"

Oh God. He must have spoken to Paula. Well, at least now I know. I stare back, holding his gaze, refusing to be intimidated.

"Paula was *extremely* upset on the phone this morning. Thank you, Rose."

Presumably that was the news Chris imparted to Carne in the garden a few minutes ago, along with the heavy gesticulations and a few warnings, I wouldn't be surprised, to stay out of it, *I'll deal with the problem. Keep your mouth shut.*

On the sofa, Carne crosses and uncrosses his legs. Considers standing, then thinks better of it. Anger slithers up my throat.

"So, how's it work, Chris? Is Penmaris the price you had to pay for Carne's silence? Part share in the cottage and he keeps stumm about your little affair with Sally Hendry? About all your murky little affairs down here in the sticks while your posh London fiancée remained in blissful ignorance?"

"You have no idea what you're talking about, Rose. I really would advise you to stop before you say something we'll all regret."

"Are you threatening me?" I take a step forward, conscious that my head barely comes up to his shoulders. "Was that what Sally did? Was that her mistake? Did she threaten to make waves, spoil your nice, neat plans for the future? Society wedding, fresh start in London. Very respectable." Chris is bending down, pretending to ignore me, picking bits of mud off the carpet. "Poor Sally. How she must have come to hate everything to do with London. The very word.

313

Because she was going to lose out again, wasn't she, she was going to lose out to London?" I'm shouting now. "First Alec McConnell, then you, relegating her to the ranks of village bimbo, the bit-on-the-side whenever you were slumming it down here in *Hicksville*."

Chris recognises his own expression, and the contempt in my voice. His arm moves.

"Oh, yeah, that'd be right." I need to shut up, stop taunting him, but instinct makes me carry on. There something more here, more than casual sex and notches in his belt. "Yeah," I hiss, egging him on, daring him. "Yeah, come on, then. This what you do, Chris? This your way with women, is it?"

Rising in a smooth arc across the space between us, his right arm smashes against my cheek, sending me staggering backwards. I crash into the coffee table, then collapse awkwardly on the floor, banging my head on the table as I fall. When Chris steps towards me, Carne is out of his chair in a bound.

Momentarily stunned, all I can see is a blur of grown men scrapping, but the air reeks of an anger strong enough to overwhelm Penmaris and bring the walls down.

"Stop it, stop it!" My cheek is on fire and I wonder if I've broken a tooth. The entire right side of my face feels flat-ironed.

From inside the puffing and panting comes an animal growl: "Don't you ever…" as Chris struggles to throw Carne off his back. Though younger and probably fitter, he has no answer to the years of pent-up misery that fuel Carne's rage.

"Stop it, both of you! Stop fighting!"

I grab the edge of the coffee table, which has skidded across the room under the impact of my weight, and I haul myself upright. Chris's head has been yanked backwards, exaggerating the absurd lump of his Adam's apple; his arms flail ineffectually as he tries to grab Carne, to grab anything in order to free himself, but his assailant clings on, a demon on his back. They are locked together, gasping, and I get the impression neither man knows what to do next. Earlier I thought Chris seemed like a playground bully; now the pair of them remind me of overgrown louts, amateurish, belligerent, out-of-breath, made vicious by the heat of the moment. I charge at them and elbow Carne in the ribs, making him grunt. Inserting myself in the space between, I try to separate them.

"For God's sake, stop it. Stop it!"

A backwards kick gets Carne in the groin and when he lets go, I manage to push Chris against the wall where his body grows slack as the anger dies.

"Bloody hell, Chris, is this how you deal with things? This how you handle women? Did Sally make you so angry you hit her?" I'm panting from the exertion of holding Chris at arms' length and because my head is about to explode.

And then it does. The whole cottage shakes. From far, far away I hear a woman cry out.

"Oh my God!" My hands shoot to my face. "Oh my God." The realisation knee-caps me and I sink to the floor.

Chris is babbling, "Sorry, Rose. I'm so sorry. I'm so sorry. I didn't mean to touch you. You've gotta believe me, Rose, I'd never hurt a woman, I'd never…" He's trying to help me up, but I shrug him off.

"That's what happened, isn't it? You hit her. You hit her, didn't you? Only one day you hit her too hard. And you killed her."

Aaaaahhh… The keening I heard yesterday has started again. *Aaaaahh…* Carne has retreated to the other side of the room and is collapsed against the kitchen door, his head buried in those huge hands from which leak the most dreadful sounds.

"I shouldn't have come here." Chris grabs his things. "I'd better go before I—"

"That's it, isn't it?" I glare at Chris, then spin round to face Carne. "And you knew all along." His body jerks as though hit by a bullet. "You saw what happened, and all these years you've been covering up for—"

"You don't know what you're talking about, Rose." Chris is pulling his coat on. With shaky but deliberate movements he fastens every button, turns the collar up. Precise. Controlled. And I stand there like a fish with my mouth open. "I repeat, you have absolutely no idea what you're talking about." He opens the front door, seems to hesitate for a second, then turns round to spit out a farewell. "I didn't kill her, you stupid bitch. He did."

Chapter Twenty-Six

Carne has popped out to the kitchen, his fifth visit in as many minutes, and this time when he comes back he's carrying his wet jacket. So far he's brought me a glass of water, filled a tea towel with crushed ice for my face, fetched the dustpan and brush to sweep mud off the carpet, cleared the tea things away and let in a startled HeCat who fled past him up the stairs.

Collapsed against cushions in an armchair, I have the crocheted blanket over my knees. Now Carne drags the fan heater close to keep my feet warm.

"One last thing," I whisper. My face hurts. "Aspirins? Upstairs in the bathroom…"

Carne watches anxiously while I swallow two capsules. Then, from his inside jacket pocket he takes a leather wallet, opens it and extracts a much-thumbed photo. He looks at it like one spell-bound and runs a thumb tenderly across the surface as he's probably done a million times before, which accounts for its crumpled state. I pull the blanket over my arms and snuggle, content to wait till Carne is ready to talk. I don't for one moment believe Chris. I don't think I'm sitting next to a murderer.

"Ice!" Carne says.

I protest. "But it's cold."

"It'll keep the swelling down. You'll regret it tomorrow, if you don't."

Obediently I lean my right cheek against the freezing pad of the tea towel, wincing. I remember Oliver once with a packet of frozen peas clamped to his eye following a careless rugby scrum.

Carne passes me the photo. "He did that."

It's a photo of Sally Hendry.

It's also my sketch, the one currently propped on the dressing table keeping me company at night, the one that's unfinished but never forgotten, the drawing Carne has never seen. The same face, with head and shoulders slightly in profile, the same age, the same hair and eyes, the same wound carving the right cheek, the same terrible damage. The same.

"I took that a couple days before she… disappeared." Carne says. "To prove to her she were still beautiful." He seems much calmer now, as if the storm which threatened to overwhelm him has blown away and he's grateful to be left standing on a quiet shore. "Chris'd chucked her, told it were all over 'cos he were moving to London to get hitched. Had the nerve to thank her, can you imagine? *We've had fun,* he said, like it were a game he'd been playing. Sal lost it and they had this big fight, up on the cliffs." He nods in the general direction. "She slipped on the wet path, fell against a rock and nearly put her eye out. Least, that what she told me. She *slipped.*" He shakes his head.

"Only prised that much out of her after weeks of asking. She wouldn't let on to anyone, just made up some story."

I recall Jan's version of the same incident; evidently Sally had spun her a yarn too. "It's a dreadful injury," I say, "it must have been agony."

"Hurt her pride as much as her face. I was all for reporting him to the police, but Sal said, no, I was to leave it. He'd be gone soon, and good riddance."

"But at least she had you as a friend." I try smiling and wince again.

"She got depressed after that. Big black moods. The eye wouldn't heal, and it made her really ill, really sick. You know how pain can actually make you want to throw up? The scar embarrassed her and she wouldn't go out, 'cept after dark. Said she felt old and ugly and fat…" The word stalls him. "Said she felt… fat… So that's why I took her photo."

I hand it back to him. "Sometimes," I say, remembering my own experience, "no amount of love or support can make any difference. We get trapped inside our misery, and there's no way out. I'm sure you did your best, Carne."

He's staring at Sally's face. Like a fish gulping, his mouth opens then closes again. Opens. Closes. I wait.

"Tell you what, Carne, why don't we light a fire? Cheer ourselves up."

He gestures for me to keep still and busies himself with the task, glad to have something to do. Crouched in front of the hearth, arranging wood and lumps of coal, his voice almost disappears with the smoke, up the chimney. "I still wanted to marry her. Second time in my life I'd proposed, and to the same woman! But she

319

weren't having it. Her pride again. That's all it was, her stupid pride." He coughs, dusts ash off his fingers.

Feeling woozy, I half-hear, half-understand what Carne is saying. The extra heat from the fire is sending me to sleep. My attention drifts.

"I realised after, that's why she were getting so fat. That's why she felt sick all the time." Once the flames catch, he sits back on his heels. "There. Proper job."

I try a wonky smile. "I love that expression. Sounds just right, somehow. Thank you, Carne."

"You're the sort just accepts folk. You let 'em be. But people round here, they'd've gossiped and judged her. She always reckoned she could feel the weight of their frowns dragging her down. But, as my wife, she could've held her head up high. That's what I tried to make her understand. That I'd have cared for her." He throws a log on the fire. "Why didn't she tell me?" he asks the flames. "Why didn't she tell me she were... I'd have looked after her." More softly he adds, "And the babby too. I'd've loved it like my own. Wouldn't have made no difference it were his."

I realise what he's saying. "Oh, Carne." The ice pack cracks on the hearth.

* * *

"I followed her one night, just before 'e were s'posed to be leaving for good. I knew she were meeting 'im, and I just wanted to keep an eye."

Carne is still addressing the flames, as if fire might clean the past and burn bad memories to smoke and ash. Sally must have persuaded Chris to meet her. Did she lure him with the promise of a final fling, one last scratch of the itch?

"Lucky chance, really. I spotted her setting out along the cliff towards the bay, so I followed, at a distance, just keeping her in sight. Where the path turns, I heard her stop and speak, then I heard Chris's voice, then Sal saying '*no, don't*'. I nearly dived round the corner there and then to punch 'is lights out and make him pay. But I reckoned I were close enough. Even crept a bit closer so I could listen and be there, ready if I were needed. 'E weren't ever going to hurt my Sal again. But I thought, hang on, let's wait up a bit, just nip behind this rock and see what happens."

Does jealousy make liars of us all? Because of his frustrated longing for Sally, he eavesdropped on the lovers' last tryst; because of a prurient, masochistic urge to experience what was denied him, he held back, waited a moment longer. And heard Sally confess that she was pregnant.

"'*Your baby*', she kept saying, like that would soften his stinking rotten heart. '*It's your baby, our baby.*' She was begging him not to leave her and all he could say was *'get rid of it'*. The more Sal pleaded the colder he sounded. *'Not my problem.'* Can you believe the bugger, saying something like that? And his voice, it were cold enough to freeze your blood. Then came a slap and feet scramblin' on the path, so I was round that corner faster than you could spit and I went for him, my fists on his head, and I were kicking him, too, anything I could get hold of till I 'ad 'im on the ground."

Just like earlier today. History repeating itself. And I bet there was no contest then, either. Carne worked the land and would have been strong and fit without even trying, and he had surprise on his side. I expect he bashed the daylights out of Chris. Years of frustration must have turned him savage. He'd probably have beaten him to death, if Sally hadn't shouted at him to stop.

"She dragged me off down the path, crying and blubbing that she were sorry. She were sorry… But I reckon she just wanted to pull me further along the cliff and give that bugger a chance to run away. Let 'im escape. Then… he came at me, out of nowhere. Cannoned straight into the back of me and sent me flying. I couldn't help myself… I couldn't. I fell forwards and I… I knocked her over and she…"

He shakes his head, unable to go on. So I sit very still and try to imagine the scene, the three of them toppling like dominoes, and Sally tumbling over the cliff edge. Winded, flat on his face, with the weight of Chris Benning on top of him, of course Carne let go of Sally's hand. In fact, as she fell, it would have been wrenched from his grasp.

Responsibility. Guilt. I know exactly how Carne feels.

"We, er, we found a sandal dangling from one of the gorse bushes on the cliff. Where the branches had snapped, you could just about trace a line. It was a bit too dark to see properly, but we went on searching all night, up on the cliff and down on the shore, in the rocks, everywhere. Come daybreak we searched again, but there weren't no sign of her 'cept for that shoe, so we… we sort of convinced ourselves she was probably all right. Thought she'd somehow made her way home."

"So there *was* a baby," I whisper. "Chris's baby."

"She could've told me. I'd have stuck by her, Rose, I would. It didn't have to end like that."

322

I try to imagine the two men combing the beach night and day, getting more and more desperate. "But you didn't go to the police?"

Carne shakes his head. "After a couple of days we told ourselves she'd run away. She must be alive, we had to believe she was alive but she wanted to disappear, to hide from all the village gossip, make a clean start somewhere else. We'd've believed anything rather than think she… Chris said I was to keep my mouth shut and if anyone asked, I was to say I hadn't seen her since she came into Mary's shop, the week before."

"But that was—"

"Or else he'd tell the police it were all my fault – that I'd been stalking her and I'd deliberately picked a fight with him 'cos I was jealous of the pair of 'em. That I'd nearly killed him and I'd shoved Sal over the edge. His word against mine. Said he weren't doing time in jail 'cos I couldn't hold Sally's hand tight enough. And he were right. It *was* my fault." Carne tosses another log on the fire as if he wished it were his right arm. "All my fault."

"It was an accident, Carne. You can't blame yourself. It was a terrible tragedy, but it was an *accident*." I pause, listening to the words coming out of my mouth. And I realise it's time I listened to them more often, started taking my own advice. "And you certainly shouldn't have let Chris threaten you—"

"When they found her, years later, he came knocking on my door again. He still did a bit of business down 'ere and he dropped by one day to make sure I'd keep my mouth shut."

Exploiting Carne's simple devotion, Chris had proposed buying Penmaris and putting Carne's name on the deeds as well, so he'd have part-ownership of the cottage. He could come and go as he wished, tend the garden (which at that time Carne firmly believed to be the site of his stillborn baby's grave), stay over whenever he wanted, keep an eye on the place, supervise any summer visitors. The place would be his to use for most of the year. He, Chris, would pay for the purchase, renovation and upkeep, and when Paula eventually tired of her little cottage in the country, he'd pretend to "sell it off" to Carne and no one would be any the wiser. In the long run, Carne would own Penmaris outright. What Chris called a win–win situation.

What I'd call blackmail, I think to myself. Chris must have been mighty relieved. At long last he knew Sally wasn't going to turn up one day out of the blue waving a paternity suit at him, spoiling his nice, neat marriage. He bribes Carne and hey presto, end of problem.

"I feel sorry for his wife," Carne says.

"For Paula? Why?"

"Seems like a nice lady. For a Londoner. Does she know what a bastard she's married to?"

Despite the pain, I laugh out loud. "She does now."

Chapter Twenty-Seven

Upending the Boots carrier bag, I tumble its contents onto the duvet. About time. I've been procrastinating for days. The oblong packet seems to draw attention to itself. Why did I also buy three different shades of lip gloss, a tube of handcream, cottonwool balls, liquid and powder foundation? That perfume spritzer thingy?

And Tampax.

Just in case.

My hands are shaking so much I can't get the stupid packet open.

I know, and I don't know. I'm almost too scared to find out.

Oh, bugger. Bugger, bugger, bugger… just rip the thing apart.

I extract the slim plastic gadget; carry it carefully, like a bomb, into the bathroom.

* * *

The days are growing short and time is shrinking in upon itself. Life is slowing to the rhythms of the earth. Like the countryside around me here in the far south west, I am hibernating, brooding over a year that has passed in alternating brief stabs of reality and long, grey, comatose shadows. Some of those shadows are clearing now, and I await what will emerge into the light of a brand new year.

Jan Freeman should be round any minute. I couldn't think who else to call.

From the TV screen a volley of gun shots – the six o'clock news reporting a hostage situation gone wrong, several injured and one fatality. This is followed by a report on teenage knife-crime in inner-city ghettos. HeCat totters upright, stretches in front of the fire then flops down again, thankfully none the worse for last night's ordeal. I mute the set before the newscaster has time to elaborate on financial gloom, the collapse of the property market and rising unemployment. Such fragility, so many disturbing problems I don't wish to contemplate. I'm after the local news, which might be bad enough. Are they going to forecast sub-zero temperatures again tonight? It felt icy when I went into the garden just now, that almost-crunch of grass underfoot. My breath had bloomed on the air. December, and I am experiencing mild panic about such issues as frozen pipes, being snowed in and cut off.

The brand-new, flat-screen television is a recent purchase. Deciding I'd better get organised, I drove to Penzance last week to acquire some essentials in the pre-Christmas sales: an electric blanket, a second and more powerful heater to keep the whole place warm,

326

extra kitchen equipment so I can cook properly, a coal-store and an order of coal to eke out the wood. A lanky youth installed the TV for me and patiently explained the intricacies of the remote control; another less lanky and less patient middle-aged grump finally agreed, for what seemed like an exorbitant fee, to erect the coal-store against the side wall of the cottage, near the back door. Another job done. I am working my way through a mental list. Being sensible. I must look after myself, and Penmaris, during the long winter months. Perhaps the TV wasn't entirely sensible, but I needed a moment's madness, a bit of retail therapy. What the hell; it's only a telly.

Waiting for the regional news to start, I go into the kitchen for a glass of water. HeCat appears by my ankles as if summoned by bells and scoffs a tin of Whiskas in record time before returning to duties. Poor soul. I shudder to think what might have become of them, had I not ventured out first thing this morning for wood and coal, and come across the desperate family huddled inside my dwindling pile of logs. Last night saw the first real frost of winter down these parts, and frost will kill those with only a tenuous hold on life.

The kittens are minute and scrawny, barely visible against their mother's fur, though one, the smaller of the two, seems to have a white patch on its foot. Otherwise they are jet black, like mum. Three other scraps didn't survive. When I lifted the plastic sheeting for sticks to start a fire, a bundle that proved to be HeCat and babies wriggled and squeaked at me. Off to one side, rejected and wretchedly frozen, lay three dead bodies. I've consigned them to the dustbin. The idea of digging a hole in the garden seemed a tad melodramatic for just a few grams of flesh. Besides, it would be all too reminiscent of recent events in the grounds of Penmaris. Not a road I want to go down at the moment.

The new family is tucked up warm in a blanket inside a cardboard box in front of the fire. Now I shall have to think of another name for the cat. Doubtless Jan will have some ideas. I hadn't expected such loud fits of purring, nor such a state of bliss. If it's possible to ascribe rapture to a cat, then that's HeCat right now, in feline heaven. Not, of course, that I had *expected* anything at all. To drift down one innocent Wednesday morning and find a family, ready-made. Once over the shock of discovery and my own stupidity (why had I assumed a neutered male?), I set-to creating suitable accommodation for my house guests. Because I'll have to keep them at least till the kittens are old enough to go to new homes. I'll have to look after them. Shoulder that small responsibility.

Another sick joke life is playing on me.

HeCat is certainly a lot thinner, never having really been *fat* in the first place. And should no longer be called He-anything. What an idiot! How come I didn't realise? When I stroke their fragile bodies I can feel them move beneath my fingers, burrowing for milk.

The news has started so I unmute the box in time to hear about long delays on the A30 where it crosses the Tamar. A serious accident on the west-bound carriageway means traffic is backed-up for miles. Commuters returning home will be late this cold winter's evening. I wake sometimes in the middle of the night, my mind traffic-jammed, gawping at the enormity of what I've decided to do.

As if acknowledging guilt, Oliver has agreed without protest to buy my share of our Clapham house. This will provide me with enough cash for Penmaris. He's being very businesslike but not ungenerous, and seems anxious, now that he's persuaded of my determination, to be seen to be doing the right thing. Ellie, on the other hand, replied to my letter of resignation with a long, rambling, exculpatory whinge that has soured any lingering regrets for our lost friendship. Before reaching the last page, I scrunched the whole lot up and threw it on the fire.

A rap at the back door. It opens and a "Hi there, Rose. Only me," blows Jan into the sitting room on a gust of freezing air that billows her coat into a bright red sail. "Where are they, then? Let me see them! Oh, Rose. Oh my goodness, they're *gorgeous!*" A heap of Jan and coat and scarf and handbag crumples to the floor beside the kitten box. Startled, HeCat hisses at her.

"Careful. I don't think she wants you to…"

But she's already picked one up. "I'll have this little cutie," she says. "I absolutely must. I swore there'd be no more pets after Magnus. You get so attached, don't you? But I've just changed my mind, right this very instant. Haven't I, you gorgeous little thing? Who's a beautiful little—"

"It won't survive." She's taken the runt, the one with a white paw and the weakest hold on life. I can't see it lasting many days. Nothing lasts.

"They're stronger than you think, Rose." She's smothering the thing in kisses. "Life clings on, no matter what. Life persists, life endures. And sometimes the most fragile turns into the strongest. And the most beautiful. Look at that cute white sock! Oh, you're just…" She yanks its tail up. "Oooh, you're a little girl. Perfect! I'll have to think of the right name for you." The kitten fits snugly, curled in the palm of her hand. But HeCat is pacing round shouting at her, so she puts it back next to its sibling then looks up. For the first time she notices my face.

I turn away and head for the kitchen. I hadn't expected Jan to be the sort who went soppy over animals. Perhaps I can persuade her to look after them at Christmas, when I go and stay at Megan's. And perhaps Meg might take the other one; the kids would love a to have a cat.

"What's the matter?" Jan's hand is warm in the centre of my back. I hunch over the sink, turn the tap full on.

"It's nothing," I mumble, and brush the tears away. But her arm goes round me and it's all I can do not to howl. I splash cold water over my cheeks. "Tea or coffee?"

"I'm here, you know, if you ever want to…"

Her voice breaks my heart. "It's just… Oh God, I thought I… I was pregnant, but…" and the rest is lost in the tea towel. I rub my face. Dry my eyes.

"Oh, Rose, I'm so sor—"

"Well… that's that. There's no baby. Never was. Never will be. Coffee, I think." A frog in my throat needs blasting. "Strong coffee." I hurl the tea towel to the floor.

Bitter blackness from my new cafetière blasts several thousand volts through my bloodstream. Yanking the rubber band off my ponytail, I free my hair so I can hide behind it.

"Rose, talk to me. You'll feel better if you—"

"Sorry. Can't. Can't go there."

"But you rang me, you must have wanted to…"

Muscles clench. Pelvic floor, gut, stomach. With an effort I release my jaws. "You sure about having that kitten?" A second gulp of caffeine.

Jan sighs. She'll play the game, if she has to. "Of course I'm sure. It's ironic, really, a litter of kittens after all that business about the cat's skeleton in the garden. And to think Carne's spent half his life… " She shakes curls highlighted today with vivid purple streaks the same colour as her nail varnish. "Though of course Sal adored cats, so I'm not surprised. There's probably a few more animals buried out there. The Hendrys always kept pets." She sips thoughtfully. "It might sound daft, but, well, having one of these little… it'll be like… like a gift from Penmaris and from Sally. An unbroken line." She lets her gaze walk the room. "When I'm here, I can sense her, you know? As if she's still in the cottage, still somewhere close by? You've given her back to me, Rose. I'm very glad you've decided to stay."

Her smile is wide and I feel my resolve weakening again. Why is it so hard to keep the floodgates closed?

Because I've decided not to tell Jan all the business about Chris and Carne or about Sally's baby. She must have had enough, dealing with Sally batting for both sides, knowing she shared the love of her life with an unspecified number of men. There are confidences to be kept, and Carne's feelings, which deserve sensitivity. Some secrets are better left unspoken.

An awkward silence settles.

331

Eventually, "Bet your London friends are glad to be getting shot of this place," Jan mumbles through biscuit crumbs. "Bit of an albatross round their neck, these days. Why have a holiday home you never use, specially in today's financial climate?"

Selling Penmaris is non-negotiable, as far as Paula is concerned. In return for Chris severing all ties with Cornwall, she has agreed to a six-month ceasefire during which the future of their marriage will be considered. As she said over the phone, there's no point throwing twenty years away on a knee-jerk reaction. Chris being the jerk and her right patella being ready for action. She'd sounded a bit overwhelmed. "It's sad enough you and Oliver splitting up, darling. I'm going to miss you so much. I can't face any more right now. And it *was* all a long time ago, wasn't it? Though I'd still like to kill him. Oh, sorry, Rose. Bad choice of verb."

Jan places her coffee mug on the table and flops back on the couch. "Okay. Tell me about your plans for the future."

I shrug and remain guarded. "Not quite sure I stretch to *plans* or *future*. At the moment I've got as far as next month. Which is also next year. I suppose that's progress."

"Stop right there." Jan bounces upright again. "Before I forget, what are you doing next week? I need someone to help me paint the backcloth for the nativity play."

"Oh, no, I ca—"

"I'll rephrase that. I *desperately need* someone to paint the backcloth. The whole bloody thing. You know Trish, teaches Year Six? She usually does my scenery,

332

but she fell off the garage roof and broke her arm." Jan rolls her eyes. "Don't ask! Anyway, I can't paint and time is running out. But I'm very good at giving orders, so you won't have to think about a single thing. I'll tell you exactly what needs doing. And we'll have such fun! Go on. Say yes. You know you want to."

I recognise an immoveable object when I see one. "Oh, all right then. I'll help. It probably will be fun, sloshing paint around on a grand scale. Mac would approve."

Jan cocks an eyebrow. "You sure you trust that man, Rose? With your work, I mean, your precious paintings? You really think he'll put a word in for you and get you commissions?"

"Why not? He made the offer; I didn't exactly have to twist his arm. Why? Don't you?"

She frowns. "There were some articles a while back in the *Gazette*. When he first moved down here. Paper claimed to have dug up the dirt on kick-backs for foreign works of art. Nothing came of it, mind you. Probably just a rumour, usual media gossip. Young journalist looking to break a scandal and launch his career. 'Art-fraud prof turns beach-comber.' They printed a photo of Mac down on the Bay collecting driftwood. He went ballistic and there was, shall we say, an exchange of views in the local press." Her eyebrows arch higher. "Trouble is, mud sticks, doesn't it? No smoke, etc."

A few more pieces of the Alec McConnell jigsaw fall into place. I decide to be partial. "Well, as far as I'm concerned, Mac has useful contacts and people seem to rate him. I can't imagine he's got anything to gain by supporting me, and a bit of influence in the right place might make all the difference. I'm prepared to give it a go, anyway. I reckon I can afford a year or two to see what happens. I'm not looking any further ahead. Who can, realistically?"

"Realistically! Goodness. There's a big word."

"Yeah, well. I lie awake at night worrying about the big fat chunk of reality I've just bitten off. I don't mind admitting I'm scared. It's weird juggling sensible decisions about mortgages and insurance policies alongside this feeling." The floodgates nudge open a fraction. "You taught me about the spirit of place, the way it speaks to us." I hold Jan's eye. "And Sally's poetry has helped me hear the words. Stone circles, the mist and landscape, all this endless sea and sky, everything round here, everything speaking with one voice. So here I am risking a couple of years on a voice. My parents are horrified. There'll be ructions at Christmas, sparks will fly over the turkey." The thought makes me laugh.

"Any projects in mind, or will you paint to order?"

I take a deep breath. "I think I'm going to illustrate Sally's poems."

Give her her due; Jan doesn't even blink.

"Well, in some cases I'll be more… interpreting them, painting what they say to me. I'm stealing Mac's idea, but he's been quite enthusiastic. And at the bottom of each painting, or maybe down one side, I'm not sure yet, I'm going to put a copy of the original poem." I watch for a reaction. "Then whoever buys my picture will also be buying the work of a local poet. I can promote Sally's poetry at the same time as selling my art. Who knows, she might even become famous. Well, in Cornwall, anyway." My off-the-cuff attempt at levity.

There's a long pause while I chew my bottom lip. Perhaps I've blown it, taken too much for granted. Jan's face is drained of colour. Then she reaches out and grabs me, smothers me in the tightest of hugs. "Thank you," she whispers. "Thank you. I can't—"

"Hey! Don't get too excited." Though I feel absurdly relieved. "I haven't painted any yet, let alone sold one."

"But you will. I know you will."

Extracting my head from clouds of silk and patchouli, I wriggle free. "More?" I ask, picking up the cafetière.

But Jan's mind is racing. "I could do some sort of promotion for you in the shop," she begins, ideas flickering before her eyes. "I'll put posters up to advertise. Make sure everyone who comes in knows all about you. Word of mouth, Rose. We may be a small shop, but in summer you'll be amazed how many people… ooh, it'll get round in no time, you wait and see. You'll need to make sure there's plenty of stuff ready for the start of the tourist season, so we can capitalise on…"

Pressure, expectation. Warning bells. I'm not going down that road again.

"Let's not get carried away, Jan."

"An overnight success doesn't happen over night, Rose. You need a plan, a strategy."

"Now who's sounding horribly realistic? Come on, I've hardly put brush to canvas and you're busy organising my publicity campaign."

Leave it, Jan, just leave it. Back off.

And as if she reads my mind, that's exactly what she does. "Okay. Fair enough. I can see your point." She gives my hand a reassuring pat. "I'll take a raincheck, as they say. But I won't forget. I'm determined to do my bit. So if anything occurs to—"

Her enthusiasm is interrupted by the phone. Serendipity.

Colm Brian's baritone rings out, upbeat as ever, announcing success. "Think we've found you a good deal, Rose. Yeah, really. Checked her over this afternoon. Sound as a bell. Do you for the next couple of years, I reckon. And Derry's lined up a buyer for the MG, so… any time next week."

I've decided to sell my car. Much as I love it, a two-seater sports is not the vehicle for my future needs. Replacing it with something bigger, older and more prosaic will mean cash in hand that I can put to good use. Having spotted a For Sale notice on an old hatchback in the village, I reluctantly asked the Brians for help. Derry's been bragging for weeks he could get top dollar for the MG and it seems he's done it. Two more jobs off my list.

"That's great! I owe you. What? Tomorrow night? Well, yes, I suppose I could. Okay. Eightish? See you then. Bye."

Jan has a kitten snuggled to her breast. "Was that who I think it was?" She croons adoration into the heap of fur.

"Colm Brian."

"Yes, that's who I *thought* it was. And was that *a date* I heard you making for tomorrow night?" More purr than question.

336

Can I be bothered denying it, explaining myself? After all, what's a drink down the pub? I'm playing Colm Brian along because he's useful, and once my plans are accomplished I'll let him down gently. But firmly. And hope not to lose a friend.

I walk over to the fire and throw more logs on. "When Penmaris is actually mine, Colm has promised to help me move the stone back to its proper place. In the dance. I'm going to return it to the field with the others, to the circle where it belongs." Jan is planting kisses on the kitten's head. I wish she'd stop. "God knows how one does that, which is where a mechanic with some serious lifting gear comes in handy."

HeCat jumps from her box, mewing loudly, but all I hear is *Let the maiden join the dance, join the dance.* I hear it every time I'm by the stone; plaintive, hopeless, such a sad, sad voice. Someone moved that stone and I'm going to see it gets put back. I grasp for what I'm trying to say. "It feels like a last gesture, I suppose, something that I can actually do, like righting a wrong. It's something for Sally or whoever else it is whose voice…" I shake my head, give up. "Er, Jan, I think you ought to put that kitten back. Mum's getting frantic."

HeCat is pacing and shouting at Jan who wrinkles her nose. "It's all your fault," she says. "Your babies are just too cute. How can I be expected to resist." She's nearly in the box with them. Suddenly, from over one shoulder, she shouts, "Got it! I know what you should call her," but I'm miles away thinking about stones and, oddly, about Mac and how it felt when I was in bed with him. "The cat, Rose. Do concentrate."

"Sorry. What do you mean, you've got a name for your kitten?"

337

Purple and black curls bob and dance. "No, no, no. You were almost there yourself. With HeCat. Just add one more letter and make her female." A grin, as if expecting me to solve the puzzle.

"Oh I see, I think. Oh no. No, I don't like SheCat. Sounds spiteful and hissy and far too human. Sort of scratchy."

"Wrong letter. Add an E." She waits for me to catch on. "Makes Hecate? That's what you should call her. It came to me in a rush, just now. It's an old name, Rose. The name of a goddess not a human. Three syllables: Hec-at-ee."

"Hmm. Rings a bell, but…"

"Well, you chooses your mythology and you takes your choice." Jan enumerates on her fingers. "Hecate: deity of earth, sea and sky; chief witch, mistress of magic and necromancy; guide at the crossroads between this world and the next; queen of ghosts; Greek goddess of the wilderness. And of childbirth." The word makes me jump. I hear my heart race. "Think back to when you first arrived, Rose. Your first impressions. What you saw and thought and felt. Then remember everything that's happened since."

The garden in moonlight, a woman singing far away, the shadow of a black cat slip-sliding across my path. A presence in the house. A bringer of ghosts. Sally's ghost. The voices of Penmaris.

"Hecate. It's perfect, isn't it? Sums it all up. I should have realised sooner."

"Well…"

"She's been here with you all along, Rose. You can't reject her now."

"I thought I was pregnant," I say. And I cry and cry.

Chapter Twenty-Eight

When Jan finally leaves, I head for Mac's and the comfort of strong arms. Hopefully he'll be sober. I need him to hold me, to knit my bones together and fill the hollow spaces where I'm in danger of becoming transparent, as though I might vanish into the stones of Penmaris and become another ghost inhabiting its fabric. The evening is cold and brittle. Down Porthallen's empty lanes my breath spins fantastic shapes in the frosty air, my own spectre preceding me and luring me on. I am weightless; my feet, my legs seem to carry me effortlessly along the unlit road so that, although I can scarcely see in the dark, I have no fear of stumbling or getting lost.

Having revealed to Jan a few of my hopes and plans, I feel closer tonight to the spirit of Sally Hendry. The woman I sense she was and her legacy to Penmaris have become like a guiding light, one of the reasons perhaps why the darkness holds no fears. For a few days I allowed myself the dream of a baby, but that's all it was. A dream. And one that probably makes no sense given my current circumstances. I truly believe that this time I shall get over the disappointment, the shock, and not crumble the way I used to. I have to believe I can start again. I chant the words to the rhythm of my footsteps – start again, start ag…

My head comes up – the faintest of sounds from far, far away.

The sound of the woman singing.

Her voice, thin at first on the icy air, has the ring of pure crystal, mellifluous, hitting impossibly high notes that soar above the bare winter trees and ragged hedgerows. As always it thrills me, a magical sound that seems to emanate from another world even as it grows stronger and draws closer. It is a siren song which, tonight, I have no option but to follow.

Carne's place lies straight ahead, a dark shadow in the darkness. Normally I would bear left at the corner to get to Mac's house, but the singing insists and I carry on, brushing past overhanging branches that creak and snap back like whips. I bury my hands deep in my coat pockets. Despite wearing gloves, my fingertips ache with cold and my nose is numb; there are probably icicles hanging off the end where my warm breath is freezing on the spot. With each step I take the voice gets louder. To my surprise I'm walking fast now, panting as though I'm in a race, as if the winning post is in sight. Almost I sense her presence, the weight of another sad soul within reach, so close in fact that I stretch out a hand to touch her and am astonished to find only air. The voice urges me on, promising a welcome. *Nearly there, Rose. That's right. Keep going. I'm waiting for you.*

"Sally?" I hear myself say. Security lights flare as I open the gate to the front path.

Although I've passed this way many times, I've never been inside Carne's house. Exaggerated now by the dazzling spots, it seems huge, its outlines fuzzy where they fade into gradual darkness. Halfway along the path, I can see a light is on in one of the downstairs windows; otherwise the place mocks the night, a shadow among shadows. I tiptoe up to the lighted window and lean against the windowsill, hoping to peer in. A pair of thin curtains are drawn and all I get is a reverse pattern of multi-coloured stripes.

But I can hear her. The woman is in there, in that room, singing. And suddenly I realise why I've never been able to make out the words. She's singing in another language. Of course! Thinking back to a conversation with Mac, I realise that she must be singing in old Cornish. What did Mac call it? Kernowek? The ancient language of Cornwall, kept alive today by a few enthusiasts. And he made the point about songs. The woman whose lovely voice carries across the cliff tops, whose plaintive melodies have haunted my days, she's in there now, in Carne's house, singing in Kernowek.

The realisation hits me like a physical blow, sending me rocking back on my heels. I crash into a hydrangea bush whose bare, brittle stalks crack and snap off. Gravel underfoot rattles when I try to regain my balance. Shit! A small cry escapes me.

The singing stops.

With a hand clamped across my mouth, I creep backwards, holding my breath as a figure passes the window and one of the curtains flicks open before dropping back into place. Crouched down I guess I'm pretty much invisible out here.

But I don't want to be out here. I want to be inside. I want to meet… her.

This is crazy. It has to be. The most absurd thoughts jostle in my mind and they keep on coming. They assail me. They invade my head and I can't block them out. Was that Sally's voice I just heard, that I've been hearing all these weeks? Is Sally in there right now with Carne Tresawna? Could Sally Hendry still be alive? The idea makes me gasp. It's almost as fantastic as the spectral shapes formed by the frost, as the shifting sounds that have haunted Penmaris, and the nightmares that have stalked me.

A sharp gust of wind rattles the bare branches and I shiver; I hug my coat tighter and bury my nose in its fleecy collar. Closing my eyes against the icy blast, I see Carne searching for days, then finding Sally, her body crushed and disabled among the rocks. He could have brought her back here somehow, couldn't he? He was strong. He could have carried her. And he would have cared for her and kept her hidden, safe from the threat of Chris Benning. If her injuries were so severe, if she'd been crippled in the fall, disfigured maybe, well, in that case he'd've had to…

But Mac said the police found her skeleton and identified it from dental records. Besides, my little Hitchcockian scenario makes no sense. Why would Carne maintain a vigil at Penmaris if Sally were alive and living with him here? To get his own back on Chris Benning? To fool everyone into thinking…? What kind of warped vengeance is that? Though Mac always reckons Carne's a bit…

My jaws are juddering and tremours shoot up my spine. Fear knee-caps me and I stumble, grabbing hold of the first thing that comes to hand. Solid brickwork. The corner of an ordinary house. It feels good and firm, the way it should, and I pat it for reassurance, shaking my head to clear the nonsense out, all these stupid ideas. Honestly, if I'm capable of thinking like this, then I really must be going ma…

No. No. I refuse to let myself…

I stand straight, square my shoulders, and march up to the front door.

* * *

"Rose! What are you…?"

Somewhat taken aback, I think, Carne leads me into the warmth of the sitting room. His hands dangle then fan out and flutter round. He shifts from one foot to the other as we murmur conventional nothings. The expression on his face is hard to read; it could suggest embarrassment, awkwardness, surprise, or plain confusion – what on earth is this woman doing here, uninvited, on a cold winter's night?

There's no one else in the room, of course. Nor any sign there ever was. "I hope you don't mind me…" One ear is listening for tell-tale creaks from the floorboards above. "Just passing. I thought I'd drop in and let you…"

Then I spot it. On top of a display case full of books (books? I hadn't taken Carne for a reader), open ready for use and plugged in, an old reel-to-reel tape recorder. The brand name is clearly visible in chunky metal letters along one side. Grundig. A name I recall for some reason. A Sixties or Seventies must-have. High-tech toy, once upon a time.

Carne swells. "My pride and joy, that ol' thing. Got so many tapes I needs a bit of a clear out, really, only it seems a shame, you know?"

I bet he has no intention of throwing anything away.

From the floor, down by the side of a wing-backed armchair, Carne grabs a handful of tape boxes, each meticulously labelled along the edge. "Look at this lot. Go back to the dawn of time, they do."

I've never heard Carne try to make a joke before, and I grin. "Stone diaries, eh? Any artists I might've heard of?"

"All the commercial stuff's in there." He points to the display case. "Classics, they are. Nina Simone. MJQ. Dizzy, Sachmo. All the greats."

Yes, I can see now – books on the top two shelves, piles of tapes jammed onto the bottom one. Carne's a jazz-lover. Well I never…

"Made these myself." He shakes the boxes he's holding and they rattle like teeth.

Suddenly I'm sweating. Two double radiators are blasting out megawatts and, having been frozen only moments ago, I now have to yank my scarf off and unzip my fleece, or I might pass out.

Carne drops the tapes into the armchair and springs to my side. "Sorry, Rose. Forgetting my manners. Don't get too many visitors these days." He takes my coat, folds hat, scarf and gloves into it and lays everything carefully over the back of another chair. "Can I get you…?"

"No, really. I'm fine. I didn't mean to disturb you."

"Oh, I weren't doing much." A sheepish look now. Slightly guilty?

"The Brians have sorted out my transport," I tell him, for the sake of something to say. "Going to get that old banger Phil Vickery's been trying to sell." Carne nods. "Makes sense, don't you think?" I wander over to the tape recorder, where two spools hold a tape that's half wound-on. "What's this one? Trad or modern?"

Carne comes and stands next to me, bringing his warm, musky scent, slightly feral but not unpleasant. A man of the earth. His voice, when he next speaks, is so quiet I have to listen hard. "We used to have a folk band," he says. "Back in the day. Me and Danny and… and a few of us. I'd record some of our practice sessions," his arms start flapping again, "record our gigs, too, specially when…"

He looks up at me, waiting for me to understand. And this time there's no mistaking it. The look of love. And pain and such weariness.

"When Sally sang?"

For answer, he presses a switch and her voice spirals.

* * *

Apparently Carne often plays his tapes of Sally singing, sometimes in Cornish and sometimes in English, her own interpretation of local folksongs. He tells me that when weather permits, he opens the windows wide, turns up the volume and releases her voice to soar across the fields and out to sea. The spirit of Sally Hendry, still floating over Porthallen. Many of her favourites songs, he says, were about the sea.

345

She had a wonderful voice.

Carne invites me listen to several tracks and we talk companionably about the gift of true talent, about the wonder of it. After half an hour or so I take my leave. It's time to go home. Sally accompanies me through the gate and down the lane.

Carne's windows had been tight shut against the cold, so the sound was blocked from travelling very far. But even if they'd been open, do I seriously believe an ancient Grundig could belt out enough volume to carry all the way to Penmaris, to Porthallen Bay, over miles rather than metres?

I shiver. Another explanation that explains nothing. Stuff happens. Let it be.

Back at Penmaris, I make my way along the garden path to sit on the stone. Bundled in coat and scarf and gloves, with a woolly hat pulled down over my ears, I'm just about warm enough and will stay outside until the late-night freeze drives me in. Immense above the garden hangs the endless sky, and from its depths the endless stars shine. Carne and Chris and Oliver and Ellie and, who else? We will all have to accommodate to the burdens of conscience. The stars don't give a damn. And the stone is just a stone, tonight.

About the Author

Shirley Wright was born and brought up in London. After graduating from university she taught French, relocating to Bristol when she got married and has remained there, on and off, for most of her life. It is only in recent years she has been writing full-time.

In 2007 she was short-listed for the Impress Prize for Fiction, and in 2008 was the national winner of the *Telegraph* Poetry for Performance competition, judged by Andrew Motion and Ben Okri.

She has poems published in various magazines and also short stories in both the traditional medium and via epublishing.

Time Out of Mind is Shirley's first published novel.

Lightning Source UK Ltd.
Milton Keynes UK
UKOW040500190912

199247UK00001B/9/P